IF I
EVER

HELL or HIGH WATER: BOOK 4

SE JAKES

RIPTIDE
PUBLISHING

Riptide Publishing
PO Box 1537
Burnsville, NC 28714
www.riptidepublishing.com

If I Ever

Cover art: L.C. Chase, lcchase.com/design-portfolio.html
Editor: May Peterson
Layout: L.C. Chase, lcchase.com/design-portfolio.html

ISBN: 978-1-62649-871-6

First edition
January, 2019

Also available in ebook:
ISBN: 978-1-62649-870-9

IF I
EVER

HELL or HIGH WATER: BOOK 4

SE JAKES

RIPTIDE
PUBLISHING

This one's for my readers, for waiting for me to be able to complete this series, and for trusting me to make good on Prophet and Tommy's HEA. Thank you for cheering me on!

Hell is empty and all the devils are here.
— *The Tempest*, William Shakespeare

TABLE OF CONTENTS

CHAPTER ONE

I n the story of Prophet's life, he'd played his own hero enough times to know that waiting to ride off into the sunset with one of his own was both unrealistic *and* stupid.

But *shit*, he'd still hoped for it every single time.

At least that's what he'd always thought, even if he'd never said the words out loud. Everyone wanted a hero, no matter how goddamned capable they were. If anyone said differently, they were goddamned lying.

But the man he was currently leaning on for support as he navigated the snow-covered sidewalk with bare, numb feet wasn't a lie. Farthest thing from, and Prophet had bet his own life on that enough times to be sure of it.

"Come on, Proph—got you," Tom said quietly, his voice a soothing drawl that Prophet had come to depend on.

That would bother the fuck out of him some days more than others, but he'd have to remember the times it didn't. Like now, as he let Tom guide him the whole way back into their building, lock the door behind them while never mentioning the fact that he still held Prophet's boots in his hand even as Prophet shuddered from the cold.

Instead, they stood together in the hallway for a moment, processing. Assessing. Having his best friend turn into his biggest enemy had been a betrayal he'd known about, but discovering that man had been in his house, with Tom, with Remy?

Now, it was war.

His wrists ached, the way they always did in extreme cold, but he'd be damned if he'd pay them any special attention. Instead, he directed his burning hatred of the guy who'd once been his best friend like it could inject itself directly into his bones and heal them. That anger? That would pull him through hell every time.

But the cold had fucked with his head, the thaw happening too slowly for his own good.

"What's in the basement?" Tom's interruption to his thoughts was quiet but Prophet heard the tension in his words, felt it in the arm of steel wrapped around his rib cage. "Cameras?"

Prophet blew out a harsh breath, his lungs still pained from the cold. "Yes, but there's no egress in the basement."

"Think maybe *he* made one?" Tom refused to say John's name. Prophet couldn't blame him. He eased away from Tom's hold, forced himself to stand steady on his numb-as-fuck feet and only then did he draw his weapon. Tom followed suit and took point on the steps, Prophet following close behind. They found the big room empty, save for the boiler and water heater, along with the generator and electric panels and several storage boxes that Prophet recognized as Cillian's. It was clean and dry with no place to hide.

"Cameras seem to be in working order. I'll have Cillian run the footage," Tom said. "I'm surprised neither of you thought to make this a panic room."

"Cillian had plans drawn up, but we'd need elevators. Secret panels in the wall. It got complicated." But now that Remy was in the picture, those complications suddenly didn't seem so complicated.

CHAPTER TWO

Tom knew full well that ordering Prophet back up the stairs and to their apartment before he died of hypothermia wasn't the way to go. Instead, Tom waited—with a patience he didn't know he had until he'd met Prophet—as his partner continued to stare around the room like he was waiting for the answers to appear on the walls in front of him. Finally, Prophet blew out a muttered curse and headed back up the stairs to the main hallway.

In turn, Tom followed, locked the basement door, hit the alarms for the main doors and waited for them to arm. And waited some more until Prophet finally said, "Let's go up and check Cillian's place by camera," and Tom again followed him up the stairs. Even though Prophet's feet still held an unhealthy tinge of dusk, the interior hallway was warm enough that he'd stopped involuntarily trembling.

Still, he paused at the top of the stairs to let Tom open the loft's heavy steel door. Tom walked inside but Prophet paused, shook his head.

Because as he'd unfrozen, so had his anger. "We're going to end this," he promised. "I'm finding John and I'm ending this. Do you understand?"

"Let's take it one step at a time," Tom urged him.

"He's been in my house," Prophet growled. "Near you. Near Remy. So no, I'm not going to take time to think about the next step."

"Fine. What is the next step?"

"Check the cameras. And stop treating me like a bomb you're trying to defuse."

Tom bristled at the orders, but he did as Prophet asked, on both counts. "Then put your goddamned socks on."

"Yes, daddy," Prophet said absently as he headed toward the bedroom. He was in there for a while, long enough for Tom to call him a motherfucker, out loud, several times, and run the searches on the computer connected to the cameras in both Cillian's and Prophet's apartments, as well as the one pointed out from the building, and pour two mugs of coffee.

Finally, Prophet wandered out of their bedroom, socks in his hands and the envelope with John's jacket in it under his arm, and Tom could practically hear the wheels moving inside his head as he headed to the kitchen.

"Cillian's apartment's clear now. I went back several hours—no disruptions in the tape," Tom called over his shoulder.

No answer. He glanced over and saw Prophet leaning against the countertop, writing something. Then he rooted around inside the envelope, pulled the jacket out and instead slid the paper inside. He left the jacket on the floor, yanked on socks and boots.

And then he went back into the bedroom, opened the window, and went outside via the fire escape. By that time, Tom was watching him jump down off the final leg of the metal ladder in order to slide the envelope into its original place behind the dumpster, and scale back up the metal scaffolding.

Tom moved aside to let him climb inside, then watched him carefully close and lock the window. Only then did he go past Tom and into the living room and Tom muttered at the ceiling for more patience before joining him.

"Can you sit down now?" he asked, and Prophet actually did, let Tom wrap a blanket around him, and took the warm coffee from the table. Then he pulled Prophet's boots off and tugged his legs up so Prophet could settle them into his lap. Tom attempted to rub some circulation into Prophet's feet through the socks.

Finally, Prophet informed him, "I told John that it's his turn."

Tom frowned. "His turn?"

"This whole time, I've been trying to catch him. And he's been evading. Poking at us. That's what he's really good at. I forgot that. In the beginning, I was desperate to get him back, to prove he had nothing to do with it. To show everyone I wasn't an asshole for caring about him the way I did."

"And now?"

Prophet gave him a lopsided grin that made his heart skip a beat, and answered in a way Tom didn't expect. "You and me? We chased each other."

Tom swallowed hard as he processed that. It was obviously a major difference in the two relationships. "Yeah, we did."

"With John, it was one or the other. Always. Cat and mouse. Trying to prove to the other who cared more. The guy could hold a grudge. And as long as I was doing the chasing, he'd hide. Now I have to turn the tables and force him to catch me."

"And that will help?"

"John sucks at being the hunter. Don't get me wrong—it's a relative suck. Better than ninety percent of people. But not better than me."

"Where do I fit in here?"

Prophet paused, but it didn't matter—Tom knew exactly what he was going to say. "I think you need to stay here."

"Because of Remy."

"Because of Remy," Prophet repeated, his eyes haunted.

"Not because you're worried about me."

"If I thought John would come after you, I'd never leave you here without me," Prophet said honestly.

"*We're* going to do this," Tom said fiercely. "Remy needs both of us to come back."

Prophet blinked. "You think this is my version of a suicide run?"

"Is it?" Tom pressed.

Prophet stared at him, gray eyes like rising smoke. "I have to end this. It started with me. It has to end with me. If that makes it a suicide run, then so be it . . . but since I plan to come back and drive you fucking nuts for the rest of your life, then no."

Tom smiled. Reached out and touched Prophet's bottom lip with his thumb, stroked it. "Just needed to hear you say it."

"Maybe I just needed to say it," Prophet countered. They sat in silence for a long while, Prophet staring out the window and Tom rubbing his feet. "No one ever noticed the paint, just like I didn't," he said finally.

"Proph, the guy was practically invisible. He used your dreams."

"John always said he felt invisible."

"Did you?"

"Nah. I was never melodramatic. Besides, people noticed me."

Tom held his tongue on the melodramatic part but couldn't help adding, "You were always an asshole too."

"It's one of the most endearing qualities."

Tom stroked a hand through Prophet's hair. "Most definitely." Prophet smiled in satisfaction. "Did you ever consider he was real before this?"

"Not until the night we left for Djibouti. Right before you came in."

"I know you have flashbacks. PTSD episodes. You said you hallucinate during them. I've seen some of them. But this? This is different."

"It's happened like this before," Prophet insisted. "I just didn't realize it, but it's happened for a while."

Tom softened, because Prophet was already frustrated as fuck and he wasn't helping. "How long?"

"When I was first rescued, if you want to call what the CIA did a rescue, I was in the hospital. Recovering. John visited me. I figured it was the pain meds." Just how much Prophet hated revisiting that time showed clearly in his face, and the flash of pain and anger, the barely contained hatred in his voice at his circumstances made Tom immediately flashback to the video that had given him his first glance of an angry, young Prophet being interrogated by the CIA, and nearly killing the agent stupid enough to believe that Prophet wouldn't break his own wrists to kill him.

"And what, he assumed you're going to have flashbacks like this, so he visits you?"

"I've been having them for a long time. Before Hal," Prophet confessed. "Not this bad, but John was always there. My shrink said I manifested them for comfort."

Tom shook his head at the absolute irony of that. "Maybe you forgot to turn a camera off. What if Cillian saw a flashback incident and he's playing with you?"

"Even you don't think Cillian would pull that shit. He wanted to drive me crazy, but he doesn't need to fuck with my flashbacks to do it."

Tom knew that, but he wanted to believe anything other than the fact that John had been *here*. "What does it mean that he's been this close to you—to me—and we're still alive?"

"I have no goddamned idea what to think of that, Tommy."

This was serious—especially because Remy was now here. And there was nothing to stop John from hurting him. Just because he'd left Prophet and Tom alone for now meant nothing. John would figure out a way to threaten Remy so they'd leave John alone. "Do you think . . . he missed you?" Tom asked hesitantly.

Prophet stared at him. "Staying hidden's tough, you know? You can't show who you really are. If violence happens, you can't help anyone. For someone used to walking into the fire, it's torture to survive like that."

Tom pretended not to notice Prophet had ignored the original question. "And John's not like that?"

"Just the opposite. Like he was relieved not to have to carry that burden of who he was all the time," Prophet explained. "On one level, I caught the appeal. I just couldn't do it. I just kept moving after I showed my hand. I'm good at escaping." He stared at the window, but Tom noticed his fingertips—there was still black paint on them from where he'd touched the windows, and he was touching his pointer to his thumb as if feeling the stickiness. "Should've fucking known."

"What?"

"The paint was my trick, to cover our tracks when we snuck out. You always end up scraping off paint when you break in or out. He knows I would've noticed."

"And these windows aren't alarmed?"

Prophet shrugged. "Fourth floor. I mean, hell, why would anyone bother? You want me dead, you'll shoot a bomb through the glass. Besides, he was bypassing cameras already. I'll bet this system's not a problem for him, but he's not behind all of my flashbacks."

"How do you know?"

"I don't think you'd sleep through a firefight," Prophet said wryly.

"So John was the trigger. He'd leave and then . . ."

"Yeah, and then the fireworks started. But they'd start without me seeing him more often than not. Even though I know he's the cause of the shit going down all around me . . . I still look for the bastard . . . every single time."

CHAPTER THREE

Prophet practically spat his last words, not sure if he was angriest at himself. Probably so. He'd been told numerous times throughout his career incarnations that having a conscience would fuck him over every time.

They were right, but hell, where John was concerned, the time for worrying about his once best friend was long gone. Now, it was about not being able to ignore John any longer. Because of him, Mal and Ren and King and Hook couldn't safely remain in the US—or anywhere else, really—because they all had a bounty on their heads. Their work remained on the down low, and suspicion would always dog Prophet as well. Suspicion—and secrets that lived inside of him.

And even if they could continue to live with all of that, as they'd been doing, the fact that John might have a plan that could impact thousands of lives? That was something Prophet and his teammates couldn't turn their back on. Especially because they carried the weight of the crimes John had already committed, and that albatross was strangling them.

"I still look for the bastard . . . every single time."

PTSD: the bitch that kept on giving.

Tom had stayed quiet, just watching . . . but when he finally spoke, there wasn't an ounce of judgment or jealousy there. "You want to save him before you can't," was all he said of John, and it was nothing like what Prophet expected to hear, or even deserved, and his throat got too tight to speak, tighter even when Tom added, "I wouldn't expect anything less from you."

Finally, Prophet managed, "You're not on the 'Prophet's in denial' team then? Because you'd be in damned good company with Mal and King and Ren." His team, the men who'd stuck with him even as they'd been dragged through hell because of him.

Tom shook his head slowly. "Never have been. Never will be. But I can see why they are. It's because you want them to be there, on that in-denial team. You've always got your reasons. But you've got them fooled with this one, because they think John's your kryptonite."

"Doesn't everyone have a kryptonite?"

Tom tapped his fingertips on his thigh thoughtfully. "I guess my partners always dying was mine. My curse."

Prophet shoved aside the thought that maybe Tom's curse was Prophet himself, because that was too maudlin for an already maudlin afternoon. But Tom's fingers stilled and he narrowed his eyes at Prophet.

Fucking Cajun voodoo bastard. "Shut up, Tommy."

"Fine." Tom pressed his lips together before continuing. "Are you in on this with John?"

Prophet leaned back against the couch—a nondefensive posture to be sure, but that didn't stop the hurt from flashing for the briefest of seconds in his storm-filled gray eyes. "You and your fucking voodoo shit—why don't you answer that question for me?"

It was probably the hardest question Tom would have to ask him. Prophet gazed at him, his eyes cool, and for a split second, Tom saw the machine behind the man, the special forces operator, trained, bred to kill, to follow the mission to its logical end.

And then Tom answered his own question. "No, you're not."

Prophet's jaw clenched. Tom ran his hand over Proph's cheek, and the jaw unclenched, expression softened. "So what do we do now?"

"It's not your war."

"It involves you, so yeah, it is."

"It's getting harder to . . ." He motioned to his eyes, and Tom told him, "Then let me be your eyes on this."

"There's never been a choice, has there?" Prophet asked him. "Not from the goddamned beginning." He sounded half-angry, half-pleased as Tom shook his head. "John's not my kryptonite, Tommy. Not by a long shot. But you . . ."

"Yeah, but I don't make you powerless, *bébé*."

Prophet gave a wan smile, but his mind was obviously moving too fast to settle onto anything. "What if this fucks up the adoption?"

"I don't know."

"You and Remy could go into official protection."

"By the time all this goes through, we hopefully won't need it. And while we're away, the foster visits . . ."

Prophet sighed. "We'll just have to say we have jobs out of town sometimes and that he's got significant supervision."

"Mal is considered 'significant supervision'?" Tom groaned.

"He's an adult. We don't have to use the word 'appropriate,' but man, you've got a Special Forces operator and a doctor watching this kid. How could he be safer?"

"Don't you think we might need Mal with us?" Tom asked.

"Shit." Prophet frowned. "I'm trying to keep all of them away but . . ."

But life—and John—didn't always work like that. They might need all the resources they could muster.

"How long, Proph? Really."

"Could be a week. Three weeks. A month. Depends on his timetable. But John's escalated. My gut says under a month. And if I press, we can bring him out sooner."

"Then press."

"I will, T. Dammit, it hasn't been a game, ever. But he's treating it, and my life, and Mal's and the others' lives like it is." Prophet sounded firm, not defeated. "I've been looking through his things, looking for a mistake, a sign, *anything* that links his banking to any of this. Mal's got some hits in offshore accounts, but beyond siphoning out his money, there's not a lot to go on."

Tom nodded. "He seems to be spiraling."

"As the plan comes to an end . . . this spiral, this letting us get close? Could all be an act." Prophet shook his head. "He's still the same . . . as much as he's changed, he's stayed the exact goddamned same."

"Would I have liked him, back then?"

Prophet glanced at Tom like he'd asked a trick question. "You'd have hated him on sight."

"I feel closer to Mal than I ever have."

Prophet snorted. "John's an acquired taste. We didn't love each other as much as we hated to love each other. It was complicated, and not in the good way." He looked at Tom meaningfully. "We need to end this."

For so many reasons.

"We will," Tom promised him.

"Tell me what you want. Spell it out," Prophet told him.

Tom gazed at him, so full of goddamned trust, with none of the wariness like there'd been the first time they'd done this. "I want you, Proph. All of you. Good, bad, sick, well. You. That's all. You're my goddamned family. You, Remy. Doc. Even Mal."

Prophet smiled. "Even Mal?"

"You tell him I said that and—"

"I won't. But he knows, T. He knows." He ran a thumb along Tom's bottom lip. "So you're in it."

"Long haul."

"Suppose it gets ugly?"

Tom gave a small, lopsided grin. "I've seen ugly, Prophet. We'll get through it."

Prophet believed it, believed Tom meant it. *But sometimes when you're in the thick of it . . .*

He stopped mid-thought, because Tom's voodoo-meter must have pinged. Tom was palpably angry when he grabbed Prophet's biceps, hard. "Don't you fucking underestimate me. I'll fuck that right out of you."

"I'd like to see you try," was all Prophet got out before Tom's mouth was on his, as rough and punishing as his grip. And Prophet relished it. Wanted all of what Tom could give him, wanted him to leave marks all over his goddamned body.

Wanted Tom to erase this day, purge the memories and leave Prophet whole again . . . for as long as that would last.

He was beat down exhausted. Fragile. Pissed and sad and on the verge of losing it completely, and Tom knew it. Prophet wanted to throw him off, buck him away, but Tom would fight him every step of the way.

There was nothing else he could do—nothing *to* do—but let Tom take him, anyway he wanted to.

He surrendered into Tom's fierce kiss and unrelenting grip, to accept the warm slide of Tom's tongue along his as Tom forced him toward the bedroom. There wasn't an escape, not into himself, because Tom wasn't going to let that happen, like he knew it was too dangerous for Prophet to disappear into there . . . because if he went down that road, he might not come back.

Instead, Tom set about keeping him on the damned road, crawling, cut and bleeding, instead of walking, but going down the road just the same. Stripped him down physically, and set about doing the same to his mind.

"Knees, Proph," Tom told him in a tone that brokered no argument. Prophet turned reluctantly, forehead pressed to the mattress as his arms were pulled behind his back, not roughly, but enough to remind him that leaning on them wasn't an option. Tom wrapped the leather cuffs around his wrists, and there was enough chain between them so Prophet's arms didn't feel the strain. But he was still bound. Open. Vulnerable.

God, it fucking hurt to do that, especially now. He wanted to glance over to the window where John had come in God knew how many fucking times to violate him, over and over again, but he didn't. Instead, he screwed his eyes tight and just breathed as Tom spread him, buried his face in his ass in a way that forced Prophet to whimper, helpless against the onslaught. Forcing him to feel, to react, to need.

"Fuck you, Tommy," he muttered and Tom dug in deeper, letting Prophet know it was message received. His tongue took Prophet until his balls tightened and he ached to come, thrust his hips into air, needing something to touch his dick, to grind against him and let him release.

Frustrated, he cursed—at the ache, at Tom, at everything—and with the pull to the window becoming more possible to ignore, he didn't. He turned his head and opened his eyes and stared at the reflection of Tom lording over him in the glass. He saw another figure there, above them, and he blinked and forced himself not to say shit, because it wasn't real.

He had no right to be there, but every goddamned reason to be.

Suddenly, Tom stopped, but it took Prophet a few seconds longer than it should've to realize it. The room chilled, even as Tom's hand swatted Prophet's ass several times, hard as hell, bringing him back to earth.

"You want to stare at the window?" Tom taunted. "I'll do you one better." He grabbed Prophet roughly by the biceps and dragged him up and toward the window, slamming his upper body against the glass. With a palm on the back of Prophet's head, he forced Prophet's forehead against it and said calmly, "Open your fucking eyes and look for him. Look at him, for all I give a fuck, because I'm the one who's here with you. Inside of you. You're mine, goddammit it. So say it."

Tom thrust up into him and Prophet growled at the invasion, the taunts, the orders. But Tom wasn't having any of it, thrust up into him over and over with an unrelenting motion until Prophet mouthed, *You're mine.*

He didn't say shit out loud, he hadn't even been able to hear his own goddamned voice, but somehow, Tom did.

"You're mine, Proph. And better than that? I'm yours." With that, Tom pulled out of him entirely and then entered him again, and Prophet cried out, eyes staring down at the alley below until it blurred under his gaze and melted away into nothingness.

Only then did he smile.

With Prophet pressed against that window, Tom fucked the ghosts out of him—all of them, the best he could, until Prophet's body relaxed, part bliss and mostly exhaustion, and Tom didn't care so long as Prophet found momentary peace.

When he helped Prophet back into the bed, Prophet stared at him for a long moment . . . and Tom didn't see any of the ghosts there, just a reflection of himself before Prophet closed his eyes.

For Tom? No such luck, at least not tonight. He lay there, a leg thrown across Prophet's body, staring at the window John had been sneaking into and wondering how the hell they'd all missed it. If Prophet really had, or if John's stranglehold was stronger than anyone realized.

Discontent grew in Tom's gut as that last *maybe* took hold. Prophet was the strongest man he knew, but everyone had their kryptonite, their breaking point, their weakness. For a while, Tom thought he was Prophet's, but now he realized that was something he never wanted to be.

CHAPTER FOUR

Prophet opened his eyes in the darkness, the weight of Tom's leg grounding him, and even so, Prophet had to simply lie there and fucking breathe so he didn't trigger himself into any kind of flashback.

When he felt steady enough, he pushed Tom away, murmuring, "Bathroom," and Tom grunted and moved. Prophet took a piss and grabbed his jeans, leaving Tom in dreamland.

Prophet had places to be. People to yell at. And he knew exactly where to start, he thought as he walked grimly down the steps and began to pick the lock to Cillian's door, even though he had a copy of the key, just to piss the guy off.

Cillian had his ear to the ground . . . and so did Gary. Gary knew the kinds of things to look for regarding John and what exactly his plans were. But Gary wasn't here, and the asshole at his disposal slammed his loft door open and glared at Prophet.

"What the hell? You've got a key."

"Figured it would be rude to just let myself in."

Cillian rolled his eyes and walked back into the apartment. Prophet joined him, closing the door and roaming through the rooms on the current floor.

"I'm alone," Cillian called. When Prophet came out of his bedroom, Cillian shook his head. "Who were you hoping to find? John?"

Prophet stared at the couch, if it could even be called that anymore. It'd been thrown out of a window in the rain, pushed up stairs and thrown down them, and otherwise defiled—and put together again with pink duck tape. "That looks pathetic," Prophet informed him.

"I keep it to annoy you. Good to know it works." Cillian paused, and then sighed, obviously knowing why Prophet was there and admitting, "John's got more of a stronghold since Sadiq was killed."

In the ultimate irony, killing Sadiq had actually helped John, a fact that hit Prophet like a physical blow. Cillian had been right to tell him, even though Prophet could see the reluctance to share in his eyes.

Prophet, in turn, threw the first thing in his path against the wall, which was hopefully some priceless sculpture or some shit like that. It went whizzing by Cillian's head and fuck, he had to work on his aim.

"If you're going to destroy something, can you make sure it's in your own apartment?" Cillian asked, seemingly unperturbed. Prophet took a step toward him and Cillian stood his ground.

"Don't tempt me. Not now," Prophet warned.

"I'm shaking." Cillian threw up his arms and frowned.

"Did you know? Did you know John was really here?"

Cillian's expression went serious. "Prophet, if I knew John Morse was here, flesh and blood? I would've killed him with my bare hands."

Prophet believed that. What worried him now was the skill level John had achieved, and while survival could give a man an edge, John had received some serious training. Maybe even more advances than the CIA could've given him. "Could SB-20 be employing John?"

"I've thought about it, yes," Cillian said slowly.

"And?"

"If they did bring him in and train him? They lost control of him rather quickly. And once that happened, they wouldn't own up to it for fear of being exposed to the CIA, thus compounding the problem."

"And the CIA was already in fear of being exposed. John screwed them all over and forced them to keep quiet."

"And prepared you and your team to take the fall," Cillian added. "SB-20 wanted him alive—as though they were doing the CIA a great favor, but John's got to have something on them too."

"Maybe you could ask your old boss, Trent—oh, wait, you can't, because you killed him," Prophet pointed out.

"What are you really asking? Because the man I know wouldn't dance around this shit."

"My bedroom window. It's been opened. Painted over. You'd know that because you've got the same alarm access I do."

"Yes, Prophet, your bedroom window's been opened many times since you've lived here. You're allowed to open your bedroom window. You do it often."

"But it chimes."

"So you didn't hear the chimes."

"No. I heard a lot of goddamned things during my flashbacks, but I'd know the chimes. I fucking listen for them, because I'm not completely out of it. I'm always waiting for the chime, so I can know if someone's coming to really kill me."

Cillian stared at him. "Say what you mean."

"You and I are the only ones with access."

"Really? You haven't given codes to Tom, Doc, Phil, Mal, King, Ren . . ."

"Right, because they're all far more likely candidates to let John come in here and fuck with my head."

"What do you want from me? Go through the codes."

"You could doctor them."

"True." Cillian crossed his arms. "Say it."

Prophet had been fighting this urge. Couldn't anymore, not after this. "It was you."

Cillian raised his chin. A haunted look flashed in his eyes. "You need to trust that I have reasons enough to want John dead, more than anyone. Except maybe you."

"Or Mal."

Cillian's eyes got that haunted look again for a fleeting second. "But why would I let him in? What would I gain?"

"I don't know, Cillian. Money? Power?"

"*Bullshit* you don't know." God, his brogue was so heavy these days. Must've been weird for Mal to finally hear that. He'd freaked the first time he'd heard King's brogue, and had tried to drown him in the ocean during a BUD/S exercise, and no one noticed because the instructors were all regularly trying to drown them anyway.

"I'll leave," Cillian said.

"Right. Convenient."

"You don't trust me to leave. You don't trust me to stay."

"Maybe I should do what Mal can't."

"Won't," Cillian corrected him. "I have no doubt that Mal could, in a heartbeat. But he won't, for several reasons."

"What are they?"

"Ask him. This question-and-answer period is done."

And there was John, ruining another relationship, because whateverthefuck happened between Mal and Cillian had to do with John. He was always in the way.

Because yes, John and the CIA framed their team, but John saw Mal as competing with him for Prophet's attention, much more so than Ren or King or Hook. Because none of them loved John, but Mal's hatred was instant and absolute.

He'd protected the team—and John at one point—but he was always suspicious, waiting for John to fuck them over. And while Mal never said anything to Prophet outright, Mal was protective as hell over Prophet.

The reverse was also true.

Now, back in his own apartment, he sank onto the couch, closed his eyes and found himself picturing the night before the Hal mission, the night he and John had the worst fight they'd ever had— and they'd had some bad ones. But before that, he recalled hanging out with Mal, who'd been sitting on the trunk of the Hummer, staring up at the stars, rifle around his neck without the safety engaged. Mal was big on the whole "my finger is the safety" argument.

Mal had never come with a safety.

He was also deeply unhappy with the idea of Prophet and John riding in the front car, since Prophet was point and therefore needed his team protecting him. But the mission specified that provision . . .

"All set?" Mal asked, Boston accent rough and strong. Prophet could listen to Mal tell stories for hours, mainly because of the voice.

But tonight, neither was in the mood for a chat. When Prophet didn't answer, Mal simply said, "Yeah, me neither."

Prophet's discontent had grown all day with a vengeance, one he couldn't afford to ignore. It was uncomfortable, a nudge he couldn't shake. He'd avoided Hal but doing so for much longer was putting off the inevitable.

He'd avoided John for longer.

Mal seemed content with Prophet's inability to face what he had to do, simply lay back on the hood with Prophet and watched the sky. Simple, quiet moments, the kind Prophet would reflect back on and miss desperately.

He wanted to tell Mal his fears, but being point meant brave face and no fear and don't fuck with your teams' psyche.

But of course, Mal knew. Prophet never asked him and Mal never said but Prophet knew.

They both knew their beast was marching toward Bethlehem.

Inevitable.

Indestructible.

Prophet finally got up and walked back toward his tent, looking over his shoulder only once.

Mal was still there, silent, immovable force that he was. In that moment, Prophet realized that Mal would always be there and it gave him the most comfort of anything he'd ever had in his life. He silently promised Mal he'd give the man the same thing.

Hal was in his own tent, now guarded by Ren and King. Prophet was up next on guard duty, but he had to talk with John before that.

John was lying on one of the cots in their tent, eyes closed but not asleep. He didn't open his eyes, not until Prophet told him, "I think we need to change the route."

"Why? Because Mal wants to?" John sneered.

Prophet stared at him calmly. John had been fucking with him the entire trip, prodding him, pissed that Prophet was going to Mal more and more. "It's a gut feeling. You used to trust my gut."

"'Used to' being the key words. What? Do you call Mal every time you need to take a piss to make sure it's okay?" John continued. "Mal's not running point and you and I have our mission. It can't change. We need to make sure we get from point A to point B. If he doesn't understand that—"

"I understand everything. It's not Mal who's questioning it, John. It's me."

John was up, on his feet, in Prophet's face. Prophet slammed against his chest to move him away, and that's when the fight started in earnest.

Later, Prophet will recall this conversation when Lansing threatens him, accusing him of changing the route in order to sell Hal to the highest bidder and killing John in the process. Now, all he could do was take the brunt of John's brutal punch—a mean right hook. But he didn't go down, just wiped his lip with the back of his hand and stared down at the blood on his knuckle.

He spat blood at John's feet, the too-familiar metallic taste stoking his anger. "I'll take you off the mission."

"Yeah, you try that."

If Prophet followed through, they'd be a man short, and for this mission wrapped in a mission—with implications Mal and the others didn't know about—that wouldn't be the way to go. LT would be pissed. Either way, John was going to compromise everything.

"Stop being an asshole," Prophet told him. "Or I'll tell LT you were set to sabotage the entire mission."

"Like he'll listen to you over me? Hell, his own brother got fucked up on a mission and LT retired him quick."

As if Prophet needed reminding. Thinking of Dean now, recovering in a hospital bed in some private hospital—the best LT's money could buy—made him sick to his stomach. Because Dean was now blind, and since Prophet knew that was his fate as well, the coincidence was eerie. Chilling.

Fuck. He should just scrap this entire mission, cite intuition, which had never been wrong, but this was a military op and a CIA one as well, and neither institution wanted to be told what to do. Neither paid him for his decision-making skills, just his ability to follow orders and follow them well.

And it was the nature of those orders—their rigidity—that was why Prophet was starting to bristle. "Not another word," he told John.

John nodded as if acquiescing, and then he came at Prophet, fast and furious, slamming his body into Prophet's, knocking them both to the ground. Then his hand was between Prophet's legs, the other on Prophet's throat. Prophet didn't resist, mainly because he didn't want the others coming in and seeing this—it would ruin what was left of team camaraderie, and the night before one of their most important missions *wasn't the time for that to erode completely. So he let John unzip his BDUs and told himself this wasn't anything they hadn't done a hundred times before this.*

"*I was always there for you. Always,*" *John told him, his hand pumping Prophet's dick and no, he didn't want to come but John knew him intimately. His voice had softened and he bit down lightly on Prophet's shoulder.*

It wasn't sexual—it was power, pure and simple, and in that moment John had all of it. Prophet was left to wonder if he'd given it away so easily on purpose, or if he'd needed John to think he was compliant.

Should've canceled the mission right then and there.

He was numb. "*It's over. Really fucking over.*" *It was a surreal moment, one he'd never forget thanks to what happened hours later.*

"*It's been over for a long time, so fuck you, Prophet. Just get the fuck out of my face,*" *John spat and started walking away, although for some reason he was still speaking.* "Just get up. Come on, Proph, you need to wake up . . ."

"Proph, come on." It was Tom's voice, in the middle of his fucked-up flashback. He opened his eyes and saw Tom, not John, and relief washed over him.

Tom watched him carefully, unmoving. Smart man, because Prophet could kill him in a second if he thought he was fighting John, and fuck, Prophet hated these flashbacks, hated that there was no way to fix him.

They were untouchable.

Untouchable.

When he and John were young, as young boys did, they'd decided that being important—untouchable—was the way to go through life.

As they got older, they watched men who they'd thought untouchable get touched by so many factors in life that it became unbearable.

Prophet reasoned that maybe you could only be untouchable in certain situations . . . or for certain periods of your life.

But John? He never let go of the idea of being untouchable. The one thing Prophet was sure of? The men who John surrounded himself with knew John was important. Untouchable. And John never believed Prophet would be able to change that.

But Prophet had more faith in himself than John ever had, and even more in the man standing in front of him now. His eyes blurred for a second, maybe more from exhaustion and anger than anything, but these days, the blurring came around more and more often.

So he closed his eyes again, heard the hoarseness in his voice when he told Tom, "It's okay. I'm okay."

He felt the weight of Tom sink next to him on the couch. "Yeah, you are okay." Tom's arm went around his shoulders and Prophet sank his head against Tom's chest. "What else can I do?"

Prophet didn't hesitate. "Bring Remy home."

CHAPTER FIVE

L ess than twenty-four hours after finding the envelope, Remy came home . . . and Remy's Crazy Uncle Mal came along with him, and they all pretended everything was normal when they all knew it was far from it. Remy had been with them as soon as they'd gotten back from killing Sadiq. After initially finding the envelope from John, Prophet had made sure that Remy got safely to Doc's straight from school instead of coming back to them.

Tom had complied with Prophet's request because they both needed to see Remy, to be around him and reassured while planning their own personal version of hell.

It was late by that point, and Remy settled into his room quickly, like he was imprinting himself back onto the apartment before anyone could stop him. Prophet wanted to tell him not to worry, that he'd already imprinted on them, probably from first meet, but Prophet knew Remy would still worry.

Prophet knew two things in particular were bothering Remy, but the first was the most important. Remy knew what they did for a living, and the travel (read: danger) involved. That kind of family life he could deal with. It was another instability that most worried him. So Prophet went into the bedroom where Remy was drawing, lying on his belly on the bed, legs up and crossed, shirt off, headphones on and music pounding out of them, which meant the iPod was turned up to deafening levels.

Mal would come in and sleep next to him in a bit, but for the moment, Prophet welcomed the quiet time. And when he sat next to Remy on the double bed, Remy pulled off the headphones and turned off the music, but not before Prophet recognized the blare of classic rock—AC/DC's "Dirty Deeds Done Dirt Cheap."

He wanted to look up at the ceiling to ask if that was a joke or a sign but decided it was a little of both. He looked back at Remy and noted the small tattoo, low on his inner calf, a nautical star, not unlike Tom's.

Remy jerked his head toward it. "Cool, right?"

"Did Etienne give you that?"

"He was there but no—I did it."

"You did that?" Prophet leaned in to study it. "It's really good, Rem."

Remy beamed. "Tom said we could open up a shop."

"Yeah, I've heard that's the eventual plan."

"What about you?"

"I don't tattoo," Prophet said seriously. "Want to tell me what's bothering you?"

Remy narrowed his eyes. "How do you do that?"

"It's a gift. Spill."

Remy sighed and leaned up on one elbow. Prophet's eyes shifted momentarily to the scar on Remy's chest, the one made by the man who'd also killed his father. The scar was pink now, much less angry looking, and still a constant reminder of how close they'd come to losing him. As if Remy knew what he was thinking, his fingers brushed over it as he asked, "Is everything settled? With my mom."

"It will be, because I've got some information."

"About the drugs?"

"Yes." Prophet paused, wishing Remy didn't have to know any of it. "How long have you known about it?"

"A long time," Remy admitted. "So does that come out in court?"

"The only other thing I can have her do is keep it out and have her sign temporary guardianship until you're seventeen. That's probably the easiest option, lets her save face and it doesn't put either of you through a trial."

"And then what?"

"You emancipate."

"What about . . . adoption?"

That surprised Prophet, but not in a bad way. He hadn't wanted to broach that, not this close to Etienne's death. "I don't know if we both can."

"One of you can though, right?"

"We can do that, Rem, if that's what you want. I can adopt you after you emancipate."

He frowned, obviously trying to take it all in. "You can do that after I emancipate? It wouldn't matter then."

"It would to me."

Remy blinked fast. Nodded. "It's important."

"Then consider it done."

"You really don't have any tattoos?"

"No. Tom draws them, but I don't think he wants to settle on any one thing."

"Well, you can't do names."

"I know that superstition." Prophet paused. "What about the initials of kids I adopt?"

"I'm not a kid," he said seriously. "Besides, are you planning on roaming the countryside looking for fucked-up kids to adopt?"

"No. And you're not fucked up, Rem. Not even a little bit."

His soft smile looked a lot like Etienne's. "But my mom is."

"Yeah, well . . . sometimes that happens. People can't always help their addictions. Doesn't mean she doesn't love you."

Remy seemed to take a moment to absorb that before hitting Prophet with, "What about your mom?"

"What's with all the hard questions tonight?"

Remy shrugged. "Remember this the next time you ask me all the questions."

"Smart-ass." Prophet sat back against the headboard and wondered if this kid was some kind of truth serum in the form of a teenage boy. "My mom's bipolar. Do you know what that is?"

"Sort of."

"It's a mental disorder. It's not uncommon and a lot of times, it's really treatable. Her case is tougher than most. She needs medicine to regulate her moods, but a lot of the meds she's tried don't always work on her. And, even when they do, she doesn't always take them because the disorder makes her confused." Prophet said it that way as a reminder to himself, because she'd been addicted to drugs while he'd been younger. Because she hadn't been diagnosed, she was always attempting to self-regulate, and twenty-twenty hindsight was a definite bitch. He'd hated her when she was using—and yet he'd always made sure she could get her fix and that she stayed safe. Knowing that she couldn't have helped herself made him feel guiltier. "When I was younger, she didn't know about the disorder, so she did a lot of drugs to make herself feel better."

Remy processed that. "But that's not why my mom does them."

"People do drugs for all kinds of reasons, Rem. I'm not an expert on it—I just know why my mom got addicted. I didn't back then."

"Where is she now?"

"She lives in a place where they help her remember to take her meds and they keep her safe."

"Did you make her go there?"

"No. She put herself in there. She didn't want me to have to worry about her." Not one hundred percent truth but relatively speaking, it was close enough.

"So she's fine now?"

Prophet sighed. "Depends on the day, kid."

"Does that run in your family?"

"My mom says no, but it can be inherited."

"Because you're always moody."

"Bipolar and blind? What the hell are you trying to do to me?" Prophet joked.

Remy laughed, then got serious. "Where's your dad?"

"Third fucking degree," Prophet muttered, wondered if Tom was standing by the door gathering all this information. It was what he'd do if the roles were reversed, and hell, it would take care of him ever having to talk about it out loud again. "He died when I was around your age."

"Was he nice?"

"No, he wasn't. He wasn't anything like your dad," Prophet told him honestly, then realized that, at some point, Mal had entered the room and was sacked out in the corner chair, looking at an iPad. Later, Prophet knew he'd lie on the floor at Remy's bedside. He'd put a cage around Remy and sleep on top of it if he thought Remy would let him . . . but Mal also knew the importance of not living like you were in prison.

"Sorry, Proph."

"'S'all right, Rem. I've got a lot of chosen family around me." He glanced up at Mal, whose only indication that he was listening was a small quirk of his mouth, like he was trying to hide a smile. "Why don't you try to get some shut-eye?"

Remy complied without complaining, but only after he seemed to realize that Prophet would hang until he fell asleep. He put his head down and closed his eyes and after a few restless minutes where he complained that he would never be able to sleep, his breathing went deep and even.

It'd been a long day for all of them.

Ain't family grand, Mal signed, the sarcasm heavy in his fingers.

This one's not bad, Prophet signed back so as not to wake Remy and Mal gave a sharp nod.

Nope, not bad at all. But lying this close to a teenager made Prophet feel like he was back in his old bedroom, in his old skin, in a life that seemed so far away that it felt like it belonged to someone else at times . . .

Joe Drews had talked a good game, and from that Prophet learned the importance of talk. Didn't mean he didn't take something from every encounter.

Judie Drews wanted people to believe she was fine. She was a horrible liar, and from that Prophet learned to be a really good one. He also learned the importance of pretending to wholeheartedly believe someone's lies, whether it was because they desperately wanted him to or because his life depended on it.

The former happened a lot to him before the age of sixteen, the latter almost exclusively after that. And while his father was always all too fucking predictable, he never knew which Mom he was going to get on any given day. The cycles were unpredictable, the manic phases easier than the depressive ones, but truthfully, they all sucked.

But the move to Texas from New York made things worse. Joe Drews had an opportunity, which really meant his scams had gotten them run out of another town.

So now, they were stuck here. But John made it marginally easier at first, and then much more so after Prophet began spending most of his time at John's house.

Childhood games of hide and seek gave way to evading the truant officer and finding a way to make some cash. At first they'd done some low-level gambling—mainly street dice, and it was from those associates they'd learned about the underground fighting. They'd both liked it a lot in the beginning but as time went on, John liked it more. Prophet recognized early his friend's need to get out his aggression, and hell, who was he to judge?

Joe Drews was alternately a shitty father and semiabusive, but not as bad as John's father. Later, after Prophet learned that John's father had molested him, he realized just how many degrees of shitty there were.

Joe'd been a sailor. Prophet liked the idea of following in some traditions. The genetic eye disease that'd been dogging the men in his family for generations and made them form the blind suicide club? Not so much. In fact, Prophet went so far as to sit down with Joe Drews at the age of nine and was granted an answer to a single question.

Prophet had asked, "Do all the men in this family die from the eye disease?"

And on that day, he'd learned that the eye disease hadn't caused the deaths, which made him feel better, and way worse, because Joe had told him, "They all killed themselves before the disease took their sight."

"Are you going to kill yourself too?"

Joe said, "I agreed to one question."

Prophet took that as a yes, of course, and said, "So that's what Drews men do? Join the Navy and kill themselves? Gotta say, not all that enticing."

"So do more," his father told him brusquely.

"You suck as the head of this family," Prophet informed him, knowing he'd get a knock on the head for that later, and not caring.

But before Joe had done just that, he said, "One day, when you're staring down the barrel of this gun, you'll understand."

Prophet had stared down the barrel of many literal guns since that day. Now, he was staring at the only one he'd never be able to control . . . unless he followed in his family's footsteps.

And yeah, he got it, the whole *don't judge till you've walked in my shoes* thing. But he was here, walking in those goddamned shoes, having gotten further in life in general . . . but he was younger than Joe or his grandfather.

Maybe that was why he'd packed so much into his life at such an early age. Like he'd known he would only have so long for one kind of life.

Whether or not he'd accept another kind was anyone's guess.

Seven years after the conversation with Prophet, Joe killed himself, a single shot through the temple with an unregistered gun. There was a short note in his hand that the police brought to them when they knocked on the door.

It's your legacy, son. Make the most of the time you've got.

Joe hadn't lived with them at the time, had moved out when Prophet was ten but was never far. The police had contacted several of his known associates, who told them that Joe had been playing poker and talking about his death. He'd given them his deck of cards and his chips. He'd made a check out to Prophet, which one of them handed to Prophet soberly.

"Any idea why he'd plan his suicide?" one of the older cops asked Prophet.

"He was going to go blind," Prophet told him. "Runs in the men in my family. He's fourth generation."

Prophet saw the look of pity flash across the cop's face and he fucking hated that more than anything.

"Don't take that way out, son," the cop told him. "My father's in a wheelchair and he's doing just fine. Plenty of people are fucked up in one way or another. No reason to leave everyone you love behind."

Maybe he didn't love anyone. Maybe the Drews men were all too selfish, or not built for love. Because hell, Judie was left behind more than Prophet was. Judie couldn't take care of herself, no matter how badly she wanted to. And she did try—Prophet saw that.

Even when Prophet decided to enlist at seventeen, Judie hadn't begged Prophet to stay—had even signed the papers the Navy needed—and that probably made him feel guiltier. She was working part-time, collecting disability and Prophet would send her home money regularly. He'd banked a lot of his fighting money and there wasn't real cause for him to spend it on the Navy's dime. He saw the world—too much of it, probably—and he learned shit no one should ever have to learn. And he'd long ago realized that was his lot in life and accepted it.

That didn't mean he didn't fight it every now and again.

CHAPTER SIX

Something happened daily, and although there was no sign of John, it felt like a petulant child was trying to get their attention, like the bomb threat at Remy's school that made Tom and Prophet side-eye each other.

"Probably nothing," Tom ventured, wanting it to be true.

Prophet didn't argue, but they both decided that school was off-limits for a bit. Remy, of course, didn't mind a damned bit. Mal offered to tutor him in the interim and that actually worked out quite well. Then again, for all Tom knew, *math* was a code for *bomb building*.

When he mentioned that to Prophet, all he got in response was, "They're both useful life skills."

And still, there'd been no sign of John taking the package. Prophet's plans remained in limbo. They kept things as normal for Remy as possible, dealt with lawyers and the foster care system. They were making plans, or rather, Prophet was and Tom was trying not to get pissed that he wasn't a bigger part of the process.

It was slightly similar to the way they had been in what Prophet began to refer to as the good old days. But in the beginning of their relationship, the good old days were full of lust and hate and the thin line those rode.

Not that that was a bad thing.

Prophet's PTSD flashbacks continued—and escalated—including a pretty nasty one with Prophet nearly strangling Tom, who was only relieved that there was no sign that John had actually been there in the aftermath. Afterward, Prophet claimed to not remember what the flashback had been about, and Tom hadn't believed him but they'd both pretended otherwise.

Beyond that, their lives were oddly domestic, for lack of a better word, Tom surmised, if he could ignore the fact that every day, twice a day at least, Prophet checked for the envelope that remained untouched.

Finally, on the eighth evening, when it still remained so, Tom found Prophet talking to his connections to charter a private plane, off the radar.

"Takin' me on vacation?" Tom drawled, leaning over his shoulder to bite his partner's neck.

Prophet turned to him and narrowed his eyes. "You just want me to drink those umbrella drinks again."

"I wouldn't mind."

Prophet conceded, "Me neither," and then, more seriously, "It'll be over soon."

Tom leaned against the table so he was facing Prophet—and not looking at the screen. "I know. Then what? Because I'd much rather plan for that."

Prophet smiled, but Tom knew there was something bittersweet about leaving these days behind. Because of so many reasons, but most especially because of Prophet's sight. If there was anything Tom could do to fix it, he would. He'd tried, of course, read up on the genetic condition (fairly rare, running in families) and then gone into full-on research mode, and Prophet had let him, almost like he somehow knew Tom had to go through the same steps of grieving that Prophet already had. Granted, it was a different level of grief.

One night, Prophet had found him sleeping, head down next to the computer. He'd woken, expecting Prophet to be angry that he was contacting doctors on Prophet's behalf. Instead, Prophet turned the computer off and said, "Take me to bed."

Tom had, fucked both of them into the mattress. He wanted to do that now, but he had a feeling Prophet had other plans.

He did. It went: Check on Remy. Call Mal. Check cameras. Cillian's apartment. Alarm the place. Brace the bedroom window shut.

And then Tom found himself stripped, tied and fucked. And yeah, that was more than okay.

Finally, Prophet had gotten Tom to fall asleep first. The guy would stay up all night, every night, just to watch over him, like he was a child, which Prophet found both endearing and utterly fucking annoying.

Jesus, almost strangle a guy once . . .

He glanced over at the big man, whose arm was slung over his eyes, taking slow, deep breaths, still looking flushed and handsome.

Prophet was grateful Tom had pushed to come along on this very unauthorized and highly necessary mission. If Tom hadn't pushed, Prophet would've gladly left him home with Remy, and there were times he wished Tom would change his mind. But he knew how bad his eyes were getting—really fucking rapidly—and the thought that he might leave for a week, a month and not actually be able to physically see Tom again after that . . . that made him curse John and all of this more than anything.

But the longer he waited, the more sure he was that John would get away with everything, that the past eleven years, from the way his team had been forced to live to Mal almost losing his life, and Chris losing his, would be in vain.

"You're thinking so loudly," Tom murmured.

Fucker. "You were pretending to sleep so I'd sleep."

"Yes." Tom opened his eyes. "It's what you'd do, right?"

Again, fucker. "You get cranky when you don't sleep."

"Right, I'm the cranky one." Tom turned on his side and threw his arm across Prophet's chest. "Can we talk about where Remy will go during the next however many weeks? And yes, I'd love to stay here with him but no, because you need me more. I told Remy I'd get you back safely."

Prophet sniffed. "Funny, I told him the same thing." He rubbed a hand along the scar on back of his neck, an old habit he'd gotten into shortly after someone had tried to chop his head off. With a machete.

Tom once told him that he could completely sympathize with the guy who'd been holding the machete. Prophet guessed he could too. "I think Remy should go with Della for a bit," he said finally. "It'll be all around easier."

"Unless he stays with Phil," Tom said.

Prophet's face hardened but he made no comment. "How about Mal's until he's got to come to us? He can hand him off to Doc or Della, depending on what's happening."

"I trust that."

"Think he'd be okay at Della's if that's where Mal decides? Because of his mom?"

"He can at least have a visit with her. It's what the social worker wanted to see happen. Wants to see us making an effort to keep Remy close to his roots. Plus, Della's not going to let those visits happen without supervision."

Yeah, Della would protect Remy as fiercely as she once had Tom. Plus, Remy was almost sixteen and soon enough, they weren't going to be making decisions for him so much as advising him. "We'll tell him first thing. Ease his mind."

"He's not going to be happy about it."

"Yeah, well, neither am I." Prophet rubbed his neck again. "If he ends up with Della instead of Doc, I'll call in a favor. Have someone stay with them, just in case."

"Someone I know?"

"Jin. Easy enough to underestimate him but whoever did so would be damned stupid." Jin was a former Navy pilot who'd explained about Prophet's bad luck with flights. Jin might not look the part of a bodyguard, but he was pretty lethal in his own right.

Tom agreed. "Della would probably appreciate that."

"We can say he's a cousin of mine," Prophet added.

"And if the social worker really looks into that?" Tom asked and Prophet just waved his hand with a *pffft* sound. "Like that's really going to magically take care of it?"

"It just might, Tommy. It just might."

CHAPTER SEVEN

Tom woke early the next morning but Prophet was already out for a run and Remy was just stirring. Tom made him breakfast and watched as he ate three helpings of it and yes, they might need to take out loans to feed this child.

"Is there any more?" Remy asked hopefully.

Tom handed him the eggs he'd made for Prophet, a not so subtle attempt to get him to eat something other than sweets for breakfast.

Remy grinned and downed what was on the plate. After he finished, Tom broached the subject of leaving. "Hey, you know that Prophet and I have a job that's coming up—one that will take us away from here for a little bit."

"How long?"

"I'm not sure. Less than a month, we're hoping."

"You guys have been walking around with your heads together and whispering, so I'm guessing it's a big job," Remy said.

"Yes."

"What makes it so big?"

He knew Remy deserved to know some of the truths. "He's got to hurt someone he was best friends with."

Remy pushed a little away from the table, pulled his knees to his chest and wrapped an arm around his knees. "And he can do that?"

"The guy's not the same person anymore."

"Still. I mean, somewhere in Prophet's mind, wouldn't he be the same?"

Tom ruffled a hand through Remy's hair. "Proph'll be okay."

"You'll make sure of it, I know," Remy said, with more trust than a fifteen-year-old should have to have. He'd be sixteen by the time this was all over. "Did you know that Prophet eats Twizzlers for breakfast sometimes?"

"It's not breakfast. It's like a pre-breakfast," Prophet explained as he walked in, wearing fresh clothing and hair wet from a recent shower. Tom hadn't even heard him come in from his run. "Where do you think I'm going to get all the calories that my body needs to keep functioning. Kale? I don't think so."

"What's kale?" Remy whispered to Tom.

Prophet frowned and told him sternly, "Don't think about shit like that—you're too impressionable."

Tom shot him a look, then turned and left them to their own devices.

"Somewhere in Prophet's mind, wouldn't he be the same?"

Prophet had been listening to Tom's explanation, and Remy's questions, especially that one, sat uneasily with him. Probably because the innocence of Remy's observations were like a knife point in his conscience, and the loss of innocence was impossible to explain.

Prophet refused to be the one to take Remy's innocence away. "You know I don't want to leave you, Remy. Neither does Tom."

"Then tell me what's happening."

"What did Tom and Mal tell you?"

"That there's some asshole who hurt you—and now he's trying to hurt all of us."

"Pretty much the way it goes," Prophet said. "I can't give you more specifics now though, Rem."

"I understand." But he didn't, not really. At that age, Prophet wouldn't have either, and would've demanded answers (and gotten ones he'd had no idea what to do with). "It's like the guys who hurt my dad and his friend—more than once."

"Kinda is," Prophet agreed. Etienne had lived through hell in high school and then lost his life because of those same events, many years later.

Remy was watching him carefully. After a second, he said, "Listen, I knew you were both leaving, before Tom told me."

"How?" Maybe Remy had Tommy's Cajun voodoo shit.

"Mal told me."

Yeah, thanks, Uncle Crazy. Prophet wasn't sure if he wanted to hug Mal for that or kill him, which was pretty much his everyday feelings for the man who'd become a brother to him. They took care of each other, and Prophet could draw a parallel to the way he and John had once been, but he and Mal were different. Prophet could easily see that now. Mal watched out for him. Worried. Cared . . . and all because he wanted Prophet to be okay. It wasn't about owning him, cutting him off from the world. "I want to stay."

"I know. But you can't." Remy was up and pouring him a mug of coffee . . . and handing him a donut.

"Why are you buttering me up?"

"You can't worry about me."

"Unfortunately, that's never going to happen." Then he added, "If there was another way . . ."

"Is there?" Remy asked.

"Sit here, let the world blow up and hope my one-time best friend leaves me and my family alone," Prophet said. "Plenty of people step back every day."

"But that's not you."

"No. Sorry."

Remy nodded. "Will Mal be here, like he says?"

"Until he can't be. From there, we'll let him decide if you stay around here with Doc or head to Della's—or a combination of both? Are you okay with him choosing what's best for you at the time?"

Remy nodded. "I'm cool with that. Because it's only temporary." He clearly meant it, as much as any fifteen-year-old who'd lost their father and was worried he was about to lose two more could be.

Prophet's heart squeezed. "You're not. Neither am I."

"This guy—John? He really fucked up?"

Prophet ignored the curse because there was no better way to say it. "Yes. And at one point, I'd do anything to help him."

Prophet had met John in middle school . . . in the principal's office. On Prophet's first day of school after moving to Texas. He could see himself clear as day trying to break into the attendance office . . . just to prove he could. For him, it was never really *why*, but rather, *why not.*

John had lived in that town his whole life and would sometimes tell Prophet that he felt like he was in trouble for simply being alive.

At times, Prophet thought that was pretty damned accurate for both of them. From that day on, they just tended to get into trouble together. And they were extremely talented in doing so. As the years went by, they got even better at not being caught. They got bolder, but while Prophet got stealthier and more cautious, John got more reckless.

Once, when John was drunk, he'd admitted what had happened to him, and then never spoke of it again. After that, Prophet realized perfect families never existed—the facade was just that. The dose of reality helped him in several ways, but nothing could've prepared him for his father's suicide.

Because that brought the spectra of the disease he was living under into direct focus. Prophet was no longer *next in line*. He was first in line.

He was just *next*.

So he put himself, literally, on the front lines. It was both freeing and devastating. Any invisible leash that might've once tethered him to the edge of caution was cut . . . but that didn't mean he didn't learn to self-protect.

He'd protected John. Stayed safe so he could watch over his best friend. So being a team leader was a natural fit. No one under his watch was getting hurt.

Remy prompted, "And now, you want to hurt him?"

"Actually, I'm going to help him." Saying that out loud for the first time crystalized it for him. *Because that's your job—you retrieve people from hell, and if they can't come back, you save them from future suffering.*

Remy frowned, attempting to process it all. "Kind of like me with mom. I want to help her, but I don't want to be with her."

"Yeah, Rem. Kind of like that."

"So help him then. That's cool," Remy said simply. And really, it was that simple. Prophet had let his feelings complicate everything.

Now, it was back to basics. Remy could read between the lines that John was somehow dangerous. There was no need to tell him outright what Prophet's definition of *helping John* was.

There were some things the kid didn't need to know. Then again, Prophet thought about the things he knew at that age, which was, at times, more than most adults gave him credit for. At Remy's age, he'd already been living in Texas, had known John for three years and within the next year, his dad would also be dead.

Remy got up from the table and disappeared . . . and reappeared with a gun. And a cleaning rod and other supplies. "Mal's taking me to the range this morning," he said by way of explanation. "Oh, and I never plan on joining the military. Just FYI, dude."

Dude?

Remy started cleaning the gun on the kitchen table and Tom reentered the kitchen and stopped short at that sight.

"No, Prophet didn't teach me this," Remy said without looking up from his task. "You grew up where I did, Tom. Dad taught me this for Bayou living."

"No gators here," Tom murmured, but Prophet shot him a look that made his cheeks heat. Remy, thankfully, kept his head down.

"Mal's been taking me shooting," Remy continued.

Mal? Tom mouthed to Prophet.

Prophet shrugged. "He's a good teacher."

"Really good," Remy added, eyes still on the gun. "He should've been a sniper."

"He was," Prophet said. "He was our sniper. He didn't want to leave us, so he didn't do much formal training."

"They would've pulled him from your team?" Tom asked, unable to keep the surprise from his voice.

"Yeah, imagine that," Prophet said, a wry quietness in his tone. "Imagine that."

"I don't think Mal ever wanted to." Tom put a hand on Prophet's shoulder, both of them watching Remy expertly put the newly clean handgun back together.

He looked up at them and smiled . . . and then teenager-narrowed his eyes and asked, "What?"

"Good job," Prophet told him, shrugging off Tom's hand. But Remy looked down and smiled again at the genuine compliment in Prophet's tone before moving to return the gun to its proper place in the gun safe. In the locked room that Mal had shown him how to get into.

To be fair, Mal had turned it into a panic room of sorts.

"You're a better father than I am," Tom told him. "I worry too much."

"I just don't let it show," Prophet said. "For the record, you're a great father, Tommy. And it didn't have to be that way."

"Guess we both broke the cycle," Tom agreed. "We won't fuck this up."

"I thought being a parent meant you got to fuck up. We've only got a little time left to do it while he's still impressionable, so we'd better hurry." He frowned for a second, then smiled as the idea hit. "I'm going on all his dates."

"Yeah, that'll do the trick," Tom said dryly.

CHAPTER EIGHT

The night before they left, Tom finished packing his most important piece of luggage—his go-bag. Prophet had given him considerable help in filling it with several weapons that Tom was grateful for. He zipped it up, put it into the locked closet and away from Remy's curiosity, and found himself drawn to his dresser . . . and the small box he kept on top of it.

It held odds and ends, things from his life before Prophet and also present-day trinkets. Coins from countries he'd visited. An old bullet slug taken from his Kevlar vest—the first time he'd been shot at on the job. Old motorcycle keys. He also kept the bracelet Prophet gave him in here too, because he didn't want anything to happen to it. Now, he put it on his wrist, over the tattoo, and finally found what he'd started this hunt for.

It was a key—nondescript. Brass. Round top, with the number 456 on it. That didn't matter. It was actually a key to nothing, and something he hadn't looked at in a long time, something he'd always seen as a kind of talisman before moving in with Prophet and realizing he had a living, breathing blond one with him the majority of the time.

"What's that?" Prophet had come up quietly behind him and was now looking over his shoulder.

Tom stared at it, feeling slightly stupid. "It's nothing. It's just . . . Ollie . . . you've heard me talk about him, right? He was my unofficial mentor at the FBI." *Unofficial mentor* was putting it lightly. Ollie was probably the reason Tom stuck it out for so long, was probably the closest thing to a real father Tom had, because his real father was for shit.

"Yeah, you've mentioned him."

"Well, before he left, he gave me this. He told me that when I didn't think I could do something, to remember I was the key to my own challenges." Tom fingered the key and turned to face Prophet. "Corny, I know. I can't believe I kept it."

"I can, T. You should bring it."

"Really?"

"Something made you seek it out."

"I used to carry it everywhere. I was carrying it when I met you."

"Maybe it's a sign you need to do so again." Prophet gave him a small smile and hadn't made him feel stupid at all. Tom slid the key into his wallet and tucked it back into his pocket.

Remy sat with his sketchbook, taking furtive glances at Prophet as he worked on his laptop. Remy had a book of tattoos next to him, and he pretended to be drawing them, but he was actually drawing the man who was trying to adopt him. Tom would let Remy sketch him—had already—but Prophet wouldn't and that made him an appealing target.

It was also hard as anything to capture Prophet. Remy likened it to catching the ferocity of a storm in motion, and something that changed and moved constantly was hard to capture. It was more complicated, like a 3-D drawing come to life. So he'd settled on trying to draw several pictures of Prophet in motion, like a time lapse. Maybe he would make a flip book to animate the energy.

Or maybe he could slow down and work on one portrait at a time.

It was what he remembered his dad saying out loud, to himself, when he was deep into one of his paintings. His father had been tattooing since before he was Remy's age, and he'd taught Remy. But Remy had no one to practice on now, and he was afraid of getting rusty.

"Hey, Proph?"

"Yeah?" Prophet's eyes didn't move off the screen.

"I need to practice my tattooing. It's been a while and . . ." He trailed off because Prophet didn't have any tattoos.

"Can you do something small that will heal fast?"

Remy was almost afraid to look up. *Was that a yes?*

"Rem?" Prophet prompted.

"Yeah, I can do something small," Remy told him.

"So what are you waiting for?"

"Wait, you want me to do it right now?"

"Unless you've got other plans."

Remy collected the things from his room—his father's tattoo guns and ink. He'd use black ink because it would heal fastest. He also grabbed alcohol pads, gloves and salve.

He laid it all out on the table, where Prophet had closed and moved his laptop over. "You know this is permanent, right?"

"I've heard that's how it works," Prophet said, but there wasn't any sarcasm in his tone.

"This is your first," Remy said. "Maybe . . ."

"What are you going to do?"

"You don't have to do this."

"Rem? Do I seem like the kind of person who does things he doesn't want to?"

"No." *Except for people you care about.* Remy swallowed the weird lump in his throat. "I know what I'll do. It's not tiny, but thin lines. Easy healing."

"Where?"

"Shoulder." Prophet pulled his shirt off and Remy studied the skin there. "Over the scar."

Remy studied the thin, light-pink line. It was maybe an inch long, but barely raised. Still, scars were always tricky and he really didn't want to mess anything up. "It's still pretty new . . ."

"Just give it your best shot. You can always go over it again when we get back, right?"

"Right," Remy told him, bolstered by Prophet's confidence in him. Reminded him of his dad. Reminded him how lucky he'd gotten to have both Prophet and Tom in his life, despite the unluckiness that'd taken his dad away from him forever.

He heard his dad talking in his head, something he used to say to customers who came in with scars—usually much bigger than this one on Prophet's shoulder—and wanted them covered. *Some scars never heal . . . but we cover them with other things and we move on.*

Prophet had switched the chair around and leaned his chest against the chair's back. "This okay?"

"Yes. But you can lie down too."

"I'm good."

"You're busy though . . ."

"Rem."

"Okay." He wondered if maybe he should do a stencil first. It was too important to mess up . . .

"Don't worry about that," Prophet told him, jarring Remy into realizing he'd spoken his fears out loud. "If you mess up, you can always fix it. Life's never perfect—that's what keeps it interesting, right?"

As the needle buzzed against his skin, Prophet wondered about the parenting rules of letting the kid you were trying to adopt tattoo you.

Ah, fuck it.

He could see why this was Tom's jam—the slight, constant buzz of pain.

"You're leaving soon," Remy said quietly over the noise of the small machine.

"Yes."

"To where?"

"Africa. To Dean's. But you can't tell anyone."

"Except Mal?"

"Except Mal," Prophet agreed.

"And this John guy will stop hanging around here?"

"He'll follow me."

"Like hide and seek."

"You're a lot smarter than I was at your age."

"Can I visit your mom?" Remy asked suddenly and Prophet forced himself not to tense up.

"Why?"

"Because."

Prophet sighed. "Let me think about it."

"That's parent for *no*," Remy informed him.

"No, it's Prophet for *let me think about it*."

"Fine."

Christ, teenagers were moody.

"It's done." Remy was wiping a layer of salve across his shoulder. "I'm going to wrap it for a while. I'll clean it later."

"Thanks, Remy. Now you'll be with me every step of the way."

Remy blinked a few times. "And that's important?"

"You have no idea how much."

Tom let Prophet herd him, out of the house, into the airport and onto the plane, because it was easier than arguing. Being bossy was Prophet's natural state, and if it helped to take his mind off what they were headed toward, even for a second, Tom would allow it.

Their plane was next in line for takeoff. The pilots were Mitch and Jin, the ones who'd taken them to Dean's before, the last time he was kidnapped. Except this time, it wasn't a plane LT commandeered, mainly because Dean didn't want his brother hovering over him, asking questions. LT's protectiveness had kicked up, understandably so since the kidnapping, but Dean was a grown man. It was a battle Prophet wasn't getting in the middle of, he told Tom as they settled into their seats.

"And Dean trusts them to not tell LT?" Tom asked.

"They like Dean better than LT."

"I knew I liked them." Tom's phone beeped and he saw Remy's text.

"Everything okay?"

"It's from Remy." He looked up. "Proph, I've got something to tell you about your mom."

"Okay," Prophet said warily.

"She's gone from her facility. She checked herself out. Remy got the call off the machine a few minutes ago." He wanted to ask why Prophet wouldn't have gotten the message on his cell phone, but Prophet always had his reasons.

"What exactly did the message say? Word for word? It's important."

"Hang on." He texted Remy and a few minutes later, thanks to the teen's fast fingers, Tom had a transcript. "'This is Mary Lambert, a night supervisor from the Ward Home and Health Facility. I'm calling to let you know that Judie Drews checked herself out today at 6:34 p.m.'" Prophet checked his watch and Tom kept reading. "'Since it was a voluntary hold, we could not keep her—she declined to leave a forwarding address and you have been contacted, as per our agreement, after she left the facility. Thank you.'"

"Okay." Prophet breathed the word, as if something made sense to him. But fuck, none of it did to Tom, least of all Prophet's reaction.

"Prophet, do we need to send someone to go find her?"

"No. She'll be all right, T. Promise."

"You said that without her meds . . . Remy's worried." Maybe that would get Prophet's attention.

"Please tell Remy for me that I swear on my life he doesn't need to worry about my mom. And I'll explain it all when I can. Come on, Tommy—you used to trust me with shit like that."

"I trust you—"

"There's a 'but' in that sentence." Prophet put his head back. "Go fuck yourself then. Go home if you can't handle it. I don't need your shit."

Not the response Tom was expecting at all, but he had a feeling that everything that would happen on this trip would exceed expectations. Everything was changing rapidly, sides were shifting, and Tom felt like he had to hold on to something steady because the ground underneath him was constantly threatening to swallow them both.

Instead of fighting about it, he closed his eyes—and shut Prophet out purposely, in reaction to the shut-out he was feeling. After takeoff, Prophet was moving around restlessly. Tom glanced over, hoping it wasn't another flashback and found Prophet pulling his shirt sleeve up and trying to look at a bandage on his shoulder. "What's that from?"

Prophet glanced at him. "Shit, my tattoo. You've got to clean it."

"Your what?"

"Are you going to just sit there with questions or will you help me?" Prophet demanded. "Remy gave me stuff to—"

"Wait, you let Remy tattoo you?"

"He was worried about getting out of practice."

Tom stopped himself from saying anything further about that. "What did you get?"

"I don't know—he picked it."

"You don't know," Tom repeated.

"Are you done playing parrot?" Prophet asked irritably.

"Asshole." Tom ripped the tape off without ceremony and stared at Remy's creation.

"So." Prophet continued trying to look at it over his shoulder, like a dog chasing his tail. "What is it?"

Tom felt an odd sense of satisfaction settle in his chest. "Nautical star."

"To guide me home safely," Prophet finished quietly.

"He didn't fill it all in."

"I told him it had to heal fast."

"He left parts of it to finish when we get back." Tom took a picture of it and showed Prophet his phone screen.

"He's good."

"Very." Tom stared. "Normally, I'd let it out for the open air, but I think we'll go old-school for this, and wrap it for a couple of days. You've already taken something?"

"Yeah, Doc put me on antibiotics anyway before this. You too?"

"Yeah," Tom confirmed. "So, a piercing and a tattoo. You're finally coming out of your shell."

That made Prophet laugh, longer and harder than Tom could remember in a long time. Then he told Tom, "Sorry—about the Judie thing. It's just . . . a lot."

"I can imagine."

"I promise it's fine. Not unexpected. It's just . . . now, more than ever, I'm really going to need you to take some leaps of faith. And I'm the last one who would handle that well if roles were reversed. But this . . ."

"It's the culmination of all those years you spent searching," Tom finished. He leaned in and kissed Prophet. It was meant to be quick, but Prophet pulled him in hard, until they were full on making out, Prophet maneuvering into Tom's seat, Tom's lap.

The plane banked a hard left. Prophet cursed into Tom's mouth and they both heard the pilots laughing over the speaker system.

"Assholes!" Prophet called, then grumbled, "Ruining my fun."

"There's always the bathroom," Tom suggested as Prophet sank to his knees. "Proph—"

"Shut up. You need the distraction."

"And you don't?" Tom managed as Prophet yanked on his cargos until he'd carefully freed Tom's dick, piercings in full view.

"This definitely helps," Prophet murmured, fingering the metal, making Tom shiver, and when Prophet put his mouth on him, the plane could've flown upside down and Tom wouldn't have cared. For all he knew, it did.

CHAPTER NINE

Cillian was in his own apartment, packing, no doubt getting ready to try to find Prophet. Why, Mal didn't know, because no one had invited Cillian . . . and Mal thought that maybe killing him would stop him from going. It was definitely the best option, but then there'd be a lot of blood to clean up and Remy was still in the apartment . . .

You do realize you're typing all of this directly to me, right? Cillian asked him.

Just thinking out loud, Mal typed in response. *Isn't honesty the best policy?*

Not in this case. Then again, maybe it's better I know to sleep with one eye open.

Which eye? Just curious? And what time do you plan on sleeping? Just asking for a friend.

If that didn't work, Mal would simply superglue his doors and windows shut. Well, he only had the windows left to do anyway.

There was a long pause and Mal sat back, staring at the screen. It was easier like this, when Mal couldn't see him, could pretend that there wasn't history between them.

Unsettled history at best.

Tom knew what had happened and Prophet was beginning to suspect but Mal telling Prophet would mean Prophet would probably kill Cillian for sure.

And that was Mal's right to do so, when and if he pleased.

"Hey Mal?" Remy called. "Why is Cillian coming up the fire escape?"

Fuck. *Give us a minute, Rem*, he signed, and Remy looked at Cillian with narrowed eyes, but his expression relaxed when he looked back at Mal. *I'll be okay.*

"I know where the guns are if you need me. Just press that button I gave you and I'll come running," Remy told him.

The device beeped on Remy's end and flashed and vibrated on Mal's. Remy had given it to him—it seemed like the equivalent of friendship bracelets but Mal had to admit it was a cool thing. They'd worked out a systematic code for things like *run now* and *call Prophet* and *I need donuts.*

Remy always needed donuts.

Up until now, Mal had tried to avoid Cillian—both in person and through texts—as much as possible. It wasn't hard, because Remy kept him busy and Cillian was avoiding him too. But now he felt Cillian's eyes on him through the glass. Mal figured he could get off a clean shot but hell, that would be anticlimactic. Better to make him suffer . . .

Cillian knocked impatiently and Mal reluctantly went over and unlocked the window . . . and only pulled it up the slightest bit, forcing Cillian to have to work to open it and climb in.

And Mal still hadn't looked at him, not the way he wanted to. In person, Cillian had exceeded his expectations—the man was handsome as fuck, refined in that spook way. It had definitely made things exciting when the guy you were fucking could kill you as easily as you could kill him . . . until you found out he actually *had* tried to kill you, nearly succeeded *and* left you for dead.

Cillian was claiming mistaken identity and they both hated John with a fury like no other for what he'd done. But no matter that, it was still an albatross between them, an insurmountable brick wall, Sisyphus's rock.

Except Mal wasn't the one who'd be rolling a fucking rock up a hill in Hell on a daily basis. No fucking way was he Sisyphus.

Now Cillian tilted his head to the side, staring at Mal, like he knew exactly what Mal was thinking. He sighed a little and started with, "How's Remy doing?"

Ready to shoot you, Mal thought. Signed instead, *Misses his dad. Tom and Proph. Tough being a kid.*

Cillian nodded. Mal wanted to ask if it had been tough for him too but he told himself he shouldn't care. Couldn't, anyway.

"You don't seem surprised to see me come up the fire escape," Cillian noted.

Mal shrugged. *Whatever floats your boat. You could probably use the exercise. You're not exactly young.*

Cillian's eyes narrowed, and his brogue clipped when he said, "I can't open my apartment's front door."

That's a fire hazard.

"Yes, I realize that."

You seemed to be unscathed. Was there a fire? Do you have any burns?

"Why do you look hopeful?" Cillian muttered. "Never mind. I'm—"

Leaving the country.

"Yes. And you can't trust anyone."

The fucking irony. At least he didn't say anything stupid about Mal needing to hold down the fort. *Anyone in particular?*

"Doc's clear," was all Cillian said. "Beyond that . . ."

Got it, Mal signed. *Go.*

"Mal," Cillian started, then shook his head and muttered, "No— not now," to himself.

Yeah, not now. *Not ever,* Mal thought, then called himself a motherfucking liar when Cillian went back out the window and Mal closed and locked it between them. For a moment too long, Mal caught his eyes through the glass, and then he didn't want to be the first one to look away. Because he wasn't fucking weak.

Finally, reluctantly, Cillian broke the gaze and went quietly down the metal steps and only then did Mal close his eyes and press his forehead against the cool glass.

CHAPTER TEN

Tom woke when Jin announced descent. Prophet was texting—on two separate burner phones that he broke in half as soon as he sent messages on them—and then shrugged at Tom like it was business as usual.

Which Tom supposed it was. He glanced out the window as the ground began to show through the haze. He hadn't been back to Africa in months, not since he and Prophet had gone in to rescue Dean and Reggie after they'd been kidnapped.

LT and Dean were from a very wealthy family, and Dean had chosen to live and work in Africa, mainly living and working in Djibouti and Eritrea, with occasional aide trips to Somalia and Ethiopia, despite the dangers—or because of them. Dean helped to fund the building of clinics and refugee camps and the like, and because of that, he was often a target for kidnappings.

Tom liked Dean. LT? Not nearly as much.

"There's Reggie." Tom pointed out the window to the man in khaki shorts and a dark T-shirt coming into view along the airstrip, which was pretty much in the middle of nowhere and still on Dean's massive property. "Did he serve with Dean?"

The plane rumbled along the dirt runaway strip after final descent as Prophet unbuckled his seat belt. "Reggie's former Force Recon, but he and Dean met in the field on some joint missions. Dean reached out to him after his accident and vice versa. From there, the two of them started reaching out to other vets who were considered retired under special circumstances."

"I'm sure that entails a lot of men and women these days."

"Yeah. The saying is that there's no such thing as an uninjured soldier." Prophet pointed to his own head. "Every soldier has PTSD. It's the one thing they can't inoculate you against. But damn, they try. They do try."

Tom put a hand on his forearm. "We'll get through this."

"No choice, right? Let's go, T."

They deplaned, the humidity slapping them like a wet blanket as Reggie came over to meet them.

"Good to see you, Proph." Reggie gave a hug to him, then turned to Tom and did the same. "You both look good."

"You too, Reggie," Tom told him.

"Work's treating me right. Come on—car's right here." It was much different seeing him under these circumstances. He was obviously back in his element, so much so that if Tom hadn't known about the prosthetic arm, he'd never have noticed it, not the way Reggie hauled their bags—insisted on it, actually.

The truck was a white Range Rover that looked old but definitely had the right machinery under the hood. Once they started rolling, Tom felt the extra pickup.

Prophet sat in the back and Tom knew he hated not being in control or behind the wheel. Tom wanted to tell Prophet that he was always in control, no matter what. It was just something Prophet had been born with—he exuded *in charge*.

As they drove to the house over the dirt roads, Tom stared at the empty plains mixed with greens that had been driven back from man-made means as Reggie and Prophet talked about the new security measures Dean had put into place. It sounded like a major upgrade, and all since the kidnappings, which made sense, and it was about an hour away from the old place, on the border between Djibouti and Eritrea.

"Here we go. We just moved in a couple of months ago, although Dean kept the other place. But this one has the airstrip," Reggie explained as he motioned to the high gates, a necessity in this part of the world. Tom heard dogs barking—more deterrents—and he'd bet there were armed men watching from all sides. It was both comforting and eye-opening, because living like this, in a fortress, couldn't be easy.

Tom figured it was a testament to Dean himself that he chose to stay and continue doing the work he did under dangerous circumstances.

"Last I talked to Dean, he sounded like he was back up and running at full speed again," Prophet was saying to Reggie now.

"Better than ever," Reggie confirmed. "But he takes a lot more precautions now. Knows we can't afford to lose him—he does too much good out here."

Prophet nodded and Tom watched the gates open after Reggie typed a code on his phone. The men came out to watch the road—and their six—as Reggie drove through and the house loomed before them. It wasn't huge in height but it sprawled.

"Looks like a vacation house," Tom murmured.

"Or a fortress masquerading as one," Prophet added.

"He's waiting for you," Reggie told Prophet, who started to walk toward the front door.

"You coming?" he asked Tom.

"I'll be right there—I'll help Reggie with the bags," Tom told him and Prophet nodded. Tom knew he'd appreciate a minute or two alone with the man.

Reggie nodded in Prophet's direction. "He givin' you trouble?"

"Wouldn't be Prophet if he wasn't."

Reggie laughed and shook his head in agreement.

Prophet tried—unsuccessfully—to sneak into the room where Dean sat, but the fucker clocked him the second he stepped inside.

"About time, Prophet."

"How the hell do you do that?" Prophet asked, walking toward the couch and sitting next to his old friend.

Before Prophet met him, Dean had been a SEAL, mainly working in conjunction with the CIA in moving specialists around the world. He was good at it, maybe better than Prophet'd been but they were cut from the same cloth. That was apparent from the first night they'd met—although by then, Dean had retired from the SEALs and covert ops—when he called Prophet an asshole within three minutes.

Probably because Prophet had called him one first. But hell, it was the truth.

From that point on, he and Dean had remained close. Checking in on each other's lives regularly. Outside of Prophet's team, Dean had been the only other one who knew all about John and what was happening, knew more than Phil or LT or even Tom, at points.

Now, he assessed the dark-haired, light-eyed man who'd always been tall and wiry but strong as fuck. He looked better than the last time Prophet had seen him, but hell, no one looked their best after being kidnapped.

"Been working out, Guns?" Prophet asked. Dean threw an ice cube at him—it hit Prophet right between the eyes. "Asshole."

"And don't forget it." Dean sat back. "I've always worked out."

"Yeah well, Reggie says you're doing more than ever."

"Reggie needs to keep his mouth shut," Dean muttered, then shrugged. "I got complacent. I like working the clinic. Like the guys working around me. I trust them, because I have to, but if they can't trust me . . ."

Prophet nodded, even though Dean couldn't see him do so.

"Your eyes are getting worse," Dean said finally.

"Faster than I thought," Prophet agreed.

"I hope you're not going to whine about it the whole time you're here." Dean picked up his beer bottle. "I'll have to kick your ass in front of everyone. And you might cry."

Prophet snorted. "Pump a few extra weights and suddenly you're America's Top Merc? Hey, that'd be a great show . . ."

Dean shook his head. "Don't look to me to fund it." Only then did he turn to the door where, seconds later, Tom appeared. "Hey, Tom—can't believe you're still dealing with this asshole."

Tom raised his brows as he came farther into the room. "Looks like I'm not the only one dealing with him."

"Touché," Dean said before turning his attention back to the open doorway. "Come on in, Nico. We've got company."

Tom saw Prophet's expression harden and he was off the couch, asking, "Nico?" as a tall, dark-blond man walked into the room and faced Prophet.

Nico's expression was unsurprised, his voice lazy when he answered, "Hey, Proph."

Prophet's response was nowhere near as calm. "The fuck?" burst out of him, and then Prophet grabbed Nico's arm to stop him from turning away. "You don't get to come back from the dead and act like it's not a big fucking deal."

"Right. Forgot that's something only for the Prophet Drews bucket list." Nico spoke blandly, which managed to put his sarcasm into sharper focus.

If Prophet hadn't been so pissed, Tom definitely would've laughed. Instead, he stepped toward Prophet, but not before looking back toward Dean, who was facing the disturbance as if watching the show, and what the fuck was happening here?

"I don't get it, Nico. How the fuck could you do this to Doc?" Prophet demanded, his voice a low growl.

Nico stared at Prophet, his eyes seeming to hold a million secrets and kept his voice even. "Doc knows."

"What the fuck do you mean?"

"I thought you were losing your eyesight, not your grasp of the English language."

Prophet lunged with an almost inhuman speed, taking down Nico. And a table. Tom managed to save the sculpture, though Nico was on his own. And Nico was being strangled, his face turning a shade of purple Tom didn't know existed in nature . . .

And then Dean was there, literally turning the hose on them.

"Prophet, could you not kill my houseboy?" Dean demanded.

"Not your fucking houseboy, you asshat." Nico's voice was gravel as he shoved Prophet off him. "Assholes. The whole fucking group of you."

"Right. The SAS is so much nicer," Prophet bit out, then looked at Tom, who was still holding the sculpture. "Nice catch."

"Thanks. Want to tell me why you're randomly yelling at people?"

"You act like my temper's something new, Tommy," Prophet answered seriously as Tom reached down and hauled him to his feet.

He was soaked and smiling. And Tom had to admit, seeing Prophet in his element like that was always a fucking joy to see.

"Nico—the kitchen." Dean was leading Nico by the elbow, but not before Nico mouthed, *I'm going to fucking kill you* to Prophet . . . who in turn flipped him the bird and mouthed back, *You and what army?*

"Will the two of you stop?" Dean called before leading Nico out of the room. "Or I'll kill you both myself. Prophet, go find your room. Now."

"I'm getting a seriously . . ." Tom glanced over toward the doorway before following Prophet out another door and down a long hallway. "A *seriously* different vibe from him than I did the last time we met."

"What you're seeing is the real Dean. He puts on a damned good act when he needs to." Prophet stopped at a large wooden door before opening it. A king bed was in the middle of the room, carved wood, mosquito netting and handmade rugs on the floor.

Their bags were already in there. Tom closed the door behind them. "You have a lot of explaining to do."

Prophet groaned, rubbed his temples. "I think I have a concussion."

"Then throw up, grab an ice pack, and start talking."

Prophet narrowed his eyes. "You had a lot more sympathy when we first met."

"I guess I put on a good act when I need to."

Prophet smiled. Tugged him close, and not gently, as he growled, "No way, Tommy. Not with me. Never with me."

Tom melted against Prophet, immediately as soaked as Prophet was and unable to disagree. Prophet's mouth covered his and he didn't care about information or broken tables. After the fight with Nico, Prophet was revved up; Tom would bear the brunt of some of it . . . if he was lucky.

"You upset because Nico almost killed you?" Tom asked innocently.

"Maybe you're the one who needs to worry about his sight, T, because, from where I stood, I totally won." Prophet shoved him against the wall and Tom grinned at how easy it was to rile him back up.

"Really? I could've sworn he had the upper hand."

He barely got the words out before Prophet was throwing him onto the bed, climbing on top of him and shoving his shoulders down to the mattress before leaning in and kissing the hell out of him, his tongue dueling with Tom's. It was part fight for dominance and all surrender . . . to each other.

Tom held fast to Prophet's hips, pushed his own up to brutally grind against him, their cocks thrusting against one another's.

"Humping me like a teenager," Prophet muttered against his mouth, and Tom laughed.

"Just shut up and come." He made a side-to-side motion with his hips and then thrust up again, wrapped a leg around Prophet's thigh so they were moving in unison.

Tom came first—or Prophet would've never lived it down, but he wasn't too far behind, his muscles stiffening before allowing himself to just ride his orgasm out.

"Now I'm sticky," Tom mock complained, even as he reached his hand in between their chests to tweak Prophet's nipple ring, loving the way Prophet growled. "You need to take this out."

"Definitely not now," Prophet told him.

Tom pushed him so they were both lying on their sides, and he sucked on Prophet's nipple, playing with the piercing with his tongue, sucking and tugging and twisting until Prophet's dick throbbed hot against him again.

"Better watch out—I'll have you yelling my name so the whole house hears it," Prophet murmured, reaching down to play with the piercings that ran along Tom's cock.

Tom hissed. Smiled. "Wouldn't mind. They know I'm yours. I know it too."

Prophet stared at him, and then smiled too, one of those rare, true ones that broke him open like the sun on a warm summer's day, basking Tom and making him shiver just the same.

Fuck, he loved it when Prophet smiled. More so when he could be the one who made Prophet smile.

He wasn't disappointed when Prophet basically manhandled him onto his stomach until he was ass up on the bed, Prophet buried in him, fast and hard, with no other foreplay except the fight. It was all either of them needed right now.

With his arms behind his back and Prophet plowing into him, Tom began to groan uncontrollably and he definitely did scream—Prophet's name, and other more graphic things.

"Like that, baby?" Prophet murmured against Tom's cheek.

"Huh—uh-huh."

Incoherent? Check. Tom needed it. They both did.

And then Prophet let go of his arms, flipped him and re-entered. Forced Tom to wrap around him or slam his head against the headboard with each of Prophet's thrusts. "T—"

"Something smart-ass to say to me?"

Tom nodded, then opened his mouth . . . but bit Prophet instead.

"Yeah, just how I like it." He thrust harder, loving Tom's grunts and general whimpering with pleasure. It wasn't often these days that he was able to get him into this headspace, so this was a goddamned miracle.

Tom came first, his muscles straining until his body jackknifed and then come warmed their bellies, which was enough to make Prophet shoot, so hard he saw spots for several minutes.

He collapsed, half on Tom, and when he was able to see clearly—or as clearly as he did these days, he glanced up to see Tom smiling at him. He noted how Tom's eye color appeared more unbalanced after he came—wild, abandoned, and fuck, Prophet never wanted to stop seeing that look.

But you will.

"Sorry," Prophet murmured finally.

"Take as long as you need, Proph. Take the picture in your mind."

Something hitched inside of him and he stared for several minutes, noting the slice of Tom's cheekbones, the fullness of his lips . . . and he brushed his thumb over them. Tracing. Feeling.

Memorizing. He closed his eyes and did the whole trace again, the way Dean had taught him, mapping Tom's face, recalling with his fingertips. He felt Tom's smile under his attempt and he traced that too. He could feel the emotion.

And Tom pressed his lips up to Prophet's, and Prophet kept his eyes closed, kept his fingers in place as Tom deepened the kiss. For a while it felt like it would never end. But this one would. And there would be more behind it. Prophet had to believe that.

Tom watched the change in his partner happen. Maybe he'd sensed it even before that. But he knew Prophet, could tell that his eyes weren't terrible blurry, that he was just practicing instead.

Because of that, he wouldn't let Prophet stop kissing him. Not now. This was Tom's version of a lifeline and it extended both ways—and Tom was never letting go of his end.

He'd hold on, for both of them, if need be.

Prophet moved to lift Tom up and Tom let him, and they stumbled, laughing and kissing, to the bathroom.

Prophet's eyes stayed closed . . . until they got into the shower, and then he opened them under the running water.

Tom was glad. Because he didn't want Prophet to waste his sight pretending he was blind. Even so, in the aftermath, it was all about Prophet tracing Tom's body relentlessly. Restlessly. Creating a sightless map, measuring everything for precise placement and distance. It was why Tom had decided not to add any more tattoos—Prophet needed his map and Tom wouldn't bring confusion to the memories.

It made Tom sad but it reassured him. Prophet was preparing for the future. He wasn't looking for a way out.

"Any fucked-up psychic vibes?" Prophet asked when they were back in bed.

Frustrated, Tom shook his head. Beyond the constant, ominous forbidding that pushed into his brain like a relentless drill set just high enough to buzz and torture him. "Now are you ready to tell me about Nico?"

Prophet sighed and rolled over. "Way to kill the mood. And no, I'm not ready. At all. I think the concussion's back."

"Start talking."

"Fine." Prophet stared at the ceiling. "Obviously, I don't like Nico. At all."

"Got that loud and clear. Tell me about Nico and Doc and the dead thing," Tom urged, rolling onto his belly so he could watch Prophet.

Prophet finally lowered his gaze to meet Tom's. "Look, the shit between him and Doc is Doc's—Nico's—to tell." He drew out Nico's name sarcastically. "But Nico was part of a joint task force."

"He was SAS?"

"Yeah."

"But—"

"The American accent is fake. He's British, which never sat well with King or Mal. But Doc was part of the task force and that's where they met."

"And?"

"And what?"

"The dead part," Tom prompted.

"Oh. Right. We thought he was dead but I guess Doc knew he wasn't, the end." Prophet jumped him and Tom figured that he'd gotten all he could out of the man for one night.

Tomorrow. They always had tomorrow. And he refused to think any differently.

CHAPTER ELEVEN

Prophet eased out from underneath Tom and went to find Dean. He tried not to do too much sleeping these days, because he never knew what would trigger a flashback and nobody wanted more of those.

Nico was nowhere in sight, which was good, because Prophet didn't think Dean would allow him to strangle the fuck out of Nico . . . but hell, if he could cover Nico's mouth while he did so, how would Dean ever know?

"Stop planning Nico's murder and get your ass in here," Dean called into the hallway.

Prophet didn't bother denying it. "Lucky guess."

Dean snorted. "Come sit down and eat something."

There was a spread of food on the coffee table by the couch and Prophet happily obliged him. There were plates of shrimp and stews and breads and rice. All the good stuff. "Delicious."

"How's Tom?"

"He's good. Sleeping. I'll try to save him some." Prophet ate in silence for a few minutes, then sat back and asked, "So, what the fuck happened to you?"

"I'm assuming you mean when I was kidnapped? Why are you bringing this up now?" Dean glanced at him. It was unnerving, but every once in a while, he'd fucking turn his gaze so direct, Prophet would swear he could see.

Now, Prophet realized that was simply wishful thinking . . . on both their parts. "You know what I mean."

"No, I don't. I was kidnapped. It wasn't fun."

"But you know enough . . ."

"To what—fight that many men off? Risk my life? For what?" Dean challenged.

"Forget it," Prophet muttered.

"You want me to give you hope, Proph? Tell you everything's going to be exactly the same? It's not."

"Great. Thanks for the newsflash." Prophet got up and walked away from him onto the back porch, because everything here was safely behind bulletproof glass.

Dean didn't leave him alone, walked up next to him. Slung a heavy arm around him. Prophet stood stiffly, still angry.

But Dean pulled at him until Prophet was putting a head on his shoulder, a finger running along Prophet's cheek to wipe the tears that'd come so silently they'd surprised him.

"It's not the same, Proph. Sometimes, it's better."

"Yeah? How? Because you can't see the kidnapper's faces, so they know you won't be able to identify them?" Prophet challenged.

"Well, yeah," Dean answered seriously. "Nobody bothers with a blindfold. People take for granted that you're entirely disabled. Treat you like a princess. Serve you."

Prophet's eyebrows shot up and Dean snorted, apparently feeling the surprised expression on Prophet's face. "Figures you'd like that part."

"Fuck off."

"You can still do that too. Better, even."

"Better? I'm already pretty fucking perfect."

"And yet so humble," Dean added, without a trace of mockery.

"At least you're still smart enough to agree."

"You know, I didn't realize I was bi until I was blind," Dean said.

"I'm not going to realize I'm straight, am I?"

Dean laughed at the horror in Prophet's voice, although really, Prophet saw nothing funny about it. "I don't think so."

"I'm sorry my hotness confused you."

"Jesus, you're such an asshole."

"Thank you," Prophet replied automatically. "Most of the time it comes naturally. Occasionally, I've got to work at it." He paused. "So, you're blind and fucking men. Any other surprises I need to know about?"

Dean considered that. "I fuck women and men. And you've definitely got a lot to learn."

"Says the man who thinks fucking men is something you can do without practice."

"There's no app for that," Dean said seriously.

Prophet patted Dean's chest. "You've still got some asshole in you left."

CHAPTER TWELVE

When Prophet went back into their room, he had a plate of food for Tom, who he found awake, dressed and kneeling on the bed that was now covered in paper maps.

"Thought you were sleeping." Prophet put the plate down on the night table.

"I thought the same of you. And these maps of Dean's are better than anything I've seen." Tom grabbed his phone and started taking pictures of them, until Prophet took the phone and threw it onto the nearest chair.

"Bed's too damned crowded," he said as he grabbed Tom. The wall would have to do. Because his single-minded focus was all on the man in front of him. He was ripping Tom's shirt off—literally. Yanking down his cargos that hit the ground with a heavy thud of hidden weaponry stores.

Tom, naked.

Score.

Prophet couldn't wait, just unzipped his pants and grabbed Tom's hips.

Lube. Shit. He turned to see if there was any in arm's reach— because that was definitely not out of the realm of possibility.

"Do it." Tom's voice was a low rasp, his eyes glittering with need as he reached under Prophet's shirt and tugged hard on his nipple ring.

It was a straight line of jolting heat from nipple to cock. "Jesus fuck, Tommy."

"Do it," Tom insisted, wrapped a leg around him. And tweaked the piercing again.

He swiped pre-come off Tom's cock and mixed it with his own to slick himself, then shook his head. "Don't want to hurt you, dammit. So wait." He pushed Tom's leg off, found the lube and was back in position in seconds.

Still not fast enough for Tom, who demanded, "Do it," again.

"And here I thought I was in charge," Prophet murmured.

"I . . . let you think . . . fuck!" Tom yelled as Prophet seated deeply inside of him in one push. And there wasn't time—or energy or breath—for talking. Just sweat and grunts and prickles of pain that gave way to intense pleasure. Prophet sucked several red spots that blossomed along Tom's shoulders like symbols of everything—a map over Tom's heart, around the compass, his own way to protect Tommy—and Tom continued to tug on that damned nipple ring until Prophet started coming, hard, grabbing on to Tom and the wall.

Tom laughed and came moments later, spilling his load between them, leaning in to bite at Prophet's shoulders. Prophet's muscles shook from exertion, but the relief was intense. He felt too good to move and for several long moments, they just remained, propping each other up.

Until Tom urged, "God, again. Come on," and Prophet's dick stirred.

"You're lucky I'm younger."

Tom nodded in agreement because he obviously needed more. God, they were like fucking teenagers around each other. Since the beginning.

"Don't see it changing," Tom said, reading his mind.

Prophet smiled. "Don't need it to. Want it to." Ever. "Come on." He pushed off Tom and went to the bed. Tom helped him quickly move all the maps onto the floor and then Tom was under him and Prophet was fucking him. Again. Staring at Tom's different-color eyes, refusing to break his gaze.

This time was far less frantic but no less heated. Prophet took his time, lazily pressing into Tom, teasing him, taunting him, twisting his nipples, biting them, getting off on Tom's groans and protests.

Finally, Prophet began snapping his hips, a driving rhythm that got them both panting and ready.

Marry me.

Prophet thought it with every stroke. Tom writhed against him, slick with sweat. Barely holding on and neither of them letting go.

Marry.

Me.

Tom managed, "Yes, Proph. Yes." And then his orgasm swept him as Prophet watched his body arch with pleasure. "Come on, Proph—Lije—your turn."

It didn't take much to bring him over the edge. He bucked, cried out Tom's name, and finally buried his head against the crook of Tom's neck. Tom reached around to cup the back of his neck, stroking it, murmuring, "Thank you," and whether it was for the sex or the proposal, Prophet didn't know. And it didn't matter. Tom was *his.*

Finally, he lifted his head and slid out of, and off, Tom, ending up on his back next to him. Tom turned onto his side, a hand on Prophet's chest. "We getting married here?"

"Fuck, I'd love that. But . . . I want Remy there when it happens."

"Agreed."

As soon as this is over. Prophet didn't want to voice that thought again, was tired of putting his life on hold for John, but knew it was a necessity.

"You're already mine," Tom reminded him with a tug on the nipple ring. "No matter . . . the ceremony's for everyone else. We already know."

"Yeah," Prophet drawled, but in perfect Tom cadence, because it made him smile. "Shower?"

Tom shook his head. "Want to smell like you for a while."

"So dirty, Tommy."

"Yeah, *bébé*. Only for you."

"Won't be like this forever."

"Better not be," Prophet muttered thickly, heat and sand turning his mouth into cotton. He blinked as if it would get the sun out of his eyes. But that just made things worse as the grit seemed to make everything feel raw and scraped. On fire.

Getting away seemed to matter less and less, because his mind wandered. Neither man could walk in a straight line, and this getting captured crap? Way better at teaching shit like survival and E&E than any drill ever could.

Prophet knew then and there he could learn to survive things way worse. Why he should have to was another story altogether.

His feet were strangely numb—maybe it was the chains, the scrape of bare feet across hot desert sand. Later, his skin would swell and peel, the results of burns and blisters that would heal, despite Prophet's not caring much about what was happening.

He was delirious. Dehydrated. Half the time, he wasn't sure who leaned onto who, but when they heard the chopper, they had to reassure each other that it was a rescue, not a recapture.

After that it was a blur. What he recalled most was sand. So much fucking sand . . . Prophet remembered finding it everywhere for weeks after he got home. He tried brushing it off his hands, his body but it seemed to multiply . . .

"Proph, come on. You're home. You're safe, so wake up before Dean and Nico come running in here," Tom urged now, and Prophet was back in Eritrea, in a bed in Dean's house, Tom's hands on him despite how dangerous a prospect that was.

Prophet realized he was attempting to grab hold of Tom as well, like he'd been reaching out, needing Tom to pull him out of the sandpit and back into reality.

Sand. *Motherfucking sand* and blood and *fuck*, would this ever be over?

"Same one, or something new?" Tom asked after several quiet beats. He was sitting on the side of the bed, fully dressed, had probably been preparing to leave the room and let Prophet sleep.

"Shit." Prophet avoided his eyes, stared at a point over Tom's shoulder, like he was watching a movie. When he started, he was aware that his voice sounded odd—distant. "All that fucking sand, T. It never went away. Kept multiplying."

"The sand we found in the apartment?"

Prophet nodded woodenly. "I kept some of it but it kept multiplying . . . like it did when we were walking . . ." He realized he was slipping back into the past, tried to shake it off but remained in that space between the two, off-center and vaguely threatening.

"Proph, you don't have to—"

But he did. They both knew it. "We'd been captured—me and John."

"Fuck, Proph. You never . . ." Tom brushed the blame off quickly, maybe realizing that Prophet was planning on plowing ahead with the explanation and not wanting to stop it.

"I never. I couldn't, T." Prophet touched his face but still didn't look directly at him. "'S'what started all of it—for John. For me. Our first mission."

He took a deep breath and spilled it all. "We were the only two sent in. We finished with SERE training and some of the other schools you go through for qualification training. Because John and I were pretty much tied for top of the class in close-quarter battle, weapons training, unarmed combat and demolition, we caught the eye of the CIA director. They needed two men to bodyguard an embassy official. Military. So John and I were handpicked for the detail." Prophet grimaced. "Seemed like a great thing at the time. Never an easy mission because you never know."

The US Embassy, located in Kinshasa, was being used for training purposes, care of the Marines, when a riot started outside by locals, deeply unhappy at some new policies they believed the Americans had instituted. It was really fucking bad—so bad that, as he was watching it unfold, he knew it would haunt his dreams for the rest of his life. The swell of people was the kind of angry mob no military man wanted to be caught in—and they'd be unhesitating in tearing Prophet and John alive, limb from limb, dragging them through the streets just to prove their hatred of American military men.

"We were told to hunker down until the Marines controlled the crowd, which took hours. Maybe half a day. At the time, we thought the powers that be knew what could happen during those exercises, even though our op was supposed to be a simple one. But while it was happening, we had no doubt that the CIA knew this particular attack would happen. So we sweated it out—the ambassador obviously hadn't been let in on the plan, either. It wasn't just about him then, even though it was supposed to be. But there was no way

I was following orders and leaving the ambassador's wife and kids behind."

Tom frowned. "You said 'I.' Was that because you were point or..."

"I overrode John," he said brusquely. "Finally, the Marines got the riots under control and we left the embassy—we sent out cover cars—red herrings—and we had the entire family with us. We didn't use a full caravan, because that would've been a dead giveaway. And we got to the LZ in time. Just in time, actually."

He swallowed, hard, and Tom touched his arm. "Stay with me, Proph. Stay in the present."

"Trying." He shook his head, but couldn't shake the feelings of being back there, head down, loading the family onto the chopper. "They had three kids—the youngest was three years old and he was holding on to me for dear life when the rebels started firing. Didn't matter what rebels, because fuck, that's all the Congo was—different groups of rebels all fighting for their slice of power for that day or week or month. But once we got to the LZ, we realized that we wouldn't have room on the chopper they brought."

"They didn't account for the wife and the kids."

"Right?"

"I'm assuming you and John stayed back—without question."

"John and I held off enemy fire and let the chopper get away safely. Took down the guy with a rocket launcher by running him over." He glanced at Tom, who smirked and shook his head.

"I can so picture that."

After the bird took off, he and John had begun the long hike back to the embassy... until they were ambushed. "It wasn't the rebels."

Prophet knew then, deep down, that it had been a setup. He'd spotted a Mossad agent earlier that afternoon, and when he and John were held, it was to obtain information.

"They were going to leave us, Proph," John told him after they'd been rescued. "One of our first missions and the CIA gave orders for us to be left behind. We weren't even their men at that point and they still found a way to screw us over."

"The CIA had their eyes on you early on," Tom said quietly. "Both of you."

And that's why John had turned so easily when the time was ripe for it. He'd just waited for a way out—a way to play and pay back the CIA and the government for fucking him (and Prophet) over the first time, and at the same time.

"What happened to you during your capture?"

Prophet shook his head. "Can't talk about it."

"Can't—or won't?"

"Both," he managed. Tom had seen only a small portion of his torture at the hands of the CIA, but that had come much later. As the saying went, *You never forget your first time . . .*

That's exactly what the agent who'd tortured him for those four weeks, three days, two hours and forty-six minutes had whispered at the start.

You never forget your first time . . .

Prophet sat up and Tom wrapped around him. "We could run from all this shit. Better yet, we could all just stay here."

"Remy?"

"He'd love it."

"He would," Prophet agreed.

"Mal, King, Ren too. We could just . . ." Tom lost momentum. "Sorry. You guys have been running for ten years and I'm acting like I can make it better."

Prophet ran a hand through Tom's hair. "Mal tried it first. Then King bought us all a place in Bali. Do you know how fucking hot it is in Bali?" Tom ducked his head and smiled. "The fact that you want us all together? That means a lot. I'm fixing this, T. Once and for all."

"Maybe you should let me."

"Between me and John. Trust me, though—if I could give this job away, I'd trust you with it."

"Are we done after this?"

"I am, Tom. I won't take it away from you."

"You're not."

"Fuck, we're sappy."

"Yeah. I like it."

"You would." Prophet nudged him.

Tom froze.

"What?"

"It's ah . . . nothing." He glanced at Prophet. "Something. Just not sure what yet."

Prophet's gaze slid out the window and over Dean's land. Tom was tense. Waiting. Phone out of his pocket, in his hand although Prophet would take bets Tom hadn't even noticed he'd done it.

That happened so often, Prophet was used to it at this point. "Any messages?"

"Huh? Oh." Tom checked his phone. "Nothing yet." Then he turned to Prophet. "How many more secrets are you holding, Proph?"

CHAPTER THIRTEEN

Tom watched Prophet squirm until he finally admitted, "Enough of them."

"But there's something—one of them—you're trying to figure out how to tell me, right?"

"Fuck, I hate it when you do that."

"Only when it's something that doesn't suit your purpose," Tom pointed out.

"Touché, T. You win. Guess now's as good of a time as any." That last part was more to himself than to Tom. And yeah, Prophet was twitching a little. Tom rarely saw him this nervous, so fuck, this had to be big. "Look, I couldn't tell you before. Shouldn't be telling you now, except . . ."

"You're killing me here, Proph. Seriously."

"It's about Ollie. And Hal."

"Okay." Tom frowned. "What do they have in common?"

Prophet sighed. "A lot more than you realize."

"Like . . .?" *Like fucking pulling teeth.*

"Like everything. They have every single thing in common . . . because they're the same person. Ollie is Hal. Was Hal. Fuck, you know what I mean."

Tom stared at him for a long moment, and when he spoke, he didn't recognize the slash of anger in his own voice. "No, Prophet, I don't know what you mean."

"Not sure how to make it clearer. Want me to draw you a picture?"

Tom grabbed Prophet's arm, hard, and Prophet stared between it and Tom. "Oh no, you don't get to be pissed at me. Don't even try to turn this shit around."

Prophet held up his free hand, like he was surrendering. But he wasn't.

"How long, Prophet?"

"How long was Hal Ollie?"

"Fuck you, you bastard." Tom was ready to pin the fucker down and make him talk, and not in the fun alligator games way.

"I've known . . . as long as I've known Hal. But I didn't know you, Tom."

"So you knew—the first time I mentioned Ollie, you knew who he was . . . what happened to him."

"Yeah, I did." Prophet's tone was defiant, something Tom would normally back the fuck away from.

Now, he was too far gone to avoid the danger. "I get why you wouldn't tell me back then when we first met . . . but fuck you for not telling me before this."

"What does it matter? What does it change?"

"Everything. Because it's all about trust." He shook his head, still reeling over the fact that Ollie was Hal and not fully comprehending exactly what that meant . . . until right this second.

Prophet stared at him warily, like he'd been waiting for Tom to process the full value of what he'd been told.

"You killed Ollie," Tom managed. "All of this, with John, started because of Ollie."

"Yes. And yes."

"So over ten years ago, killing Ollie—*Hal*—was your job."

Prophet nodded. "That was my job, yes. Looking back, if I hadn't, John would've taken Hal and set off a worse chain of events. As it was, I made John's life harder."

"And you took the FBI's word for it that Hal was too valuable, too much of a threat to world security, to stay alive?"

"At that time? Yes. Now? Yes again. So you can think what you want. You knew who I was and what I did. What I do. Suddenly, because it was your mentor, it's murder." Prophet shook his head. "What the fuck do you want from me?"

"Honesty."

"I just gave you some."

"None of this is a goddamned coincidence," Tom said, and Prophet didn't disagree. Which made Tom even angrier. "Tell me everything."

"You know what happened to Hal."

"Tell me about the first time you met him," Tom demanded.

Prophet looked like he was considering not complying, but finally, he began to speak. "I wasn't briefed on the mission until maybe six hours before we left for the desert."

"Is that unusual?"

"No, not for those kinds of missions. Everything is kept hush-hush, because that cuts down on leaks." Prophet laughed as though seeing the irony in that.

"And you met Hal then?"

"We didn't fly in with Hal. He was already transported to the tents. We pulled in the night before we were supposed to roll out with him and took him over from the FBI, who surrendered him."

"Why? Why did they surrender him, Proph?" Tom asked. "Because he was doing good things at the FBI."

"They don't tell us shit like that, T. I wish they did. But I'll tell you something—they don't pull men like Hal without a preceding threat, okay? Someone made him, or maybe he was dirty and working in conjunction with a foreign government—"

"He wasn't like that."

"Maybe he was forced into it. Did you think about that? Any guy like that who has family has a vulnerability," Prophet told him and Tom's head began to pound. "I'm not going to sit here and justify my jobs to you, so if that's what you're waiting for—"

Tom cut him off coldly. "Just tell me what Hal said when you met him."

Prophet nodded. "First time I met Hal . . ." It was almost like he was going into the past, like he was having a flashback while he was awake. And while Tom hated that, right now he thought he might hate Prophet more. "The first time we met, he was in the tent, waiting for me."

"Before John?"

"Before John, yes. I sat down with him and asked if there was anything he needed. He said he had plenty to tell me, but not right then. He wanted a beer, so I got him one. And after he drank it, he started telling me about himself. Shit I didn't want to know—shouldn't know, but when men know the end might be near, they feel the need to unload on the nearest safe person."

"Right—you were so safe."

"He knew I was the man who'd kill him if he was in danger of being captured by the enemy," Prophet told him, an edge of anger in his voice. "It was the first thing I said to him."

"Why didn't you mention that first?"

"Because you asked me what Hal said to me."

"Fuck you, Prophet. Don't you dare start mincing words—"

"And don't you think you're interrogating me. Unless you want to tie my hands down? Re-create the tape you saw before you met me? Is that a kink of yours?"

Tom shoved him, hard, both palms on Prophet's chest, and Prophet stumbled back but caught himself and warned, "I wouldn't do that again, T."

"Keep talking about *Hal*."

"He wouldn't shut up." Prophet closed his eyes, and Tom knew he was picturing Hal sitting across from him, explaining himself. "He told me, 'First, I was Sam. Then Cal. Right before this, I was Ollie, the man who taught young FBI agents how to remain calm under pressure.' And then he'd laughed at how his hands trembled and continued. 'It was the cushiest job I ever had, pretending to be a pretender. Except I was damned good at it by that point. Wasn't allowed anywhere near a lab or computer. Not allowed more than one call a month to my family.'"

Prophet opened his eyes. "By that point, he was shaking a little, and then he asked me, 'So why now? Why, after all this time?' And I couldn't answer that—not for sure."

"How does it happen?"

"Maybe someone got comfortable, breached security protocol, or maybe someone sold Hal out. In the end, it didn't matter in terms of what my job was—get Hal to his new, secure location. And if that proved an impossible task? I had orders to kill the specialist. I didn't have to call in and ask if I should—my judgment was trusted to make that decision."

"Keep going." Tom heard the coldness in his voice as he talked to Prophet like he was a stranger, and Prophet looked visibly upset about it for a second.

But then he seemed to shake it off and said, "I told Hal to get some sleep. That we were moving out in the morning. And that's when he said, 'Not until you promise me three things.'"

"Three? I know one of them was keep his son—Gary—safe."

"One was to not hesitate to kill him if capture was imminent."

"He made you promise that?" Tom asked doubtfully.

"They all do. Even though they don't want to die, the thought of being captured and tortured or worse, having to work against their country? Is terrifying in the abstract."

"And what—once they're captured, it's easier to cooperate?"

"Yes," Prophet said, his tone clipped.

"Okay, so what's the third?" Tom asked but Prophet didn't answer. "We're back to this shit? More secrets?"

"It has nothing to do with you, T. It's about my—"

"No. No fucking way. Don't you dare say it's about your job."

Prophet looked like he started to say something—maybe *I'm sorry*—but then he stopped. "It was. It is. Fuck, I'm not supposed to be telling you any of this. I'm never supposed to tell you. Don't you think it's more fucked up to tell you this shit? I'll gladly keep the burden, T, but you insist. And then you get pissed."

Prophet got up then, picked up the closest thing—a glass—and threw it hard against the wall, where it shattered in a million pieces.

Tom remained unimpressed, kept his gaze stony, even though he knew how dangerous Prophet's temper, once unleashed, actually was. So Prophet picked up another glass, and another, before a night table felt his wrath.

Finally, he turned back to Tom. "I keep everyone's secrets because they ask me to. Because I fucking have to. So this might not be the last, but you can either deal with it or get the fuck out."

Tom chose the latter.

CHAPTER FOURTEEN

om just stuttered an angry laugh and walked out, which was probably better for both of them. But maybe not for the furniture that Prophet hadn't yet managed to break, so he went in search of some, and more of a fight.

But Tom was standing in the middle of Dean's main room on the phone, his face serious. Nico lounged near the window, a bruised cheekbone giving Prophet momentary happiness.

And Dean was staring at Prophet. He signed, *He's on with Phil.* And Prophet immediately texted Natasha with, *What's up at EE today?*

She didn't hesitate to give him intel he shouldn't have been getting. *Call Elliot—he saw men take Doc and Cope. Phil called Tom in to help.*

Elliot was steady—knew his country and its people, knew the territory and said he could literally smell trouble. Still, because the order—and intel—came from Phil, Prophet wanted to hear it from him directly. He called Elliot while Tom was still on with Phil.

"Prophet, it's trouble." Elliot's accent wasn't thick—it sounded smooth and calm and as though he'd been waiting for Prophet's call. "I recognized the soldiers."

"Not Boko Haram?"

"No. Gaetan's cousin, Kamuzu. He's powerful. He's been trying to take control up north. Rumor is the son is badly wounded and they needed a doctor."

And people in the area knew Doc, but still . . . "And they don't have another doctor in their pocket?"

"I know it's suspicious, Prophet, but the bottom line is—"

"Tom's got to go get him out. I know." Prophet rubbed his eyes.

"I need to keep my cover with the region," Elliot said. Because even though it was known he worked with the Americans at times, he usually turned it to his advantage by telling everyone that he was simply using the Americans.

He was their best source in Africa, so sending him in to rescue Doc and Cope was out of the question. "Tom will be there."

Elliot was silent for a moment. "Not you?"

"I can't, Elliot. Watch out for him, okay?"

"I will, Prophet." Elliot cut the line and Prophet glanced over at Tom, who was also ending his call.

Nico and Dean remained quiet. It was obvious they'd heard the yelling but both men knew now wasn't the time to discuss it. But the tension was thick as hell, and Prophet didn't see a way to clear it anytime soon. Especially not with Tom leaving. "Everything okay?" he asked Tom, trying to keep his voice neutral.

Tom's was the same. "It was Phil. He needs me."

"Glad you two are so close." Prophet couldn't resist and Tom just shook his head.

"You know exactly where and why, so why don't you brief the room?"

Dean let out a low whistle and Prophet shook his head. "Doc and Cope were called out to help a warlord's cousin's son. More than called out—they were taken."

"Phil authorized Doc and Cope to help the boy," Tom said.

"What are you talking about?"

"They needed Doc to perform a surgery on the boy. They asked Elliot for help. Elliot called Phil, who approved it. But then the men stormed in and took Doc and Cope by force. Blindfolded them and put them into cars. Elliot said that the men said Doc and Cope were the only ones they trusted for this."

"That's Phil's version," Prophet told him.

"Just because you hate Phil—" Tom started.

"I do not hate Phil," Prophet broke in.

"I hate it when Daddy and Daddy fight," Nico drawled.

"Shut up," they both told him at once and then Prophet told Tom, "That's the first logical thing you've said in the past hour."

"Prophet, shut up. I believe what Phil said." Tom's eyes snapped with anger.

"Why'd Phil authorize it?" Nico said tightly.

"Better question is, why would Doc do it?" Prophet mused.

"Because that's Doc," Nico shot back. "Someone needs to protect him from himself."

Prophet just stared at him, one of those pot-kettle looks that needed no further explanation, then turned his attention to Tom. "Who's Phil sending to meet you?"

"No one. It's just me."

"No way, T—"

"Fuck you I'm fine." It came out in a rush, like it was all one word, and the room silenced.

Prophet started with, "I'll go with—"

"Not necessary."

Nico crossed his arms and watched them, looking from one to the other like it was a tennis match. Prophet locked gazes with him, then instructed, "Nico, go with Tom."

"You're not the boss of me," Nico said without a trace of irony.

Dean snorted.

Tom glanced at Prophet, then said to Nico, "I'll take the backup, if you're willing."

Prophet watched as Nico considered it. They hadn't gone into detail when they'd arrived about why they were there, but Nico knew the bare bones of the story of John from years earlier, and he'd been involved in the underground world of special ops long enough to know an unsanctioned op.

In truth, he'd be a good one to leave here and help him, Prophet mused. Except they'd probably kill each other first.

Now, Nico looked at Prophet questioningly. Prophet motioned his head silently toward Dean, who said, "Prophet, I'll be fine. Nico, help Doc. Prophet will help me here."

Nico glanced at Prophet. "Leaving you with Dean is like literally the blind leading—"

The knife whizzed through the air, but Prophet didn't open his eyes until he heard the *thunk* as it lodged into the wall. Right next to Nico's ear.

Prophet stared at Nico. "How's that for literal?"

Nico grunted out, "Asshole."

"Good shot," Tom told him, and Prophet slid his glance over and mouthed, *I missed*, while tugging at his ear and pointing to Nico, who watched him and ground his teeth together, his jaw working painfully.

"Prophet, enough," Dean said. "Nico, please—go with Tom. I know you won't regret it."

Nico sighed unhappily but ultimately nodded at Tom before walking away to collect his things.

With a nod in Prophet's direction, Tom began to do the same . . . but Prophet followed him into their bedroom.

Tom turned on him at the door. "Nico doesn't work for Phil."

"Neither do I," Prophet pointed out, barely concealing a sneer. "But you and I both know it's better to take him."

"Because of your eyes?"

Prophet shrugged. "I can fire an AK-47 more easily around here. I don't need finesse."

"And John?"

"He hasn't killed me yet."

"So 'yet' translates to 'never'?"

Prophet nodded. "So far, yes."

"And Doc? Is he going to feel better seeing Nico?"

"I don't give a shit how he feels. People need to stop keeping shit from me." He watched Tom grit his teeth to ignore the obvious irony of those words, but hell, in this case it was the goddamned truth.

Finally, Tom managed, "How bad's it going to be with Doc and Nico?" while still looking like he wanted to strangle Prophet with his bare hands.

Which was kind of a turn-on. "Pretty fucking bad." Prophet dragged a finger along Tom's cheek, then down to his biceps, tracing the dreamcatcher through his shirt without breaking their gaze. "Check in as soon as you can."

"If anything happens . . ." Something in Tom's tone unnerved him, but he couldn't figure out exactly what.

"I'll check in, Tom." The color difference between Tom's eyes seemed to grow more pronounced, but Prophet convinced himself it was just a trick of light.

"Yeah, see you soon. Guess we've got shit to plan." Tom's voice was gruff and unforgiving, but it wasn't unkind.

Unkindness would've been easier to take. He took his fingers off Tom's arm. "We're planned, T. You're good to go."

Tom snorted and brushed past him on the way out.

CHAPTER FIFTEEN

O f course, Prophet drove Tom back to the airstrip they'd landed on less than twenty-four hours ago. Nico got into the back, grumbling about Prophet's driving, and Dean insisted on going and called shotgun, no doubt purposely so Tom didn't have to sit next to Prophet for the ten-minute-plus drive.

Dean and Nico discussed the land surrounding them, with Nico pointing things out to Tom, showing where there were plans to expand things. The conversation definitely eased the tension in the truck, so Tom was grateful.

He still had so many goddamned questions—about Ollie, about Ollie and Prophet—but he supposed that most of those would go unanswered. Not that the answers would actually change anything.

Focus, he instructed himself harshly. He owed Dean to get Nico back in one piece. And when Prophet pulled the car up to the steel bird they'd seen upon landing, Nico touched Dean's shoulder before getting out of the car.

Tom got out without glancing in the front seat and Prophet didn't try to stop him.

Tom refused to look back after he walked to the bird, stowed his gear and climbed in. He put on the headphones and Nico started the propellers and the engine, the deafening roar and shake both welcomed sensations.

Only then did he look straight ahead, see the two men lined up against the truck, watching them take off.

"Ready?" Nico asked.

"Ready," Tom confirmed, and watched the men as the chopper rose, higher and higher, until they were out of sight.

But never out of mind.

"We're going to hit some rough weather in a few minutes," Nico called.

Tom nodded, had seen the swirling clouds as they'd driven and knew they'd be in for something on this trip. For several minutes, there was silence, and then the first pings of rain hit the windshield hard. The iron bird bounced a bit with the wind, then rocked back and forth, and Nico turned and smiled. "Beautiful weather we're having!"

Everyone Prophet knew was crazy. Tom supposed that made him crazy as well.

"So why'd you really let Prophet stay behind?" Nico asked as he tilted the bird purposely and roared through the incoming storm with ease.

Tom was surprised it had taken Nico this long to ask, since he was used to being surrounded by men and women with the uncanny ability to slice through the bullshit in life, to see right to the heart of the matter. It was honed by training, sure, but Tom had met enough of these guys to know that most were born with it, then gravitated toward each other . . . and the professions that appreciated it most. "This is an EE mission. Prophet doesn't work there anymore."

Nico nodded and was silent for a while before continuing. "You and Prophet seemed to be having a major disagreement."

"What clued you in? The yelling or Prophet's breaking things?"

"That's his MO, so if it was just that, I wouldn't have thought anything. But you were bound and determined not to have Prophet come with us."

Fucking perceptive asshole. And he'd upped his game sure, but . . . "I don't know what you mean. Prophet hates Phil. I'd never expect him to come."

Nico nodded. "Never expected you to leave him now."

"Prophet can take care of himself."

"Then why are you trying to do it for him?"

"Is it going to be awkward for you to see Doc again?" Tom asked pleasantly.

Nico's face remained placid. "Depends on if he's in one piece or not. I need to know what I'm walking into."

Nico clearly didn't trust EE—or Phil. He and Prophet might not get along but obviously he trusted Prophet's feelings about Phil.

"I don't know what we're walking into, Nico."

"I guess we'll find out when we get there."

"That was a tough one," Dean said finally.

"Tell me about it," Prophet agreed, unable to tear his eyes away from the empty airspace as he and Dean remained standing outside.

Prophet automatically followed Dean as he walked forward and assured him, "You trained him to handle himself."

"He was already there, Dean. I just gave him a few tricks."

"So what's wrong?"

"Something I can't put my finger on."

"Besides John?"

"Yeah."

Dean stopped walking, put a hand on his shoulder, his face still trained on the empty field. "You think John's going to find you here?"

"Bet on it." Because even though no one knew his location, that wouldn't matter where John was concerned. Granted, Remy and Mal knew, but hell, that wasn't hurting anyone. He'd lay bets that Cillian could also track him here. And his entire team. It was hard to get away from all those fuckers.

"Why now?"

"John's getting pissed. He's already off his game, especially with Ren and King fucking with his business. Takes a lot for the men John works with to trust Americans." Once they'd taken Sadiq down, John needed to reassemble and reassess. That time gave Prophet exactly the openings he'd needed. "He thinks I'm running from him. And I'm fine with that."

What he wasn't *fine* with was being separated from Tom. But hell, the safest place for Tom was away from him, even if he didn't trust Phil all together. "Tom thinks we're in on this together."

"Aren't we?" Dean asked.

"Not his battle."

"You're his battle, and I mean that literally." Prophet tried to shush him but Dean wasn't having it. "And so your battles are his."

"I'd have more fun if you were mute," Prophet said glumly.

Dean laughed. "You're so non-PC."

By force of habit, Prophet flipped him the finger. "Fuck off—I'm disabled."

"You know I can't see the finger you're holding up."

"Then how do you know I am?" Prophet demanded and Dean just smiled. Prophet decided he hated him. Again. "Let's go back."

He didn't wait for Dean but somehow, Dean made it into the car before him, the uneven grounds not a deterrent.

"Want me to drive?" Dean offered. "Because I'm sure it'd be better than your driving."

Prophet ignored him, took off down the dusty back roads that led from the airfield to Dean's house. He got the all clear from Reggie before he and Dean went back inside the house. There was food spread out on the table, and Prophet sat and sulked and ate, at least until Dean sat across from him and asked, "So why'd you really let Tom leave you behind?"

"Get your bat senses outta my shit," Prophet grumbled. "I already cried this trip. Isn't that enough? Place is becoming like some sort of wellness retreat."

"God forbid." Dean feigned horror.

Prophet sighed. "John's close. I can feel him and it's not pleasant. He was always heavy-handed when he stalked."

"Isn't that the point, to get him close?"

Prophet shifted restlessly. "I need to be the bait, not Tom."

"In this equation, you've made me bait too," Dean pointed out.

"You're blind—what the fuck else do you have to do?"

"Such an asshole."

"Aren't there any blind assholes?"

"None like you."

"Good, I like being special."

"You're definitely special." Dean sighed. "What's he want from you, Prophet?"

"I don't know. Never really did."

Dean frowned, leaned on his elbows and stared at Prophet, unnerving him. "Bullshit. You just don't want to remember."

The observation was so spot on, it was like a physical pain. "Maybe."

"You're holding the key. Why not use it?"

"What're you talking about? Is this blind-code?"

Dean sighed again. "Come on, Proph. He's been able to fuck with you because he's never forgotten what he knows about you."

That was true. And after he admitted it, Dean made him go over everything that happened, start to finish, in painstaking detail. He'd told Prophet to get the fuck over himself and not worry about putting Dean in danger, and by the time Prophet had finished talking, his voice was raspy and it was dark outside.

Dean had listened intently, interrupting when he needed clarification and Prophet hadn't given him any of the classified bullshit. And when Prophet said, "That's it," Dean had waited several long moments before speaking.

When he did, his voice was calm, his back straight, like he was going into battle himself. "You talked about everything John did to hurt you—how he preyed on you . . . but you didn't say anything about what you can do to turn the fucking tables."

"I'm here, aren't I?"

"After how fucking long?" Dean volleyed.

"Jesus, Dean. I can't—"

"You can, dammit." Then his voice softened. "You loved him. You feel bad thinking about any of that in front of Tom . . . but this is about survival. Yours. Tom's. Remy's. Mal's . . ."

"I get it, okay? And I'm going to need to drink if we're doing more of this." He wasn't sure how he'd gotten through it this long without.

"Go get it. But close your eyes. If you cheat, I'll know it."

"How?" he asked, and Dean gave him that look, so Prophet remained sitting because it was too much to deal with now.

"You've been avoiding it." Dean just as easily could've been talking about Prophet practicing with a blindfold, but they both knew he wasn't.

"Fuck you, Dean. It's not like I've been hiding."

Dean stared at him, his unseeing gaze cutting through the bullshit. "No—you didn't hide. You went after him."

"Fuck. You."

"Ah, Proph, I knew you were grieving. Angry. Ready to burn it all down to the fucking ground . . . but you and I both know it was an exercise in self-flagellation. A fucking fine effort, yes, but still a punishment to yourself, nonetheless."

Prophet fisted his hands.

"You can still punch me if you want," Dean said helpfully. "Proph, I didn't say you were wrong to do it. But it's time to stop dicking around now. Going after John was easy. Welcoming Tom into your life? That's the hard part. That's what you need to do."

Prophet knew that. He'd figured it out last week. That was why he was here . . . but until Dean told him all this, Prophet's sense of purpose hadn't been very clear at all.

"Thanks," he said quietly to Dean, who didn't look surprised. Prophet sometimes forgot how long they'd known each other.

"Don't mention it. Now go get us that drink."

CHAPTER SIXTEEN

The trip to EE's Eritrea office was relatively uneventful once the storm passed. Elliot was waiting at the airstrip, and he explained more of what happened as he drove them back to the office.

Tom barely listened; his memories of his time spent here came swirling back immediately, and the guilt still washed over him when he thought about how he'd given Prophet up. He'd been the one to back away from his partner after Phil had given him the choice. And then he'd agonized over it, written Prophet emails daily, telling him how he'd fucked up, all the while watching Cope bounce a tennis ball against the ceiling.

And you had a choice to stay with him after he told you a secret and you left him.

Again.

But fuck it, Prophet had pushed him to go, acted like he and Nico were a new dream team.

Asshole.

"Just a simple extraction," Elliot was saying.

"Nothing's simple in this country," Nico muttered.

"You can take this truck—try to get it back to me in one piece," Elliot told Tom.

"I'm not Prophet."

Elliot laughed. "You know how many trucks he's wrecked?"

"I can only imagine, given his special gift of driving like an insane person," Tom said dryly. "Any idea where this medical facility is, by the way? General idea?"

"Yes, but I can do you one better. Doc keeps a tracker in his bag." Elliot ushered them inside the offices, past the alarms with codes and into the computer station. "See that dot? It moved for an hour or so, then stopped . . . and then moved, but more slowly. Like Doc was walking. It's been steady for the past two hours."

"Staying in one place while he's performing surgery," Nico observed.

"I heard him mention that the surgery could take up to six hours, depending on the conditions of the facility, and how badly the boy was injured," Elliot told them.

"Then we need to move," Tom said. "Weapons in the usual spots?"

"Of course. Cash as well." Elliot nodded. "Please keep me informed."

"Will do." Tom and Nico got into the truck, with Tom driving. Nico extracted one of the AKs from under the seat and held it below window level, adjusting the mirror so he could watch for ambushes from behind as well.

Just as Elliot noted, the ride to the pinpoint took slightly over an hour. It was still light but that wouldn't last much longer. Dark would be great for an escape, but Tom would rather get in and out before that.

They parked far enough away to not be detected, less than a klick, and walked the rest of the way, weapons and grenades in tow. They slid into the makeshift clinic from the sides, where there were no windows and hence, no guards. Nico moved easily, as if being an operator was born into him. It was easy to be good following someone this trained, and Tom was glad for that.

Still, the things that Prophet taught him had sunk in, become as much a part of him as breathing. The way it needed to be in order to be effective.

And it was. Because when they assessed the situation, he told Nico, "Three cars. Maybe ten men. Maybe more."

Nico nodded. "As long as the surgery's over, we go in. We'll have an easier time of it if the boy is alive when we take Doc and Cope back."

"The back way's easiest—two guards to go through."

"Majority up front," Nico agreed. "Let's start quiet."

Tom's hinky feelings went into overdrive, but nothing about them indicated imminent danger. On the contrary, it was more of a *go now* response screaming in his brain.

So he did. When Nico slit the first guard's throat, the second, dressed in battle BDUs, had turned toward him. Tom used his knife in the man's neck, pushing down toward the carotid, twisting fast and hard until he crumpled to the ground. Tom searched him, found a gun and a knife. He pocketed them, dragged the men into the brush so they wouldn't be seen at first glance and kept moving. Nico was already using the keys he'd taken from the first guard to slowly open the door. He motioned Tom in behind him and together they moved silently through the dimly lit hall, stopping outside the first room.

There was a small window in the door, and Nico ducked under it so he could wait on the other side. From their positions, they could look in but not be immediately seen.

It looked like the outer room of an OR, with a big metal sink and shelves of medical supplies. Doc was in there alone, sitting on the floor with his bag at his side, his head back, eyes closed, scrubs bloody. He appeared to be exhausted.

He's not asleep, Nico mouthed. Both men moved back slightly when a guard came through a side door and into the room with Doc. He didn't look menacing, seemed to be just walking through . . . but in seconds, Doc was up, grabbing the guard by the throat, hitting the spot on the man's neck with such precision that had him passing out and hitting the floor with a solid thump before looking at Tom through the window.

"Is he going to be happy to see you?" Tom asked, palm on the door.

"Doubtful." Nico said the word like it didn't matter, but every bit of the man's positioning said it did. "Let's go."

Tom pushed the door open and held out a weapon to Doc, who took it and grabbed his bag simultaneously. He stared at Nico, a bit like he was seeing a ghost. He quickly shook it off in favor of clapping Tom on the shoulder and saying, "Thanks."

There was no time for awkwardness. They were on the move, taking down more guards, although the majority of them seemed to have vanished, and grabbing Cope—who wasn't tied at all and the door to where they'd kept him wasn't locked, as evidenced by his meeting them in the hallway—and headed out to the LZ.

It was too fucking easy. None of them said it as they hustled out, but based on the quiet that surrounded them, they were all goddamned spooked.

He was already at the door, opened it to sweep the hall. When he motioned to the others, he noted they were all lined up behind him. They moved down the hallway as a unit, no one speaking.

"I think we need to move," Prophet said suddenly. He'd had one drink, three hours ago, and since then he'd been sitting on the couch next to Dean, eyes closed, thinking about Tom and relaxing. But suddenly, the need to get the fuck out of there was intense.

Dean didn't argue. "I'm ready. I'll have Reggie get the truck packed. Should take ten minutes."

"Do you have a safe house?"

Dean nodded. "The only ones who know about it are me, Reggie, and Nico."

Not LT. Prophet wanted to ask why but hell, Dean had his reasons to not want his brother to even consider Dean's need for a safe house. Not after last year's kidnapping. And that's why Prophet suspected Dean put the measure into place after all.

Prophet nodded. "New car too."

"Got one of those. Plates registered to a diplomat."

"Great. Either no one will fuck with us or we'll get kidnapped."

Dean shrugged. "Hopefully kidnappings are like lightning strikes." He walked off in search of Reggie and Prophet tried—and failed—to shake off the feeling of John. He went into the room he'd shared with Tom, grabbed his go-bag that he'd packed earlier, and met Dean back in the main room.

"Reggie said five minutes and he'll pull around back," Dean told him. "Want me to tell Nico?"

"Not yet."

"You don't want Tom to follow."

"One of us needs to be free, for Remy."

Dean frowned. If he suspected Prophet's plan, he didn't say anything about that except, "Remy's a lucky kid."

"Nah, I'm the lucky one."

"Then stop waiting for fate to take it all away."

"You first," Prophet told him. And got no answer but silence.

The ride was a long, bumpy, dusty-ass one where Reggie went behind the wheel and Prophet's brain worked overtime in an attempt to tamp down his PTSD tendencies on these types of roads . . . and even still, some part of his brain was living the Hal fiasco, over and over.

The shots. The time discrepancies he couldn't reconcile. The trucks coming out of nowhere to ambush them. Ending up hanging by his wrists and later, in a CIA cage.

"Come on back, Proph." Dean spoke quietly, calmly, talking the feral wolf that lived in Prophet's brain back into its cage. A gentle coax, a prod, the promise of safety . . . it all brought him back. "Prophet, we're here, in the house. In the garage. All clear."

"Christ," Prophet muttered when he realized how much time he lost. How much risk he put Reggie in, the only one with good vision—and one arm—in charge.

Reggie didn't seem to mind, just nodded at him and pulled a gun. "Going to check the house. You both stay here."

What a crew. "Fuck."

Dean handed him a bottle of water. "You would've come out of it if there was danger."

"And if I didn't?"

"The way you looked, all I had to do was hand you a gun and tell you to fire." Dean shrugged. "We'd have been fine. Do you think he's close?"

"Probably, but not enough. He was always last with the chase. It bored him," Prophet explained.

"So you turned around and made it your strength purposely."

"I'd rather be hunter than prey. John actually thought that prey had the majority of the power. He's onto something."

It was still light outside. Tom, Nico, Doc and Cope continued to move fast through the single-floored but surprisingly intricate clinic.

Doc pointed to a closed door and mouthed, *Patient's room* and Tom swore he felt Nico's desire to enter.

He put a hand on Nico's arm and shook his head and Nico complied, but didn't look happy about it.

After what seemed like an hour, but was under ten minutes, they were all out the back entrance and into the bush, crouched low, checking to see if they were being followed.

Which they weren't.

Again, spooked.

They got maybe halfway to the truck before Nico turned to Doc and demanded, "What the fuck happened? Elliot said you just complied—no arguments. You let yourself be taken. Trying to be a fucking hero to the locals, or you've got a sudden death wish?"

Nico's voice was low and angry, and for a brief second, anger flashed in Doc's eyes, quickly replaced by a false calm before he answered, "My job."

"You're losing it, old man." Fighting words, and Nico was definitely looking for the fight. Whether Doc would give him the satisfaction was another story.

Cope frowned, looked to Tom. "Guess they've got unfinished business. Fucking drama. Maybe we could finish the rescue first? Although this is entertaining."

Doc ignored him. "'Old man'? That the best you can do?" Doc's tone was the quiet kind that forced a chill through Tom. "I'm sure you could be more creative than that."

"Of course," Nico countered. "But why would I bother?"

"Shit, meet fan," Cope muttered.

"I took an oath, Nico, in case you've forgotten."

"You should've killed him," Nico said.

"You should've captured him when you had the chance," Doc said blithely, and Tom guessed this was an old score.

Nico hadn't mentioned he knew the man on the operating table in any capacity but was now pushing past Doc. "Right. *Do no harm*'s a convenient motto when you feel like it."

Tom wanted to strangle both of them, because the pain was so obvious, so thick it was visceral. "Let's go," he said decisively in a *What Would Prophet Do* moment, jerking his head toward the path.

He didn't wait to see if they'd all comply. His tone left no room for anything but.

They made it to the truck without further incident, Tom behind the wheel again, Nico in the passenger's seat and Doc and Cope in the back seat.

By the time he pulled onto the main road, it was dark. It made for better cover but it also kept them targets . . . albeit a moving one. None of them spoke for a while, until Doc finally said to him, "How'd you escape Prophet's protectiveness?"

Tom gave him the side-eye in the rearview and Doc whistled. "Must've been some fight."

"You have no idea." Tom glanced ahead.

"Can we discuss what a fucking setup that was *now*?" Nico demanded and no one argued with him.

Tom glanced in the mirror again and met Doc's eyes for a brief second. "Maybe John?"

"Are we telling Phil?" Doc asked quietly.

"No, that's Prophet's business."

"Which turned into ours," Nico pointed out.

"Leave it, Nico." The sharpness of Doc's tongue surprised Tom, but clearly not Nico.

"I don't take orders from you," Nico shared blandly.

Tom's phone beeped. He took his phone and Nico steadied the wheel while he checked it.

It was a text with coordinates . . . and a link to a GPS.

"What's wrong?" Nico asked.

"They moved." Tom handed him the phone and took back the wheel. "Left us a trail."

"Fuck. Now I've got to hear it from that idiot brother of his."

"Takes one to know one," Doc said, eyes still closed. "Just saying."

"But if the shoe fits . . ."

"You want to discuss my shoe size?" Doc asked, and how the hell had Tom ended up surrounding by dysfunctional relationships?

"So is faking death a common operator thing?" Tom asked Nico.

"Doc knew I wasn't dead. So did Prophet. He just likes to give me shit when he sees me."

"Why?"

"Because he's Prophet," Nico pointed out. "Because he blames me for my breakup with Doc."

"And he shouldn't?"

"Doc broke up with me, Tom. Two weeks after we got married."

"Nico," Doc said warningly, just as they pulled up to EE's opening gate. Saved—by Elliot.

Doc and Cope exited the car and Tom followed suit. Elliot would drive them the short trip back to the helo, so Nico stayed put.

"Tom, thanks again," Doc said and Cope pulled him in for a quick, hard pat on the back hug.

"Good save, T."

"Keep in touch," Doc warned him.

"I'll try," Tom said and got into the back seat.

Within twenty minutes, he and Nico were back up in the air.

"Well, that went well," Nico said irritably.

Tom was too busy checking his phone . . . to find more coordinates. "Nico, they're not stopping."

Nico cursed. "His brother's definitely going to kill me."

"Well, Dean's with Proph so . . . right. See your point." Tom glanced at him. "I'd like to swing by the house first."

"Did Prophet tell you to do that?"

"No."

"Then that's what we'll do," Nico agreed.

CHAPTER SEVENTEEN

In the time it took Tom and Nico to get back to Dean's house, the texts with coordinates had stopped. Prophet's phone was turned off and Tom was telling himself that Prophet knew what he was doing.

Didn't make him any less pissed though.

"Place looks deserted," Nico noted as he punched in the numbers on the gate and it opened. He pulled in, gun drawn until it closed. And then the large dogs, mainly King Shepherds, came racing around the property toward him. He whistled and they stopped just short of climbing into Tom's car window, teeth bared.

"Thanks for stopping them from killing me," Tom muttered.

"They would've just taken a few bites." Nico petted the biggest one on the head. "They're great backup."

"And Dean left them behind."

Nico nodded. "He knew I'd be back here for them. I'm sure there are others on the property. I'll take the dogs—can you drive the truck in farther?"

Tom got out, the dogs surrounding him momentarily before following Nico and his pied piper whistle away from the vehicle. He pulled the truck up under the carport, a protected area right against a doorway that led inside.

When he walked into the familiar main room, he saw one of the cooks who'd been there early, setting out food.

"I'm gonna grab a shower," Tom called to Nico.

"Food'll be ready by then."

And it was. They ate, realized they couldn't chase coordinates that might not be correct, and they left their phones on and got some sleep.

When Tom woke, the sun was long up and he felt more rested than he had in months. Probably because he actually slept instead of watching over Prophet for his nightmares. Not that he minded doing that, but he was slowly losing his mind from lack of sleep, a fact Prophet kept trying to hammer into his head.

Finally, he dressed and went into the main room, where Nico was sitting with food and a weapon.

Tom nodded and then stopped cold when he saw who was standing across from Nico. With a weapon of his own. "Cillian?"

"Who were you expecting?" Cillian asked. "I've already met Nico."

"Fuck off," Nico told him as he ladled more eggs onto his plate.

"I can see why you're a good match for Doc."

Nico went to get up but Tom moved forward and held him down with a light hand on his shoulder. "What the fuck, Cillian, because I know you didn't come all this way to throw insults."

"I was looking for Prophet," Cillian said.

"You're not the only one." Tom moved to sit next to Nico, but Cillian remained standing. "Can't find him?"

"No, but John's a step closer. He was here." Cillian crossed his arms.

Tom narrowed his eyes. "You saw him?"

"If so, he'd be lying here with a bullet in his skull," Cillian assured him. "The locals saw him. ID'd him."

"Prophet and Dean left, probably leading him on a wild-goose chase," Tom said. "They won't tell us where they are."

"Not yet. But they will," Nico said.

"Yes. Probably just when Prophet decides to take all the trouble on himself," Tom muttered.

"Give the man a prize," Cillian said.

"I guess assholes all hang together." Nico stood and stalked through the house, brushing a little too close to Cillian as he did so, but Tom didn't stop him.

"Seems like a sweetheart," Cillian called over his shoulder.

"Not as big of one as you." Tom let an edge of anger show through now that they were alone.

Cillian, being Cillian, didn't miss it. "You've chatted with Mal, I see."

"Prophet doesn't know."

"Yes," Cillian added. "What would you like me to do, Tom? Commit hara-kiri to atone for my sins?"

"I'm not going to help you by telling you anything."

"Right. One crisis at a time. Prophet's been in touch."

"With you?"

"Yes. And Nico? Your company's been requested ASAP at Dean's newest safe house," Cillian called.

"Come on, Tom," Nico said.

"Tom and I have other plans," Cillian told him.

Nico stared at Tom, who nodded. "I'm good. I'll check in."

"I'll do the same when I get to Dean's." Nico was shouldering his bag. "I'm guessing Prophet will wait with Dean until I get there?"

"He didn't really specify." Cillian looked at Tom.

"He won't be there," Tom told Nico. "Or else I'd be going with you."

"I'd better hurry then." Nico jerked his chin at Tom. "Nice working with you, T."

"Same, Nico."

"Well, nice to see you've got a new bromance going on."

"Cillian, I'm this close to killing you," Tom warned.

"Perhaps your blood sugar's low. I suggest you eat something to ease your pissy mood." Cillian sat, opened his computer, and motioned to a chair near him, ignoring the audible grind of Tom's teeth. "We're staying put for a bit."

"Listen, asshole—I don't take orders from you."

"Only from Prophet? I'm guessing you enjoy that."

Tom lunged toward him but suddenly Nico was behind him, stopping him. "Not worth it. Trust me—I already considered stabbing him with a dull butter knife, just for fun."

Tom let Nico keep an arm on him but told Cillian, "We're going to find Prophet. We're not sitting here waiting for shit."

"I'm waiting for Prophet to give us coordinates, Tom. I thought you could be civilized."

"And I thought you knew I don't trust you still," Tom hissed.

"I've had opportunities to kill both you and Prophet, and you're both still alive," Cillian pointed out.

"Ditto," Tom told him. "So chew on that for a while."

CHAPTER EIGHTEEN

The wait for Tom to arrive at the newest safe house seemed to take forever. Granted, Tom and Cillian were flying in from Dean's house part of the way to just outside of Khartoum, which wasn't exactly a walk in the park, and Prophet was trying not to drive everyone else crazy, but he was distracted . . . and that was the worst thing he could possibly be at a time like this.

It got so bad that Mal took him by the back of the neck and forced him to sit down on the back porch and just chill.

"Chill?" Prophet asked. "Since when do you *chill*?"

I think anyone would agree that I'm way more chill than you are, Mal signed.

"If you keep using the word 'chill,' then yes, I'm definitely going to be the more uptight of the two of us."

Mal smiled and then signed, *What the fuck did you do to Tom?*

"Who says I did anything to him?" Prophet asked. Mal frowned. "What do you know? Did he say something?"

No, but you just did.

"Dammit."

You need to fix it, whatever it is.

"What, now you're on his side? How the hell did that happen?"

You wanted us to get along.

Prophet grumbled. "I told him a secret."

Mal rolled his eyes. *Lots of them to choose from.*

"What? You know most of them, dammit, so it's not fair of you to judge."

But the one you told him involved him, right?

"So?"

Reverse the roles. You'd have thrown him through a wall.

"You don't know me that well," Prophet muttered. "Might've thrown something at him but I haven't thrown anyone through a wall since . . ."

Sully. Camp Lejeune. Joint Forces training.

"He was an asshole."

Mal shrugged. *I thought he was chill.*

Prophet rested his head against the back of the wooden chair and sighed. Mal turned his head to the door and mouthed, *They're here.*

When Prophet jumped up, Mal just pointed to him. "I'll make it right. Maybe not right away though."

Mal nodded in concession.

Prophet was in the main room when the door opened, because it was all he could do not to run out the door and drag Tom in. Cillian came in first, with Tommy behind him, and Prophet realized he was fucking nervous to see him. They hadn't left on the best note at all, and then Prophet had stopped communicating and hell, if Tom didn't understand why . . .

"Thanks for the invite," Cillian said, and Mal came out of the woodwork. Tom glanced at Prophet and nodded (*nodded*? What the *fuck* was that?) and put his bag down.

Prophet ignored Cillian for the moment, went over to Tom and dragged him into the room he'd taken over, shutting the door behind them. "You okay?" He didn't wait for Tom to answer, was patting him down, looking for blood or bullet holes, even though he knew the mission had gone fine. But traveling in country could also leave anyone with scars, especially ones that wouldn't show.

"I'm fine."

"Then why can you barely fucking look at me?" Prophet demanded.

Tom finally met his gaze, his countenance still slightly stony, but relenting. "I don't know what to say."

"I love you, Tommy," was all he could think of, touching Tom's cheek. "Just give me some credit."

"I will. I am."

"I'm on your goddamned side, okay?"

Tom nodded, leaned his forehead against Prophet's. "Fucking missed you."

"Same."

"How long do we have here?"

"Maybe forty-eight hours. Everyone's converging and then . . ."

Here they were, at *and then.*

Again.

"'S'okay, Proph. Let's go plan. Maybe we'll leave some time for later."

"Damned straight we will." Prophet kissed him lightly, but Tom dragged him into a hot kiss that Prophet didn't want to extricate from. "Don't have much time—they're getting restless out there."

Then again, so was he, dammit. He shoved Tom into the small bathroom and turned the water on to mask some of the noise. They both were pulling and yanking and tugging clothing off, forgotten weapons clunking as they hit the floor still in pockets.

Tom was covered in red dust from the drive, but Prophet wasn't interested in getting him clean. The water was merely warm, but he'd be fine with cold water as long as he could get his dick inside of Tom.

He bent his head and bit one of Tom's nipples around the barbell piercing. Tom hissed and grabbed Prophet's hair, tugging him closer. Fuck, the man loved pain and Prophet had no problem giving it to him—during sex.

Tom's dick piercings were on full display, even though Prophet told him that he should take them out for missions. Prophet knew from experience, having helped Tom put them back in, what a pain in the ass that was, and right now, he was grateful Tom ignored him about it. He played with some of the piercings, the Jacob's Ladder, making Tom groan, beg, push his dick against Prophet's palm, looking to gain some friction.

And then Prophet was pushing inside of him, Tom's leg wrapped around his thighs to help drive Prophet inside of him.

"Fuck, we're going to die in here," Tom grunted as he almost lost his footing.

"Not a bad way to go." Prophet leaned into Tom's neck, resisting the urge to mark him where everyone could see it, instead moving down to the skin between neck and shoulder, marking him hard, sucking and laving as his orgasm coursed through him, and Tom's between them, spurting up their chests only to be quickly washed away.

They needed more time—in the shower, inside each other. Prophet knew that because as they quickly toweled off and re-dressed, the silence hung between them again. Prophet had no problem with silence, treasured it during an op, because it meant everyone was focused. But Tom's quiet was still an angry one.

Tom wandered out of the bedroom before Prophet, who said he'd be out in a few minutes. He'd been on his phone, and although Tom wanted to know everything he was doing, he didn't push his luck in that regard. This uneasy truce was too fragile for him to push—not until Prophet shared the next steps. Too many people were counting on his plans, and Tom wouldn't let their personal drama get in the way of that.

Even though your personal drama is very much a part of all of this shit.

He shook his head and wandered down the hall and through the kitchen, finding the main room through which he and Cillian had entered an hour before.

This place was definitely on the higher end for a safe house, with the high gates, stuccoed walls, and open design. It wasn't as nice as Dean's, but the similarities in furnishings, the colors and the dark ebony wood–carved furniture echoed the same feel.

Although they technically weren't far from Dean's house, they might as well have been a million miles away. There was no easy way to get to the safe house in Khartoum (and the irony of anything being safe in Khartoum wasn't lost on him) except by plane, so Tom and Cillian had paid a pilot to get them there as fast as possible . . . and to forget he ever saw either man.

Still, they'd had a couple of hours' worth of driving to do beyond that, past rebels, police and other dangerous types. It was all a crapshoot and men like them stuck out like sore thumbs for being exactly what they were. Sometimes that served them well. Other times, merc equaled soldier, which prompted payback to their government.

Traveling with a guide, someone from the area, was typically a good idea. The man who'd been with them since they'd deplaned was still with them at the safe house today, and he'd worked at various times for Dean and the clinics. Prophet knew him and the other men seemed to as well.

Now, Tom stepped into the main room and all the men glanced over at him. "Hey, guys. How's it going?"

Cillian nodded, then went back to his laptop. He was in the corner at a small table, slightly separated from the rest of the group.

"Hey Tom," Ren said. King nodded and Hook smiled. Mal shot him the finger. So yeah, business as usual.

The last time he'd seen them all together had been months ago in Amsterdam, in a gay bar in the heart of the city. Cillian had been there as well, although he hadn't known that at the time.

King sat in a high-back chair with elaborate carvings. Tom thought of him as shadows and stealth. He wore a black bandana wrapped around his head instead of his usual black skullcap, probably because of the heat, with his dark hair escaping and curling around his ears. He was tanned, which made his eyes stand out even more. When Tom had first met King, he thought King had green eyes, but on closer inspection, he'd realized they were more of a bluish-green, like the color of the Irish sea.

Next to him, sprawled on the couch, was Ren, a stocky blond with piercing green eyes and a buzz of energy that carried everyone near him along with it. He and King were rarely separated, according to Prophet.

Hook's long, lanky body was stretched out on the floor, his back against Ren's couch. Even though he appeared to be the most laid-back, Tom knew that meant he was probably more lethal than Mal. He was married to his high school sweetheart, and he was magic at finding transportation, according to Prophet.

And then there was good old Uncle Crazy. Mal was wearing his usual black, but he'd stripped to a black wifebeater so all his tattoos showed. He and Cillian were across the room from each other, but Tom would bet they were having a hard time not looking at each other.

"Come on in, sit down and stay awhile. Prophet's going to come fill us in any minute now, I'm guessing," Ren told him.

King rolled his eyes and grumbled and muttered something about "beating it out of Prophet" and Tom realized he wasn't the only one pissed at Prophet at the moment.

CHAPTER NINETEEN

After a semisheepish and still slightly wet return to the main room, where everyone had gathered—and had no doubt heard everything—Prophet simply sat on the edge of a couch and motioned for Tom to take an actual seat.

"Thanks for joining us," Ren said with a grin. "You're fucking loud, man."

Prophet shot him the finger. "You already knew that, so deal with it."

"Any other comments? Let's get them out of the way," King asked.

"I've got one," Cillian offered. "Anything new and interesting to share with the class, Prophet? Perhaps something we've not been privy to?"

"No," Prophet answered flatly, but of course, Cillian had a reason for asking. And that reason was a photo on his iPhone that he held up to show Prophet walking with a mystery man in a suit. Prophet frowned and shook his head. "And still, no."

"Really?" Cillian asked dryly. "Doesn't look like anyone you might know?"

"Maybe it's photoshopped?" Prophet asked.

"A friend?" Cillian persisted. "Tom, perhaps you know this man?"

"That's Agent Paul," Tom said and Cillian nodded, and then showed it to Mal, who glanced at Prophet.

Not Agent Paul, Mal signed.

"Bullshit. That's the man I met as Agent Paul," Cillian told Mal pointedly before turning back to Prophet. "Remember when he came to your apartment, *Prophet*? I saved you and Tom by pretending to be your lawyer."

Tom glanced at the picture and back at Prophet. But like Mal and King and Ren and Hook, Tom continued to wait as well. All of them knew that waiting Prophet out was never the easiest idea, and at least that thought made him happy and momentarily distracted him from strangling Cillian.

Finally, Mal grabbed the phone from Cillian, studied the picture more closely and frowned. Prophet gave Mal a side-eye and Mal rolled his eyes and pointed at Prophet.

"New language I don't know about?" Ren drawled. King shook his head at the whole thing but his posture belied any relaxation.

Mal finally signed, *His name is Rylan.*

"Oh, Rylan. *Right.* Shoulda just said so from the start," Ren said sarcastically. "Who the *fuck* is Rylan?"

"Guy in the picture," Prophet said.

Tom made a fist and gave him a pointed look as he ground out, "So Agent Paul doesn't exist?"

"He exists. And he hates me, more than Lansing did," Prophet added.

"Proph—" Tom warned.

"Okay, look, you've never met the real Agent Paul. It was Rylan who came to our apartment that day posing as Agent Paul. Sounded just like him too—"

Tom interrupted him. "I know we found bugs after he left. What if Agent Paul—the real one—had heard the recordings . . . ?"

"Rylan took care of it on his end, the way we took care of it on ours," Prophet explained. "It was the only way for him to safely let me know I was on Paul's radar. Making contact as himself was too risky."

"And we're just learning about this now because?" Tom motioned with his hand as if pulling the answer from Prophet.

"Plausible deniability," Prophet answered confidently.

"When was *this* picture with Rylan taken then?" Cillian asked, holding his phone.

"Yesterday afternoon."

"You made plans to meet him?"

"After I became aware of certain intel, yes, I contacted him. He met with me. I gave him a heads-up and he returned the favor." Prophet rolled his shoulders in an attempt to release some of the tension, but hell, it radiated through the entire damned room.

"And he just happened to be in the right place at the right time?" Tom asked.

"He would've found me if I hadn't reached out first."

"Because of John," King said.

Prophet shrugged. "We just . . . caught up on some things."

King stared at him for a long beat and finally said, "I'm going to beat the hell out of you if you don't start telling the entire story, without skipping shit."

Prophet wanted to say, *You and what army*, but looking at the small one amassed around him, he figured he would be hard-pressed to get out completely unscathed. Still, the door was closest to him . . .

Until Tom went to it and closed it firmly. Stood in front of it. Fucking voodoo bastard.

Tom smiled, as if reading his mind. Because the asshole probably was.

"Proph?" Ren asked.

"Fine." Prophet turned his attention from the door and gave his most put-upon sigh. "I've known Rylan for a while."

"How long?" Cillian asked.

"Let's say eight or so years. Maybe nine." Prophet started counting on his fingers, a sure distraction technique he'd perfected, but the men surrounding him wouldn't fall for it.

"Just around the time you stopped looking for John," King added.

"Technically I never really stopped looking," Prophet said.

"Just around the time you joined the CIA," Tom pointed out, no doubt thinking he was being helpful, and Prophet froze as Mal's, King's, Ren's and Hook's heads swung in his direction. Tom's eyebrows rose. "Ah, was that a secret?"

"Kinda was," Prophet said under his breath without moving his lips.

"Sorry." Tom shrugged. "Not sorry."

"You said you were working in a joint task force with them through the Navy," Ren reminded him. "You said you'd never ever sign on with the agency."

"I remember that," King echoed.

"Anyway," Prophet said loudly, trying to move forward and knowing it was impossible. "I met Rylan—"

"When you were working for the CIA?"

"Kinda yes, kinda no. It was a time of . . . indecision," Prophet offered. "The best of times, the worst of—"

"Stop quoting Dickens." King's brogue was thick. "He pulls that shit whenever he's caught doing something he shouldn't."

"Are you going to shut up so I can tell you what I need to tell you?" Prophet demanded and they basically all crossed their arms and stared at him with *this better be good* looks on their faces.

And hell, it was.

"I'm not joining those fuckers, so if you're here to talk me into it . . ." Prophet started at the tall, good-looking spy who sat across from him at the café in Rome.

The man took his dark glasses off and smirked. "They told me to look for the biggest asshole and that would be my mark."

"I'm nobody's fucking mark. Asshole," Prophet muttered. But the guy was staring at him, and flirting with him too, because Prophet knew the difference between being recruited and being recruited to fuck. "You could buy me a coffee though."

The guy smiled as the waitress appeared with Prophet's favorite coffee. And a piece of cheesecake. Prophet sighed and began to eat. "Go ahead, give me the whole 'why I should work for the agency,' spiel. I'll pretend to consider it and then we can go do whatever else we're going to do."

The man leaned forward on his elbows. "I knew I'd like you. I'm Rylan. And I'm not trying to talk you into shit. I'm here to ask for a favor."

"Really?" Prophet pushed his plate back. "You don't look like you've got to beg for it."

"Yeah, I don't." Rylan gave a subtle glance around, like he was enjoying the view. "Can't discuss it here. But it's outside the purview of the agency. I think it's something you'd be comfortable doing."

A favor for a man he barely knew. But Rylan was right about one thing—the favor was something Prophet was uniquely qualified for.

"So you slept with him," Tom interrupted.

"Who's telling this story?" Prophet crossed his arms now.

Mal pretended to bang his head against the wall.

Cillian pretended to snore.

King took out a knife and exposed the long blade. Ren put a hand on his arm, then shrugged and took it away.

"Fine," Prophet said.

Rylan waited until after they'd slept together to ask for the favor. And Christ, the guy was good.

Rylan snorted, like he knew what Prophet was thinking. "Trust me, you're pretty damned good yourself."

"'Good'? Christ, defame me more, why don't you?" Prophet groused, secretly pleased with the look on Rylan's face.

"I need you to hide someone. Bury them completely."

"I can do that."

"It's someone already in CIA custody."

"Is this a setup?" Prophet asked mildly.

"No."

"Okay." Prophet stared at him, knowing he was going on gut instinct by trusting Rylan. And hell, if he'd listened to instincts about John all those years ago . . . "Is this person going to be killed otherwise?"

"Yes." Rylan's eyes clouded then.

"This is personal." It wasn't a question. "Is the specialist dangerous?"

"In the wrong hands? Lethal."

"Current location?"

Rylan gave coordinates, and Prophet memorized them. "I won't be in touch when it's done."

"Best that way," Rylan conceded. "But—"

"I'll play go-between. But not too often."

"In return, I've got something for you," Rylan said.

"I don't accept cash."

"No, it's intel. I think you need this," Rylan told him. "It's about your friend."

Prophet got a knot in his stomach, knew exactly which friend Rylan was referring to, but he remained casual. "I've got a lot of friends."

"I think this one's special—you've gone AWOL for him, right?"

"Rumor is that he's alive. I'm pretty sure he's one of yours."

Rylan confirmed his suspicions by not answering that question—not directly. "You need to leave him be. If you do what we think you're trying to do, it'll be a problem."

"Like I worry about the CIA and their problems." Prophet paused. "What exactly is it that you think I'm trying to do?"

"Get him out of hell, anyway you can." Rylan sat back. "We've got similar jobs, Prophet."

"If I do my job, the CIA's worried about intel that might go public, right?"

"If we knew that . . ." Rylan shrugged. "The CIA wants him to do what he's doing."

"And Lansing?"

"Lansing is about as in the loop as you were."

"You're not supposed to share any of this shit with me, right?"

"None."

Rylan was taking a big chance . . . but he also wasn't. Because he knew Prophet would gladly take a specialist out of the CIA's clutches. "Is the intel that might leak . . . is it also about me?"

"No. But it involves members of your team." Prophet frowned at that. "Two members are under WITSEC."

"Fuck," Prophet breathed.

"I can't give you more than that."

"No need to." Prophet waved him off.

"We've got the room for the night," Rylan said.

"That's enough," Tom said.

"Why would you stop him when he's getting to the good parts?" Cillian demanded.

"Who else knows? About WITSEC? And how does Rylan know? How close to John was he?" Ren asked in a machine-gun barrage.

"Close enough to know about the probable dead man's switch John's got over the CIA's heads. Did you stop to think—" King started.

"That it's Rylan?" Prophet shook his head. "No way. I've got enough on him that he wouldn't risk it. And that's all I'm saying."

"And Agent Paul doesn't suspect Rylan?" Tom asked.

"The entire CIA doesn't trust itself." Prophet leaned forward, elbows on his thighs.

"The biggest problem in all of this is Agent Paul. It's always been him working with John."

The men were all silent for a long moment, digesting the information.

Finally, Cillian broke the quiet. "So, which one of you two are in WITSEC?"

"Like they'd tell you," Tom muttered.

"That takes you out of the running," Cillian said.

"No one say another word about it," Prophet warned. "Agent Paul discovered the kill switch for his own purpose—to cover the CIA's ass. Finding out the other intel didn't further his interests. Giving it over to Lansing would've been like admitting Paul'd been lying about his mission, so . . ."

"Fuck." Hook shook his head. "And you've kept this secret for eight years?"

"Nine, technically," Prophet said.

Asshole, Mal signed.

"Fuck it, Proph. The CIA doesn't need protection," King said.

"No, *they* don't," Prophet said quietly.

Mal got it first—judging by the fact that he threw Cillian's table against the wall and watched it shatter. He always got pissed when he thought Prophet was taking the weight of the world on his shoulders, but Prophet wouldn't apologize for any of it.

King stared between Mal and Prophet. "Fuck, lad, how long have you known this?"

Prophet shrugged.

"And you kept it to yourself. You knew and you backed off without giving us a chance to know. To do things differently." King's brogue was heavy. Tired.

"I'm lost," Tom said to Cillian.

"John's got a dead man's switch," Cillian told him.

"And I've been trying to find out who holds it since then," Prophet added.

"Yeah, I got that. Maybe it's just software?" Tom suggested.

Prophet shook his head. "Too easily destroyed."

"Like people aren't?" Ren asked.

"Maybe it's a bluff," Tom argued. "He's enough of an asshole to do that."

"Want to take that risk? Because I wasn't willing to expose two of my teammates. Two of my best friends," Prophet answered, his voice tight. "And I'm still not. I'd do it again in a second."

How do you know the intel is airtight? Mal signed.

Prophet sighed. Pinched the bridge of his nose.

Tom looked like he wanted to punch all of them, but he probably also understood their frustration better than anyone. "Proph—"

"Yeah, I know." He knew that Tom's voodoo was on the rise—that he agreed that Prophet's guy was on the money. "I couldn't let you all get any more hurt."

"Isn't it enough that he worked for the CIA to help you?" Tom asked and all heads swung in Prophet's direction. Except for Prophet's, whose swung toward Tom.

"You've *got* to stop mentioning that." Prophet slowly edged away but was stopped by Mal, who'd somehow gotten behind him. "Hey, Mal, didn't see you back there."

Tom continued, "I'm just defending you. Because you were helping—"

"And you're not," Prophet told him. "You've done enough, T."

"Yes," Ren echoed. "Thankfully you've done the dirty work by exposing Mr. Weight-of-the-World-On-Our-Shoulders. Now answer Mal's question—how do you know the intel is correct?"

Prophet looked at Mal. Mal looked at King, who semifroze. Prophet admitted, "I didn't want to believe it either, but the files had been hacked. Rylan showed me the code."

Who else knows? Mal signed.

Prophet sighed. "Well, now *I* do. You. King. John. And I'm guessing the dead man's switch person might—or might just let it all out into the world mindlessly."

And Rylan?

"He gave me the intel in exchange for something. He'll never give up what he knows."

Why's that?

"I have a kill switch on him." Prophet sat back down.

Everyone groaned.

Cillian looked impressed.

"Christ, Prophet." Hook downed his beer. "Anything else you're holding back on?"

When Prophet didn't answer, another collective groan went up.

"What the fuck am I missing?" Tom demanded.

"Kinda wondering the same thing," Ren asked. Hook nodded in agreement and Mal and King—and Prophet—all looked like proverbial deer in the headlights.

"Apparently, they're the reasons for the dead man's switch. Mal and King—and their WITSEC protection," Cillian clarified. "Prophet could be on John's death list too, but I doubt it."

"He's definitely on mine," King muttered.

"I'm guessing this is because of the Irish thing," Cillian offered.

And you'd know about that, being from Belgrade and all, Mal signed.

"I was stolen from Ireland. Brought to Belgrade," Cillian corrected.

Mal shot him the finger and Cillian grunted.

Tom stared at Prophet. "You didn't know before Rylan told you?"

Prophet shook his head. "I didn't know for sure after Rylan either but..."

"The Irish," Cillian finished. King took the knife out again and Mal pretended to bang his head against the wall again. Or maybe he wasn't pretending this time since they could hear the actual sound of a head hitting a wall.

"Wait, so if you knew this already, then what was the most recent meeting with Rylan about?" Tom asked, turning to Prophet.

Prophet glared in Tom's direction. "Jesus Christ, Tommy—maybe you could not point unanswered shit out among the psychos."

King jumped off the table carrying the knife. Ren got in front of him to ostensibly slow him down and Prophet put his hands up. "Fine—okay? The specialist that I hid for him? Disappeared forty-eight hours ago."

"Taken?" Cillian asked.

Prophet shook his head. "Ran."

King cursed. "So there's a threat."

"A big one," Prophet agreed.

"Your specialist's left the building," Prophet told Rylan as soon as he sat down across from him. The restaurant was small—open air—with lots of noise around them from the surrounding markets.

Rylan didn't look surprised as much as troubled. "Then my needing to contact you seems to make more sense—to me, at least. Your expertise is needed to take care of a problem. One we discussed many years ago."

Yeah, none of this was a coincidence. "Funny, since you all told me to back off."

"You didn't exactly listen—and I didn't tell you to back off. I just gave you reasons to consider."

"Right. An even exchange," Prophet groused, but there was no heat behind it. "He's alive, right?"

Rylan gave a small smile. "If we have our way, not for much longer."

"You're going to have to do better than that," Prophet told him. "You know why I haven't finished the job. You know what's going to be uncovered when he dies."

"We know. And we've decided it's worth the risk." Rylan stared at the sky. "If we could control him, we would've."

Which meant that Mal's and King's days of anonymity were about to be over. All the enemies held at bay before would be unleashed. But if the CIA was willing to let it happen to their secrets, then whatever John was planning? Must be really fucking bad. Worse-than-they-thought bad.

"So now the CIA wants us to do their dirty work with no promises that we'll be free once it's done?" King glowered threateningly and threw the knife so it wedged into the wooden front door . . . but not before it whizzed directly past Prophet's head.

"Way to keep it under control," Prophet muttered.

King looked him in the eyes. "I missed."

"What the fuck do you want me to do? We had to do this anyway. Agent Paul wants us to kill John because he's lost control of him. He won't interfere. And if we do our jobs right, we'll have intel on the CIA . . . enough for them to leave us alone for good."

"Right—because they've always been so transparent in the past," Hook drawled.

"So we've got Agent Paul—who, for all intents and purposes is working with John," Cillian started. "And John's got triggers, but was never able to find a specialist to complete the bombs."

"He's found a substitute," Prophet said.

"The new specialist?" Ren asked.

"Not a bomb-maker. The substitute is the substance of the bomb." Prophet paused. "Rylan said there was a break-in at a government facility. He won't say where or how, but what's missing? Sarin."

Fuck me, Mal signed, and it rang out as clearly as if they'd all yelled it.

"So we've got active triggers and a missing specialist who . . ." Cillian trailed off.

"Builds black sites . . . with secret exits only she knows about," Prophet finished.

It was like the air was sucked out of the room. For a long moment, no one spoke. King and Mal both made the sign of the cross, an instinctive reaction for both men, who probably hadn't set foot in a church since boyhood.

"Jesus," Ren muttered finally. "And Agent Paul doesn't seem to give a shit about the bombs. Or the specialist."

"Which is why *we* need to," Prophet emphasized.

"If we split up to look for her, we're stretched too thin," Tom said.

King nodded. "He's right. Besides that, there's too many high-value targets locked up in black sites—some we don't even know about—to choose from. We're going to have to stop the immediate threat, which is the triggers."

"Do we know where they're placed?"

"We will," Prophet assured him.

"There's too many variables," King started. "Too much can go wrong."

Prophet stood. "You can all figure out right now if you're in or out. Either way, there are triggers out there and I know we all agree we can't let thousands of people die because we're pissed at the CIA."

CHAPTER TWENTY

Tom remained among the disgruntled after Prophet walked away, mainly so he could avoid Prophet for a little longer, but also so he could give his partner the general mood of the discussion post-departure.

Dramatic departure at that.

It *had* made them all shut up, for several minutes at least, until finally Ren sighed. "I hate when he does that."

"Which part?" Tom asked.

"All of it," Ren confirmed. "But especially that last bit."

"Because it gets you every time," Hook added.

Mal nodded and leaned back. He seemed the least upset by all the revelations, which made Tom immediately suspicious that he probably knew about most of them anyway.

Which also made Tom angry. Unreasonably so, perhaps, but angry nonetheless. It wasn't a great way to start out his evening with Prophet, but it was close to midnight and they no doubt planned for an early morning. They were all on constant alert, go-bags packed and at the ready for evac.

Prophet was lying on the bed, legs crossed, arms behind his head and staring at the ceiling. He didn't look at Tom when he came in through the door, not even when Tom closed the door and asked, "The specialist disappeared forty-eight hours ago, right?"

"Uh-huh."

"That's around the same time you got that message. The one about Judie."

"Oh. Right." Prophet nodded. "Did I tell you that I got another call? She's back in place. It was just a momentary lapse."

"Really?" Tom's drawl was exaggerated. "Isn't it funny how both your mom and the specialist disappeared on the same exact day?"

"I know. Life is funny sometimes."

"How do you even say that shit with a straight face?"

"How about you keep your dirty voodoo shit to yourself?" Prophet barked. "Okay, fine. Judie—the real Judie—is safe."

"And you knew that when you got Remy's message on the plane. That's why you weren't more worried."

"Trust me, I was worried."

"So the specialist?"

"In the wind."

"Jesus, Prophet."

"Fuck you, Tom. I've had enough people doubting me today."

"I'm not doubting you. I'm trying to help."

"Sadiq, when he was alive—or John—they were calling Judie," Prophet admitted after a pause. "The real one."

"If they have the number . . ."

Prophet shook his head. "Until now, they've been unable to find her. I bounce the signal too well. But the numbers . . ."

"You know how they get them?"

"Someone in the CIA's giving them out."

"And you know who."

"Agent Paul."

"That's why you don't visit her—the real Judie."

"That's not the only reason, but yeah. I mean, there's only one person who knows me well enough to track me."

"John." Tom shook his head. "Proph, you really think?"

"I didn't want to. I tried not to for the longest time. But I don't see any way around it."

"Is that how the specialist was compromised?" Tom asked.

Prophet shook his head. "There are more than two Judie Drews. And the real one isn't under her real name. Listen, the specialist ran. Maybe she caught wind of a threat or maybe she got an offer she couldn't refuse. She wasn't a recluse there. She had access to the dark web, mainly to keep track of chatter and keep herself safe."

"So why now? You have to know that."

"You don't think my team's thinking the same thing, Tom? The difference is, they trust me." Prophet's voice was cold and Tom hated that. "If we all know the same intel, then the intel's compromised. But since you have a burning need to check my work . . . Rylan said that someone tracked down and threatened the specialist's son. That would be enough for her to turn herself over in exchange."

"And she's counting on you to find her and save her—and her son."

"Her son's safe. Rylan's got him secured," Prophet said.

"Did Rylan tell you that John was recruited by the CIA?"

"Not exactly. It's more implied. It's always gray with that agency."

And with you, Tom almost bit out. Instead, he managed, "John never told you either? Didn't even hint that they'd tried to recruit him?"

Prophet shook his head. "He wouldn't have been able to. And by that point, he was angry with me." He winced at whatever memory he'd had and Tom instinctively moved toward him. But when he put a hand on him, Prophet brushed it off.

"Sorry." Tom pulled back and Prophet stared at the ceiling again.

"I'm tired, T. Really fucking tired."

"So let's get some sleep."

Prophet moved over and let Tom lie next to him. Neither man touched the other. "Did you talk to Remy today?"

"Yeah. You?"

"Yeah. He sounds good."

"Time with Della will do that to you," Tom agreed. He tried to stay awake for a while after Prophet fell asleep but the past days proved too much for that. And he dreamed his own dreams, none of them good at all, with faceless men trying to drag Prophet away and Tom running after him, only to realize he'd lost him.

He woke with a jolt, sucking in a deep breath, the awful sense of foreboding pervading every pore. It seemed like Prophet felt it too, was in a restless sleep of his own, tossing and turning, arguing loudly.

Tom heard, *John* and *no* and *not like this*, and edged gingerly away. Because this was different—there was something dark and dangerous in Prophet's tone, an edge that gave Tom a flutter of anxiety.

Even though he was strong, maybe inherently stronger than Prophet and usually angrier, but Prophet was still a savvier fighter. Tonight, Tom had a feeling he'd feel the brunt of that if he didn't slide away from this living, breathing PTSD flashback. But as he started a slow roll, Prophet was on him, faster than Tom could've thought. Prophet had grabbed for him once during a flashback, but it'd been more of a reach-out-and-flail grab.

This had Prophet sitting on his goddamned chest, hands around Tom's throat, pinning him to the bed and choking him out at the same time.

He stared up into Prophet's eyes, dark with anger, and begged, "Prophet, please. It's me."

"I know who the fuck you are," Prophet spat. "Always fucking known, John."

Oh, fuck that. "Prophet—it's Tom, not John. You're dreaming. Wake the fuck up." Tom tried to buck him off but Prophet was too angry, too filled with adrenaline. And Tom figured this might be it, he might fucking die at Prophet's hands because Prophet thought he was John, and that's what pissed Tom off.

Because no way in hell was he anything like John. He'd never betray Prophet or hurt him or leave him.

Motherfucker.

Because fuck that noise.

Tom reared up with all the anger he felt for John behind it and he smacked Prophet on the side of his head. He'd been trying not to hurt Prophet's wrists, because he had enough strikes against him going into their next phase of battle . . . but John.

Prophet's hand closed around Tom's throat again—hard.

But then he got distracted by something else, a something to the right that only he could see, and Tom quickly took his opportunity—and the upper hand. He realized he was fighting with the man he loved, trying to kill his ghosts and Tom wishing nothing more than to let that happen. They rolled off the bed together, a loud bump on the wood floor echoing through the room. Prophet landed under him and finally he was able to pin Prophet down, straddle his hips and hold his wrists against the side of the bed . . . and only then did he see the fear in Prophet's eyes.

Only then did he know for sure what John had done . . . or attempted to in whatever hellish flashback Prophet was reliving.

Immediately Tom pushed away and off him, and Prophet blinked. Tom saw his haze clear as Prophet realized where he was.

It was only then that he saw Mal in the door, watching, a look on his face that let Tom know that this episode had confirmed something horrible, something Mal had no doubt either long suspected or knew about for sure.

You needed to do that, Mal signed.

Tom figured that was Mal's way of letting him know that he probably wouldn't have let Tom die, if for no other reason than fear of the guilt Prophet would bear.

Prophet gasped, like he'd emerged from a deep dive, stared at Tom, horror and agony etched all over his face.

"Fuck." He closed his eyes. Whether they blurred now was anyone's guess, and he lay there, breathing hitched, ashamed and angry, with Tom wanting to go to him, comfort him, but unable to unfreeze himself. He'd made so many wrong moves this trip with Prophet, he refused to make another one.

Mal brushed past him, sat on the floor next to Prophet, put a hand on his shoulder. Prophet seemed to know the touch instinctively, opened his eyes so Mal could talk. And Mal did, fingers moving rapidly. Tom's guilt at watching the intimacy happening here didn't make him turn away though, and he wanted to get on the floor with them but fuck, the secrets kept building the walls higher and higher and Tom had lost his footing way back at Dean's house.

But with Mal, the walls just fell—and fast—because Mal was helping Prophet up, holding him as he half collapsed in Mal's arms. And sobbed.

The two men, brothers-in-arms, were in their own world, a place where Tom couldn't go. His shoulders sagged with the weight of that truth and he walked away. He went into Mal's room and lay his head on Mal's C-4 pillow, understanding for the first time why Mal would find it comforting.

Prophet was never more grateful to climb out of a flashback than he'd been that night, even with Tom on top of him, holding him down. And just like that night back then, Mal stepped in to help. Mal, who'd seen the aftermath that night the events had really happened . . . only to then quickly lose Prophet to the desert for months.

He'd heard Tom leaving the room, and as much as he wanted to call to him, tell him to stay, or even go to him, he couldn't. Instead, he held on to Mal as though they could go back in time, fix it, change it. Make it so it never happened.

But as he finally stopped shaking, he knew that going back had never been an option, not for any of them.

"Fuck, Mal," he managed finally.

I know, Mal mouthed. Prophet touched Mal's scar and Mal gave him a lopsided smile.

"Yeah, you do." Prophet sighed. "Fuck. Fuck."

He hurt you. Bad, Mal signed. *Should've killed him that night.*

Prophet couldn't argue, but hell, they'd have been in the same trouble if John had already been recruited by the agency. Fucked by the CIA either way. An unstoppable destiny.

Want me to get Tom?

Prophet shook his head. Mal sat back against the headboard and pulled Prophet's head into his lap. Prophet curled and let Mal comfort him, the wedge growing wider between him and Tom, with no way to stop it.

Fate.

Destiny.

John had hurt him beyond belief, more than anyone who loved another person should ever. And Prophet had figured he'd never open his heart again to anyone, especially not the way he had to Tom.

The ghosts of the past were impossible to ignore. "It's too fucking hard."

I know, Mal tapped against Prophet's shoulder, a shorthand they often took on for times like this. *Tom's a good man.*

Prophet murmured, "Maybe too good for me."

He could say that to Mal and not be accused of being too dramatic because Mal understood—good things were for good people. For them? They didn't get the families. They watched out for them instead.

Then again, Tom understood the hell out of it too. "I'm losing him."

Mal shook his head. *Not yet.*

"We haven't been connecting."

TMI.

"Since when is anything TMI for you?"

True. So fuck him till he screams. I'll bet that helps. Helps me.

"Now who's TMI?"

Mal rubbed the tips of his fingers together, the way he always did when he was pondering something. Usually, it was when he was thinking about John and all the fucked-up ways he wanted to kill him. Finally, he signed, *I wish I'd stopped it. Him. If that mission hadn't happened . . .*

"But it did. And you couldn't have," Prophet assured him, the way he had every time this topic came up. Mal made the shape of a gun with his hand. "And then you'd have been in jail."

Mal shrugged. *Would've escaped. Wouldn't be all that much different than it is now.*

Prophet snorted at the truth in that, and then they remained like that, in silence, until the sun rose.

CHAPTER TWENTY-ONE

Prophet went into the main room and the conversation stopped. Whether it was because of what they knew happened last night with Tom, or because of Rylan, he didn't know or care. He needed to get—and keep—his head in the game, and these motherfuckers were going to start playing along.

"What's the good word?" he asked, and Mal handed him a mug of coffee. He took a sip and surveyed the faces around him, only glancing at Tom for a quick moment because hell.

"You know we're in," King grumbled.

"But the CIA's coming for you soon, right?" Ren asked.

Prophet nodded. "We don't have a lot of time to get Tom and Cillian to the next safe house."

"We're ready," King confirmed.

"Hold up here," Ren reasoned. "Let's say John's intel can embarrass the CIA. They'll just bury it, the way they do everyone and everything. It's got to be something else he knows—besides what he's got on our team."

"Well, we don't know what that is, so we've got no choice," Prophet countered. "You have to let Agent Paul get me to John so you can disable the bombs."

"Suppose he sets them off when he gets you, Proph?" King asked.

"He won't," Prophet said quietly. "He'll want me to watch. To know what he's done. If he thinks you're all neutralized . . . he'll play with his prey for a while."

There was a heavy silence for a long moment. Finally, King spoke. "So your job is to stay alive until we dismantle the triggers. Then you do what you need to. And then we all go after the specialist."

What you need to do . . . King's unspoken *and kill John* hung in the air.

"So we keep this mission about the triggers," Prophet said firmly. "Let John think I'm vulnerable."

"You are," King reminded him, without rancor, reaching out to touch his cheek.

It was the first show of softness Prophet had seen King render this trip, and it made him ache . . . for all of them.

But they had a damned job to do, and sentimentality had no place in it. "Remember that time we were in Yemen?" Prophet started, and everyone, save for Tom and Cillian, groaned.

"Do we get to know about this?" Cillian asked and Mal signed, *Never.*

"Great. What now?" Tom crossed his arms.

"We move out tomorrow. At first light." Prophet looked calmer than he had earlier.

"I have one more question," Cillian said quietly. "You told me that the man you knew would never have turned."

Prophet gave a wan smile. "That's true. But John stopped being the man I knew a long time ago, Cillian. Once he left Mal for dead, I knew it was too late. It's why I tried to save him right away. Because I fucking knew what would happen if this was all part of a mission. But you've got to give me a little credit for feeding you what you wanted to hear. You're not the only one good at planting seeds, you know."

"Asshole," Cillian muttered.

"And on that note, let's go get some food," Ren suggested, with a not-so-subtle nod in Prophet's and then Tom's direction. King nodded, and he and Mal followed out the door. Cillian sighed and muttered something about "drama" but he, too, went the way of the others.

"Where are they going?" Tom's voice was a rasp in the suddenly too-quiet room.

"We have the house next door too. Seemed safer that way," Prophet explained.

"Does Rylan know?"

"About the houses? Yes."

"I meant . . ." Tom looked around to make sure they were alone. "About us."

"You think I fuck for intel?"

"I know you do."

"Fuck you, T. Just . . ." Prophet moved to brush past him but Tom stopped him with a flat palm against his chest.

"That's not an answer."

"If you have to ask me that—"

"I do."

Prophet yanked Tom's wrist to move the outstretched palm over his heart. "No, Tom. I haven't been with anyone else, on or off the job, since you."

"But if you needed to . . ."

"To save Mal's life? Or King's, Ren's, Hook's? Remy's or Doc's? Yours? You'd better bet your life I would. I'd do anything to protect all of you. I hope you would too."

Tom narrowed his eyes, his tone dripping sarcasm. "So Rylan giving you intel wasn't about helping to save our lives?"

Prophet shook his head. "If you don't trust me on this, T . . . I don't know what we've got."

"Yeah, me neither."

"You're going to take this Hal/Ollie shit out on me forever, right? Unforgivable?"

"That's not—"

"Of course it is. Doesn't take a genius." He avoided the *I'm not blind* analogy because he'd have to say *I'm not (that) blind yet* and he didn't think Tom was in the mood to appreciate the varying degrees of thought and subtlety that went into the statement.

"Good thing, because you're definitely not."

"You're looking for a way out. Told me you could handle this and—"

"I can handle—"

"Nothing!" Prophet yelled. "Classified secrets aren't spilled just because we're fucking." Tom's fists clenched. "Getting pissed at me again? Just like the old days, right?"

"Fuck you."

Prophet grunted as Tom's fist slammed him hard in the solar plexus and knocked him to the floor. "Makes you feel better, T?"

Prophet fought to his feet and slammed his body into Tom's, since he couldn't do other important things, like breathe, for several moments. The momentum was enough to send them both sprawling to the ground, hard.

Tom spat blood and went for Prophet's throat, his palm closing hard around it. "How's *this* feel, Proph?"

Prophet elbowed him in the jaw, forcing Tom to release him. Tom made another grab for him, trying for a headlock that Prophet squirmed and evaded by throwing himself against Tom again, causing them to crash and roll into a wall. Tom's forehead slammed against it and Prophet laughed. "How're you doing, special agent?"

"Swear to fuck," Tom muttered, reaching out to grab for him.

In a few swift moves, Prophet ended the fight, leaving Tom flat on his back, Prophet's knees pressing the insides of his elbows, and his palm on Tom's throat—not hard, but enough to keep him in place and force Tom to look at him. "Tell me how an FBI agent deals with classified missions, Tom? Got anything you'd like to share with the class?" Prophet goaded. Tom's jaw remained stubbornly clenched. "So it's okay for you to keep classified job secrets, but not me. Got it. Makes perfect sense." Prophet felt himself winding up, which meant he was probably (read: most definitely) going to fuck this all up. Probably part purposeful sabotage and part temper getting the best of him, mainly mixed with guilt and anger at himself for even feeling guilt and anger over a situation he couldn't have controlled or anticipated.

"You're telling me you don't already know what I did for the FBI?" Tom asked slowly, his voice half-strangled.

"I'm not one to play games with people. I love you, you dumb-fuck. So no, I don't have your file. Never did."

Tom looked completely surprised and started hesitantly with, "You know Ollie taught me."

"Interrogation tricks, yes."

"My temper was unpredictable, to say the least. Especially back then." Tom rolled his eyes. "So you'd figure . . ."

"You were the muscle. The hitter. Yes, you'd be useful in that capacity. But having you only do that would be a complete waste of your talents," Prophet started and Tom's cheeks reddened slightly. "Your gut instincts were great. Tracking too. Also, your ability to get a confession without beating the fuck out of someone was probably impressive as hell to your sups. But did the FBI utilize you in that way? Or were you too busy worrying about your curse to be effective?"

"Fuck you, Prophet." Tom's voice was hoarse, eyes bright with anger.

"Truth hurts."

Tom glared at him. "Guess you'd know all about that. I caught a lot of cases—good cases. I made a goddamned difference. If they'd let me work alone, I'd be fine. I'd be a better agent."

Prophet's eyes narrowed. "You're using present tense," he noted.

Things were fucked already, so Prophet figured, might as well keep going.

Tom's heart hammered, and his mind told him to stop, to not say what his temper pushed him to say . . . but that latter urge was too strong and definitely in charge at the moment. "Yes. Present tense. Present company included."

Prophet's face blanched slightly, but then he nodded. "If you were alone—or stayed with Cope—you'd do a lot of good for Phil. I'm guessing that's why you stayed. Being with me . . . well, fuck, nothing but trouble, right?"

Tom's hand shot out and caught Prophet by the throat, holding him in the same way that Prophet held him.

Prophet didn't struggle, but rather, waited calmly.

Tom wanted to break him. "You've known from the first time I mentioned Ollie that you were supposed to kill me."

A clearing of the throat behind them made them pause.

"Yes, Ren?" Prophet asked.

"I'm sure this is a sweet moment you'll all remember forever, but we need more of a plan than just killing Tom."

"Thanks, Ren," Tom said sarcastically.

"Welcome," Ren said, then added, almost as an afterthought, "Because Mal's trying to drive off alone and King's body on the windshield won't be a deterrent for much longer."

"Dammit, Ren—why do you always save the important part for last?"

"Because it's the only way I can truly annoy all of you," Ren deadpanned as Prophet ran past him, and Tom heard King's cursing as he reached the front door.

Mal was driving in circles, trying to buck King off. Lots of shouting ensued.

"Way to stay covert," Prophet muttered.

"It's a wonder we haven't gotten killed before this, right?" Hook asked, arms crossed as he leaned a hip on the porch. "How much longer before King tires himself out?"

"Too long," Prophet said.

"Shoot the tires?" Hook suggested.

"Then I'd have to change them." Prophet walked to the truck instead, got into the circle, and tried to punch Mal and take the wheel and hold on at the same time.

"Dumbest thing I've ever seen." Tom stood next to Hook.

"Stir-crazy," Hook said. "'S'why I used to pray for missions. Sitting around for too long is never a good thing for any of them."

"They'll tire out eventually," Ren assured them.

"Or I could just start shooting rubber rounds." Hook already appeared to be locked and loaded. He raised the rifle and fired, hitting a glancing blow off King's ass. "Don't want to piss him off completely."

"Nice shot, but Mal's the problem here," Tom reminded him.

"Prophet's blocking him," Hook said, as if that logic explained everything.

"Then shoot *him* in the ass," Ren suggested.

Tom sighed with frustration. Then he stopped the entire thing with one word. "Remy!"

The truck screeched to a halt. King almost fell off. Mal opened the door and Prophet went flying, and Mal stormed up the steps, throwing Tom a dirty look.

"Prophet would've stopped you eventually," Hook told him. "King too."

"Until you shot me in the ass," King growled, coming up behind Mal, with Prophet following him.

"Rubber rounds," Hook shot back.

"Still hurt like a bitch," King grumbled.

Ren nodded at his other half sympathetically. "Want me to rub it for you?"

"Not now, babe," was all King said, and Tom couldn't decide if King was utterly serious, sarcastically deadpan, or both.

Prophet slapped a hand on his shoulder. "Don't think about it too hard. It'll hurt your brain. Seriously." Prophet rubbed the side of his head and truth be told, Tom's head had started to ache that familiar, goddamned ache.

"Who's psychic now?" Tom muttered.

"C'mon." Prophet led him away. Tom heard the others arguing, yelling at Mal in the background, but to his surprise, Mal was in this room, running an IV. He motioned for Tom's arm.

"Are you going to kill me and think I'll just assist you without a fight?"

Mal rolled his eyes, motioned again for Tom's arm and Tom decided his head hurt too much to care.

The bag said *saline*, and the others seemed to be some sort of vitamin concoction, and for all Tom knew there was formaldehyde and he'd be embalmed to death. Slowly.

Mal rolled his eyes again, like he knew what Tom was thinking. Signed, *I'd snap your neck—that's way easier.*

"Good to know," Tom muttered.

"There's also propofol here," Prophet told him. "It'll break the migraine fast."

Why tell him that shit?

"Why try to leave?" Prophet shot back.

"We going somewhere soon?" Tom managed drowsily, not missing the look that passed between Prophet and Mal before he dozed off . . . and seemed to wake minutes later, with the migraine gone.

He tried to sit up but Mal was there, shaking his head, holding his shoulder. *Give it a minute. Might be dizzy.*

Tom nodded. "Got it." He took the water Mal offered and drank some cautiously. When he didn't get sick, he gulped it like it was the best thing on earth. "Everyone okay?"

Except for King's ass, yes, Mal signed. *But you and Prophet? Not so much.*

Tom didn't even attempt to counter that. All that kept running through his mind was that Prophet knew Ollie . . . and Prophet killed Ollie because he had to. And Tom tried to reconcile Ollie as the dangerous man Prophet knew. Tom knew in his heart that Prophet was doing a necessary job. But the Ollie he'd known, the man who'd shaped his life as an FBI agent, taught him strategies he'd use until the day he died.

Prophet had once told him, *"My job is to take out specialists, and the people who knew them and were trained by them. Most of the time their family members are exceptions but not always."*

"You could've been my son," Ollie used to tell him.

If Prophet had known about him—and Prophet never did any kind of half-assed research—he'd have known just how close Ollie had been to him. A mentor, and so much more.

Prophet had drawn a line in the sand. Broken rules. Made judgment calls . . . or Tom wouldn't be standing next to him today. It was something that Tom both understood . . . and something that infuriated the fuck out of him.

CHAPTER TWENTY-TWO

Prophet was so wound up and had already tried to kill him. Tom didn't know how much worse things could get . . . but he knew they could.

We just need more space between us . . . just until this is done. But Prophet obviously didn't agree, because suddenly he was in the room with Tom.

"Proph, let's not do this now."

"Oh, we're doing this now. We didn't get to finish," Prophet said stubbornly.

"You tried to finish me last night."

"Good one, Tom. Maximum impact." Prophet spoke casually, but Tom knew he'd wounded him.

It was the only way to bring the damned wall down, and if Prophet came back to play, Tom wasn't going to drop the damned ball. "What did he do to you, dammit?"

"What didn't he do?" Prophet shot back.

"Again with the secrets." Tom immediately regretted his words at the look on Prophet's face.

Because he knew exactly what had happened, and while he believed it, he couldn't believe the levels John had sunk to. "After . . . after he did that, you still looked for him?"

"Fuck you for judging me."

"I'm not."

Prophet gazed at him warily. "I can't afford to hate him, T. Too close to love. I'm indifferent to him—but I can't be indifferent to the deaths of innocent people. I swore I wouldn't let that happen. And I'm probably the only one who knows him well enough to take him down. Otherwise the CIA would've gotten rid of him a long time ago. They'd all but admitted that."

Tom suddenly felt weary, all over. The migraine was gone but the aftermath hit him hard and defeat coursed through his body the way the IV had. "I'm in the way."

"You are the way," Prophet told him. "The only way."

"Don't humor me." Tom was shoving clothes into his bag. "I'm going home to Remy."

"Yes, you are. But not today."

Tom shouldered his bag, ignoring him, walking away.

"You're doing what you said you never would," Prophet said.

"I'm doing the best for you, for the team. For Remy. I don't belong in this."

"For a while, I thought that too. I wanted to protect you—from John, my past, the ghosts." Prophet shook his head. "I've done things for survival, for the job, but I've stopped short of doing things I don't believe in. I have no regrets. None. But if you leave—if I let you leave . . . I'll regret it for the rest of my life."

"I'm bringing you down, Prophet," Tom yelled. "I'm making things worse. The dreams are getting worse."

"Maybe. But I don't care. I wouldn't have it any other way," Prophet yelled back before striking.

Tom didn't see it coming. One minute, Prophet was standing still and the next? Tom got hit by what felt like the wall he'd been so desperate to climb, tackled to the ground. He went flying through the air and slammed down on his back, momentarily knocking the wind out of him. Prophet kept him there with a knee pressing his chest.

"You going to sit on me like this all day?"

"Can't get out of it with all the training? Guess you weren't paying close enough attention," Prophet goaded him, then yanked Tom's pants open, leaving him exposed, and, of course, hard . . . the way he always was with Prophet when the goddamned man touched him.

Prophet's hand curled down his cock. "Can't help yourself, can you?"

Tom averted his eyes to stare at the ceiling. "I'm not doing this."

"I'm the one doing things. I'm not asking you to do anything . . . but come," Prophet said reasonably, and Tom was pretty sure he hated him in that moment.

"We don't have time for this."

"For this? I'm making time."

"Let me out of this if you want a fair fight."

"I don't want a fair fight—I want you."

"Afraid I'd kick your ass?"

"You'd try. But I fight dirty."

"Even in your sleep?" Tom bit out. Prophet stared at him, an expression even Tom's voodoo shit wouldn't let him read. It was a low blow, deserved, maybe or maybe not but . . . "Get the fuck out of here."

Prophet just shook his head and smiled like a predator. Tom shifted because he recognized this look, and tried not to get harder.

Prophet stared at him like he knew.

Fucker.

And then Prophet wasn't letting him recover, was fucking mauling him, sucking hard on his nipples, biting them while grinding pelvis to pelvis. Tom closed his eyes and tried to get his breath but his cock had other ideas. Prophet's mouth was warm and wet as he alternately bit and sucked his way along Tom's chest, leaving dark-red marks as he went.

"You're still pissed," Prophet informed him.

"Damned straight." He bucked up and caught Prophet by surprise, and now it was his turn to slam Prophet to the floor. He straddled Prophet, then leaned in and bit Prophet's shoulder—hard enough to leave marks.

"Fuck, Tom—you're the one who likes pain, remember?"

"Right. You're the one who likes to inflict it." Tom straddled Prophet, a reversal of the way he'd been awakened that morning, and stared down at him.

"You look like you don't know who the fuck I am," Prophet snapped.

"Because I don't."

"Fuck you and your melodrama," Prophet told him evenly.

"Right. Forgot you're all about the job."

"I thought you were fucking me. Because your talking isn't going to make me come."

Tom raised his brows. "Really? Is that a challenge?"

Prophet groaned as Tom put a palm over his throat to hold him in position as he yanked Prophet's pants down. He grabbed for the lube Prophet had prepared to use on him and spread Prophet's legs, fingering his ass, spreading him.

"You keep treating me like I'm going to break," Prophet protested. "I wasn't . . . I didn't—"

"Yeah, you did." Prophet's voice was hoarse with lust—and some anger—and he stroked a hand along the side of Tom's cheek. "I know you've thought about leaving."

"Not . . . not like before," Tom promised.

Prophet looked unsure. "Seemed like it."

"I'm bad for you, Proph. I'm bringing your dreams back."

"It's not you. It's John. Dammit—if you're always going to let him come between us—"

"I'm not."

Prophet hissed a breath between his teeth, then demanded, "Do it, Tommy."

Tom's pants were already open, his cock still hard, and he responded to Prophet's order by bearing his teeth and hitching Prophet's legs higher on his hips. Breaching him roughly, causing Prophet to meet Tom's thrust. In one roll of Tom's hips, he was fully seated inside of Prophet, and for a long moment, the two of them just stared at each other.

Tom pulled back and entered him again, harder this time. Prophet's back arched, letting Tom know that the bite of pain to pleasure roared through him. And Tom continued rocking against him, thrusting his hips, holding Prophet's, calling Prophet's name as Prophet called his, seeing stars, even as fireworks lit off in his body.

"Don't leave, Tommy. Please . . ."

"I'm here, Proph. Here," Tom murmured, dropping Prophet's legs and leaning forward, letting Prophet grab hold of him as they fucked each other into the ground.

Tom held on to Prophet tightly in the aftermath. He heard Prophet's breaths return to normal, and then Prophet snarked against his ear, "Told you I wouldn't break."

"Asshole." Tom refused to roll off him, and besides, he was still half-hard and still half-inside of him. And thinking about fucking him again, at least until Prophet was too tired to talk. "You knew, Proph. As soon as you figured out the Ollie thing, you knew you'd have to kill me."

"We're back to that?"

"We never left it."

At his words, Prophet dipped his chin in acknowledgment, but he looked like he'd taken a punch to the gut at Tom's words. "I wanted you to know . . ."

"But you didn't think I'd put it together," Tom finished for him. "And you think partnering us was a simple coincidence."

Prophet shrugged.

"So the person who put me in Phil's path is possibly the dead man's switch," Tom paused. "Phil found me because of that vet—the crazy one from the bayou, back when I was still sheriff. That wasn't planned."

"Fate?" Prophet offered.

"Does John know? Am I part of the dead man's switch? Is there intel that's been planted somewhere that I don't know about that can ruin your life?"

Prophet stared into Tom's eyes. "I don't know for sure. Doesn't even matter, because this kill switch that points to me and Mal and the guys—"

"Also points at me." Tom stared. "I hate him."

"You should."

"You don't."

Prophet sighed. "It's an old wound. Too much wrapped up in it to worry about feelings. But I'm going to take care of him, make no mistake about it."

"And then?"

"I don't think you're a danger to this country. Same way I know I'm not, Mal's not . . ." He trailed off. "I mean, not really."

"I'm still pissed at you."

"I know. Hopefully we'll have years more time in which you can take it out on my ass," Prophet reassured him quietly.

"Plan on it."

"I do."

CHAPTER TWENTY-THREE

Prophet showered and was rubbing his hair with a towel when Tom joined him in the bathroom. Both men bore the bruises from the earlier fight, and although they'd fucked the anger out of each other—and the mistrust too—it was still an odd time for them. The walls had tumbled but there was more than enough left that it was a hike to get over it just to get to each other.

Tom ran a hand over Prophet's chest. "Hey."

"You okay?"

"Better now. You?"

Tom nodded. "Everyone's back."

"Figured that. Come on." Prophet motioned for Tom to follow him. He found everyone gathered again in the main room, sprawled on couches and in chairs, go-bags packed and ready. The tension in the air came from what lay ahead of them, not between them. No, they were all ready, willing, and able.

"What's the good word, Proph?" Ren asked.

"Because I feel like we're being herded," King said.

"Yeah, by me," Prophet told him.

"You sure?" Ren asked.

"For now, yes. John thinks I'm somewhere else."

"You know that—for sure?" King demanded.

"I have a theory." Prophet crossed his arms.

"He has a theory," King repeated slowly, brogue heavy, which never boded well.

How do we know they're not sending a clean-up crew to get us this time? Mal signed.

"They tried that before twice," Ren reminded them. "They lose too many men on us and decide it's easier to leave us alone."

Prophet sat on the back of the couch Mal was reclined on. "It's not a clean-up crew—but they are coming—for all of us. Except for Cillian and Tom, not yet."

"Then Cillian and Tom need to get the hell out of here," Hook confirmed. "And I'm not letting myself get taken."

They all nodded. Hook was better off free.

"If some of us aren't out within forty-eight hours . . ." Prophet began and Hook waved a hand.

"Point taken." Still, Hook looked serious and a serious Hook was never what any of them wanted to see. "And then what? Once we're all free?"

"Yemen," Ren reminded them and everyone groaned again.

"At least we know what we're in for," Hook said then turned to Tom and Cillian. "Well, you guys don't but trust me . . . you're better off."

"I still want to know exactly what happened in Yemen that makes it so bad," Tom said.

It's because we weren't actually in Yemen, Mal signed.

"I give up." Tom turned to Prophet. "Is this all Agent Paul's doing?"

Prophet nodded. "Agent Paul's taking his orders from John—or vice versa."

"So you're going to surrender yourself—and us—and wait till Paul releases you to go kill John?" King asked, and Prophet nodded.

"And then I buy time until you escape and take out the triggers. I guarantee John's got a system in place—if I kill him too soon, the bombs will trigger," Prophet said heavily.

"How do we know that that's not exactly what Agent Paul wants?" Ren asked. "He needs someone to take the fall. You fit the bill. Let's say they offer you money and you refuse. Then there's no trail. And if you take money, there's a trail *to* you. He's good."

"We're better," Prophet insisted. "We'll do this and then deal with the new fallout."

"I'd feel better if we could figure out a way to lay blame at Agent Paul's feet, where it belongs," Ren said.

"Two birds, one stone," Hook murmured.

"If only we got him on tape," Cillian mused.

I'd rather kill him, Mal signed.

"Cillian or Agent Paul?" Prophet attempted to clarify, because he'd lost track.

"I'm sitting right here," Cillian reminded him.

So does that mean you don't want the answer? Mal signed. Cillian rolled his eyes, and Prophet made a mental note to get to the bottom of that mess once the current one had been sufficiently mopped up.

Plans were made fast after Tom walked out of the bedroom with Prophet. Trucks were arranged and the men set out two by two, in staggered intervals, to the new safe house several cities away. Which could take hours on the short side.

Tom and Cillian were the last ones to leave. Cillian had been tense during the wait, and Tom had been too, but for other reasons. Mainly because there was something else happening during this transfer of houses, something he couldn't put his finger on.

Something Prophet wouldn't tell him.

"Feels like you're saying goodbye," Tom told him.

Prophet leaned in and nipped his shoulder. *"Feels fucking good to me."*

Tom had let it go but couldn't help feeling Prophet was slipping away. Then he told himself to shake it off, stop being dramatic. They'd made up. Held each other.

Three hours and plenty of silent brooding later, Tom pulled into the driveway of the safe house and Cillian got out to open the gates. He walked through, weapon drawn, and Tom drove slowly behind him. The other cars were parked there, a good sign . . . but the three men who hung out by the front steps were not.

None of them appeared to be armed or threatening, not at first sight. They were all in their late fifties to early sixties, and deceptively harmless looking . . . definitely so now that Tom was closer.

Cillian had drawn his weapon on them and they eyed him calmly, for the moment. "Identify yourselves."

"He must be Cillian." One of the men stepped forward and turned his attention to Tom. "Tom?" The black man was the shortest of the three, with a shaved head and a wry smile, and his drawl had a cadence Tom recognized. Another bayou boy, right in the middle of the dark continent.

"Who wants to know?" Tom walked toward them, hoping to see Prophet pop out of the house but knowing he wasn't going to. Dammit. "Where are the men who belong to these cars?"

"Saw them take your boys." Another man with bright-blue eyes and blond hair mixed with white confirmed, and Tom's gut tightened, because knowing something was going to happen and having it happen were two different things entirely. He'd been hoping for a Hail Mary.

"Who are you?" Cillian asked, gun still drawn.

"Could be your goddamned father," the first man shot back. "And I sure as shit have more experience than you, so secure your damned weapon, son."

"'Son'?" Cillian repeated in his heavy brogue as Tom put pressure on his arm to lower it.

"Who's 'them'? Do you know our boys?" Tom asked, because this shit had Prophet—or Mal—all over it.

"One of them," the first man confirmed.

Tom practically groaned as Cillian said, "Let me guess which one. Prophet?"

The men shrugged, neither confirming nor denying, but the smallest one had a smirk on his face worthy of a Special Forces operator.

"This is either very good," Tom started.

"Stop tempting fate." The dark-skinned man pointed a finger at him, his voice reminiscent of a drill sergeant's. "I thought you had more sense, being the superstitious one."

Had Prophet been talking about Tom to these men? *Great.*

"Need anything?" The third man's voice was a rasp. He was the quietest. Maybe, if what Tom had come to learn, the most dangerous.

"I need Prophet back. All of them, but Prophet especially," Tom told them. "And I need him to stop acting like a one-man wrecking ball, but nothing I say to him about that gets through."

Cillian stage-whispered, "I feel like they were just offering you a refreshment, not counseling."

Tom shot him the finger and realized he'd never felt closer to Mal.

"I'm Xavier. And Prophet's working on that one-man-wrecking-ball thing," the bayou-drawling man told him.

"They'll all get out. Right now, they're where they need to be," the blond man said vaguely.

"And you are?" Cillian asked.

"Elvis." He pointed to the gravel-voiced man. "He's Cahill."

"Where are they?" Tom demanded. "You have to tell me."

The men glanced at each other. "We're not supposed to," Elvis admitted. "Normally, we wouldn't but this time, we're overriding Prophet. For his own good."

"He's gonna hate that," Xavier muttered. "But Elvis is right. Come on." He started walking into the house, motioning for Tom and Cillian to follow. Elvis and Cahill strolled behind them.

"Make yourself comfortable," Xavier told them.

"So, just to clarify—they were all taken?" Tom asked, once inside.

"They were each taken after they'd parked," Elvis supplied. "First in were King and Ren. Hook never came this way—he's a smart one."

Xavier nodded. "He'll be in touch when the time is right."

"Wait, you were here when they were taken?" Cillian asked, and Xavier nodded. "So why didn't they take you?"

"It's not like we announced our presence," Elvis said indignantly. "We're old, not stupid."

Tom sank into one of the closest chairs. "Who took King and Ren?"

Xavier shrugged. "Maybe SAS. Two different cars took off in two different directions, so they're separated."

"Mal and Prophet?"

"Looked like CIA. Same MO as the SAS."

These guys knew more than they were saying. Tom had no doubt about that, or the fact that he couldn't push them without running up against a giant brick wall. *Fucking Yemen.* "Are we safe here until we figure out next steps?"

"Yes," Elvis assured them.

"Elvis, what did you do before you retired?" Tom asked.

"Navy."

"Just Navy?"

"Various jobs within that scope," he said vaguely.

"And Xavier?"

Xavier murmured, "SAS."

"And last but not least." Tom cut his gaze to Cahill.

"I built things. Secure things," he said. "Some of them float."

"Things like black sites?" Cillian asked.

Which meant Cahill could have resources with everyone from the US Marshals to the CIA, not to mention foreign governments. Tom sighed. At least the rest of the team would have backup, which left Tom and Cillian—and these men—free to help Prophet.

Elvis pressed a light finger to the side of Tom's head as if he knew what Tom was thinking. "Use this less." Another finger pressed his gut. "This more. You've let go of a lot of your confidence this time around, son. Get it back—and fast."

CHAPTER TWENTY-FOUR

When the hood came off, Prophet tensed for a fight. He didn't think John would be on the other end of it, but hell, these days he could never be sure.

But it was Agent Paul—the real one—in his three-piece, looking pissed off, as usual. "Nice of you to join us, Prophet."

"Always appreciate the invite. The transportation methods have a few kinks, though." Prophet rubbed the back of his neck. "The manhandling's a little much."

"Funny, I heard that's how you like it."

Prophet let a smile edge across his face. "You've got time? I'll show you exactly how I like it."

Paul frowned a little. "You're not in control here."

"Then why don't you tell me exactly why I'm here?"

"You know why."

"John."

"He needs to be put down," Paul said bluntly. "You know what he did to Lansing."

"You know for sure that was him?"

"Best guess," Paul said vaguely. "Lansing was too busy looking out for you to see it coming."

"So Lansing didn't know shit."

Paul shrugged. "Part of the plan. But John losing control?"

"So your protégé is out of control. You take him down."

"The master can't control his creation." Agent Paul looked loath to admit that.

"But you think I can?"

"Yes. That's why I had to separate you two," Agent Paul said thoughtfully. "LT thought you were the best. You were, but not for my purposes. We were looking for a different type of black ops soldier. John fit the prototype."

"Angry?"

"Yes," Agent Paul agreed.

"How's the recruitment going these days?" Prophet asked.

"Varies."

"So the project is still in existence?"

Agent Paul smiled. "I suspect if you'd stayed, you'd be told to find a recruit."

Prophet closed his eyes and tried to imagine himself a handler to someone like John. "He's killing more than just Americans. How've you been able to explain that away?"

"John needed to do a few acts of terror in order to prove himself. Some of his attempts were more toothless than others."

"And you think he's a double agent?"

"I wouldn't expect anything less, although I think he's more a general spy for hire at this point. He's good but he's also left too much damage in his wake . . ."

"For over ten years, dammit."

"In the beginning? No."

"He framed me."

"Some collateral damage is necessary for the greater good. Always. You know that, Prophet, but your inability to like it is what held you back."

Prophet snorted. "I'm fucking fine with that."

"Right. Because there was never any collateral damage on your end, right?"

"Fuck off now. This isn't Prophet's life story. You want me to be your clean-up crew. And his." Prophet took a page from Mal's book and growled wordlessly.

It worked, because Agent Paul looked like he wanted to back up a few steps but, to his credit, he didn't. "That's exactly what we need. You know as well as I do that military intelligence is all about risk and reward."

"I think you all need to stop using the word 'intelligence,'" Prophet muttered. "Is this a one-off? Because I suspect saying no to this job means a sudden death."

Agent Paul's smile didn't reach his eyes this time, and Prophet wondered how many men had been sent to their deaths, promised backup and never seeing any. "This job is what I need done. Let's not bullshit each other—you were going to kill him anyway."

"So now I'll get paid to do it?"

"When I see a body."

Prophet closed his eyes. He'd never take the money, but he'd do the job. Whether the CIA ever saw a body was questionable, because he'd make sure nothing would be traced back to him. "What about my team? The consequences?"

"I'll do the best I can," Agent Paul said. "No promises."

"You sent me and John into the desert to get captured. It was a test, for John more so than for me. You didn't count on how much John could exploit you. Underestimating John proved to be your biggest mistake." Prophet wondered how much longer it would be before John killed Agent Paul . . . and if that was why he was being pulled in now. "I hope your family is protected."

"You don't need to concern yourself with me."

"Right. But see, since you had John's brother killed in order to try to get his head back in the game"—Prophet knew he was right on the money by the look on Paul's face—"John's not going to be in a forgiving mood."

"He'll never forgive *you*."

"I know. I'm content to live with that."

"I don't understand you, Prophet."

"Something to be grateful for."

Agent Paul snorted. "Someone will be in to let you go. You'll be on your way to find your mark immediately."

"Alone."

"You'll have an escort."

"Figures," Prophet muttered.

Still, he wished the black site luck on his way out. If they wanted Mal to escape on his own, he wasn't sure the place would remain afloat for much longer.

"Remember that time we were in Yemen?"

Prophet's words rang in his ears as King was separated from Ren, hooded, tied and tossed unceremoniously into the trunk of a car. It slammed shut and the car moved at a sickening pace—King judged it was going at least 100 MPH for about half an hour. Over these roads, that was a miracle, which meant they were in the more populated parts of the closest cities.

Which still meant *middle of nowhere.*

At one point, there was a bone-breaking slam—not an accident, he realized when his body had stopped fucking bouncing, but a giant pothole of some kind. He heard cursing and then the truck was being raised and he realized they were changing a tire. In the background, he also heard music—rhythmic, native to the region for sure.

They'd gotten back on the road quickly. After driving at least ten more miles, if his assessment was correct, the car finally stopped. He'd been taken from the trunk, finally, and walked blindly into a tent with a cot, as he'd learned when his hood was taken off. His wrists and legs remained bound and he'd been told to "Lie there and keep your mouth shut."

The men around him were so silent that if King hadn't seen them move with his own eyes, he'd think he was alone in the room. Most of them were born into circumstances that necessitated them disappearing into the woodwork—to avoid abuse, the police, and anything or anyone that could harm them. Now, that silence helped them gain the upper hand, and King didn't intend to let them keep it.

Still, he lay back against the cot, his hands cuffed to the metal pole embedded in the dirt with cement, and surveyed them carefully. There were five, which meant there could easily be ten more in the wings. Then again, SAS traveled in small groups because they didn't need the manpower. One man could equal ten with their kind of training, especially in this type of situation.

"So." One of the men pulled a chair next to the cot and sat. "Want to tell me about it?"

King watched him as dispassionately as he could, and in his best American accent said, "I don't even know why I'm here."

"Because you're a threat to national security." The man's brogue wasn't as thick as King's—when King let it out. "Why're you playing an average American former military man?"

"I'm not playing."

The man laughed. "Ah, don't be like that, lad."

"Not your lad." King could be out of the chains in seconds and he'd already cursed Prophet left, right, and center for forcing him to lie here and pretend to be helpless. "Do you have any intel for me?"

"Maybe. Hungry?" He reached up and undid the chains. "Figure I'll save you the trouble, but thanks for officially playing along."

"There's something important I need to do from here," King said, finally letting his brogue out. "I need confirmation."

The man stuck his hand out. "I'm Brock. I'll be glad to help you out. But first things first." And then he pulled a knife from his pocket and moved in toward King.

CHAPTER TWENTY-FIVE

Cillian made a few inquiries while Tom sat, watching their three hosts chat quietly among themselves. Those men were both to be admired and feared, and Tom was glad he was on the right side of them. For the moment, at least.

Cillian hung up the phone. "Got a little intel. They were definitely taken as they arrived here. Prophet and Mal were taken by the CIA. They're in a black site."

Tom shook his head. "King?"

"SAS has him. And God fucking help them," Cillian added.

"Ren?"

"Last I heard, the NSA nabbed him. Which means they're in worse shape than the SAS . . . especially once King gets there. Although they might welcome King taking Ren by the time that happens."

Even after only meeting Ren a handful of times, Tom could still confirm that Cillian was right—about all of it. "Hook?"

"He's, ah, MIA."

"Still in play then. And Prophet and Mal are still definitely at the black site?"

Cillian's expression tightened. "Yes. I'm sure they'll release Prophet to get John—he was banking on that. But Mal? They're not going to let him go that easily."

And that was what worried him—and obviously Cillian—the most. "Can you get him out?"

"I could, but I'm guessing he'd rather us spend our energy finding Prophet—and John. He's got his job to do and he knows that."

Tom nodded, his fists clenching at the mention of John's name. "Will Mal be all right?"

"If he doesn't act like himself, he'll be fine."

"Shit," Tom muttered.

Cillian just looked grim.

Brock let King go and commandeered him a vehicle—because he knew King would do it on his own anyway. King was never more grateful to the SAS in his life, especially when Brock added, "I think the NSA is done with your friend. Done interrogating him, I mean. Sounds like they're partying with him."

"Christ," King muttered.

"Doesn't seem like it's the first time. Good luck with that."

"Thanks for the intel." King shook his hand—and those of the other men who'd been silently listening to what he and Brock discussed—and then he grabbed Ren and got the rest of the mission moving.

"So John thinks we've been picked up by the CIA?" Ren asked. True to form, Ren had quickly endeared himself to the NSA and had informed King that he'd gotten multiple job offers before he left.

"He believes we're all out of commission," King said. "And he's probably on his way to Prophet."

Ren grew quiet then. "I guess we knew that would happen. I was hoping . . . that there was another way."

"There's not," King said shortly.

"Is Mal out?"

"Not yet. I'd give it another few hours. Let's get into place. I heard from Hook—he's where he needs to be. We'll get in touch with Cillian and Tom and loop them in."

"So we're still going after the triggers," Ren confirmed. "And John has no idea we're coming."

"Best-case scenario," King told him. "So . . ."

"So . . ." Ren echoed.

King rolled his eyes. "I'm waiting."

"For what? Applause? I got myself out of there."

King stared at him, wondering where he got the patience from when it came to his friend and teammate. Because there really was no one else he could deal with—not like he did with Ren. And Because he used all his patience up with Ren, it often made King want to strangle Prophet. "I'm talking about me. Prophet's announcement."

"Oh." Ren glanced out the back window, as if checking their rear, but something made King come up cold. "I figured you'd talk about it when you were ready."

King gripped the wheel tighter. "Prophet never came out and said it was me. Everyone just assumed, and I didn't say anything to challenge it."

"If it's not you, then who is it?" Ren asked carefully.

King looked over at him. "Why didn't you tell me before this, Ren? How worried do I have to be?"

"For yourself?"

"For you?" He pulled the truck over and turned to Ren, who frowned. "You haven't asked me a single question about WITSEC."

"I was waiting for you to be ready to talk about it."

"I know it's you, Ren," King said sharply and Ren just stared at him, almost defiantly. "So tell me."

"After this is over . . ."

"It might be too late then. Tell me now."

"So there's this cartel," Ren started.

"Cartel?"

"There's always a cartel." Ren shook his head. "It's not the time, King. We've got shit to do. One thing at a time. We take care of the first mess, and then we deal with mine."

"Suppose it's too late by then?" King demanded, without much heat behind his words.

"It was always too damned late," Ren told him before turning up the radio.

Two humorless men in suits dropped Prophet off at the airport with tickets, a passport in his own name, and cash. No weapons, since he couldn't board a plane with any and hell, that's what the cash was for.

The ticket would get him to Burundi, but he knew he wasn't going to get that far.

Even so, he acted complicit, went into the airport and checked in through security and then planned on checking out and driving to a secure location where he could decide if they were leading him to the right place or not. But halfway through the packed terminal, his vision began to blur.

It's just stress. He forced himself forward, concentrating on the people he was following, the air flow, just like Dean taught him to do. He could smell the outside air, which meant he must not be far from the door, and he took a deep, ragged breath to stave off what could easily become an inevitable panic attack.

Finally, he put a hand out to the left, brushing past people, muttering "Excuse me" until his palm found a wall. He stopped. Breathed. And then an arm slung over his shoulders, familiar and yet not at the same time . . . but there was no mistaking John's voice. "You look good, Prophet. Whatever you're doing agrees with you."

Prophet almost said, *Losing my sight*, but instead he nodded as the haziness took over, the people walking ahead of him with suitcases blurring into one another.

John tensed, then relaxed. "Jesus, Prophet. Come on, I've got you."

Right—lead me to your kidnapping, like fucking Stockholm syndrome . . . but Christ, it was all so familiar. Normal. Civilized.

"Fuck, man, breathe," John instructed, and Prophet did, until the need to hyperventilate dissipated.

He'd known this was going to be hard. He hadn't realized it would be impossible. "I'm fine. Let's go."

John stopped him by grabbing his wrist and touching the bracelet on Prophet's wrist. "Anything you need to tell me?"

"Not here." Prophet's throat tightened.

John pressed a kiss to his temple. "'S'all right—I've got you."

That's what Prophet was worried about. But still, he let John lead him through the crowds and out into the air, which cleared his brain a bit but not his eyesight. It was one foot in front of the other, the inevitability driving him onward . . . and into John's truck.

He settled in, the absurdity of John buckling his damned seat belt not lost on him. "Not a fucking child," he muttered and John snorted.

Prophet blinked, alone in the truck for seconds until John got into the driver's side. "The CIA's long gone, Proph. Just in case you were waiting for the cavalry."

"They sent me for you."

"They sent *me* for you," John told him and Prophet turned to stare at him—or at least attempt to.

From what he could make out, John looked the same—older, but the same. "Long time no see, brother."

John smirked, and for a second, a single second, they were fourteen, just finished fighting, headed to a week's worth of in-school suspension . . .

And then Prophet blinked and he was staring at a man he didn't know at all anymore . . . and one he'd known better than anyone in the fucking world. Until Tommy.

"Took you long enough." John lit a cigarette. There were no BDUs, but this was the same John from his dreams and flashbacks, from his waking hours when he saw a ghost of this man leaning against the wall, causally correcting Prophet, taunting him. Forcing him to see truths he never wanted to see. "We've got a couple of hours' worth of driving to do. Make yourself comfortable."

Prophet put the seat back as John threaded the truck through the dirty, busy streets.

"No bodyguards?" Prophet asked.

John automatically raised his eyes to glance in the rearview, giving Prophet his answer. "You shouldn't have looked for me."

"Really?" Prophet fought the urge to punch him in the throat—he didn't need to fucking see for that. They'd go off the road into a ditch but it'd be worth it.

"I'm protecting my throat, so don't try it," John said. "Tell me about Tom."

Prophet's heart seized. "Not much to tell."

John laughed. "Right. You're just fucking him."

"He's my partner. Easy access." God, the bitterness in his mouth as he spoke the lie threatened to choke him.

"Nothing more?"

"I've never stopped looking for you," Prophet said quietly—that was the truth and John knew it. "Where are we going?"

"Someplace nice, Proph. Take a rest."

John was still a good driver. Prophet closed his eyes. He wouldn't be free for long. John would cuff him. Maybe break his wrists. It wasn't all going to be old home week.

It never was.

Inside the newest safe house, tensions were rising. Tom was attempting to keep a lid on his temper—and barely succeeding—and Cillian was trying his best to be patient with him, Tom knew. And it made Tom want to strangle him even more.

"We've got to do something else besides sit here," Tom told Cillian for the fiftieth time in fifteen minutes.

"You're not sitting," Cillian pointed out—for the fiftieth time—then reminded him patiently, "We don't even know where we'd be going, Tom. Waiting here is for the best."

"Until what? You get something on that stupid computer of yours?"

"I'm still running airport footage," Cillian said, pointing to the laptop that showed a map and a stupid, stupid whirring circle that Tom supposed meant it was working on something. "And I'm trying to activate his tracker too."

"If you're not seeing it, then it's not working."

"It's purposely not that easy to do. It's not on all the time, in case he's wanded for it," Cillian explained. "We've only got a short window of time."

Tom looked over Cillian's shoulder at the program that showed the device moving a million miles a minute and still too slow. "He shouldn't be alone."

"For this, he has to be," Cillian told him. "He resigned himself to that a long time ago."

Tom knew it, but he'd hoped Prophet could change his mind, the way he had about bringing Tom along in the first place, the way he'd shared his secrets.

Because you handled that so well.

Cillian banged his hand on the back of the laptop, like that would speed shit along, and the men sitting at the table just shook their heads and continued playing cards.

Two hours later, when Tom had paced a hole into the floor and Cillian had begun muttering to himself in languages Tom didn't recognize, Elvis's cell phone beeped.

He took out his reading glasses to peer at it, before looking up at them over the lenses. "Most of them are sprung."

"How? When?" Tom asked.

"King and Ren were released an hour ago. Prophet before that," Xavier confirmed.

"And Mal?" Cillian demanded. Cahill gave him a long look that Tom likened to a mental gouging from stem to stern, and judging by the way Cillian paled, it felt like it too.

"I suspect he'll be out shortly," Xavier said smoothly.

Tom sighed. "Are they coming here?"

"No."

"Are they in contact with Prophet, at least?"

"No. Doesn't matter though. The others will follow the plan," Xavier said. "There are thousands of people at risk if they abandon what they're supposed to do in order to save Prophet. He'd never let that happen. Neither would they."

Tom drew a harsh breath, knowing they were all correct and hating it just the same. All he could do was follow the men into the state-of-the-art bunker in the basement that put doomsday preppers to shame.

Xavier pulled up a computer. "This is the first footage we got."

Tom and Cillian moved closer. "The airport," Cillian said. "I goddamned knew it."

Xavier panned out into the crowd, then began zooming in. "This was two hours ago."

"There," Tom said, because he'd recognize Prophet's walk anywhere.

"What's wrong with him?" Cillian asked as Prophet lurched. "Is he drunk? Drugged?"

"His eyes," Tom murmured. "Shit." He watched Prophet reach for the wall that was too far away and finally, almost by sheer force of will, find it, and Tom needed to be there, dammit.

He froze, a cold chill slamming up his spine as a man momentarily blocked his view of Prophet, a man as tall as Prophet, who threw an arm over his shoulder and gave him what would look like a hug to most.

"I don't see a gun," Elvis muttered.

"But it's John," Cillian confirmed.

"Prophet wouldn't put people at risk," Tom said. "Especially if his vision's blurry."

And Prophet, being Prophet, allowed John to touch his wrist and then lead him out of the airport, seeming like they were two old friends.

Because they technically were.

At that moment, John looked up at the camera, like he knew they'd identify him that way. Looked up and smiled, and Tom forced himself to keep watching Prophet and John walk together through the airport toward the exit. "They're going toward the parking garage. Which means he's still in country," Tom breathed. "He never boarded."

"His seat is filled—ticket was checked. Which means John boarded one of his men in his place," Cillian added.

"We've got someone on the case." Elvis pointed to a dot on the screen and then opened it up to show . . . Blue. Who waved at them, then reassured the group, "I'm on this. Pinpointing and will send coordinates when I have them."

The screen went out and Cillian turned to Tom. "Does Phil know about this?"

Blue came back on the screen. "That's a big N-O. Mick and I are off the grid for this one. We're technically on vacation."

The screen went blank again and Elvis shrugged. "Kid's way better with technology than we are."

Tom stared down at his phone. "There's no text here."

"He wouldn't send it to a phone John could track," Cahill informed him, slipping him a burner phone. "It's here. I think you need to let this play out."

"For how long? How the fuck can I do that? Sit here and do nothing?" he asked no one, and everyone.

All the men nodded, including Cillian, but remained silent. Tom did a half turn and paced toward the window. *Think, Tom, think. Everyone else is getting into their position. By 1300 it will all be over.* That's the amount of time Prophet needed to distract John . . . the amount of time Prophet had left before John killed him. Because even if John still loved Prophet—which was obvious—Prophet was still expendable in a John versus Prophet kind of way.

"Can we get a live feed?" he asked now.

"Audio for now—safer," came Blue's voice. "I'm tracing the location as we speak. It's going to take me some time."

Tom nodded at the screen as though Blue could see him and wandered out onto the porch, visions of John with his arm around Prophet running through his head, led there in part by a low whistling. He'd heard it somewhere before and was drawn to it now, a tune he could almost place, a tip-of-his-tongue song that escaped him and still managed to bring him back to a moment in time that threatened to crystalize and then, just as suddenly disappeared . . . because the whistling stopped when he walked outside.

Elvis joined him several minutes later, sitting next to him on the low bench and passing him a warm soda in a glass bottle. Fanta. "This is the good stuff."

Tom took a swig and wished it were scotch. "I'm guessing I won't hear from any of them until their parts are over."

"If things go well, you won't." Elvis patted him on the shoulder and left him . . . with Cahill. Who Tom didn't even notice sitting across from him, the ever-present cigarette dangling from his mouth.

Tom figured Cahill would make him work for every word and he didn't feel like pulling teeth. He'd wait to see Prophet again for that kind of treatment.

Cahill glanced over at him, pulled out a bottle of scotch from under his seat—and two glasses. He poured one for Tom and one for himself, and Tom gladly put the soda aside for the warm burn of the alcohol.

Finally, after an hour, in which Tom traced all possible routes to get to Prophet in his mind and thought of all the terrible forms of torture John could put him through, Cahill broke through his thoughts.

"Feel better now that you've run through every possibility?"

"No," Tom said honestly.

"So go back and think through every possible way you can rescue him and kill John. Every single way. And think up some new ways too, just for good measure. That shit's going to keep you alive." Cahill poured them each a second drink, and Tom figured it wasn't the scotch that made him talkative. So he listened carefully to the man who was speaking more now than he probably had in the last month. "You know, I was the one left behind once."

"What does that mean?"

Cahill's lips pulled to the left, which was probably the closest to a smile he'd ever get. "I was left behind in country. Military units pulled out fast—too many skirmishes. I was a spook, so I got left behind with no cover. No money. Nothing. I didn't need much, mind you. But hell, getting out of this place with no help?" He shook his head. "Those two? Elvis and Xavier? They were tasked with bringing me out alive."

"They did what Prophet did," Tom breathed. "Is that why you're all still here?"

Cahill grunted. "We don't only stay here, but I stayed with these guys. Helped them, because there were a lot more people who needed help getting out. Prophet's official work is a little different . . . but what he does on his off time . . ."

"He's worked with you guys."

"Prophet doesn't really work well with others. Guessing you know that." Cahill took a sip. "Then again, you're still around, so he hasn't killed you yet. Good sign."

"Yeah, thanks." Tom downed the scotch. "Did you ever meet John?"

Cahill turned to face him, his dark eyes turning endless. "Met him once. Never wanted the pleasure of doing it again. I applaud Prophet's loyalty but I would've stopped supporting this mission long ago if it wasn't a danger to people I care about."

Tom nodded. "I've never met him and I hate him."

"Start thinking of all the ways you can kill him. Over and over again, until you can do it in your sleep. Feel free to get creative." Cahill lifted a glass toward Tom. "When in doubt, let the scotch help you."

Tom snorted softly.

"You don't understand why Prophet has to be the one to find John."

"Of course I do."

"Logically, you do. But in here." Cahill tapped his heart. "You still think if he would just give that up, everything would be better."

"I know it wouldn't be, Cahill."

"You know, I was almost John," Cahill said finally, his voice a rasp in the dark. "If these guys hadn't gotten to me in time . . ." He shook his head and then stared at Tom. "You understand—they still would've come for me if it hadn't been in time, right? It's something they have to do."

"Rescue men from hell," Tom said.

"Even if it's of their own making," Cahill agreed.

CHAPTER TWENTY-SIX

M al had learned early in life to never rely on actually seeing the outside to know what time of day or night it was. Being locked into terrifyingly small places as both punishment and necessity had forced him to learn to count minutes and hours, to reorient himself the way one might after taking a tumble in the ocean—you had to quickly trust yourself to find which way was up.

By his calculations, he'd been locked inside this floating fucking box for twenty hours—and counting. Prophet had no doubt come and gone. They were doing catch and release for him because they needed him to kill John. As for Mal, and the rest of the team, he supposed it was a crapshoot.

He was definitely the one not getting released until last, if at all. If Agent Paul had anything to say about it, the terms would not be anything Mal would agree to.

After another forty-six minutes, a knock on the door was a preview of that young agent—Warren something—coming in. Mal thought about convincing him that not knocking was most effective, that knocking gave Mal an easy chance to kill him . . . but he saved his sage advice for someone who'd actual benefit from it.

Finally, the agent poked his head in, murmuring that his name was Warren. Like they were fucking best friends in the making. Warren was armed—and easily disarmable, but patience was good for the soul.

He came bearing food, or something that resembled it. Something sandwich-like with water, which Mal ate because it wasn't drugged— fuck, he could only hope. He'd asked for drugs immediately, which of course insured he got none.

"Your friend's gone," the agent murmured as Mal ate. "Didn't even look back or think of asking about you."

Right. Like Mal was going to believe this dumb-shit's dumb shit. He stared hard at Agent Warren, who looked like a fucking puppy dog, and wondered what kind of experience it would take to rip the big-eyed innocence out of his expression, wanted to meet this man again when he was dead-eyed and steely, and then say, *Now you fucking get it.*

This guy probably wouldn't make it that long or that far. Mal could usually sense the ones who could and right now, he wasn't sensing anything impressive.

"Anyway, all they want is some intel. Any intel," Agent Warren continued earnestly, which was step one in the CIA interrogation's handbook: *make friends with the captive.* "So even a little bit would go a long way."

Mal stared at him until Warren squirmed. Then he smiled and Warren backed up a little, because Mal's smiles were probably more terrifying than his deadpan stare.

It was an art form. So was lying. But man, this guy wasn't even good practice. Target practice maybe.

Fuck it.

Fine. I'll give you some intel, he signed. When Warren frowned, he mouthed, *I have intel*, and Warren's face brightened. Especially when Mal shook his leg up and down, which Warren would chalk up to nervousness or impatience, the first sign of weakness Mal had given them. And he was certain Warren would take the gift without seeing the Trojan horse he'd wrapped it up in.

Agent Paul was a different story, but Mal had bigger plans for him.

"Can you tell me what, exactly what you've got intel about?" Warren asked.

Upcoming assassination attempt, Mal mouthed.

"Okay, this is good, Mal. Really good. Great. I'll go let Agent Paul know. And thank you for your cooperation."

I'm going to strangle you on my way out, Mal signed. Agent Warren tilted his head at him uncertainly and Mal knew then and there the kid could read sign language.

Hell, maybe Agent Warren had a chance at life after all.

After another three hours, the door opened and Agent Paul strode in. He was a big motherfucker, thin though, and he was also a stuck-up prick who appeared all world-weary and exhausted in his three-piece suit.

"What is it now, Malcolm?" He slammed the door behind him.

Mal'd bided his time, watched Prophet get sprung, and stayed jailed up until the agreed-upon time limit. Now, it was time to get the fuck out.

He was told to do it any way he could, because he wasn't getting let out like the others, escorted to a waiting car and driven safely back. No, he'd have to beat his way out, a true escape, because that was the only way for this to work. The agents would never believe Mal. Prophet was only let out because the CIA still thought he was their bitch.

They were going to be so disappointed.

I've got intel, Mal signed, then shook his head and motioned for a pen. Instead, the bastard called for chalk and a board.

Mal could kill him with chalk just as easily as a pen. Chalk and tracheas were pretty much the same size. Round peg, round hole ...

Paul interrupted his pleasant thoughts. "So, what did you feel the need to share today, Mal?"

Assassination going down tomorrow, he wrote carefully. Even included a smiley face, which made Paul frown.

Could he frown with chalk in his trachea? Probably until he lost consciousness.

"Mal, elaborate." Paul snapped his fingers and yeah, time was up. Both their time.

Maybe your obituary can read "death by another man's underwear," Mal signed.

Paul looked at him, tilted his head because he no doubt recognized some of the signs, and hell, if Mal had a prisoner who only knew a certain language he'd be damned sure he learned it pronto because if you wanted something done ...

You've got to do it your damned self, he signed. In seconds, he was up, cuffs dangling off one wrist uselessly, his own shirt off over his head and wrapped around Paul's, cutting off his airway by tightening the fabric around his trachea.

He'd have to try the chalk another time. He held on to Paul as the man tried to struggle, pull away, create some kind of ruckus, and Mal knew the cameras for the cell wouldn't be on now. Paul hated being watched and judged, especially when dealing with someone he thought could get the better of him.

Stupid, stupid man.

After Paul slumped, Mal checked his pulse and cracked his neck, just to be sure dead was dead. He sat him in the chair, back to the camera and re-dressed them both in each other's clothing. Now he had Paul's BDUs, cap, credentials, and gun as he took to the hallways.

On the way out, he passed Warren, who paused. And stared. And then signed to him, *You owe Agent Rylan one, but I owe you one for Paul. Even.*

Fuck. He'd let the kid live this time. *Couldn't have just let me out earlier?*

More fun to watch you in action. I need to learn shit, right?

Huh. Maybe all this kid needed was a little seasoning. *Your math's a little off. I owe Rylan and you owe me. And I need to collect on my favor now. I need your clothes . . . and you need mine.*

Warren frowned, but complied. And then Mal explained exactly what the favor was.

"After this shit, we'll definitely be even," Warren told him.

See you on the other side, War, Mal signed. It was time to get off this fucker, even if he had to swim to shore.

Which he did, at least part of the way. A fishing boat picked him up—just in time since they were chumming the water for sharks. Mal liked swimming as much as the next SEAL but hell, he was all for no blood in the water while he was doing it.

"You runnin' from something?" the captain asked once Mal had boarded and gotten checked out by the crew.

Mal had asked for a pen and paper—or a phone—and now he typed in the guy's notes, *Aren't we all?* quickly followed by, *A thousand bucks in exchange for your phone.*

He got full agreement on both items, plus a quick trip to the dock and dry clothes. Score. Borrowed a car to put a few towns in between him and the black site, found some new IDs and made his way to the next stop on the Prophet Does Death World Tour.

It was going to be a good day.

CHAPTER TWENTY-SEVEN

After several hours of driving, they were back over Eritrea's border, in the slightly more industrial area, if you could call it that. It was dark as hell, except for a few lights around the building, and Prophet saw movement, which no doubt meant John had a couple of guards placed strategically out front.

"We're here, Prophet." John got out and came around and opened his door. When Prophet got out, John instructed him to turn around, and tied his hands behind his back, a little harder than necessary. "Too tight?"

"Just perfect." Because Prophet wouldn't show him any weakness. He squinted as he surveyed the building on the way inside. "Love the *no one gets out alive* theme."

"You'd expect nothing less than wired to blow." John kept a steady hand on the small of his back as he led Prophet up the concrete steps and through a metal door. The room opened up—a large space with a bed, a fighting ring, and computers.

Every teenage boy's wet dream and hell, at least he had the sense to not say that out loud.

John sat him down and roped him into a chair. His eyesight hadn't cleared much, but he'd been automatically scanning the area anyway. He tried to soak in as much as he could, because he didn't know when the blurring would intensify again and he needed something—anything—he could use for a weapon, besides the obvious. He'd be looking for weapons and exits until he was an old man—if he made it that long.

You have to . . . for Remy.

He finally understood why being a parent was the hardest job imaginable. You didn't think for yourself anymore—every single decision was meant to put you in a position to continue caring for the person who depended on you. It made you raw and vulnerable.

Tommy made him that way too, but he'd trained him to take care of himself.

"Here are your friends, Prophet, in case you're interested." John pointed to a spot on the computer. "That's King, I believe. And here's Ren—he can't keep still but the movement is within a cage. And this, way over here? Mal."

Prophet kept his voice indifferent. "Glad you're so scared of them that you had to get them locked up. Not scared of me? I'm upset I didn't get the same treatment."

He was pretty sure John frowned at that. He sat there and watched John rifle through his bag, pulling out the money before moving closer, telling him, "Hey, I found these drops in your bag. Need me to put them in?"

The drops were supposed to help with the blurring and hell, he could use all the help he could get, but why the hell would John want to help him now? Definitely a trap. "I'm good."

John grabbed his hair and yanked his head back. He tried to throw himself—the chair—off-balance and struggle to get away, but John still managed to get a drop into each eye . . . and if Prophet was a betting man? His eyes would be blurrier than they'd been soon enough. He pushed away from John and blinked. "What are we going to do now? Play cards? Watch people die?"

"Funny. First, we're going to get out our aggression."

"In the ring?"

"Can you think of a better place?"

"Yes. Many of them." He thought about the last time he'd seen a ring like this one . . . Tom, almost killing a man. About Chris too, and John hadn't brought that up at all.

Prophet wouldn't either. Not yet.

John was over by the computers, angling a camera and then hitting a few keys. "When Tom gets this email and he opens the link, he'll be able to see and hear everything in this room."

Shit. "Seems unnecessary. This is between us."

"I know you're trying to keep Tom away from big, bad me but I think he won't be able to resist coming to your rescue."

"Why not invite Mal here instead?" He shrugged. "He'd kill to see you."

"Still a funny guy."

"I wasn't laughing when you took off. I wasn't laughing when I looked for you for two years, almost killing myself in the process."

"See? I can hear the anger in your voice. You'll welcome the opportunity to beat me."

"I'm sure you'll keep it a fair fight, won't you?"

"You never had faith in me." John's voice was cold, ice, like the night before Hal's mission. He kicked his shoes off and Prophet did the same, readying himself for when John untied him.

"I did—for too long." Prophet tensed as John walked around him . . . and untied him from the chair. He kept his wrists bound though, and he pushed him into the ring.

Prophet ducked as he turned, and caught the tail end of a blow to the jaw. "They want you dead, John."

"Someone always wants me dead. Then they decide I'm too good to kill off." John shook his head. "Still a company man? Deep down inside, where it counts?"

"Go fuck yourself." Prophet spat blood on the ground between their feet. "None of this is worth it."

"The money is."

"How're you ever going to use it? That's been the holdup, or you wouldn't've been working for ten years killing people."

"You don't know me as well as you think you do."

"I know you better than I know myself," Prophet hissed. "Let me go. Take the money I've got in my bag and get the fuck out of here. Get plastic surgery. Go off the radar."

"You're here to get me out of hell, not let me go. I take the money, you shoot me in the back."

"I'd never take the easy way out."

"Then why offer?"

"Because I knew you wouldn't take it." Prophet stared at him.

John smiled. "After this, the CIA won't know what the fuck is going on. But I will. I'll fuck them all over, the way they've all fucked me in the past."

"Fucked you?" Prophet asked. "Well then, at least they used lube, because for me and the rest of the team, it was raw."

"I thought you didn't mind that."

"And you fucked us all over just so you could play hero?" Prophet asked and at that moment he finally realized what this was all about. For him, anyway.

Punishment. For him. For getting close to the team. For getting close to anyone but John, and for pulling away toward the end. "You're still a jealous bastard."

"Don't flatter yourself. I didn't take the job to punish your friends. That was just an added benefit," John confirmed. "They never believed in me. No one did, not even you."

"You're wrong," Prophet told him, aware of how dead his voice sounded. At least he knew the majority of the plan—it was very close to what he and Mal had surmised. There was a plan already in place to stop him, but that depended on what happened now, in this room. "How's Judie looking these days?"

John shrugged. "Same. She doesn't age. Must be the meds."

"Still out of it then?" Prophet asked and John nodded.

"Your family was always as fucked as mine," John told him. "Like Christopher."

"Tell me that was a mistake."

John's head snapped like Prophet had slapped him. "Of course it was."

Prophet was long done believing him. "John, Agent Paul said he had Christopher killed. Did you know that? Or is that what you told him to say?"

"Don't, Proph," John warned, but Prophet was through with being careful. He might not be able to see but goddammit, he could hear the tension in John's voice . . . and the lie.

"You had your own brother killed," Prophet spat and John lunged and tackled him. Prophet swung and heard a crack, knew he'd broken John's nose, would like nothing better than to shove it up into his skull . . .

John slammed him onto his back and got up, bouncing on the balls of his feet. The John he once knew? Gone. Prophet had mourned Christopher, and now he said a prayer to him—for him—and rolled to his own feet.

"You look serious, Proph. Thinking about your boyfriend?" John laughed. "He know all your secrets? You finally let him in? Hell, I thought for sure it'd be Mal you ended up fucking, but hey, to each his own."

"Leave Tom out of this."

"You're not in charge here. And you're the one who brought him into it."

"You have me. You don't need anyone else."

"Hal started this—I didn't. If he didn't keep secrets, I wouldn't need to either. You would've been cut free of all of this years ago, but you just had to try to protect the asset's interests."

"It's called being human."

"Right." John sighed. "Anyway, none of us are getting out alive."

"Then what's the point of bringing Tom here?" Prophet asked calmly, trying to tamp down his panic.

"Because it'll kill you," John said simply. "He can see this, by the way. Watching everything. He's almost as worried about you as you are of him. But once he sees me hurting you, he'll do what he needs to."

"Why, John? What the fuck happened to you?"

"You happened. You and your fucking team, always trying to make a fool of me."

"Mal was always the best at exposing you."

"The trouble started when you began to believe him."

"It started when I realized it was the truth. Your dad was a psychopath, but I didn't realize it was passed down."

"You're one to talk mental illness."

"Fuck, I used to love you, John."

"But you don't recognize me?" John mimicked.

"I do. You were always the same. I guess I changed."

"Touché, Prophet, if that makes you feel better . . . but no one changes that much."

After that, Prophet stopped talking . . . and began to fight for his life.

"Hey, Dean? There's someone here who says she needs to see you." Nico's voice sounded . . . odd at best. Dean tensed but then Nico added, "She looks like she's in trouble."

"Bring her in the back room," Dean called and double-timed it to meet Nico and Trouble.

"She's not armed," was the first thing Nico said. Dean felt the air redistribute as two bodies came into his space. Nico was standing next to the woman and Dean put his hand out.

The woman grasped his. Her skin was cool, not clammy, but her breathing was slightly hitched. Nerves. "Nico, get her something to calm her down. Ma'am, have a seat."

Dean heard Nico shove a chair in her direction and he continued holding her hand until he felt her sit. He smelled the bourbon Nico poured, heard her noisy gulp . . . and for several seconds, he let the silence hang between all of them until he asked, "What's your name?"

She cleared her throat. "I've gone by so many now, I'm not sure it matters. But my real name? Karen."

Dean frowned as the voice cut through him, deep into the muscle of a memory he didn't want accessed. But the wound had been reopened. His head began to pound and he leaned in, putting his hands on either arm of her chair, locking her in place. He couldn't see her, but the tension flared between them. "Did you come back to try to finish the job?"

CHAPTER TWENTY-EIGHT

A couple of hours later, Cillian and Tom got a Skype call from King and Ren.

"You guys all right?" Tom asked. Both men looked suspiciously unharmed.

"We're fine, Tom. Hook's here with us too," Ren assured him. "We got away, no problem."

"Really?"

"Ren was showing the NSA men how to do the hustle when I got there," King informed them.

"Wait—seriously?"

"Would I lie about shit like that?" King grumbled. He was sitting on a chair slightly behind Ren, who was at the table behind the computer.

"And you were worried about me." Ren turned and knocked King on the shoulder. "I was halfway out of there."

"You were hanging out to finish the dance."

"Can't leave on the good part of the song, man," Ren told him solemnly. "Any word from Mal?"

"None," Tom admitted.

"Doesn't mean he's not out." King peeled an apple with a KA-BAR. "Just means he's staying away so comms don't pick him up."

"So how do we know?" Tom asked.

"We have faith." King offered Ren a piece of the apple. "If Mal is still at the black site, that just means he knows it's where he needs to be."

Tom accepted that, because there was no choice.

Ren appeared to as well. "As soon as you find out where that fucker John has Prophet, we want to know."

"As soon as you disable those triggers, we want to know," Cillian told him.

King nodded. "We've got the intel we need. Ren's taking Hook and I'm going with Rylan. Then we'll meet up. Hook's got us air or ground support when we're done."

"We'll stay in touch," Tom promised him.

"Tom, don't worry about Prophet—he's strong," Ren assured him quietly before he cut the feed.

Tom knew how strong Prophet was . . . but he also knew how strong John's ghost was. "Dammit. We can't just sit here."

"We're working on finding him," Cillian repeated and put a hand over his heart. "Boy Scout's pledge."

"Asshole," Tom muttered.

Cillian ignored that, reached into his pocket instead, muttering something about a pen, and frowned as he pulled out a yellow folded piece of paper. He unfolded it and it turned out to be legal pad sized. "Mal's writing."

Tom glanced at it. "Yeah. While everyone was planning the other day, he was writing a list of all the ways he could kill someone. 'A good memory exercise,' he called it. I asked him for a copy."

"But he gave it to me."

"Maybe it's a reminder. Or a love letter," Tom pointed out.

"Or both," Cillian said grimly.

"Probably." That thought made Tom happy. "Mind if I refresh my memory? I'll give it back to you for your hope chest."

"Fuck you, Tom." Cillian handed it to him.

At first, Tom thought there might be some kind of secret code embedded but it appeared to be a very extensive and teachable list of ways to off someone, written in perfect Catholic school penmanship and organized impressively in categories like *guns*, *poisons*, *strangulation*, *how to make it look like suicide*, *bombings*, and *other*. Plus two sections devoted to *improvisation* and *torture*.

Finally, he handed it back to Cillian, who folded it and pocketed it again carefully, and look at that, Cillian was a romantic. He was about to tell Cillian that because hell, he could drive that knife in deeper all day long for Mal's sake, but Cillian was telling him, "Tom—you've got an email. From John."

Tom moved next to Cillian to stare at the screen. He hesitated briefly, then glanced at Cillian and opened the email. There was a single link inside it, and Tom clicked it and waited. After a brief hang, it opened to reveal a room, a black-and-white picture that at first didn't appear to be a video. But then the figures in the foreground moved . . . and Tom realized they were watching a live video feed.

"Bastard," Cillian growled. Tom punched a few keys and brought the room into sharper focus. Prophet lay on the floor, staring at the ceiling.

"Is he knocked out?" Tom asked, more to himself than anything. Both men leaned in toward the screen as if that would give them the answers.

And then another figure walked onto the screen. "That's him. John." And suddenly, Tom was watching a scene that was eerily reminiscent of the fight club where he and Prophet had worked their first case together. Except there was no one to watch this—not in person, anyway. Prophet was already in the ring, on the ground, his hands bound behind his back, his lip already bleeding and John looking slightly bruised too.

And this was just the beginning.

"You don't have to watch this, Tom."

John was torturing Prophet—and inviting Tom to watch. In that way, he could torture Tom too. "Of course I have to. If Prophet's going to live it . . ."

Then so will you.

"Come on Prophet, get up," he muttered. He noticed Prophet's arm twitch, and realized he was fisting his hands so hard they were shaking. "Cillian, where's this happening? You have to find out."

Cillian was on the phone. "I'm already on it. Sent it to Blue to try to get a trace."

As he spoke, Prophet struggled to his feet, and that's when Tom realized Prophet wasn't seeing well.

Cillian noticed too. "Are his eyes that bad?"

"Sometimes but . . . I'm betting John did something. Maybe drugged him."

"He's still putting up a hell of a fight."

Not enough, though, and they both knew it.

A cry from Prophet seized Tom's heart. John had punched him in the gut and then the jaw, causing him to buckle again. "This isn't right."

"Looks like they've been at it a while. John's tired too."

"But not drugged. John tipped the scales. Couldn't do it without cheating." Tom slammed his fists on the table, his temper rising to almost unbearable levels.

As if John could hear him, he turned and looked back at the camera. And smiled, blood between his teeth.

"I'll get you, John. You fucking coward—tell me where to come and I'll take care of this now," Tom yelled, then forced himself to calm down.

Focus.

Look around the room.

Private house? Not a hotel—he could see land outside the window. A truck. Truck. He glanced over his shoulder at Cillian, who was distracted on the phone, and then Tom brought the truck into focus . . . and the license plate.

It was a long shot. Just because he had a plate number didn't mean the plate would be registered to the house John was at. Especially in this country—nothing would be easy to find.

Triangulate the feed. That was the best shot. And he had no doubt Blue was working as fast as he could but . . .

"No," Tom whispered as John pushed Prophet over and climbed on top of him. He'd made sure Tom would have a ringside seat to this.

"You have to trust that Prophet knows what he's doing."

"What the fuck is he doing?"

"Buying time," Cillian noted.

"Not like this." Tom shook his head. "He can't sacrifice himself like this. Dammit, Prophet. I should be there with you." He put the volume on the computer all the way up and heard Prophet telling John, "You handicapped me."

John stroked some hair out of Prophet's eyes. "You want out?"

God, that question had so many variable answers . . . and Tom winced when Prophet whispered, "Sometimes, yeah." Because he knew it was an honest answer.

"Me too," John agreed and Tom itched to break his fingers, one by one, the more they touched Prophet. "But getting out now? All that time wasted? No, especially when it was going to happen at this point with or without me. It's done."

"This is your big fuck-you to the CIA?"

"You want to give them a hug, a pat on the ass, and send them on their way? After what they did to you? Punished you for knowing what happened?" John shook his head. "You should've just not looked for me."

"Would you have?" Prophet asked.

John swallowed. Never tore his gaze from Prophet's. "Never."

Tom went cold, because John was lying. "And I know he's lying. I *know* that but I'm fucking believing him."

"John's gift," Cillian agreed.

"Why'd you come here, Prophet? Really?"

"I want to understand why, man."

"Trying to keep things safe for your team, no doubt."

"They're *our* team, John. Our brothers."

"You were my brother, above all else."

John wasn't wrong to expect loyalty but . . . "I was there for all of you. And brothers keep each other from going off the rails."

John snorted. "It's all a big chess board. I'm just keeping the pieces I control in play. It's what they wanted from me. It's what I'm good at."

"Undermining their own missions."

"Then they had deniability. You know how it works." Unfortunately, Prophet did—John did too. "You shouldn't have come."

"I know."

"But that didn't stop you." John shook his head. "The only person I couldn't ever break was you."

"And that pisses you off? At least you can still feel something."

"Still trying to be my conscience?" John asked.

"It's a lonely job."

"Then fucking quit. Like I said, you shouldn't have come here."

"No choice."

"Funny, but you always said—"

"You were my choice. I chose to come here. This isn't about following orders. This is about my cleaning up a mess I should've a long time ago," Prophet murmured.

"If it wasn't me . . ."

"But it was. And it's not going to end well for you."

"Or you. I've made my peace. Have you, Proph?"

Only since the move to this new safe house had Tom noticed that the bracelet with the wrapped leather ropes he carried with him everywhere—the one Prophet had given him for protection—was missing from his bag, leaving Tom with only the inked version around his wrist.

There was no way he'd lost it. No, Prophet had taken it purposely. He was going to meet John, wearing the bracelet.

Hoping it would give *him* some protection.

"Tom's not a part of this," Prophet said, instead of answering John's question about finding peace.

"Of course he is. Willing player or not," John reasoned. "He can hear you—tell him to come on down. I'd be shocked if he doesn't discover my hiding place soon."

"No. He's not coming here. I want him alive." Prophet's words were directed to Tom and John knew it too, because he smiled.

"No one gets out alive, Prophet. But better to die with the one you love, right? Or else he's going to mourn the rest of his life and ruin his own anyway."

Tom swallowed hard and put all of the other shit aside. Prophet needed him, needed his concentration and prayers and anything else Tom could think of. "He'll get out of this," he murmured.

Next to him, Cillian didn't say a word.

"Dean? What the hell's going on here?" Nico's question demanded an answer, his voice low, but Dean sensed the unmistakable danger the woman had brought along with her. It was palpable, hung in the air over them like a cloud of debris from a bomb . . . the last thing he'd ever seen.

Dean had allowed Nico to pull him aside, with assurance that he still had eyes on Karen. He'd also informed Dean that he'd handcuffed her to the chair until he could figure everything out, and Dean saw no reason to change that. "This woman's the reason I'm blind."

"Yeah, I caught that." Nico's voice sounded deliberately casual. "Care to elaborate?"

He reached for his phone instead of answering. "Is your GPS on?"

"No."

"Check mine—make sure it's still off," he instructed.

Nico took it from him and then pressed it back into his palm. "Still off. Now what?"

"Now, we have to deal with this."

"Who is she?"

After what seemed like hours, he finally managed, "She's the woman who nearly killed me. And who saved my life," his voice sounding weak and hollow to his own ears and *no*, this was the time for strength. For him to put his money where his mouth was, just like he always urged Prophet to do. "I used to do the same kind of missions as Prophet did—when I was a SEAL and right after I got out as well. LT had been running those kinds of missions for a while and he had an important one coming up. I was running point on it— actually I was the only operative on it. Supposed to be an easy in and out, and I did the research. Was in the right place at the right time. Didn't know the asshole planted a bomb. LT told me I should've been more careful, that a lot of these specialists are resistant to being relocated . . . but hell, most of them don't bomb the agent relocating them."

Nico drew in a sharp breath. "What were you told about her beforehand?"

"The usual. That she was a scientist who was trying to develop a virus that could kill people. That the government wanted her contained. To avoid syringes. I mean, fuck, I was ordinances. I looked out for bombs in my sleep no matter what, but I wasn't carrying out an assassination. I was her next security detail, bringing her to the next spot on the tour, unless something happened. She wasn't violent."

"So she had no reason to know anyone was coming for her."

"Not unless someone told her ahead of time, which obviously, someone might have," Dean confirmed.

Nico put a hand on his forearm. "What do you need from me, Dean?"

"I'm okay. I've got this. But you can—should—stay."

"Trust me—I'm not going anywhere," Nico told him.

"But you want an explanation," Dean said, this time loud enough for Karen to hear. "I do too, actually."

"That's why I'm here." Karen called over to them, her voice smoother than it had been earlier, probably thanks to the bourbon, but the rough edge revealed the panic pulsing underneath. "I didn't know where else to go."

"I was told you were dead." Dean heard Nico's breath subtly quicken . . . but Karen gave no such sign.

"I still don't know who I can trust—I'm taking a big risk here."

"If you thought I was in on it, why come back to me?"

"Because you still owe me one."

Dean laughed. "I owe you?" He pointed to his face. "You took my sight."

"And you set me up to be sold."

"Never," he said tightly. "Who gave you my information?"

"A man who's been keeping me safe for years. His name is Prophet, and he gave me your name and basic coordinates. He told me you might move around a bit but that you'd never leave the general area."

"Why not contact him when you were threatened?"

She sighed. "Because I think he's been compromised. That's the only way someone could've found me."

At the words *Prophet* and *compromised*, Dean felt the hairs on the back of his neck rise, felt the worry coming off Nico as well. "And how do you know that I haven't been compromised?"

He swore he felt her eyes burning a hole through him when she spoke. "Because Prophet has no idea that I'm the one who took your sight."

He swallowed, hard. *That* he believed. Prophet would never keep something this big from him. Prophet thought the doctor who'd done this to Dean was dead, just like LT told them both. Because LT didn't need either of them chasing any more ghosts ... "Why did Prophet say he gave you my information?"

"He said you were one of the best men he knew. I couldn't believe he was talking about you. It didn't make sense. Why would he tell me to go back to the man who'd tried to sell me?"

"Because it wasn't me," he said hollowly.

"I took care of it, Dean. The doctor's dead," LT had assured him.

A lie to make him feel better. And Prophet had been hiding the same woman for all these years? None of this made any sense. "I was told they put you down."

"I ran," she said defiantly.

"Why? Because you wanted to remain vulnerable?"

"Because someone was trying to sell me. For all I knew, it was you. For all I know, it still is."

His breathing slowed. "That wasn't my mission. For all I know, you paid enemies of the United States to take you out of here in exchange for building bombs for them."

"I don't build bombs," she said.

"Did a pretty good facsimile of one."

She sighed. "It was just enough to get me away—that's all. That wasn't my specialty."

"Tell me this, doctor—if you were that concerned about being sold, why not just kill yourself and save the world?" he challenged.

"My son." Her voice shook, and that shook Dean, because she was telling the truth. "For him. That's why I stayed alive—for him. And even though I've only had brief contact with him through the years, it's enough that he knows his mother did the right thing and hid herself. I was hoping that one day ..."

"No one would want to use you for your knowledge?"

"I guess today wasn't that day. Or should I say, last week, when I got word that I needed to get the hell out of dodge."

"Who told you that?" he demanded. "Prophet?"

"No, it wasn't Prophet. That's how I knew I'd been compromised. Whoever contacted me was trying to draw me out. If I contacted Prophet, I'd be putting him—and my son—in danger too. So I left, and ran. I might not be young anymore but I still remember how to evade and escape. I didn't sit in that assisted-living facility only making lanyards."

"So who was it?"

"I don't know, but I'm guessing it was the same person who wanted me years ago. The intel I have, for now, is still helpful. The chatter out there is, frankly, terrifying. Coming here, to you, equally so. But I have to believe Prophet wouldn't lead me to danger."

"No, he wouldn't." Dean shook his head. "Nico?" He knew the man was still there, but just wanted to judge the tone of his voice.

"I'm here, Dean," was all Nico said, and Dean knew he wasn't losing his mind, that Nico believed the doctor's story . . . and that they were both slowly coming to the same, unnerving conclusion. "Doctor—"

"Karen," she insisted.

"Karen, can you tell me what the chatter you heard was?" Nico asked.

"If you think it will help you find who's after me . . ." She hesitated. "I've never told anyone about what I do. Prophet knows, of course. My son as well and some select CIA agents, but I guess I've already taken a leap of faith, so why not go all the way, right?" She laughed, a tense sound. "The chatter I heard is about Ahmet Mehmed-Handan III."

"The terrorist?" Nico sounded surprised. "Karen, he was—"

"Assassinated? Blown up? Buried at sea? Yes, I'd heard all that too." She blew out a hard breath. "What I do—my specialty? Was to create prisons for men like him. Boxes that could keep them away from the world at large, but alive and isolated, just in case we needed them. It's a dangerous proposition, and I took my job seriously."

"You built black sites," Dean said.

"I designed them, yes. From the ground up. I supervised every single detail. Different crews. I was the only one who knew the full floorplans for any of them."

"Rumor has it that there are back doors in every single black site you built," Nico said.

"Rumors like that are why I'm on the run," she said wanly.

"Which is why it's not just a rumor, right?" Dean ran a hand through his hair and wasn't surprised when she didn't give a definitive answer. Because he had what he needed to know—Karen Sutter was going to be forced to break one of the world's biggest terrorists out of a black site she designed . . . but for who? "You think the person after you now is the same person who tried to sell you all those years ago?"

"Yes," she said softly. "Like I said, not many people know I wasn't killed."

"What now?" Nico asked. "Because the longer we keep her . . ."

"The more danger I bring to all of you, as well as myself," she finished. "I could keep running, but if I'm caught . . ."

"I'll call my brother. He's the one who sets up jobs like this—the relocations."

"Not Prophet?" she asked. "Is he okay?"

"I haven't heard from him. He's got a job of his own, and I'm not sure how long it will take." He'd been dialing the man's number and getting his voice mail, and he'd left texts to no avail. "We'll get this taken care of."

"I don't know who to trust."

"You can trust me. And you can trust my brother to get you to safety. That's what we do. Okay?"

"Okay."

"Wait with her, Nico." He went into the next room to dial LT and explain the time bomb that just landed on his doorstep. "LT? We've got a big problem. Whoever told you that Karen Sutter was taken care of lied. She escaped . . . and now she's here. With me. And no, I'm not kidding."

Tom stood frozen and watched the live feed, refusing to look away from what was happening to Prophet. Everything around him went still. It was only Tom and the screen and it was as if he'd been sucked inside of it and was hovering, witnessing exactly what was happening, could see the sweat slicking Prophet's skin, could hear the punches hitting flesh as clearly as if he were standing right on the mat with them.

And finally—finally—Tom's phone beeped.

It was Blue. *Got his location.*

Give it to me, Tom texted back. Because nothing would stop him from going to Prophet. And when Blue gave him the coordinates, Tom announced, "I'm going to him."

And realized he was talking to an empty room—with a closed and, he was soon to find out, locked door. A metal door, dammit. "Let me out, Cillian, or I'll destroy everything in this room and get myself out."

In between watching Prophet fighting for his life and knowing that by going he was playing right into John's hands, he planned on ripping the door off its hinges, when it opened . . . and he came face-to-face with Cahill.

"Let me get you to Prophet in one piece."

"And once I'm there?"

"God help you, son," was all Cahill said before turning tail and heading out the door.

Tom grabbed his go-bag and was right behind him, ignoring Cillian cursing in the background. He caught up with Cahill, demanded, "Why are you helping me?"

"Looking a gift horse in the mouth's not the smartest thing you can do." Cahill glanced back toward the house, where Elvis came out, carrying a bag of his own.

"Xavier's staying with Cillian," he confirmed as he put his bag in the back.

"Neither of you are coming in with me," Tom told them.

"He telling us what to do?" Elvis drawled to Cahill, who rolled his eyes and got into the driver's seat.

Tom stopped arguing and got in next to Cahill. "I'm telling you, I'm going in alone. It's the only way."

"We know that better than you do. We've got different jobs to do. This is just a quick stop to let you go do what you need to do," Elvis explained. "We've all got our parts."

"It looks like John is alone with Prophet." Tom was thinking out loud.

"Appears that way, yes. Because he knows—or thinks—that everything else is happening around him like clockwork. He planned his time alone with Prophet. He knows that even if things go wrong between them, Prophet can't singlehandedly stop what's already in motion." Elvis patted Tom's shoulder from the back seat.

"So that's why you're helping me," Tom muttered. "You know Cillian's right behind us, don't you?"

"Figured that." Cahill lit a cigarette as he drove over the rutted roads like the seasoned professional he was. "I knew you were getting out of that room—that house—and to Prophet, even if it was literally over all our dead bodies. If I thought you couldn't handle it, I'd risk my life to stop you from risking yours. But I know what I'd risk for someone I loved. In this life, you've got to know what you're willing to die for. You know what that is."

Tom sighed, mainly in relief, as he leaned his head back against the seat to collect his thoughts while the truck rumbled through the night.

"You know we used to do the jobs Prophet does," Elvis continued.

Tom turned around to stare at him. "The asset jobs?" Cahill nodded. "You worked for LT?"

Cahill snorted. "That asshole? No. We found Prophet after he left LT. If he hadn't, we were prepared to take him aside and help him exit gracefully. Prophet was too good to stay working with LT, not with all the shit he pulled."

"I'm glad Prophet found you."

Cahill gave him the side-eye. "You don't understand what Prophet did—what he does, why he does it, and that's okay. Classified is hard to wrap your mind around, especially when you're close with someone. But when you are, that's when you've got to understand."

"What would Prophet say if he knew you were bringing me to him?" Tom asked.

"He'd kill us," Elvis admitted.

"Then why are you doing it?"

"Because Prophet doesn't always know what's best for him. Turn here," Xavier instructed.

"I know that," Cahill growled as he lit another cigarette from the butt of the first. "Fucking bossy asshole."

"Someone needs to be," Elvis murmured as the truck pulled over and stopped, and Tom felt like he was looking into a time machine of what would happen years from now . . . because he knew this would be

Prophet's team's idea of retirement. Like Elvis said earlier, old men like them didn't grow old gracefully, nor did they want to.

Right now, Tom was damned grateful for that.

"Prophet's location is in a warehouse ten minutes from here. Take this truck and go alone." Cahill got out as Cillian pulled up behind Tom. "I'll make sure Cillian stays here. Go in there and buy some time," he ordered as Tom climbed into the driver's seat.

"I thought—"

"Don't think. Instincts," Cahill told him. "And fight like hell."

CHAPTER TWENTY-NINE

Cillian waited inside the car, with Xavier and Elvis having pulled their truck to a different location to watch for incoming enemies. Cahill remained with him, but outside the truck, smoking and waiting. They were in a fairly deserted area, and Mal was supposed to meet them here. In the meantime, Cillian kept his eyes glued to the computer, watching Prophet struggle.

And all the while, John continued to spar with Prophet. Cillian wanted to believe that Prophet was playing at being hurt more than actually being so . . . he had to believe that, because every blow? Cillian swore he felt it.

Half an hour later—a lifetime, at this point—and John stopped beating Prophet long enough to take a phone call. Cillian tensed, waiting for John to acknowledge that Tom was there, but all John did was listen, nod and then put the phone back down. He was headed back toward Prophet when a knock on the door distracted him. He called for whoever it was to "Come in," and a man popped his head in and said, "He's here," and John told him, "You know what to do."

Only then did he turn toward the camera and say, "Cillian, are you out there? Waiting? Watching? Disapproving that Tom is coming in?" John smiled through his split lip. "Listen, I'm sorry we couldn't formally meet, but hey, I guess I owe you one for almost finishing the job and killing that fucker, Mal."

Cillian wanted to smash the computer to the ground but he restrained himself, because it was his only window to Prophet and Tom.

"Listen, I'm just letting you know that we've received Tom, alive and well, for now. And word to the wise—this place is wired to blow. Don't think about storming in unless you want Prophet and Tom to die, all right? With that, I'm afraid I've got what I want, so I'm ending your viewing experience."

The screen went black, cutting off all access. Cillian knew where he was but could do nothing to stop John without risking Prophet's and Tom's lives, and now he prepared to smash the computer, but Mal caught his wrists.

Cillian stared into those damned dark-as-coal eyes and went still, let Mal subdue him subtly and take the computer from him. "It's not good."

Mal put the computer down on the hood of the truck, then signed, *But it might be at some point.*

"How the hell did you get here so fast?"

I have my ways, Mal signed.

"I tried to stop Tom," Cillian told him.

No one can stop Tom. Or this. Sometimes, the only way to get through hell is to walk right through it.

Tom had pulled up to the building and the truck was immediately surrounded. He stuck his hands out the window and let the men open the truck door. One of them wrenched him out and tried to throw him on the ground—and Tom lunged up and slammed him against the concrete, his hands around the man's throat.

A hood went over his head. A slam to the kidneys and he was being dragged, hands behind his back, up some stairs and thrown unceremoniously into a room. He was patted down, his boots taken, his shirt ripped off. And then his hands were suddenly untied and he yanked the hood away . . . and saw the six men standing there, watching him.

He looked around and realized he was inside of a fighting ring. "Where's John?"

One man stepped forward and got into the ring with Tom. "You will need to get through us first. If you cannot?"

"Bring it," Tom told him with a sneer. "I've got some extra energy to burn."

Two hours.

Six men down.

They'd taken themselves out of the fight before he could totally incapacitate any of them, and he'd called them fucking cowards. He was hurt, of course, but he'd crawl naked over broken glass to get to Prophet . . . and that's basically the gauntlet he'd just run.

Now, broken, they'd bring him to John.

Cahill made him run the scenarios the other night purposely, knowing what Tom would be up against, and still it wasn't enough preparation. Nothing would be to find Prophet strung up—again— bleeding and bruised—and John, waiting for him in the ring.

John looked like the pictures of him Tom had seen, except older, leaner, and still Tom hated him on sight. There was a palpable energy radiating off him, and as good of a judge of character as Prophet was, how the hell had he gotten so taken in?

Prophet thought he and John were alike. For a long time, this was how Prophet had seen himself.

Tom was looking at what Prophet'd thought he was, and whether he ever could have turned out like John had he chosen a different path wasn't something they'd ever know.

Well, Tom supposed they were all just a couple of steps away from John's chosen path at any given time.

"Tom, so great to finally meet you," John boomed. "Hear you've got an anger problem."

"Hear you're a fucking asshole," Tom shot back.

"I'm definitely going to enjoy this. You picked a good one, Prophet." John smiled. "You've made it through the gauntlet, I see."

"Just so I can have the pleasure of killing you."

"You don't have it in you to kill, Tom. Not me. Not when you know Prophet will never forgive you for it. Not really." John's goading dug deep. Tom kept his expression neutral as he moved forward. He had a small knife that he'd pickpocketed off one of the men who'd strip-searched him and it was now hidden in the waistband of his boxer briefs. He figured it could too easily be turned against him and instead, he palmed it off, dropping it as he passed Prophet.

In perfect synchronized motion, Prophet pushed his bound hands back and caught it . . . letting Tom know he wasn't as hurt as he appeared.

"Back away from him or I kill him on the spot," John said, holding a gun pointed at Prophet's head.

Tom put his hands up and moved away from Prophet, who'd turned to look at him.

Tom could see the look in Prophet's eyes. He was having trouble seeing, but he was also tired. Not from the fight or lack of sleep, but rather from the internal war that'd been waged inside his mind for years. His brain was exhausted, and, for the first time in all of this, Tom was really and truly worried about Prophet.

But Tom also knew what he needed to do, and anything else that was happening was merely a distraction to the one goal he'd come here to accomplish: *kill John.*

It surprised him that it wasn't *save Prophet* . . . but his subconscious knew that killing John was the only way to accomplish that.

Kill John equaled killing the ghosts. Prophet would say it wasn't that simple but right now it seemed it was. Didn't matter that the others were out there, righting John's wrongs, that John dead or alive didn't matter to anyone but the people in this room (because he was basically toothless now, dead either way) and he was fighting the fight of the desperate. Which made him very dangerous.

That made two of them. Two very desperate and dangerous men ready to face off tonight.

"Center of the ring, Tom," John ordered, and Tom did as he was told, because it was one step closer to freedom. His body ached but need burned inside of him, hot and ready.

John nodded when Tom stood in place, and he put the gun on a high shelf behind him, out of both their reach if they were on the ground, struggling.

Buy time.

This was the beginning of the end for their plan. This fight to the death would be the culmination. Tom said a quick prayer as he moved toward John, fighting every urge to break the man's neck on impact.

CHAPTER THIRTY

I n the middle of this hellhole of a city, in a continent of complete unrest and sudden, unexpected beauty, Mal waited less than five klicks from the place where his best friend was going through hell.

Again.

The dense humidity closed around him, cloaking him. Choking him. Restless, he paced. He wasn't helpless. He was doing what Prophet had asked, had made him promise to do: stand down. And he'd agreed, knowing what would happen inside John's house of no fun . . . and now he knew there was only one way they were getting Prophet and Tom out in one piece. Even if they killed John, their escape was dependent on how everything was rigged. John wasn't going to let Prophet go that easily, if at all.

"He's going to be okay." Cillian's smooth brogue interrupted his thoughts.

Mind reader now?

"You don't believe I'm thinking the same things you are?"

Sit and wait goes against how I'm made.

"Again, Mal, tell me something I don't know." Cillian leaned against the car and Mal stopped pacing, trying to translate his words into thoughts rather than the action he wanted.

Something isn't right here, he finally signed. *John's too confident. He had to have known Agent Paul might be compromised, but he wanted Prophet anyway.*

"He's confident because he's got a fortress that self-destructs," Cillian growled, then stopped. "But does it really matter if there's another reason? We can't concern ourselves with whether or not he has the missing specialist now."

No, it doesn't matter. The time for buying time? Just ended, Mal announced. *You drive.*

Cillian nodded and neither man wasted time getting into the truck, Cillian already calling Cahill, who, along with Xavier and Elvis, was parked far enough away to avoid suspicion, and they soon pulled behind to follow, Cahill in the driver's seat, window opened, asking, "What now?"

Get as close as you can. I'm going in there, Mal signed.

"And do what?" Cillian asked, although he didn't seem averse to the idea.

I'll take apart any bombs I can get to quietly. That way, if he wants to blow the place . . .

"There are less explosives that could kill them," Cillian finished.

"I'm sure he's rigged the inside too," Cahill added.

We've got to start somewhere. Then we figure out how to get Prophet and Tom out when the time's right—but make sure we keep John and his men in.

"Then let's get started," Cillian agreed and made his way through the city in the darkness. "Blue's trying to disable the bombs at John's, but says they're too low tech."

Low tech can still cause a hell of a lot of damage.

"He's also trying to get eyes inside, to see Prophet and Tom, but no luck."

I'm not surprised. John always was a control freak—he'd cover that base first thing.

"You always hated him."

On sight, Mal agreed.

"What did he do to you?"

To me? Nothing. But have you ever just looked at someone and seen their demons on the surface? he asked, and Cillian nodded. *John? He was the demon.*

Cillian stopped asking questions after that.

The music hummed in the background, the hard drumline beating in time with Mal's pulse. He stayed inside his own head as Cillian navigated, going over his knowledge of explosives, ruminating briefly over what could go wrong and what could go right and everything in between. There were pros and cons to this plan, and Mal comforted himself that taking out the explosives outside the building wasn't the same as breaking his promise to Prophet.

"They're going to be okay," Cillian said finally, when Mal's mind cleared and fuck, maybe the guy was a mind reader.

And still, there was no reason not to be an asshole. *Do I look like I need reassurance?*

"Maybe I do," Cillian said, in an uncharacteristic confession.

This is a long time coming. Mal turned his head to catch a breeze through the opened window, letting the wind race against his skin. *But you already knew that.*

He felt Cillian's eyes on him, as if trying to discern if Mal meant any malice toward him with those words. But Cillian just let that hang between them, a wall of uncertainty that neither man had the time to climb or knock down at the moment. Hell, maybe Mal fortified it purposely, to get himself through the next hours.

Are you clear on your mission? Mal signed when they pulled in a blind spot, as close to John's building as they dared.

"You still don't trust me."

Are you clear on your mission? Mal repeated. *Because originally, you were willing to kill Prophet in order to keep John alive. So I don't know where you are on any of this. I don't know if you're still the CIA's bitch ...*

Cillian was on him, pinning him to the seat, which was a dangerous fucking move, and one that Mal appreciated. It gave him a chance to look Cillian in the eye. "I was never the CIA's bitch. Or SB-20's. I learned my lessons, Mal. Learned them the hard way." He backed off into his own seat. "Prophet didn't want this."

Since when do you do what Prophet wants? Mal demanded, assuming he meant the rescue and not the breeding suspicion, but it could've been both.

"Is he stable enough for all of this?"

It'd be worse if he was.

Tom's entire body ached, and that only served to fuel his anger. It felt good to finally unleash it, let it run wild without fear of reprisal because this time? Killing someone was exactly what he was supposed to do.

John stood in the ring across from him, Prophet still bound in the corner, watching them.

John took a step toward him. "We have a lot in common, Tom."

"What? Daddies who beat the shit out of us? Wanna bond over that?" Tom taunted, saw the briefest flash of vulnerability before the anger replaced it. "That's right—Prophet told me your deep dark Daddy issues."

John smiled suddenly. "I thought we could bond over Prophet, because, try as you might to stop it, we still share him. I'm sure he wakes you up at night with my name in his mouth."

Tom's anger rose swiftly and he could almost hear Prophet telling him to calm the fuck down. To remember what happened the last time he fought someone and lost complete control. He'd almost killed someone on their first mission together . . . and right now, that would fuck up the entire plan. "That's in the past for you. He's my future, and that's what this giant temper tantrum of yours is all about. You couldn't get your ex-boyfriend's attention, so you tried to blow up the world? Fucking pathetic."

"He's only thinking about you when you force him to. Even when you're inside of him, he's thinking about me. And he always will."

Fucking, he was playing on Tom's deepest, most secret insecurity. And wasting time, which was the point of all of this, he reminded himself. "Why? Still pissed about Daddy? Mine just used me as a punching bag. Yours was looking for pussy."

John lunged and they made contact briefly, with John slamming his forehead against Tom's, and Tom taking that and slamming John back with a hard hit to the man's shoulders.

Tom would say the most disgusting, hateful things, words he didn't mean and would never say to another survivor of sexual violence—anything to keep John angry. But rape was about power and right now, John held it. And one of the strongest counters to power? Anger. Pride, even. "You can talk about Prophet's dick all night. We all know the one you miss the most is Daddy's."

It only took a beat for John to come at him again, John's palm wrapping around his throat, squeezing and for a long moment, Tom watched the burn of pure hatred in his eyes. Even as he struggled for air, he was aware of another pain—and Prophet's yell—but he brought his elbows down on John's arms, breaking the hold.

Behind him, Prophet's protests continued. Maybe they'd hate each other for this later and Tom would have to live with that, with everything that happened in this room today.

"I've seen you fight, you know. I know it's dirty," John said with a sneer. "You almost killed Ivan that night."

Rage burned through Tom—whether John was actually there the night he fought was irrelevant. But he forced himself to stand still and make John react. "I was stronger than your brother Chris, though."

John charged like a bull, and Tom braced, took the hit, and stumbled back with John, which allowed him to wrap his arms around John's head and shoulders and semi-immobilize him as they fell, and then rolled.

They hit hard, Tom landing on his shoulder, John elbowing his chest, but Tom used the momentum to shoot a leg out and roll John under him. He used his hand to grab the front of John's hair and slam his head a few times against the wood floor, stunning him momentarily. But the man had a hard fucking head and lunged up to try to grab for Tom's throat again.

Tom evaded, jumped up from his knees straight to his feet and out of the way before John attempted to knock him down again.

John rolled and got to his feet as well in a swift moment, but he wobbled just enough to let Tom know he'd knocked something loose.

Tom brushed the hair and blood out of his eyes and suddenly, he was woozy.

Dizzy as fuck. Had John drugged him?

He blinked and his hand went to his biceps where he'd registered the brief pain earlier.

"You didn't think this would be a fair fight, did you, Tom?"

Tom blinked and saw John standing above him. One minute, he'd had John in a headlock and the next, the world was spinning. "You . . . drugged me." His voice felt thick, like he was pushing the words through molasses.

"Give the man a prize." John was trussing him up, tying knots and using metal cuffs on top of it in order to ensure Tom wasn't moving.

He had a knife now, and Prophet was calling him off, yelling for John to "Take it out on me instead," and John turned to Prophet.

"There's plenty of time for that, Proph." His attention went back to Tom, who couldn't move his body no matter how hard he tried. Even breathing wasn't easy, and that's all he could concentrate on, because John wasn't going to kill him, not now. Not until he'd made Tom suffer, and Tom knew he hadn't suffered nearly enough.

John bent down and ran a finger along the dreamcatcher on Tom's biceps . . . and then he dragged the knife across it, following the same path, like he was ruining it. Cursing it. Rendering it ineffective. Taking its luck.

John smiled, like he knew. "Bad luck, Tom? How're your other partners doing? All dead, right? This won't end any differently, but you knew that. You always do."

Tom smelled fear and pain and blood, all of it washing over him as his body became a lead prison, the mat sticky under him, the sweat and the drug making him shiver. Useless adrenaline raced through him, because he knew what John had planned now, knew it in a flash, and there was nothing Tom could do to stop him.

Not when John dragged him over to face Prophet with a clear view and told him, "Figured because you like to watch Prophet's dick so much, that you'd enjoy this. Bet you only want what's best for him."

Prophet turned his head from Tom and looked up at John, who dipped his mouth to Prophet's. And then Prophet was kissing John and Tom wanted to unsee it, wished he could look away but for Prophet, no. This wasn't enjoyable—it was about dominance—and Prophet's kisses told Tom he was desperately trying to gain that dominance.

He blinked—hard—to stay conscious, because he had to. For Prophet.

John was whispering to Prophet, telling him that he loved him, he'd kill for him—all the normal, romantic ways to Prophet's heart. Tugging Prophet's pants off, tying his legs down to match his arms, even though Prophet appeared to be so drugged he could barely move. Or maybe he was faking.

Tom prayed that he was just faking it. That he was just wasting time. Buying time . . . and still, he couldn't help but shake the feeling that they were also running out of it and fuck, they were never getting it back. Everything that happened tonight was important.

Irreversible.

Bad loque, Tom.

He tried to shove his thoughts into Prophet's brain before Tom lost it completely, until something niggled. Instead of forcing it, he stopped. Listened for Prophet's thoughts and knew that Prophet would tell him that he *wasn't bad luck.* That Tom *needed to hold on and fucking trust him.* That he hated what he was forced to do. How it was all a means to an end.

Hold on and trust. Because right now, that's all he could do.

Mal wiped sweat from his eyes as he traced his steps back around John's building, checking the wires and blasting caps. Nothing too sophisticated, which made them both easy to disarm—and yet that much more unstable.

Cillian was watching his six from a higher perch that covered the front (and only, besides the windows) entrance. John's bodyguards were all camped out inside, and in the dark, Mal was able to avoid the cameras and clip wires surreptitiously. And that was a good thing, even though he had a sinking feeling that the bombs inside were far more plentiful and probably much harder to dissemble.

His phone buzzed in his pocket as he made his way down the street toward Cillian. He answered it by tapping a code, so King knew it was him, and heard, "Mal, we're good. All three triggers have been disabled and the bombs detonated safely. I repeat—all three triggers have been disabled. How do we proceed?"

The phone line crackled on King's end, letting Mal know it was a shit connection, but relief coursed through him just the same. He tapped the phone three times to let King know he'd gotten the message loud and clear. This was where being unable to speak got frustrating, but he'd learned that letting the frustration win wasted too much time. Handing the phone off to Cillian wasn't an option. This was about his team, and he needed to push all the anger down and deal, so he continued tapping the phone—his location in Morse code—until King repeated the coordinates back to him.

"We're about three hours out, by plane," King told him.

Too long, Mal tapped.

"We're still headed your way," King insisted. "Don't turn your damned phone off."

Cillian was watching him. "Tell me it's done."

It's all done, Mal mouthed and, even in the dark, Cillian read him. That might worry Mal more than anything, but he pushed that thought aside for the other one crowding his brain.

Too easy. Too fucking easy. And he'd learned early that *easy* meant *fucked*. Yes, thousands of innocent lives had been saved—the sarin gas bombs had been rigged to blow, so crisis averted, and thank fucking Christ for that.

But there was a bigger crisis unfolding. And he'd lived shit like that one too many times for the hairs on the back of his neck not to prickle.

"Blue's trying to disable the bombs inside but they're not high tech—just dangerous as hell," Cillian told him. "Still, he managed to get us a way in that's not rigged."

A way in's a way out, Mal signed.

CHAPTER THIRTY-ONE

T*his isn't happening.*
Prophet was pretty good at living in reality, but now he was going to pretend none of this was real, that this was all some fucking flashback from hell . . . that John wasn't climbing on top of him while Tom was in the room.

"Come on, Proph." John's voice was gentle. "Like the old days."

He wanted to say, *In the old days, you'd never do this to me,* but that would be a lie. This—all of this that John had meticulously set up for him—was a callback to the night before the mission with Hal. But back then, he hadn't been drugged and tied and hurt—he'd told himself that he'd given in to John because it was easier than fighting, that letting John get him off hadn't done any harm . . . but it had.

This would as well. "The old days were a fucking lie, John."

John smiled, the corners of his eyes crinkling. "You're finally getting it—I haven't changed. This is who I always was—and you knew it. Everyone tried to tell you that. I'm flattered you still believed in me, but you shouldn't have. Not after the night before that mission. You knew then, but hell, you've got a sentimental streak a mile wide." John leaned in to kiss him again, open-mouthed, intense, demanding.

If I have to fuck someone else, it's to save lives . . . and not mine.

Prophet closed his eyes as he repeated the words he'd told Tom in his head . . . and gave in. Between the drugs and the bindings, there wasn't much else to do, and he knew it wasn't going to stay this gentle.

"One for the road," John murmured.

"You're not taking me with you? Isn't that what this is—you wanting me back? You got me."

John stilled, and the spell was broken, irrevocably, the way it'd been since the day Prophet had killed Hal. "Give it up, Prophet. You're letting me fuck you in front of him to prove your loyalty to me. I'm fucking you in front of him to prove you'll never forget me. We're definitely not on the same page."

"You don't have that much power over me," he said as if breaking it to him gently.

"Easy to say now."

Nothing was easy, but Prophet? He was done pretending. He turned his head away from John's kiss, but John grabbed his chin roughly and forced Prophet to meet his eyes. "I guess the game's up, right? No more playing nice with John?"

"Right. No more." Prophet made out the shadow of John's smile.

"Ready to watch the world blow up?"

"Show me what you've got, John. 'S'what I'm here for, right?"

John pushed off him and headed toward the computers, giving Tom a vicious kick on the way. Tom groaned and cursed John, and John just laughed and began typing once he reached the computer.

"'S'all right, Proph," Tom managed to slur and Prophet nodded, staring at his mismatched eyes more from memory than from actual sight.

"Shut the fuck up," John told him, obviously agitated. Prophet heard him hitting several more keys, then pausing . . . and then the same thing, hitting the same sequence over and over four more times.

Job's done. Triggers dissembled. Bombs disarmed. Go motherfucking team.

He forced himself to keep his mouth shut, to let John's being distracted happen so he could try to fucking free himself . . . but breaking his wrists, again, wasn't going to work. The cuffs were too tight, and when he was younger, he'd probably do it and risk the inherent nerve damage, but he was older and supposed to be wiser.

He'd find another way.

Glancing over toward the computers, he saw a light—a screen flickering—and he could make out a man. A video call, and one John wasn't bothering to hide. Prophet heard the all-too-familiar sounds of someone being beaten and then a yell.

John froze as another voice on the screen said, "I guess the guy's not a mute after all."

Then the feed was cut off and John's rage lit up the room, slicing through Prophet's triumph like a knife through butter.

"Guess time really is up," Prophet said, more to Tom than to John.

Tom snorted, and then Prophet heard the kick, followed by Tom's angry howl that sounded far stronger than it probably should, given the drugs, as John shadowed past before leaning in and telling Prophet, "You think you're so smart. So Mal escaped and he's probably lying in wait, right? I'll blow the shit out of him along with you."

"And yourself too? You're dying for your cause now? Identifying with all those suicide bombers? Because altruism isn't something I normally identify with you."

Prophet caught the movement and braced himself as John slammed him across the cheekbone. Prophet's teeth vibrated and he prepared for another kind of onslaught. He turned his head to stare at Tom, who refused to turn away. He ignored the pain (the whole *pain is weakness leaving the body* theory was surprisingly accurate, he'd learned early on) and because he couldn't stop it, he let it happened. Because the only way to go through hell was to keep going.

John walked away again, but when he came back, Prophet heard the slushing of water in a bucket.

Fuck.

Before he could take a full breath, John covered his face with a towel and began waterboarding him. Prophet had been through this countless times, both during training and in real-life situations. It taught him not to panic but it never, ever got easier. In some ways, it got harder, because he knew just how bad it was. Holding his breath wasn't enough—the water went into his nose, down his throat, and mere breath-holding did shit.

Prophet forced himself to count. Got to fifty before the water stopped and he coughed his goddamned lungs up. Said, "That all you got?" which, of course, earned him another round of water torture, and never let it be said that he took the easy way out.

After John stopped, probably because he ran out of water, he ripped the towel off his face. Prophet blinked and coughed and choked while John watched him.

Finally, when he caught his breath, he looked over at Tom, who appeared to be thrashing furiously. And when he turned his head back to John and knew what he had to do to end this. It was going to hurt like a bitch, but hey, so did life. "Just fucking do it, John."

"You want it, Proph—that what you're telling me?" Something flashed in John's eyes that even Prophet's blurred ones caught.

For the briefest of seconds the old John was with him—at fourteen and seventeen and twenty-two in boot camp, both of them scared and exhausted and exhilarated all at once, their bodies aching in unfamiliar places, their minds swimming with so much new intel about battles and ammo—the words swimming . . . but words they both knew would save their lives if they let them. Their shared time of being beaten, threatened with rape . . . of being stripped and tortured and still those words from boot camp running through his mind, telling him he could get through anything. That he always had.

Always would.

Let the words save your life. "Yeah, John, I want you. You've made me wait too long. Never found what I needed. So don't hold back now."

John entered him raw and fuck, it hurt like hell, but he bit down and refused to show any reaction. The rest of his body was numb anyway, from whatever drugs John had made him ingest, and his eyes still blurred as he tried to look at the entire scene dispassionately. Fucking for intel. Fucking to save lives. He could live through this. He would.

John began to jack him as he pumped and thrust, anger fueling him. "Just like before that mission, right, Proph? Made you enjoy it then."

"That was different." Much different, because Prophet wasn't hard this time, and it was pissing John off.

"It's never different with us. Same old shit," John panted in time with his thrusts.

"Four weeks, John. Four weeks, three days, two hours and forty-six minutes." His breath came in small hitches as he spoke of their time in captivity together. "After we got through that together, we should've been able to get through anything."

"Shut the fuck up, Prophet." John grit his teeth and continued his assault, but his rhythm faltered.

"They tied us up. Stripped us. Drugged us. Beat us. And you did the same thing to me. You're no better than them," Prophet goaded.

John went at him harder, although he was losing his erection. He put his palm around Prophet's throat and began to squeeze.

"Guess you and Lansing have a lot more in common than I realized," he managed, his voice rough and barely there.

In the background he heard Tom yelling. Thrashing. Fighting.

Neither of them knew any other way.

Prophet flailed, attempted to buck John away but only succeeded in getting him to ease up on his throat, and his voice was hoarse when he told John, "It's not going to happen."

"Maybe this isn't, but something is, Prophet . . . something bigger."

"You won't be around to see it."

"Funny, you talking about me seeing," John said, his hand going up to Prophet's throat again. He started to squeeze but his mouth suddenly froze, mid-smile, half-open and with a gurgle, and Prophet blinked at the sudden clarity.

Tom. How the hell he'd gotten out of his restraints, Prophet had no idea, but Tom was free, twisting a knife into John's armpit, pointing it downward, and then John stopped fighting and collapsed, dead. Tom had popped his heart with the knife, an impressive move.

Prophet put his head back down and struggled to breathe as a sudden panic filled him, until Tom yanked John off him, the body hitting the floor with a heavy thud. Prophet breathed, lay there, refusing to assess the damage. It was too fucking great at the moment to deal with. "Fuck. How, T?"

"Thanks to piercings that double as handcuff keys . . . and Mal's list," Tom muttered as he worked feverishly on Prophet's cuffs, trying to be quick and gentle at the same time. Prophet's arms were stretched overhead and they were numb. Tom rubbed the circulation back, and it hurt, but it was necessary pain. "Can you see?"

"A little bit. Fucking waterboarding was good for something." He shifted when Tom freed his hands, then tried his free wrist and shook his head at how badly the thumb had swelled. He tested the other, still in the cuff, gingerly.

Broken too. Again.

Tom freed his legs, did the same massage to get his blood flowing and then brought his pants over, helped shove them up and on, because hell, this wasn't over. Prophet ignored the stickiness between his thighs as he zipped up and thought about the easiest way to break the hell out of this place.

Except, at the moment, even though he was seeing better, it was just clearer shadows.

It won't be as bad as this, he consoled himself. The drops were worse than his final sight would be. He knew that because he'd asked his eye specialist to simulate it for him, and this kind of drop was the best he could do.

Of course, it could be worse, Dr. Salen had reminded him, and Prophet nicknamed him the Angel of Death.

To his face.

Now, he sat back and fought a sob, because this was far from over, and waited for the sense of relief that would wash over him soon enough. He wasn't sure he'd taken a full breath since John grabbed him at the airport. He'd been keeping it together for so long that he wasn't sure what the fuck would happen. When he finally allowed himself to let go.

So he didn't.

Instead, he did what he could, by rote. "I'm an old man," he muttered.

"But you're my old man. And you're far from helpless," Tom told him angrily. "Can you stop feeling sorry for yourself before we blow up?"

Even as he said that, Tom was next to him, holding him. Cradling both wrists. Cradling Prophet, until Prophet pulled back. "I can't, Tom. Not now. Can't fall apart yet."

And Tom, as always, understood. "Then let's go."

Prophet let himself be tugged up off the floor, but then something somewhere beeped. Both men froze as the loud sound continued, echoing in the cavernous space.

"Is that a bomb?" Tom asked.

"He said the place was wired to blow." Prophet scanned the room and saw the box on the wall. "Shit—he's got a check-in system, and it's not just for the disabled triggers—it's for inside here too."

"He was ready to blow himself up too, the asshole. What am I looking for?"

"He kept going over to the computers—check for a place to scan his fingerprints at certain intervals or the bombs detonate," Prophet explained, but Tom was already up and no doubt looking for the box.

"Found it," Tom called out seconds later, and then he ran back over, put a phone in Prophet's hand and then grabbed John. "The touch pad needs John's fingerprints. He's still warm—we'll get a little time, but it looks like this is set at shorter intervals for the rest of the night." Prophet heard him dragging John's body across the floor. "Okay, it worked. But shit, we've only got five minutes."

"Asshole," Prophet grunted. He fumbled with John's phone several times, squinting, then he took a deep breath, unfucked himself, and hit the keys by rote. He'd been trained to dial and activate calls without looking. "I'm calling Mal. I'm hoping he's close."

As he spoke, there were explosions from below, making the entire building shake.

"Are we dead?" Prophet asked.

"It's gunfire. Flash bangs. Think it's our guys?"

"Fuck, hope so." He dialed the number again and then again when it went to voice mail. Finally, the call went through, as evidenced by Prophet hearing the explosions echoing directly into his ear. "Mal? Mal—it's me—stop trying to blow us the fuck up," he said, and held his breath until Mal began to tap. "Okay—we've got it. You're trying to get the bodyguards to come out so you can pick them off. But we need to come out. Place is wired to blow in five minutes." He waited again, listened, then said, "Got it."

"Three minutes." Tom input John's fingerprints. "Five again."

"We've got to get the hell out of here. Mal's driving John's men back in."

"To where?"

"Mal said there's a crawlspace on the first floor—takes us out into a window well. He'll keep John's men occupied."

"Hopefully they don't realize John's dead," Tom said as he helped Prophet out the door and down the stairs. They were both armed but thankfully only met with two men on the way down, and Tom took care of them easily with two quick and well-placed shots. At least

Prophet figured they were, because people stopped shooting at them after that.

"I've got the crawlspace," Tom told him. "It's small, but doable. We're going to have to crawl through. It's about twenty feet."

Might as well be a million, but hell, he was already partially in the dark anyway. "You go first. If I get stuck, it's easier to pull than push," Prophet reasoned and Tom didn't argue, which was good. They were out of time for that.

Tom shimmied in and began to commando crawl, dragging himself along by the strength of his arms and upper body. Prophet's momentum was halting since his wrists were damaged, and it was a slow, painful drag of his body.

He counted down the seconds in his mind.

Fuck, he was tired, but then Tom's voice echoed inside the enclosed space. "C'mon. For me. For Remy, dammit," and Prophet pushed onward, his wrists numb, his body like lead, and then he hit concrete and strong hands were yanking him up out of the window well he'd been dumped into and he was being carried—fast. The explosions hit behind him and pushed him forward—and Tom and Mal, who'd been holding him up, and the ground came up fast to meet him. He felt the heat first and then the rain of debris cutting his skin, the onslaught like a thousand needles, and squeezed his eyes closed out of habit.

When he opened them, he was half buried under Tom, and he barely made out Mal, who was leaning over him worriedly. The fire burned hot enough for him to still feel it, and he managed, "We need to get the hell out of here."

He could practically hear Mal rolling his eyes and fuck, he was never so grateful for that. Mal and Tom got him up and into the waiting truck, with Cillian in the driver's seat. For a long moment, they all stared at the burning warehouse.

If only fire could burn away the memories too.

CHAPTER THIRTY-TWO

As they drove to a new safe house, Tom sat with Prophet and Mal in the back as Cillian drove, with Cahill, Elvis and Xavier leading the way. Of course, Prophet continued to fight any sort of help they tried to give him, arguing that "Tom's in worse shape than I am."

"Way to throw me under the bus," Tom told him as Mal tried to force an oxygen mask over Prophet's face and ended up compromising by just holding it close enough for blowby. And the only reason Prophet allowed even that was because Tom said, "C'mon—you do that and I'll call King and let him know we're okay."

"One piece, both of you?" was the first thing King asked after hearing Tom's voice.

"Both of us," Tom told him. "Say hi, Prophet."

Prophet yanked Mal's hands—and the mask—away from his face. "Hi Prophet."

"Still an asshole," King said fondly. "So . . . it's done?"

"It's fucking done," Tom assured him as he watched Prophet and Mal literally wrestle over the O2 mask.

King muttered something in Gaelic that sounded suspiciously like a prayer. "We're meeting you at the newest safe house. Keep in touch."

"We will." After he hung up, he glanced at Prophet's messages. "Proph, you've got a message from LT." He scanned it quickly because he couldn't help himself, and then he went to hand the phone to Prophet, who said, "Read it, Tom."

His eyes. Right. Shit. They were better, but when Tom looked closely, he could see that they were still slightly unfocused. "LT said that he got intel about the specialist. He's got her, Proph. He says she's safe."

"Jesus. More than I could've hoped for," Prophet mumbled, and, from the driver's seat, Cillian let out a harsh breath.

"I guess I have to hate him a little less." Tom leaned his head back, because he was just starting to notice that his entire body was one giant ache. Prophet's legs were on his, his upper body was on Mal, the three of them crammed back here "like idiots," according to Cillian.

Cillian kept talking to him though, like he thought Tom had a concussion and didn't want him to sleep. And when Cillian wasn't talking to both him and Prophet, Mal was hitting both of them. But finally, they were at the safe house.

Both he and Prophet needed a doctor—and both of them refused. Still, Tom allowed Mal to check him over once inside only because he knew then Prophet would let him do it too. Because Prophet was still attempting to micromanage and Mal was bitching silently, which was damned impressive.

Mal pointed out, by literally pointing, that Tom needed to put his piercings back in.

"So does Prophet," Tom added. He grabbed the baggie from his go-bag and Prophet reached into his pocket and pulled out his.

Mal continued cursing both of them, first as he cleaned Prophet's nipple ring and then signed to Tom, *Do you want to put this back in?*

As much as Tom wanted to, his hands were still shaking from the earlier ordeal, all the adrenaline pouring off him. He shook his head and Mal smirked and signed, *Guess I'll be doing yours too.*

"Fuck that, Mal. I'll do them," Prophet said loudly, stood, and then groaned and sat back down. "Fuck it. Touch his dick. See if I care."

Tom watched Mal put Prophet's ring back in, cleanly and efficiently. He put his own tongue ring back in, and his own nipple rings, mainly to cut down having to watch Prophet watch Mal put in his cock piercings. The hiss of pain invigorated him and, to Mal's credit, it was fast. Professional.

Except for Mal's smirk once he was done. *Nice piercing pattern.*

"Fuck off," Tom told him, but even those short moments of exertion tired him out.

They were both in bad shape. Beyond the cuts they'd sustained from the blast, which Mal stitched up before too much time passed,

Tom also had a huge bruise on his abdomen that Mal indicated was a bruised spleen and no doubt broken ribs to go along with it. Prophet had those too, along with a matching concussion to Tom's.

"God, we're fucked." Prophet took shallow breaths, sounded like he was pushing words out painfully now that the adrenaline had worn off. Mal came toward him with a wrap for his ribs but Prophet backed away and begged off. "I need to shower first, man. Please."

Such a goddamned baby. Mal looked between him and Tom. *Both of you, clean up. Then I'll finish here.* But first, he wrapped the places he'd stitched and signed, *Don't let these get soaked.*

Prophet nodded. Mal left them and it was so damned quiet . . . and Tom wondered if he should've found an excuse to keep Mal in the room with them. Neither man made a move, toward the shower or otherwise, like they were both realizing the magnitude of what had happened. And Mal probably knew that instinctively, which was why he'd tried to hang around.

Tom finally broke the silence. "How long will we stay here?"

"Till dark, I'm guessing. And then we'll get out of dodge. For all I know, the CIA thinks we're dead."

"Fuck 'em. That's not an entirely bad thing," Tom grunted.

"Something's bothering me, though."

"Besides the busted ribs?"

"Yeah." He shook his head. "It's just . . . this was . . . easier than—"

"Easy?" Prophet's voice was dangerous as he cut him off and moved to stand so they were face to face. "Eleven years, T, and none of it's been easy. It may be anticlimactic for you—and that's good. But I spent my last sighted years stopping this man from hurting people . . . and hurting himself more than he already had. I caught him because he was ready. Because it was the end. I have to live with years of failure."

"Proph . . ."

But Prophet was backing away like he didn't recognize Tom. His face was pale, his eyes stunned.

"Proph, I only meant that . . . why would John let his guard down so easily?"

"Because I did the same damned thing," he practically yelled, then grabbed his side and glared at Tom.

It was Tom's turn to take a step back, Prophet's words pushing him as hard as a physical blow. It was nothing he hadn't known, that Prophet would have to let John in to catch him, but knowing it and seeing it happen? Two different things entirely.

He turned away, needing another second to just breathe and separate before they unintentionally hurt each other more, and so he headed toward the bathroom.

"If you walk out now . . ." Prophet called.

"What? Don't come back?"

"If you fucking run because things are hard, you're always gonna run."

Tom looked over his shoulder. "I'm not running, you asshole—I'm turning on the shower. What the fuck are you doing?"

Prophet stared at him. "I'm standing here, Tommy. Forcing you to look at what's here. To acknowledge what you heard me and John talking about. What you saw us doing. To let it go."

"You don't think I didn't know what you and John . . ."

Prophet's next words were halting. "You didn't know. Not all of it. Because I didn't tell you—on purpose. Maybe even selfishly. But if you can't handle this . . ."

"Don't you dare try to make this a reason to push me away, Lije."

At the sound of his nickname, spoken in Tom's soft drawl, Prophet started. Blinked. "Don't, T."

Tom felt Prophet's pain pouring off him in waves that threatened to pound them both and drag them under. "I'll fight dirty if I have to. All those years with him versus our short time together. But I *will* make you forget him."

At the growl in Tom's voice, Prophet's chin rose. "Then make me."

"I did it once. I can fuck the ghosts out of you again and again."

"Do it."

Jesus. That was all Prophet wanted. It was all Tom wanted too. He grabbed Prophet and tugged him close. Held Prophet against him. "I know it was the hardest thing."

"No. Losing you would be the hardest thing," Prophet corrected him. "Trust me. Everything else pales in comparison."

"What you did—"

"Tommy—"

But Tom put a finger over Prophet's lips and continued. "What you did . . . we have to forgive each other. You for doing that and me for not being there."

"You were there, helping me. Besides, I planned it."

"You can't even accept a goddamned truce? I know you did, Proph. But why you had to hurt yourself like that in the process . . ."

"Just pain, T. I can live with pain. Always have."

"If you add 'always will' . . ."

"It's the truth," Prophet protested stubbornly. "Guess your curse is really gone. Or maybe I'm your curse now."

Tom smiled, then cupped Prophet's face in his hands. It was a curse he could live with. And then, because arguing wouldn't do shit, he kissed Prophet, long and hard. At first, he felt Prophet's surprise—and surprising resistance—but in a second, Prophet was responding . . . the most reassuring feeling in the world.

When he pulled back, he knew Prophet couldn't see, and that it wasn't just the drugs but the disease, the stress, taking its toll. There was a certain look Prophet got—and no doubt didn't realize he did it, because otherwise Mr. Control Freak would make sure not to do it. Hell, Tom needed to know so he could comfort Prophet without babying him.

And yeah, it was *definitely* as complicated as it sounded.

Finally, Prophet lost it in silent sobs against Tom's chest. "Make me forget, Tommy. Please."

And with that, Prophet finally let go of his hard-won control. Let Tom take him into the shower (no casts yet—just soft wraps to keep the swelling down, to stop him from flexing). Washed him down. Prophet cried until Tom went over him twice with warm soapy water, each swipe of the soft washcloth stripping away a layer of hell.

"Tommy . . . what you saw . . ."

"I know." Tom's throat tightened. "It's still a violation, even if you agreed to it."

"Yeah," Prophet said hollowly. "Please . . . just make it go away now . . . can't sleep until you make it go away."

"Yeah," Tom echoed, gently tugged one of Prophet's legs up to wrap around his hip.

He used plenty of lube, because John had been rough and still, he knew no matter how slowly he went, how tenderly, it was going to hurt.

"It's okay, Tom. A good hurt," Prophet assured him as Tom pressed inside of him. His hands rested on Tom's shoulders, and Tom saw he was still wearing the bracelet. Tom was wearing his in tattoo form. And John was finally gone. Buried. Tom tenderly fucked the ghosts away while Prophet quietly cried out "Tommy," and finally, they were alone and it was just them. Coming. Holding. Connecting.

CHAPTER THIRTY-THREE

T om had texted Remy before he and Prophet slept, but ended up calling both him and Doc, because Remy insisted.

"He's smart. Wants to hear our voices," Prophet had murmured as Tom dialed. "It's something I'd do."

"God help us. Hey, Remy," Tom had said, and after several minutes of both of them reassuring him that they'd be home soon, they managed to find a semicomfortable position.

After maybe six hours of sleep—if you could call it that, but Tom wouldn't, since Mal woke them every twenty minutes—it was time for them to get moving again. Although they'd done what they'd promised the CIA, Prophet couldn't be sure that they'd been cleared yet. For the moment, Prophet was pretty sure everyone still thought John had them, and it was too risky to contact Rylan and blow his cover. Mal wanted to keep them moving, to another safe house, until they were able to speak to both the CIA and LT directly, because as of now, he hadn't returned Prophet's call or texts. There'd been no contact with him since the texts about Karen almost twenty-four hours earlier.

But, as Prophet pointed out, "Who the hell would I call at the CIA? Mal killed all of them."

Not all, Mal signed modestly. *I only maimed most of them. But with a little more time I'm sure I could exceed expectations.*

"Christ," Prophet muttered.

Let's move, Mal told them.

Tom wasn't about to argue with Mal, so at oh dark hundred, he carried his and Prophet's bags downstairs to bring them out to the waiting truck. He was aching but refused to let Prophet risk hurting himself any more. According to the doctor Mal had brought in during the early morning hours, Tom definitely had a bruised spleen and bruised ribs, which explained the extra level of pain.

The doctor told Mal that Tom really needed to be monitored at a hospital and Tom had sworn Mal to keep that from Prophet.

"He'll just worry. The job's done. As soon as we get the all clear, I'll go into the closest hospital and get it thoroughly checked out," Tom had promised.

Fine, I'll agree as long as you stop whining, Mal had signed back.

Now, Tom heard the whistling again, outside the door, the one he'd heard back at their first safe house. The one that reminded him of the bayou and a specific, niggling memory he couldn't place. The tune had stayed in his head, breaking through when John had been killed, driving him crazy and finally, his vision seemed to blur and clear and he realized he was staring at the bayou . . . and the house where Phil had come to Louisiana to check on a veteran Marine who had severe PTSD, saw the enemy everywhere at night and subsequently used his trees as target practice. Ultimately, Tom had helped Phil get the guy some much-needed help, and Phil helped Tom step away from the bayou—and the pain—and into EE, Ltd.

In the house of the rising sun . . .

When he heard the lyric in his head, he froze. Turned. Because it was Cahill whistling the tune as he leaned against his truck, ever-present cigarette smoke rising as he stared up at the sunrise.

Cahill.

He finally unfroze, shuddered as he got his feet to move, toward Cahill, gaining momentum as he went. Cahill remained still—until Tom reached out to grab him and instead, found himself pushed, cheek down, against the truck's hood.

"Fuck," he groaned, because it still hurt even though Cahill had been gentler than he'd expected.

"Relax, Tom. I'm not here to hurt you."

"Then what?" Tom struggled and Cahill let go and helped him straighten up. "What's going on?"

Cahill gave a dry smile. "Most of the time I don't even realize I'm whistling that damned song. I whistled it every day, all day, for the three months I was in captivity in Vietnam. They played the damned thing over and over. I'm not sure if it was torture or if they just really liked the song."

"It was you. The crazy vet."

Cahill shrugged. "I was just shooting at the stars."

"Were you in the bayou...?"

"For you? Yes. So Phil could pretend to stumble on you accidentally."

"But how? Why?" Tom demanded, and then noticed that Prophet was now standing behind him and, judging by the look on his face, he'd caught most of the conversation, confirmed it when he told Cahill, "You need to start talking."

"I guess now's as good a time as any." Cahill took a drag of his cigarette. "Tom, you were brought into the fold because of your association with Anthony Carnes. You knew him as Ollie Harris. Prophet met him as Hal Jones."

"Jesus Christ," Tom muttered and Prophet sighed.

"Tony was a Marine turned CIA spook during the Vietnam War. He was also a brilliant chemist—and he went undercover, taking a specialist's identity on in order to expose the selling of assets to the US's enemies."

Prophet frowned. "So Ollie...Hal...he wasn't a real specialist?"

"No. The real man behind Ollie and Hal—and I'm not at liberty to give you *his* real name—killed himself. Left a note that said he couldn't live in fear that he might be used to harm his country. So Tony took that opportunity to take his place. He'd been helping to rescue specialists as well as POWs. He realized that the CIA was selling assets for money and saying they were killed in transport. It was blood money. Tony—as Ollie and then Hal—had the list of men involved...and the money."

"That's why they took him, in the end," Tom said, and Cahill nodded.

"And I killed him," Prophet said slowly.

"You had to. You saved him from being tortured to death." Cahill touched his shoulder. "You saved him from hell."

"Small fucking comfort."

"I'd imagine yes, for him," Cahill said calmly.

"Did you know it was going to be me?" Prophet demanded.

"I knew who was on the job." Cahill turned to Tom. "You had potential. Tony saw that. Wanted you safe. Watched."

That eased Tom's mind. His mentor really had been his mentor. But Tom watched Prophet shift, knowing the question he wanted to ask and knowing he also hated doing so. But finally, Prophet did ask, "You knew John, didn't you?"

Cahill stared at Prophet under heavy lids. "I had to hope you weren't like him."

"That was a big risk, Cahill," Tom asked, still smarting from being part of this game and still, more than grateful.

"He didn't have much of a choice. Worse came to worse, the money would never benefit the men who wanted it and the list would never come to light. Best-case scenario?"

"Those men get what's coming to them," Tom said. "If the CIA can be trusted."

"Someone can always be trusted." Cahill gave Prophet a pointed look. "I'd rather be sure of who can't be."

"Who do you work for, Cahill?"

Cahill smiled. "Myself, these days."

"But you used to be CIA?"

"I'm a Marine, son. And then I was left behind, only to be rescued by Elvis and Xavier, just like I told you. I got out, and then I went back in. Sometimes the CIA helped us and sometimes they didn't."

"And Tony?"

Cahill shook his head. "He saved my ass—and a lot of other men too. He knew where all the bodies were buried. So they killed him. At least, they thought they did. He took the place of an asset who'd offed himself before Tony got there. Assumed his identity. And assembled the evidence and the money. No one suspected him—not at first, anyway."

"So why not trust you with the intel?"

"Only one man can keep a secret, Prophet. You know that. All I knew was that I was supposed to put Tom with Phil. We were like the underground railroad—we only knew what our parts were. This way we couldn't compromise the mission, accidentally or otherwise."

Even so, it was unfolding in front of all of them as they spoke, all the years of helping to hide assets, to keep them safe . . . from the very people who'd ordered them dead and yet still prepared to sell them to the highest bidder.

"Did we get a lot of them back?" Prophet asked.

"Yes, we did," Cahill confirmed. "You did, Prophet."

"What now?" Tom asked.

"There's an asset out there who's in trouble," Cahill said. "Karen was one of us. Brilliant mind. I'd hoped she was safe."

"Was?" Prophet echoed grimly "She *is* safe. LT texted to let me know, remember?"

Cahill shook his head. "Can't be. Ahmet's free, according to the chatter. The only one who could've gotten him out with no visible means of escape?"

"The woman who built the site," Tom murmured. "But this doesn't make sense. LT would never turn her over to anyone who'd hurt her."

Prophet was dialing—first LT, then Rylan, with no answer. "It's not even going to voice mail for either of them. Like a signal's jammed."

"Try Dean," Tom suggested.

At some point during their conversation, Mal had appeared, and judging by the look on his face, he'd heard more than enough.

"Same deal," Prophet said, obviously frustrated. "Something's wrong."

"Speaking of wrong . . . where's Cillian?" Tom asked.

Prophet turned to Mal, who in turn, sighed and signed, *Why're you looking at me?*

"Because you either killed him . . ."

You want him dead most of the time too, when you're not flirting with him, Mal pointed out.

Tom growled, which made Mal smile.

Prophet pointed at Mal. "Stop doing that. I invented that shit."

And I perfected it.

"You're both assholes," Tom told them. "And there's no blood."

I clean up well.

Tom rolled his eyes. "Cillian's gone and Ahmet escaped. What're the chances this is all a big coincidence?"

"Zero." Prophet shook his head. Cillian knew Dean had called him, but would Cillian have known about Karen? He knew a lot about

Prophet's life and work, but Prophet prided himself on his ability to keep national secrets vaulted.

It would also mean that he had seriously misread Cillian's intentions.

Any of them could be anywhere by now, Mal pointed out.

"I have to look for bodies, at the very least." Frustratedly, Prophet stared at his phone.

"Then let's get going," Tom said.

"You gonna be okay? You got pretty beat up."

"And you're not?"

"Tom, the danger's over. If you want to stay—"

"I'm going, asshole. Trying to leave me behind," Tom muttered as he crawled into the truck.

I think he misses Cillian, Mal signed.

"I heard that, you psychotic asshole," Tom growled.

"He's been hanging around us for too long." Prophet shook his head.

Mal signed, *I'll drive. You still look like hell and I need you rested when we get close.*

Prophet would allow it, because it was Mal. Because he was right. Cahill was watching all of them, even as Mal readied the truck and checked the systems.

"What if Karen went rogue on her own?" Cahill asked finally.

"And took out LT on the way," Prophet finished.

"Wasn't she skilled enough?" Tom asked. "I'd imagine if I was that wanted, I'd make sure I was."

"Point taken. But she was limited in her training. It's not like she could stockpile weapons."

Help on the outside, Mal signed one-handed, a shorthand he developed with the team. They had to fill in the blanks, but they were so like-minded on their missions, it worked seamlessly.

"Help, like Ahmet's team," Prophet muttered. "Where the fuck is Rylan?"

"How can they all be out of pocket?"

All together?

"I can't see Cillian and LT playing well together," Tom said wryly.

Whether he did or didn't, something's wrong, Mal reasoned. *Why just disappear without telling any of us . . . at the same time we can't find LT or Rylan?*

"I think we need to slow this down," Prophet said calmly. "Listen, if LT's compromised, by anyone, Dean's going to need protection."

And that at least, was one thing they could get behind wholeheartedly. The rest? Speculation that none of them wanted to believe, even though they couldn't just ignore it.

Speaking of not ignoring, Tom asked, "What if it's LT who's doing the compromising?"

"Dean's going to need protection," Prophet repeated.

"Then what the hell are you all doing standing here?" Cahill asked.

Dean and Reggie had waited for LT's plane take off in the hours before dawn, taking Karen to safety, and Dean had been restless ever since. Finally, he'd slept . . . until the nightmare woke him, had him sitting straight up in bed, yelling into the darkness as he recalled the night he'd lost his sight. And yeah, he guessed when the woman who was responsible for that came back from the dead and into his house, he needed to expect some fucking feelings.

He paced around aimlessly until 0500 and then he woke Reggie and Nico. He and Reggie decided to head to the closest clinic to check on the new construction, but mainly for Dean to clear his head. It was an hour away, the road between his house and the structure was more than half paved—a rarity—and Dean spent time talking with the doctors—Pei, who'd been here for over a year now, and Dr. Ron, who'd arrived six months ago, and the two nurses, discussing a plan for community outreach and vaccinations.

He always felt right when he was on these grounds, could picture them from memory, since he'd been coming to these clinics for much longer than he'd been without sight. He knew the low, white buildings were simple, signaled medical help to the community and that they were kept pristine by all the staff. He felt the rough fabric of the brightly colored kangas they used as blankets when they could, because they washed better and seemed less like a hospital, which comforted a lot of the local men, women, and children who came through here for medical help. The lilt of Swahili dialects in the air, the fact that he swore he could hear the broad smiles of a people who never gave up despite seemingly insurmountable odds, all of it combining to center him.

This was exactly where he belonged.

Several hours after arriving, they'd vaccinated about twenty children whose parents brought them by, and he took a break and stepped outside into the sunlight as he heard a truck pull up. He waited on the porch of the main building, hand on his weapon until Reggie came up beside him and said, "It's Nico."

"Did you call him?"

"No—he was staying back at the house today," Reggie confirmed. LT had wanted Nico to shadow Dean and Reggie for the next several days, had insisted on it, actually, but when morning came, Nico'd said he wasn't feeling well and Dean hadn't pushed it. He refused to fuck with anyone's intuition, which he suspected was happening.

He'd been confident that everything was fine and so far, it had been.

"Everything okay, Nico?" Dean called to him now. "We were going to head back home within the hour."

He heard Nico's boots come up onto the porch, but Nico waited until they were close before telling him, "No, it's not. And it couldn't wait—Ahmet's escaped the black site."

The world swayed. "Can't be. You must be hearing old chatter—they probably leaked it like a red herring."

"Yeah, I thought so too but . . ." Nico paused and put a hand on Dean's shoulder.

"That's why you stayed behind."

"I had a feeling I couldn't shake," Nico admitted. "Look, I've got good sources. I don't know what the fuck's going on, but it's not good."

"That's not possible." Dean stood and grabbed his phone. "I've got to call LT. He said he got her to safety. Maybe something happened to both of them."

"I tried to call, but something's jamming the signal out here," Nico said. "I'm going to find out if something happened during construction. I put in a call to Prophet too, but he's not answering. Neither's Tom."

He walked away as LT's phone went to voice mail. Dean sank down to sit on the steps, dialing the phone again. "Come on, LT. What the fuck happened?"

Had LT been taken, along with Karen? Wouldn't someone have contacted Dean?

He wasn't sure how long he sat there, waiting for LT to call. Maybe half an hour before going inside, mainly because the rain started unexpectedly. He heard Nico talking to Reggie about some kind of jammer close by and wandered into one of the empty rooms to sit and hold his phone.

He heard footsteps and figured Reggie had come to collect him. "I still haven't heard from LT."

"We can't make calls," Reggie told him.

"Signal jammer," Nico confirmed. "We really should get out of here."

Just then, Dean heard a truck in the distance. He also heard Nico and Reggie ready their weapons too. He tried to ignore the voice in the back of his head that told him things were really, really bad and instead, he lied to himself.

It's all going to be fine. It's always fine. LT makes sure it's fine.

Maybe it's time you stopped relying on LT to make things fine.

He told himself to shut up and told Nico to prepare for whatever—and whoever—was coming this way.

CHAPTER THIRTY-FOUR

Prophet sat in the passenger's side of the old Range Rover, with Tom in the back. Mal was the only one not playing hurt, so he did all the driving to Dean's house . . . and the fact that Cillian had packed up and left while they'd been sleeping remained an unspoken worry, a new construction in light of Ahmet's escape.

The betrayal in Mal's eyes had been painful for Prophet to see. But they all forged onward, for Dean.

King and the others had been called immediately after discovering Cillian's disappearance, and they chose to fly into Dean's house, since driving would've taken them far too long. They'd landed just before Mal pulled into the house, and were waiting to greet them.

"You look like hell," Ren said warmly, touching Prophet's shoulder like he was checking to make sure it really was him. An old gesture, one Prophet recognized and appreciated. Mal and King hugged but King merely did the light touch on the back to both Prophet and Tom.

"Hear you boys had a bit of a rough time," he said.

Hook's voice boomed. "I don't care what else happens. This was a victory. So fuck the long faces. We go find Dean and then we go home. Deal?"

Prophet smiled, because that was a deal he'd take.

They learned quickly from the guards at Dean's that Dean, Nico, and Reggie had all gone to the clinic . . . and that Nico had only gone because he couldn't get through to Dean or Reggie.

And still, Prophet couldn't reach any of them. King and the others borrowed one of Dean's trucks and followed behind Mal to the clinic, which was another hour's drive.

It seemed like years, and he barely let Mal stop the truck before he was getting out . . . and Nico was heading out of the clinic toward him, like he'd been expecting him . . .

"I'm glad you're here," Nico told him.

"I didn't realize how badly you missed me," Prophet started, but Nico cut him off with, "We've got a major problem, and you look like shit." Then Nico looked over his shoulder toward the porch of the main building, where Dean sat, unmoving. He looked more troubled than angry. Defeated, even.

"Thanks for caring about my well-being. I know something happened to LT," Prophet started, trying to ignore the rising feeling of dread in his already aching body. Everything was so normal here at the bustling clinic . . . and yet, he couldn't help but feel nothing really was. Kids were playing in the dust and he was discussing escaped terrorists.

"What the hell happened to you?" Nico demanded as he glanced at Tom, who looked equally shitty, Prophet knew.

"We ran into an old friend."

Nico's brows rose and he looked between both men. "And?"

"It's taken care of."

"Finally," Nico breathed. "One asshole down."

"LT," Prophet prompted, because there was time for storytelling later. "He's okay?"

Nico shook his head. "We don't know. I saw him late last night, when he came to pick up Karen. I was at the house when I heard that Ahmet escaped, and I tried calling here, but the signals were fucked."

"That's why we came here," Prophet explained. "LT left me a message last night—said he'd found the missing specialist—"

"Karen," Nico said, and Prophet frowned. "She came to Dean's house, Proph. Said you sent her there—told her to go if there was ever any trouble."

Prophet shook his head. "I never told her that."

"Because you knew," Nico started hesitantly, glancing back at Dean.

"Knew what? Cut this cryptic shit, Nico—there's not a lot of time if LT's in trouble." Prophet pushed past him and walked toward Dean, with Tom and Mal at his heels. The others stayed back with

Nico, but they were all within listening distance. "Dean, what the hell's going on?"

"Wish I knew, Proph." Dean took a deep breath and Prophet sat next to him, turning his body to face him.

Dean didn't reciprocate. "Did you know about Karen Sutter?"

"That's a pretty broad question, but simply put, yes, I knew Karen Sutter. I knew her as a specialist who needed hiding. So I hid her, and for a long time, she was fine. A couple of days ago, she ran, of her own accord—but I'm inclined to think she had some motivation."

Dean shook his head wordlessly.

"Dean, man, you turning mute too? Because I need some fucking answers."

"You think I don't!" Dean yelled. "What the fuck were you thinking, Prophet—keeping the woman who did this to me safe and never telling me? Letting me think she was dead."

"What?" The air left his lungs and hell, with the injuries, he hadn't been pulling in much to begin with. He put a hand to his chest and in seconds, Mal was there, tapping his chest—his way of telling Prophet to fucking breathe, man, and then there was an oxygen mask over his face and he was ripping it off because it was too much, too claustrophobic.

"Prophet—please—stop." Dean's voice. Dean's hand on his face.

"Back off, everyone," Hook said. "Give them some space."

Everyone must've listened because when Prophet looked up, it was just Dean, still sitting, and Prophet was lying on the porch, facing the land—the cars—the men who'd come with him. "Dean, I didn't—"

"You didn't know. You really didn't know." Dean's voice had returned to normal, not that icy cold shit that scared the hell out of Prophet.

"I thought the guy who hurt you was dead. Hell, I thought it was a he." Prophet reached out to grab Dean's hand. "LT said he killed that specialist."

"That's what he told me too," Dean started. "He never said anything about involving you in hiding her."

"He didn't approach me to do it. Another guy from the CIA did." Prophet wasn't sure how much Dean knew—or wanted to hear—but he pressed on anyway. "Karen had a son. She made a deal—the agent would place her son in a safe place with a new family and I'd hide her. No one knew where she was—I was the only contact."

"But she was free to go anytime."

"I was told she turned herself in voluntarily because she was tired of running. Someone had tried to sell her to a terrorist—"

"So why not kill her?"

Prophet sighed. "You don't think I've been asking myself that question for the past couple of days? But at the time, I didn't know she'd hurt anyone. I don't kill the specialists I can relocate safely—you know that. I only take them out if they're in danger of being captured."

Dean ground his teeth together. "LT lied to me. To us. And he came in last night and he took Karen and he promised me she'd be safe."

"You thought about killing her."

"Of course I did. She nearly killed me. Took my sight . . . and then she saved my life." Dean shook his head at the impossibility of the situation. "When she told me she thought I was trying to sell her, I thought maybe she was bullshitting me. I think she finally realized it wasn't me, but she didn't offer up any other theories as to who it could be. And then LT came in and . . ."

"And what?" Prophet pressed.

"I can't see, Proph—I can't fucking see reactions, but I can feel them. They knew each other. Somehow. And they didn't meet when she tried to kill me—I was rescued by someone else."

"And that's when she ran."

"She and LT knew each other. And still, I let her go with him." Dean blew out a harsh breath. "There has to be a good explanation as to why LT lied to me. To us. There has to be."

Prophet wanted to agree, and for the moment, he let himself. "LT left me a message—he got her settled safely."

"Right. And Ahmet just happened to escape the black site she built without her, right?" Dean's voice was hoarse, grief and anger mixed.

At this point, Mal and the others were there, listening in the background.

"Maybe LT and Karen met when you were hurt?"

"I was rescued by someone else. She saved me and then she ran. But hey, I guess anything could've happened right in front of me since I couldn't fucking see."

"Prophet." Tom was in front of him now, leaning in. "I don't mean to interrupt . . . but something's happening."

"What?" Prophet sat up and looked around . . . and then looked into his partner's eyes. "Something bad's already happened, T."

"Something worse is going to," Tom told him. "I don't know . . . it just feels . . . it's bad. Like we need to get the fuck out of here fast, bad."

"Then we leave," Prophet said.

"We'll go to my house. The one you and I went to, Proph," Dean told him. "Fewer people know about that one."

"Does LT?" Prophet said.

"Yes," Dean said. "You think that's a problem?"

Prophet treaded lightly. "If he's been compromised, it could be."

He glanced over at Tom, who drew a stuttered breath in and looked away for several long moments. Yeah, something was really fucking wrong.

"Yeah, T, I know," Prophet murmured so only Tom heard. When he hoisted himself up, Dean rose too. Suddenly, there was a ruckus to the left and all the men were pointing weapons . . . until they saw it was a group of women and children, using the land as a cut-through.

Reggie called, "Weapons down," and Prophet saw that King and Ren only partially obeyed that request—because in other parts of the world, women and children weren't always safe. But Reggie went over to them and they were speaking to him, and pointing behind them and then other local women who worked at the clinic came out too.

"What's going on?" Dean called, and one of the female clinic workers ran over.

"Rebels are coming through," she said breathlessly. "Many of them. They evacuated their village. More of them are coming, they heard. They just want to cut through."

"How far out?" Dean asked.

"They said a woman came in from town to warn them. There's time to get away, but it's not much. They are headed this way—to the clinic."

"Let them go," Dean told her. "Tell them to go fast, and get as far from here as possible."

She complied, heading back toward the group and ushering them across the expanse and into the path on the west side of the clinic.

"This isn't a coincidence, is it?" Prophet asked quietly.

"Never is," was Dean's answer.

One minute, Tom was watching the women and children rushing through the clinic grounds, and the next, he was grabbing onto Prophet's shoulder to keep from falling.

The pain in his side had been getting worse all day but true to form, he'd ignored it, because there was far more important shit to be handled. But suddenly, upright was a major issue, and Prophet was lowering him to the ground, telling him to hang on and calling for Dean to find a doctor for Tom.

"A doctor? Good thing we're at a clinic." A young woman stepped forward as she spoke, her words just sarcastic enough to calm Prophet's panic as she knelt by Tom to check his vitals and Tom liked her immediately. "Tom, I'm Pei." She was slim. Young. Dark haired and pretty, and proved her competence immediately as her hands flew over Tom like a pro, probing and pinpointing, "Spleen." She pulled his shirt up to reveal a large bruise on his upper abdomen. "Were you in an accident recently?"

"Something like that," Tom muttered. "I was kicked. But the pain wasn't this bad yesterday."

Still, Mal and the doctor had both warned him about his spleen. Now, Pei said, "Spleen injuries can sometimes take a while to show themselves. I'd like to get you inside. I can have the OR ready to go within the hour. I need to get you stabilized first. And I'm going to need some blood."

"OR?" Tom repeated. "I can't—the clinic's under attack. This has to wait."

"We need to get out of here before they cut off the roads," Nico was telling Pei as well.

"You need surgery," Pei told Tom in no uncertain terms as Prophet listened, uncharacteristically quiet. "Putting this off means risking your life."

"Can it wait until we evac—even for a couple of hours?" Nico asked.

"There's no way," she confirmed. "We'll take him in now."

"Doc...the rebels..." Tom told her.

She waved him away and looked between Prophet and Nico. "They'll have to stop them. You just concentrate on going to sleep and let me take care of you."

"You take care of him, Doc, and we'll take care of you," Prophet promised, before he and Nico were helping to get Tom up and inside the clinic, onto a bed. Pei got him some sedatives through an IV and he was feeling better pretty quickly, but not enough to deal with the underlying anxiety that there was a disaster heading their way, and he was the one holding them in place. "Proph—you need to go—"

Prophet shook his head. "Hey, you need to deal with your spleen. I'll deal with the rebels."

"Sounds like a fair trade," Tom murmured sarcastically.

"Those drugs are working, no?"

"No," Tom agreed, then frowned. He reached up to touch Prophet's cheek. "If you die, I'll kill you."

"You drive a hard bargain, T. Love you too. Give good spleen, all right?"

"You're just humoring me. But it'll be okay. Close call . . . but okay." Tom stared at him. "Proph. I didn't want to say it—but don't trust LT. Not completely. I don't care what he says."

Prophet frowned. "Tom, you're drugged—"

"Voodoo, remember?" Tom closed his eyes, knowing that Prophet would much rather believe it was Rylan or maybe even Cillian. "Just fucking promise me you'll tread carefully. I want to be wrong on this."

"Okay, I promise." Prophet grabbed his hand and squeezed hard. "You just concentrate on coming back to me as soon as possible. I fucking need you."

"Yeah, I know," Tom murmured, and he heard Prophet laughing as he drifted off.

CHAPTER THIRTY-FIVE

Prophet waited until Tom was put under before he let Pei kick him out of the small OR.

"I've got this," she told him firmly.

And even though Prophet knew surgery was the right thing to do, all the questions he didn't want to ask in front of Tom came tumbling out. "He's got a concussion. Isn't that more dangerous?"

"It's not ideal, but if I let the spleen bleed more . . . he could lose the whole thing. And then we're talking a major surgery. He's in good health otherwise."

"What if you can't repair it?"

"Let's deal with that when we come to it. I know soldiers—"

"I'm a sailor," he said, managing to sound offended.

"Sorry. I know military men in general like to plan . . . but I also know you're taught to take things as they come and improvise when necessary. Let me take this one step at a time."

"Doc . . ." He paused. "I love him. I can't lose him."

She gave a small smile and nodded. "You work your magic out there and I'll work mine in here. Deal?"

"I don't want you to worry about anything that's going on out here. We've got it covered."

"Ditto. I trust you. Now, you need to trust me."

Prophet nodded. She closed the door and he touched it with his palm and said a small prayer to whoever was listening because fuck, John's reach was goddamned long and treacherous. And what Tom said about LT? Prophet didn't want to believe it. Hoped that LT or Rylan or both had been compromised by actions beyond their control. They always knew John and Agent Paul weren't working alone.

Both LT and Rylan—and even Cillian—had the right kind of resources and clout to make things happen.

It also made them targets.

Prophet grabbed the nearest garbage pail and threw up. Nico found him, on his knees, and Prophet waited for the smart-ass comments.

Instead, Nico wiped his face with a cool cloth and handed him a bottle of water and an antinausea pill. "This'll help," he said quietly. And he stayed there until Prophet felt well enough to stand up. "Concussion?"

"Yes."

"You've been through hell since I last saw you."

Prophet nodded. "I think you should take everyone you can and get the hell out of here. I'll stay with the doc and Tom. If you bomb so they can't get to us . . ."

"You can ask, but I'm saying no. I have no doubt your team will tell you the same thing. Sentiment's appreciated, but this is my fight too. I let LT walk off with that woman . . . and something wasn't right." Nico looked angry now at the memory.

"LT might've lied to Dean about Karen being dead in order to protect him. And no matter what, second-guessing yourself's not going to help. We don't know anything yet, so let's concentrate on what we've got to do to stay alive."

That worked, because that's the way both of them—and the men who waited outside the clinic's doors—were built, bred, and trained.

Nico helped Prophet out the door without making him feel like an invalid. His eyes hadn't gotten blurry today, which was a good sign, but fuck, he hurt everywhere.

"Tom in surgery?" King asked.

"Yes. It'll be a couple of hours." Prophet glanced over all of them. "Where's Mal?"

Hook motioned to his left. "Took off right after the women came through. Got a wild hair about something."

"Alone?"

"You ever try to stop him when he wants to do something?" Hook asked. "It's like trying to stop you. But no, Ren followed him."

Prophet frowned. Ten minutes later, his cell phone started beeping. He grabbed it to see incoming texts. "We've got service."

Twenty minutes later, Mal and Ren came out of the brush, looking triumphant.

"I'm guessing they've got something to do with that," Nico said.

"Mal found the jammer," Ren told them. "It was planted about two miles from here. Definitely done purposely. Because jammers don't just show up in the middle of nowhere. Not US Military–issued ones, anyway."

Mal was carrying it. *Need to check this fucker for fingerprints so I know who to kill.*

King came over to stand with them. Prophet glanced around to the men assembled there, Nico and Reggie and Dean, and Prophet's team. The women from the clinic were assisting in surgery. They had four trucks. Several grenades and a few bombs. Some weapons.

And God knew how many rebel soldiers headed their way with orders to raze the clinic and take out anyone there. If they ran . . .

"I'll stay with Tom—I'll get them out of here as soon as they're out of surgery," Prophet started in again, but King shook his head.

"Not happening, Proph. Don't even bother. We're in this together." His brogue was heavy but he clapped Prophet on the shoulder. "We keep going until we're all out of hell, yeah?"

"Yeah," Prophet echoed. Except that hell? Seemed to be never-ending. "Any brilliant ideas would be appreciated."

"I might have something." King was dialing his phone. "I think the SAS held me around here. Ren, that pothole you avoided? They didn't. And I heard music playing while they changed a tire."

"That's ten miles from here," Dean confirmed. "There's a restaurant—they play music nonstop. It's basically open twenty-four hours a day—it's in the middle of nowhere."

"Makes sense," King said, then, "Brock? It's King. Man, I need some help out here."

He walked away to continue his call and Ren crossed his arms and stared at his best friend's back.

"Who's he talking to?" Nico asked.

"The SAS. Apparently, there's a merry band of them not too far from here," Ren said. "Do you know them? Head guy's named Brock."

Nico frowned and walked over to King. Soon the two of them were listening to the person on the other end of the phone and then Nico was talking and nodding.

"Where'd Mal disappear to now?" Prophet asked.

"Building bombs," Hook said, and Ren nodded, like that happened on a daily basis.

Which really, it did.

"Don't keep us in suspense," Ren said when they began walking back over to the group.

"They're trying to get some air support. A drone—but it'll be close," Nico said as he came toward them. "We'd have to evac."

King added, "They'll try to get a chopper for Tom, but they can't guarantee that at all. But if they can get an evac? It's going to be small and fast, which means the rest of us will need to find our own way out of here."

"Just get them out of here and I'll crawl home," Prophet told him.

"And then you'll owe me," Nico said, but it was with a smile.

"Fuck me," Prophet muttered, and then his phone began to ring. "It's Cahill."

"You guys aren't all right," Cahill started. "The rebels are coming in your direction."

"So I've heard."

"They were called in, Prophet. This wasn't a coincidence."

"You're sure?"

"Yes. I just don't know who made the call. I've got feelers out to find out who contacted a rebel faction to make a hit," Cahill confirmed. "Don't worry though—I'm mitigating your damage. I let another rebel faction know that someone's trying to invade their territory."

"What rebel faction did you call, Cahill?" he asked, his voice rising a little too loud and suddenly everyone was crowding around, listening.

"I called Boko Haram," Cahill said calmly.

"He called Boko Haram," Nico echoed, his hands in the air in the classic *what the fuck* position.

"Of course he did." King shook his head in disbelief. "Who the fuck is Cahill?"

I'll fill you in, Mal signed to him.

"So you started a rebel war," Prophet continued with Cahill.

"You needed a distraction, right? Let them think they're each trying to kill the other and they'll forget all about you," Cahill advised. "Just duck down and stay out of the way. And I'm sending a chopper for your wounded. Give a yell when you're ready—I need an hour's notice."

"How did you—" Prophet asked, but Cahill had already cut the line. "I don't fucking believe this."

Maybe it was better when they didn't have any contact with the outside world, because hell, knowing they'd be in the middle of Boko Haram and whatever other group was headed their way?

Fuck. Just fuck.

The SAS wasn't able to send a chopper, but Cahill had one—and a pilot who didn't mind flying through rebel fire. Pei gave word that Tom would be out within an hour, but that he needed at least another before she felt comfortable moving him.

"We don't have that," Nico said.

"Any way to know how many men are coming?" Prophet asked.

King was staring at his laptop. "I almost wish I didn't know."

Prophet decided it was better if he didn't look. Instead, he pulled King off the computer and together with Ren, Mal, Hook, Nico, and Reggie, they rigged a wide arc of explosives, far enough away from the clinic to keep the rebels out for a while. It kept them busy, although nothing could stop them from thinking about the hordes of angry, heavily armed men headed their way with nothing to lose.

Or headed Boko Haram's way, Prophet supposed, if he wanted to put a positive spin on the whole thing. But he had no doubt that the military losses in this region sat squarely in the forefront of all their minds, of men whose bodies were ripped apart, dragged alive through the streets as trophies.

And here you thought you survived the worst thing you'd ever go through. Fate always found a way to keep things . . . fucked.

Still, some things were going right. True to her word, Pei had Tom out of surgery in under an hour.

Prophet popped in to see Tom, who hadn't woken yet, touched his arm, reassured how warm he was. "How bad was it?"

"There was a tear. It would've just gotten bigger and bigger the more he moved. If he rests, he'll heal fine and keep his spleen." Pei looked tired, but pleased, and Prophet had the sudden urge to tell her to get the hell out of this clinic, this continent, and go someplace safe.

But hell, they both knew there was no such place.

"All he's got to do is take a flight on a helo," Prophet told her. "You too."

"It's risky to move him," Pei told him. "But it's even riskier not to, I'm guessing."

"Yes. You'll all go on the chopper together. You don't have to go far. Just get beyond the rebels," Prophet told her. "You'll be in good hands."

"And what about the rest of you?" she asked.

"We'll be fine. Better men have tried to kill us and failed," he assured her.

"Somehow, I don't doubt that."

Before he could ask her if that was a compliment or not, she was waving him away from Tom's bed so she could tend to her patient. "He'll be up by the time the chopper comes."

Prophet went outside and sat heavily on the steps, which was probably the biggest mistake he could make. Not only did his body protest ever getting up again, but his mind started to run away, back to that dark place . . .

Fuck. The irony that he'd gotten rid of the man who'd haunted him for years only to possibly be betrayed by one of three men he'd trusted and die at the hands of random rebel soldiers wasn't lost on him.

"None of that," Nico practically ordered.

"If I'd killed Karen instead of hiding her . . ." Prophet shook his head.

"I don't want to think of a world that didn't have men like you," Nico emphasized. "It's about checks and balances. And the CIA put you in an impossible situation."

"I put myself in it too."

"There are people on your side. Tom. Me. The team," Nico reminded him. "*Your* team."

"And we're all going to die because of it."

"You seem surprised that you're going to die—did you really think you were immortal?" Nico asked.

"You still make me want to punch you." But hell, bad blood didn't matter—not under conditions like this.

Nico smiled. "Good. Keep that anger. Because as long as you're still breathing? You're winning."

"That's SAS crap," Prophet muttered.

"No, that's a plan that's coming together," Nico reassured him. "You just make sure Tom gets on that helo. And try not to worry so much."

CHAPTER THIRTY-SIX

The explosions had started ten minutes earlier, and even though they were a ways off, they still stopped Prophet and the others in their tracks. There was no mistaking the sound of hostile fire, and the imminent attack had the team waiting to run in and fight as opposed to just standing still.

Thankfully, the helo was right on time, with Jin behind the controls.

"Get them on board, Proph—and I'll get them to safety," his old friend reassured him.

"I have no doubts," Prophet told him.

"If I can, I'll come back for you guys. But the rebels are all over the goddamned place."

Prophet shook his head. "No way. We'll be riding too close to them for you to risk it."

Jin nodded and then Prophet got the doctors and Tom boarded, along with several other staff members.

Tom was still asleep and Prophet figured that was best. There was no time for a long, drawn-out scene. Instead, Prophet kissed him on the forehead and Mal signed, *How sweet. Just like the prince trying to wake Cinderella.*

"I think you've got your fairy tales mixed up, asshole," Prophet shot back, then went to help Dean board. He didn't know what the fuck to say to comfort him, but it didn't matter. Dean simply turned to hug him. Hard.

"Get your ass back safely, dammit," he growled in Prophet's ear, and then he was on board and the bird was rising through the air, hovering . . . and then gone.

They had two vehicles. They decided to split up for part of the journey; that way they had an extra truck, just in case. It would be Mal, Prophet and Nico in one, and Ren, King and Hook in the other.

"Let's roll," Ren said.

But King was just standing there, staring out into the distance, listening to the bombs going off, the gunfire . . . and they could all only imagine the screams.

"I won't go out like that," King said finally. He was holding a knife and Prophet understood, as those images of military men, beaten and dragged through the streets, burned through his brain again.

Ren put a hand on his best friend's shoulder. "We'll never let that happen."

We'll live to fight another day, Mal signed.

"How can you be so sure?" King asked.

Too mean to die. Mal had rigged the entire perimeter of the clinic and Prophet hoped he remembered where all that shit was when they left.

King nodded. "As long as you all know my plan," he muttered as Ren got him into the truck. Then he popped back out even as Ren tried to push him back in like a goddamned jack-in-the-box and said, "We all go in one car."

Prophet wasn't surprised to see this happening—it was natural and it was fine, as long as they all didn't go down that rabbit hole at the same time.

"You okay with this?" Hook asked.

"One car," Prophet repeated. And they all climbed in. Mal was driving and all Prophet could do was sit in the middle seat and try not to have a flashback, which was becoming more and more likely the closer they got to the rebels' fighting, according to King's data.

"Breathe, Proph," Ren told him.

Prophet did, then came back from the worst places in his mind to see that he was physically in that worst place too.

They'd been boxed in from two sides. They couldn't go west because the river blocked them and there was nothing but jungle the other way—they'd never get out of that.

Prophet dared to glance at the laptop's screen, only to see swarms of red heat-seeking blotches that represented the soldiers all around them.

"They're ten miles out," King told them.

"That's a million miles in this terrain," Ren added.

"Roadblock," Nico announced as Mal slowed the truck. "SAS."

"They know me—that's Brock." King got out and showed himself before they were killed on sight.

"Get the hell out of here," Brock yelled.

"We'd fucking like to," Ren said, without a trace of irony.

"Get to the bunker." He rattled off coordinates to Nico. "We're headed back ourselves—we were just trying to wait it out for you and help some of the locals evac. This shit's going to go on for days."

"Yeah, no doubt," Ren muttered.

"Fucking Boko Haram," Nico said again, almost in wonderment.

You have to admit, it's a damned fine plan, Mal signed before he started driving again.

Prophet just shook his head, and they drove in silence for about five klicks in the direction of the bunker. Finally, they saw the markers, and King showed them where to park the truck to keep it hidden, and led the way down the stairs and into the darkened room.

It was cool and dry and safe. They put their gear down and sat on the bunks and for several moments, they all just *were*.

Because there wasn't much else to do.

After they'd rested and eaten, they were still quiet. It didn't surprise Prophet, and it gave him a chance to assess his team and get a sense of where their heads were at.

Because that, at least, was a comfortable role for him.

Nico was in the corner, pen in hand, yellow pad on his lap, writing furiously, and they all knew what he was doing. At one point or another, they'd all written the same type of letter, the kind you hoped no one would ever read, and after several moments, they all went and found paper and pens and got to work.

It was a tradition on the SEAL teams—and it no doubt extended to most Special Forces teams too. You wrote the letter you hoped no one would ever get the chance to read, because if anyone read it, it meant that the writer was no longer alive.

If the bunker was bombed, nothing would survive, but that wouldn't stop the tradition. It wasn't great to have superstitions, but the letter was something no one fucked with.

Prophet figured that Doc was the recipient of Nico's letter, and it made Prophet hate him a little less.

He thought about what Tom told him about Nico and Doc, and the tension between them during the rescue.

"I just wanted to tell them to fuck," Tom had said and Prophet smiled in the middle of that dark, dank bunker, thinking about Tom. Thinking about the emails Tom had written him in an attempt to win him back—and about the way Prophet refused to read them all . . . until he didn't.

Prophet's was, of course, to Tom, and as hard as it would be to write, it would be nothing compared to the one he'd force himself to write to Remy. Because the kid deserved that . . . and so much more.

The recipient of Mal's letter would be anyone's guess. Before Cillian pulled his disappearing act, maybe it would've been him, but now?

Hook's would be to his wife.

King and Ren? Well hell, they were each other's. King would probably write to his mom, but Ren?

His paper was blank.

King looked up and saw Prophet looking at Ren. "You going to tell them or am I?" King asked Ren, who shrugged. "Ren's in WITSEC, not me."

Which explained the lack of the letter writing.

"And yet, Prophet doesn't seem surprised," Ren said slowly. "Neither does Mal. Nico and Hook at least didn't know."

"Definitely not," Hook lied.

"I didn't for sure," Nico confirmed.

"Well, there's at least one," Ren muttered.

"It was just a lucky guess," Prophet told him.

Mal shot Ren the finger.

"Is that some kind of solidarity?" Ren asked, with a shake of his head. "And no, I'm not talking about it. Not now."

King nodded and shook his head at Prophet as if to say, *Leave it alone.*

Prophet would . . . for now. Because they were stuck down there for the foreseeable future. Hoping not to get discovered.

If they could fight back, they would. But each man always had a grenade in their possession . . . just in case.

"This? Is more fun than Yemen," Ren observed finally.

"Digs are better," King agreed.

"Why do I have a feeling we're going to owe the SAS—and that they're going to collect?" Prophet asked.

Mal was uncharacteristically quiet, which sounded ironic but was the truth. Mal had never needed a voice to speak volumes. Even when he could talk, he'd been a man of few words.

Now, Prophet got up and went to sit by him. "You're worried about Cillian."

Mal glanced at him, then handed him his phone. Prophet read the message, a chill running through his body. The timestamp was three hours earlier.

And there was nothing to be done.

Tom woke at one point briefly, then promptly passed out again, and frankly it was probably better that way. He would've been a drugged-up, yelling mess, and Dean didn't have any news to tell him anyway when he did finally wake up.

Because the first thing he said when he opened his eyes was, "Prophet?"

"No word yet," Dean told him.

"No word? Where?" Tom felt dazed. "Where the hell are we?"

"My house. We were taken by chopper from the clinic. What's the last thing you remember?"

"You and Prophet talking," he said carefully. "Then the pain. And the doctor . . ."

"Pei. She's here. She operated—fixed the tear in your spleen."

Tom struggled to sit up but Dean stopped him. "Let me put the pillows behind you." He did so, managing to make Tom comfortable and then handing him water without spilling it.

"You're a good nurse," Tom told him after he took some sips of the water.

"Fuck you." But there was humor behind it. "They'll be okay, Tom. I know it. Jin wanted to go back for them but . . ."

"Prophet wouldn't let him," Tom finished.

"Jin's here, with us. Nico couldn't fit on the helo and Prophet wanted someone else here trained to shoot, just in case."

Tom nodded and tried to pretend everything was fine, but his hands trembled. He stared down at the cup of water and Dean continued, like he knew.

"Tom, listen. Prophet, Nico, Mal, King, Ren, and Hook got out of the clinic by car. It was a mess they were driving into, but the SAS was supposed to be waiting for them. All I know is that there are two rebel factions fighting now—and it's bad out there. I'm hoping our guys are underground with the SAS, waiting it out." Dean sat back. "The doctors and nurses are here with us. And Reggie. And Jin and the guards, of course. Jin can get us out of here fast if we need it, but I think . . . we're okay."

"Good. That's something." Tom took another sip of water, then asked carefully, "Any word from LT?"

"Nothing." Dean pressed his lips together, his eyes unfocused. "They'll be okay, Tom."

"They have to be," Tom murmured. "Dean, look, Prophet's specialist . . . Proph didn't know."

"I believe him. Christ, having her show up here? Threw me off my game. That's why I went to the clinic after LT took her away. I had to get my head on straight and not let myself wallow."

"I can understand that."

"I have to thank you—for coming to me. I know that after what you guys dealt with . . ."

"I'm okay. Better now that the bastard's gone," Tom said firmly.

And then Dean's phone rang and both men started. "It's LT's ring," Dean told him. "LT, where are you? What? Are you okay? You're coming here?" he said, clearly for Tom's benefit. "Okay, yeah, I'm at the south house. Yes, I'm fine. I'll see you soon."

He hung up and breathed heavily, like he was on the verge of a panic attack.

"Dean, come on, man, just breathe and we'll get through this."

"I know how it looks. But I have to know. In person is the only way I'll know."

Tom's pulse raced. "Let's tell Jin and Reggie, okay? Tell them that LT's coming here and that there might be trouble. Because even if

LT was compromised, he might not be coming alone. Whoever took Karen and called the rebels to the clinic . . . they might be with him. Forcing him here."

Dean nodded woodenly, then stood. He opened the night table close to Tom's bed and pulled out Tom's weapon. "You need this."

"Why don't you help me out into the main room? I'll sit on the couch. Pretend to sleep. That way . . ."

Tom was already getting up as he spoke and Dean was helping him. It hurt like fuck, but he wouldn't take a pain pill now. Not until it was over.

When he got settled, he tucked his gun under the blanket. And he tried Prophet and Mal.

Nothing.

"They were headed to a bunker," Dean reminded him. "Leave them texts—tell them LT's coming here in the next several hours."

. . . and pray that they can get here before that.

CHAPTER THIRTY-SEVEN

The guards alerted him to LT's arrival, and Dean tensed, as if he were sixteen years old again and waiting for his brother to show up after Dean had gotten kicked out of yet another boarding school. And LT had ripped into him, every single time, but he still came to gather him up.

Every single time.

If he was wrong about his brother . . . then he, and everyone he'd brought here for safety? They were as good as dead.

"Dean? Are you okay?" LT's voice came in before he did, and Dean stood to meet him in the arched doorway of the main room.

"I'm fine," he said, reached out to touch his brother and his hands came back wet, the metallic smell of blood unmistakable. "LT, are you hurt?"

"I've been shot, but I'm fine," LT told him. "You heard about Ahmet's escape by now."

"Let me get the doctor first," Dean tried.

"No, you need to know what happened first. I know what you must've been thinking. Some of this blood is mine, but some of it is Rylan's. He betrayed me. Sabotaged me and took Karen. He was the one who brought her to Ahmet's."

"You know that for sure?"

"He confessed—right before I shot him. Dean, he was right outside your gates, waiting to see Prophet. He was planning on killing him . . . and any other witnesses."

Dean heard the stress in LT's voice, but something wasn't right. "But Karen's gone."

"Yes."

"Why didn't you tell me you knew her? That you knew she was alive." He hadn't wanted to blurt that out, but he needed to know. To understand.

"I save your life and that's what you're upset about? I don't understand you, Dean," LT said . . . and that's when Dean knew his brother was lying.

About everything. Whether Tom did from where he was playing half-dead on the couch, or Jin from his hiding spot, Dean couldn't be sure. But he had his answer. He just needed to keep LT talking. Needed to find out more, even as a chill skittered up his back.

It was so quiet, save for the patter of rain on the flat roof. Dean could feel the heat from his brother's body as he said, "You sold her. You sold Karen. And I know you didn't need the money."

LT's next words were hardened, not the worried older brother voice but his firm, *I've got control of this and you'll shut up and listen* one. "It's not about the money, Dean. It's about doing what needed to be done to keep the world safe."

"You can't really believe that bullshit, can you?" Dean tried to picture his brother—and failed. "I can't believe it."

"You have love for the woman who almost killed you?"

"I think she had some help in that regard, right, LT?"

"She set the bomb."

"And you tampered with it." Dean fisted his hands, forcing himself to keep control of his voice, to not let it show a single sign of goddamned weakness. "And then, after you almost killed me, you lied to me that she was still alive, and then you sold her—a dangerous specialist—to the enemy. You helped a major terrorist leader escape, LT. What the fuck are you doing?"

"So fucking naive, trying to help the world," LT spat. "Just stay in your clinics and wait for people to rescue you when you're in trouble—that's what you're good at."

He'd always known his brother to be a hard man, out of necessity he'd figured. Their parents had died young and the two of them had big responsibilities at a young age. "You and John . . . all this damned time."

LT dug in, his tone harsh. "Like I said, *naive*."

"You had no problem using Prophet."

"I don't run Prophet."

"He ran looking for John."

"He went AWOL. Then the CIA tried to help him."

"Help?" It was darker inside his thoughts than it ever had been in front of his eyes.

"When he went to work with Phil, he could've just let it go."

"You framed all of them. Was that for God and country too?"

"I don't need to explain myself to you."

"Then why come back here?" As soon as the words were out of his mouth, Dean realized how naive he really was. There was a dearth of words between them, a lifetime, a cavern so deep there was a fucking echo. "I'm a witness."

"Yes."

"And you came to do your own dirty work."

"If I thought you'd understand and keep your mouth shut . . ."

"I promised her she'd be safe and then I handed her over to you. Might as well have brought her to Ahmet myself." Dean paused.

"The difference between us? I'll sleep at night."

He could feel the movement of his brother's arm, the smell of a recently fired gun. "You sent the rebels to kill me. And everyone who was with me. And you're here to do what they couldn't. You bastard." He shook his head, feeling more off-balance than he'd ever felt after losing his sight. "Just tell me why."

"It's the way it needed to be," his brother told him, as if it were as simple as that. "I train men like John and Prophet—"

"And me," Dean broke in bitterly.

"And you. At least I tried. You didn't have the constitution. Most of them don't. Not for the purpose I need."

"By not having the constitution, you mean having a *conscience*?"

"Call it what you want. It interferes, and my job is to not let it."

"For the good of the world, right, LT? That's what you always told us—we were doing it for the common good."

LT snorted. "No one who hasn't been in a position of power can grasp what the common good really means. If there weren't men like me, you have no idea what might have happened to the world as you know it, a hundred times over."

"What a sacrifice," Dean said sarcastically.

"Everyone has their place."

"Even Prophet?"

"Prophet and his team had a higher purpose. Prophet did things he needed to do and they served my interests for a while." Dean swore he could hear the smile in LT's voice. "But Prophet was going to kill himself eventually, which would fuck everything up."

"Bullshit," Dean spat. "You knew Prophet would never lose his conscience. Something you never had to worry about with John. But what I can't figure out is, why did John go along with it? Why would John turn against Prophet like this?"

"Pitting them against each other ensured John wouldn't turn against me, ensured that he'd see the mission through."

"He knew you surrounded Prophet with men who were trying to kill him," Dean breathed.

"John was aware of the consequences of this mission. Complete it, spend the years I needed him to building a reputation, a close circle of men he could command, and Prophet would remain unscathed. John didn't give a shit what happened to the rest of the men. But it bothered Prophet . . . and that pissed John off. He felt betrayed."

"But not enough to let anything happen to Prophet."

"At this point, no one's getting out alive, so in the end, it didn't matter."

"And you'll continue to profit from all of it, the way you have for the past twenty years."

"Someone's got to fund you and your humanitarian work," LT told him.

"My money's from dad's trust—I wouldn't touch your dirty money."

"But you have—no way around it."

He was right, but Dean would make sure he made up for that. "You're not as good as you think you are. You lost control of John, the way you lost control of Prophet." He felt his brother's posture stiffen, heard the man's clothing move. "The game is playing you at this point. You've got too many loose ends."

"My loose ends are too busy taking care of each other. Ultimately, John knows what he needs to do."

Does he really not know that John didn't succeed? Dean kept that to himself, saying instead, "But now I know everything."

"It's too late for that to matter," LT said, almost tenderly. Dean swore he could smell the metal of the gun, could picture his brother, arm extended, weapon pointed between his useless eyes. "Even if Prophet and his team stopped everything, there's another man like me, another plan like mine, just around the corner for another team. The men I work for? They run the world, Dean, and they'll just keep going until their pieces are in the right places. Ironic, isn't it, that we're using terrorists for the United State's gain. If the general public even got wind of one percent of what we had to do, they'd run screaming into the night."

"But you've got it handled," Dean heard himself say woodenly.

"No worries on that, brother."

"Don't have the courage to shoot me yourself, do you?" Dean challenged.

"Figured you'd want to die a hero in your precious clinic," LT told him. "But here's just as good."

"I'll see you in hell," Dean told him. "But you'll go there first."

Prophet didn't get Tom's text until they were almost to Dean's house, and he guessed that Tom didn't get his either, saying he was on his way. As soon as the rebels crossed over and went west to meet Boko Haram's troops, the SAS had urged them out. Mal followed their trucks along a new route until they were past the clinic and on the road to Dean's.

As Mal got close, Prophet suddenly said, "Pull over here. I want to sweep before we go in."

"There's another signal jammer," King added. "Something's definitely up."

Prophet's entire body was sore, but he shook it off, took one of the automatic rifles from Mal before asking him to take point. His vision wasn't one hundred percent yet—and it might never be again at any point. Until the drops fully wore off, they wouldn't know, but for now, Mal would lead them inside and figure out exactly what was happening.

Mal ran up ahead for recon and signed back to them that there were two big black SUVs with tinted windows behind the gates.

LT's vehicles, with bodyguards, Prophet signed back. *Take them out.*

Mal nodded, and he took Nico inside the gates. The guards recognized Nico, which put the bodyguards at ease . . . and then Ren and King came in behind them and took them down as quietly as possible. The dogs began to bark and Prophet heard LT call out, "What the hell's going on out there?"

"Just a cat," Reggie called back as he waved from the door twenty feet away from the large driveway packed with cars where they stood. He looked back as if to check and make sure LT bought what he'd said, and then he closed the space between them. He looked happy as hell to see them all. "Thank God, Prophet. I think there's a friend of yours over there, behind the trucks—I'll get the doctors."

Prophet went around the black SUVs and saw the man who was bleeding all over the light-colored concrete. "Shit—it's Rylan."

Mal was next to him, kneeling, assessing the damage, even as Pei came out. All of this commotion was going to bring LT out here, and Prophet needed to get inside.

But Rylan was pulling at his shirt. "Not me . . . Proph. LT . . . betrayed . . ."

Prophet's gut clenched. "I believe you, Ry. Just let Pei help you."

Ry shook his head. "Cillian . . ."

"What about Cillian?" Prophet asked as Mal stared.

"Shot . . . too. By LT."

"Where is he?"

Rylan opened his mouth but his eyes rolled back.

"I've got to stop the bleeding." Pei basically pushed them both out of the way to make room for her nurses. Mal helped them get Rylan on a stretcher and brought him into a back area of the garage, which was still behind the house and out of view.

He looked calmer than Prophet would've thought. *Let's get LT*, he signed.

Together, they inched into the house, heard LT and Dean talking. They appeared to be the only ones in the main room, until Prophet looked under a wall with decorative cutouts and saw Tom on the couch. His eyes were closed and from where LT stood, he probably couldn't see him.

Prophet didn't doubt that Tom was awake and listening to every word. Jin had to be around here too. Because Dean would've hoped for the best but planned for the worst.

From what Prophet heard, this was definitely the worst. LT was holding a gun on Dean, saying, "I should've just let you die that night when I had the chance."

"Why didn't you?" Dean demanded. "Or was it okay, because I couldn't see—and that way, I couldn't witness any of your atrocities?"

Prophet stood then. "Hey, LT." LT turned, his weapon still trained on Dean and he looked surprised as hell. "What's going on here?"

"What the hell happened to you?" LT asked, recovering quickly as Dean stood stiffly by LT's side.

"John happened to me," Prophet confirmed.

"John? Where is he?"

"He's dead, LT. But you probably wouldn't know that yet. At the very least, you knew I was with him . . ."

Which explained why LT looked so surprised to see him. "I'm sure you heard—"

"About Karen? Yes, I did." Prophet stood there, immobile, as did LT. "What the fuck did you do, LT? To Dean? To me? To all of us?"

"My job," was all LT said. He glanced over Prophet's shoulder, as if to signal to a bodyguard who was no longer there, and then his eyes went wide as Prophet heard the shot.

"Bodyguard's down, Proph," Nico called.

"So's LT," Prophet heard himself say through the rushing pounding of blood in his head as he raised his arm. Dean slammed LT with an elbow and ducked out of the way. Prophet pulled the trigger and took LT out right between the eyes, tasting the bitterness of unshed tears as the man he'd trusted with his life fell at his feet.

Tom felt like he'd been fighting to get air into his lungs from the second LT arrived and Dean got him to confess, but when Prophet came into the room, the panic eased and his breathing normalized. And then he blinked to make sure he wasn't dreaming.

Everything happened fast after that. Prophet's team swarmed the room and Jin came out of hiding. Dean sank to the floor but Nico caught him, and Prophet came around the other side.

He looked up at Tom, who nodded. Knew he needed to be with Dean right now. That there was plenty of time for them. Plenty of goddamned time.

Tom watched as Ren and King materialized, with Hook and Mal behind them. And Prophet smiled at Tom, a small, tight smile that didn't reach his eyes.

They were all supposed to be dead today, Tom realized. And they all knew it. And they'd all survived. "Thank fucking Christ," Tom said.

"Christ and the SAS," Nico added in a British accent that Tom assumed was his real one.

Eleven years and the CIA had chased the wrong men, because the ones in front of Tom didn't want power or fame.

They wanted freedom, for themselves. Their country.

They wanted life and love.

"It's over," Ren said, like he'd have to repeat it out loud a million times before he truly believed it. King threw an arm around him, and Tom wondered which of them was holding the other up.

In deference to Dean, there was no celebration—it was a solemn acknowledgment that everything they'd gone through had come at a price. And Dean and Prophet had paid a heavy one with their loyalty.

CHAPTER THIRTY-EIGHT

Mal waited as patiently as possible, which wasn't patiently at all, for Rylan to wake up. He and King had given blood, because Rylan had lost that much. He'd been minutes from bleeding out—Mal could tell that from the amount of blood he'd been lying in.

While he'd waited, he, King, Ren, and Hook had packed up the bodyguards and LT and driven them in their big black SUVs to a remote area just north of Dean's property. He had no doubt the CIA would swoop in for some cover-up or claim this victory as their own.

Either way, Ahmet and Karen were in the wind.

And Cillian?

"Mal?" Pei said, shaking him from his thoughts. "He's asking for you. But only for a minute. That's it."

That was all he needed. He nodded and walked past her.

Rylan took a pained breath. "Thank you . . ."

It's okay, Mal mouthed.

Rylan's hands came up and signed, *He was shot*. Showing Mal that it was okay to ask questions that way.

Is Cillian alive?

"I don't know," Rylan managed. "He was . . . taken. LT . . . saw. Was pissed."

Taken? By who?

"Big black helo."

MI6?

Rylan nodded. "Best guess. They got . . . to him. Fast. So maybe . . ."

So maybe. Mal nodded. *You need to get some rest.*

"He's on the right side," Rylan managed.

Later, after the men had showered and rested and eaten, they were all holed up in different rooms. Mal just stayed in the front room, staring, and Tom walked over to him, as painful as that was.

I'm fine, Tom. Go to bed. Prophet's waiting to fuck you.

"Fuck off. I'm checking on you, whether you like it or not." He leaned against the wall.

Rylan's going to make it, Mal signed finally. *Cillian was shot by LT. MI6 came and took him away. And no, I have no idea if he's dead or alive.*

"But he's not a traitor."

No. But even so, nothing's that simple between him and me.

"It never is," Tom told him.

Go to Prophet and get a blowjob or something.

"Glad you're okay too, Mal," Tom told him. Mal shot him a middle finger and yes, things were going back to normal.

He made his way into the bedroom where Prophet was. "How's Dean?"

"As well as can be expected." Prophet had stripped and showered and Tom lay next to him on the bed, both of them wanting to do more than just lie there . . . and both of them too tired and hurt to do anything but.

Tom contented himself with twining his legs with Prophet's. "Are you okay? I mean, I know you're not but . . ."

Prophet gave a small smile. "I will be, T. Are you?"

"I still don't really . . . understand it. I don't get why John was willing to give everything and everyone up for . . . for what?"

"Power. Money. Look, John always wanted to be important. Untouchable. When that's all you've ever wanted, you'll do anything to attain it." Prophet shrugged. "He wanted to win."

"But he didn't," Tom assured him and when Prophet didn't answer, he said, "You saved innocent people."

"And put a lot more at risk."

"What happened with the specialist—that's not your fault. That's another op for another day, Proph. Never-ending. We do what we can."

"Live to fight another day, right?"

"Live to help someone else take up the fight," Tom corrected gently. "Or at least, gather a team. You saved yours. Freed them."

"Mission accomplished," Prophet murmured, and Tom realized he was nearly asleep.

"Night, Proph." He propped himself up with a book he'd borrowed from Dean—*Shōgun*, Prophet's favorite—in order to keep the watch going that night.

CHAPTER THIRTY-NINE

Prophet and Tom stayed in Eritrea with Dean for another five days, as did all his teammates and Nico. For Dean, mainly. Tom was still healing but he'd been cleared to fly. Rylan was picked up by a CIA helo, but not before reassuring them that nothing was going to blow back on them.

"For whatever that's worth," Ren had told him, but hey, they had good reason to be suspicious. And then they'd all gone with Dean to the clinic to see how bad the damage was, and hell, it could've been much worse. They worked together with the locals, and with a little help from the local SAS bunker, they got it up and running in acceptable condition by the time they left.

Dean had sent them off on a private plane with Jin as their pilot.

"I'm only a call away," Dean had told him as they boarded.

"Same," Prophet promised. "We're coming back with Remy, so you can't get rid of us."

After they'd landed, their first stop was to pick up Remy from school because he and Tom and Mal couldn't wait to see him. After dropping him and Mal off at home, along with their gear, they'd headed over to EE, Ltd.

"Prophet!" Natasha was hugging him now in the middle of the lobby, grabbing him around the neck and practically strangling him, and Prophet let her. Behind them, Tom was smiling.

Prophet had told Tom last night about who Natasha really was—the daughter of one of the specialists he'd relocated. It had been a true moment of trust, without Tom having to ask and fuck; it definitely brought them even closer.

Maybe there was something to this trust thing after all. "I'm all right, Natasha," he told her now, untangling her.

"It's about time you're back." She turned and hugged Tom too. "Phil wants to see you both."

"That's why we're here," Prophet grumbled. Because really, he hadn't wanted to come in here, was planning on calling Phil instead, but Tom had practically forced him into the damned truck and drove him here.

More operatives and support staff came out of the woodwork to see him and Tom, and he hated that, because it made him miss this place and he didn't want to miss it here. He wanted to hate it. And Phil.

But he couldn't.

Dammit.

When Prophet finally went into Phil's office, with Tom at his heels, Phil wasn't sitting behind his desk, but rather, standing in front of it.

Prophet wasn't sure what to say, but thankfully, and because he knew, Tom started in with, "I hear you know a crazy man who pretended to take up residence in my bayou."

Phil nodded, unapologetically. "It was the best way for me to assess you."

"Sure glad I passed your test," Tom drawled, sarcasm dripping.

Phil glanced at Prophet. "I'm assuming you brought some feelings in with you as well."

"God forbid," Prophet muttered, but hell, it was nice to not be treated like glass. Prophet actually welcomed that, for a change. "Why's your desk so empty?"

"Because I'm moving offices. Actually, I probably won't even need an office, since I plan to spend more time in the field."

"So who's taking over?" Prophet asked.

Phil stared at him. "You are."

"Fuck that. I quit, remember?"

"I don't recall, but then again, I'm getting up there in years." Phil shrugged. "Anyway, the paperwork's been filed. You're all set. I'll be here for another couple of weeks to make the transition smoother, so you really need to get up to speed."

"Phil—"

"I consulted with Dean. Everything in the offices and the command center is the latest technology," Phil assured him. "You won't be going into the field, but you're the best one to manage it. You can get our men and women home."

"You knew," Prophet said. "You knew what was happening . . . the plans. What the CIA wanted."

"Some of it," Phil admitted. "Not all. And I couldn't tell you. That's not the way it works."

"So firing me . . ."

"I was trying to save you. Get you out."

"And back into rescuing people stuck in hell."

"Wasn't John? More so than you?" Phil offered. "The CIA wasn't going to let him go—or your team either. There was too much getting accomplished. Everyone had to come out of it looking like heroes—the timing had to be right. Otherwise, the only outcome was everyone coming out dead and disgraced."

Prophet blinked and his throat tightened.

"I never gave up on you, Prophet. I knew you wouldn't give up on yourself, either. But trust me, it was hard enough to let you go the way I did. The hardest thing I ever had to do. But I knew you were in good hands . . . with Tom. With yourself."

After a long moment, Prophet cleared his throat. "If I take over EE—and that's still an *if*—what, exactly, will you be doing?"

"Working with Cahill and the boys," Phil said, as though Prophet should've known that.

"You're going back out there, with your friends." Prophet stared at him like he was an errant child.

Phil shrugged. Like an errant child. "Just make sure you send an old man support when he needs it."

Tom left Prophet and Phil to settle more of the "EE's not mine, it's yours" argument, because, in the end, he knew Phil would get his way. And in doing so, so would Prophet.

He found Doc's door open, with Doc inside, sitting on the edge of his desk, looking down the hall and not at all surprised to see Tom.

"Guess you heard the news," Tom said.

Doc smiled. "If I tell you I was in on Phil's plan from the start, promise not to tell Proph?"

"Yeah, right." Tom gave him a quick hug.

"You don't look as terrible as I thought you would," Doc commented.

"Sorry to disappoint."

"I'm glad it's all done. You must be too."

"Yeah, I am." It was the first time he'd said that out loud, because really, being glad after all that had happened seemed almost sacrilegious. It was hard when Prophet and Dean were mourning for an LT they thought they knew . . . and hard to celebrate when a terrorist and his accomplice were on the loose.

Doc broke into his thoughts. "You here for a checkup?"

"No—not really. I'm fine."

"Sit," Doc ordered. "Or I can't clear you for work."

Tom didn't say anything about possibly not going out on missions, and neither did Doc. Instead, he let Doc check his scars and healing wounds and fuss over him—because he'd actually never seen Doc fuss over anyone but Prophet—and then he got dressed when Doc declared him fit for duty—in another couple of weeks.

"Are you going to check Prophet out?"

"I'm assuming he needs casts?" Doc asked, and Tom nodded. "Send him in when he's done with Phil."

"Will do."

Doc stared at him. "You have something else to say to me?"

"I, ah . . . it's just that Nico's staying on with Dean for a bit."

"Good for him. He can do whatever the fuck he wants. Always did."

And that was the closest Tom was going to ever get to an explanation, for the moment. "At least you know he's safe."

Doc stared at him. "Don't romanticize this."

"Me, a romantic?"

"Yeah. From day one. I saw it happening from the first second you and that other asshole started sniping at each other." Doc rolled his eyes. "It's not like that for me."

"Okay," Tom said mildly. Because something told him it was just like that—his own goddamned eyes when Doc and Nico were in the same vicinity.

"Go away before I hurt you," Doc muttered.

"Fine. I'm going," Tom said. "But I wanted to give you this." He pulled the folded envelope out of his pocket, with *Doc* written across it, and laid it on the desk between them. "It's from Nico."

"You're a matchmaker now?"

"It's not like that. This is the letter he wrote in Africa. When the rebels were headed to the clinic."

"Did you write one?" Doc asked.

"I had it easy—I was in surgery. The rest of them all thought they were going to die."

"But they didn't."

"They never gave up hope, but it was close, Doc."

Doc pointed to the letter Tom had set down on his desk. "This is a formality. We all write them. And when we come back alive, this is moot. We—"

"Moot?" Tom picked the letter up and slammed it against Doc's chest, holding it there. "Nico wrote to you in what he thought were his last minutes on this earth. That means something. You asshole."

There were several moments of standoff, with Tom still pressing the letter to Doc's chest, and Doc's steely gaze locking with his, unmoving.

But finally, Doc reached up and took the letter. Whether he'd actually open it or not was another story, but Tom had his own relationship to heal.

"Oh, one more thing." Tom pulled out a piece of paper and put it on the desk. "This is Nico's new number. I think you should use it."

With that, he slammed out of the office.

Doc stared at the number on the paper, then crumpled it angrily. That didn't matter, because once he'd laid eyes on a number, any number, it was burned into his goddamned brain, scarring it.

Fucking him over, good and well, the way his relationship with Nico always had . . . and always would.

"Sometimes secrets are a good thing," he muttered.

"And sometimes they just fucking suck dick," Prophet said from behind him.

"Another asshole, coming to brighten my day," Doc grumbled, but he couldn't help himself from yanking Prophet into a hug. When he pulled back, Prophet's eyes were wet, and truth be told, so were his.

"Look at that—you missed me," Prophet sniffed.

"No one will believe you if you tell them." Doc studied the soft bandages on Prophet's wrists. "How bad?"

"The wrists? The eyes? Or everything?"

Doc closed the door and locked it. "We've got time for everything."

CHAPTER FORTY

They discussed EE when they got home that night, over dinner with Remy. Tom, of course, brought it right up, like he knew if he gave Prophet any time to think about it, he'd say no.

Which he was leaning toward, despite Phil's insistence. And Doc's. And Natasha's . . . and everyone else's at that damned place.

On the drive home, Prophet had brought up the possibility of Tom running EE by himself.

"We'll do it together," Tom was telling him now. "I can't do this alone, Proph—just because I can see the maps doesn't mean I can do what you do. You're running this show—and I get to learn new shit."

"And me too," Remy said.

Both men's necks practically snapped to look at him. "No."

Remy rolled his eyes and threw his hands up. "Why not?"

"You said you didn't want to go into the military," Prophet reminded him. "And I thought you wanted to tattoo."

"EE's not the military," Remy shot back. "And I can only do one thing now? Because that's bullshit."

"Don't fucking curse," Prophet called after Remy's retreating back and was met by the sound of a slammed door. "Christ, he's moody."

"Yep." Tom tried to keep a straight face.

"And fuck you for what you're thinking."

"Yep," Tom repeated.

"Tommy—"

"No, Proph—I'm not going into the field, unless it's with you, or to rescue you, Remy—"

"Mal?"

Tom snorted. "Maybe. But you get the point."

How they were suddenly supposed to go back to normal was anyone's guess. It wasn't like they could just flip a switch and turn into homebodies who didn't have people who wanted to kill them.

"You still have people who want to kill you. Lots of them," Tom assured him, but even that didn't help. Not completely.

Working at EE wouldn't be the same when his sight was completely compromised—not by a long shot. But nothing was ever going to be the same.

And hell, maybe it shouldn't be. Because if things stayed the same, where would he be now? Certainly not with Tom or Remy.

Prophet sighed and sat back. "Is this going to be enough for you?"

Tom stood and leaned in toward Prophet. "You're enough for me. I'll say it as many times as you need to hear it, babe. You're enough for me—always have been."

Prophet stared up at him like he was trying to memorize his face, this moment . . . and in all honestly, Tom probably was too. "Can I get that in writing?"

"Asshole." Tom grabbed the front of his shirt roughly and pulled him in for a kiss.

The tortured teenaged groan from behind them seconds later barely registered, until Remy's voice broke in, asking, "Is this what I'm going to walk into all the time? Because honestly, it's a lot."

"I thought you weren't speaking to us?" Prophet asked and Remy looked at him like he was an idiot.

"You need to learn how to read a room," Remy told him.

"Seriously?" Prophet said under his breath. "Maybe I should go back into the field—it's safer."

"Probably will be," Tom agreed.

By the end of the night, Remy had them both agreeing to take over EE, Ltd. and make Prophet promise to take them to go visit Judie.

Prophet was currently drinking Jack Daniel's straight out of the bottle, lying against the headboard, already contemplating how hungover he'd be in the morning.

Tom pulled his shirt off and Prophet was momentarily distracted by his tattoos. But hell, Tom was treating him like he'd break, and he figured tonight wouldn't be any different. He loved the man, but dammit, he needed to be manhandled, not babied.

Plus, he was drunk. So fighting was out of the question.

Tom climbed into bed next to him and wordlessly took the bottle . . . and drank. And drank again.

"So, this is parenting?" Prophet asked, without a drop of sarcasm.

Tom nodded. "Mal's hanging out with him."

"Mal's just biding his time until we're settled. You know that, right?"

"I know. Still nothing from Cillian?" Tom asked.

Prophet shook his head. "No word. We've checked everywhere." Presumably, Cillian had left them to search for Ahmet and Karen, but it wasn't like him to totally disappear—they'd need his help.

Then again, maybe not.

"Christ."

"Why? You miss him, T?"

"Fuck that," Tom grumbled, taking another swig. "It's more for Mal."

"Yeah—more for Mal. Want to share what exactly happened between them? Besides the fucking part?"

"Nope." Tom paused. "With or without Cillian, it's not safe for Mal. At all. Not since he gave up his WITSEC status completely."

"You worried about having him here?"

"Not at all. But he is, I'm sure. His C-4 pillow's getting bigger."

Prophet frowned. "That was his choice."

"To save King," Tom said, but then his stupid voodoo shit must've kicked in, because his eyes narrowed suspiciously. "What aren't you telling me?"

Prophet sighed. "I guess you're part of the team now. It's not King—it's Ren."

"Ren? I didn't see that coming."

"I guess that's why it worked for so long."

"We're going to help Mal, right?"

"Whether he wants it or not." Prophet took the bottle back.

"What are you going to do about Judie? You know Remy's not going to give up on visiting her."

Prophet winced. "I know. Maybe I've been too hard on her." He stared out the window. "Some things are out of our control."

"She loves you, Proph. Maybe that's the consolation? Plenty of guys do what you did, but without the love."

"I've got to bring her closer." He glanced at Tom, as if waiting for him to argue.

"No reason to keep an arm's length between everyone anymore," Tom said, just as casually.

"She's not going to magically improve just because she's nearby. I know that. It's still going to be the same bullshit, the same complaints . . ."

Tom swallowed. "The nurse told me it's the longest she's even taken her medication in one stretch. Like, triple the time. She's come a long way."

"You've spoken to her nurse?"

"Yeah. Remy's actually . . . spoken to Judie. He didn't want you to get mad, but he was worried. Once I knew that Judie was actually still safe, I had Blue find the real number in your phone and I . . ."

"You looked through my shit?"

"Yeah. Problem with that? I took it out of your playbook," Tom told him, and Prophet just shook his head and took another drink. "Anyway . . . it made Remy happy. She told him how much she loves you."

Prophet believed that. "Fine. We'll visit."

"She knows . . . about your eyes. I mean, she knew before Remy told her but . . ."

"He told her more."

"How's it going with that? Your eyes, I mean."

Prophet sighed. "It's not fair. And I want to say that but . . ."

"But what?" Tom prompted finally, after a very long pause on Prophet's part.

"But look what I get in return. You. Remy. A life that, for once, isn't filled with violence. And maybe it's all a system of checks and balances. Deep sorrow fills deep scars and all that shit." Those

Gibran lines had been made for him. Prophet deserved every word he spoke.

Tom walked into the kitchen, where Prophet and Remy were already eating breakfast. Remy had made it—saved a plate for Tom too—and was showing Prophet his sketches . . . and asking Prophet about his eye doctor appointments. Telling him, "I'll go with you. To all of them."

"Rem, I'm okay," Prophet told him.

"Come on. I'm sixteen, not stupid. But you should probably let me drive."

"Knew there was an ulterior motive."

"You know I drive better than you," Remy said. "Tom says so."

Already, this sixteen-year-old had wrapped both men around his fingers. Whether or not what he said about Tom was true, the fact that he knew enough to mention it showed that Remy had the potential to do whatever he wanted in the world.

Remy already had the keys and was heading out to the truck.

"Does he even care that I don't have a doctor's appointment today?"

"Obviously not." Tom walked outside with him but Remy ran in past them. "Where are you going?"

"I'll be right back," Remy called.

Prophet was standing, staring at the truck. "Think it's time to get rid of this?"

"Does it remind you too much . . . ?"

"Of John," Prophet finished. "His name's not like Bloody Mary—he won't come back if you say it. And no—the truck doesn't remind me of him. It just reminds me . . . of me."

"That makes sense."

Prophet nodded. "Remy likes her . . . or maybe he's just appeasing me."

"Remy's not the best at hiding his feelings, so I think he'd be happy to have it."

"Her. Trucks and boats are hers, Tom."

"Right. So sorry." Tom rolled his eyes as Remy came out toward them, holding dog tags.

"I thought you got rid of those," Tom said under his breath without moving his lips.

"I did," Prophet said in the same manner. Because one of the first things he'd done after coming home was finding the damned envelope that was still behind the dumpster and destroying the contents. "What's that, Rem?"

Remy held out the tags to him. "I found these in the kitchen."

Prophet untensed, and when he looked at the tags, Tom saw they weren't John's tags at all. They belonged to one Elijah Drews. Prophet took them from Remy and smiled. "Yeah, I always kept them with the knives."

"Jesus Christ, you're deranged," Tom told him.

"You don't even know why I kept them with the knives," Prophet protested.

"You're telling me it's not some kind of crazy reason?" Tom persisted.

Prophet shrugged. "No, you're right."

"Because they were with the knives?" Remy asked.

"No, because of why he kept them with the knives. And no, don't ask," Tom directed Remy.

"Anyway," Remy said loudly, with a roll of his eyes that was perfected by teenagers everywhere. "So I kind of got used to the tags. And I think the truck misses them."

"Now who's deranged?" Prophet asked, and both Tom and Remy pointed to him. "I realize you all have this crazy bayou woo-woo shit going on but . . ."

"Anyway," Remy continued. "Can I keep your tags in the truck?"

"Yeah, sure, Rem—that's cool. In fact, keep the tags in the truck and . . . keep the truck. Okay?"

Remy smiled. "Yeah? She's mine?"

"Yeah, Rem. She's all yours."

"Awesome! Can you let me get in now?" Remy asked, since Prophet was now blocking the driver's-side door.

"Where are you going?" Prophet asked.

Remy crossed his arms in front of his chest. "Are we going to go through this every time I go out?"

"Damn straight, skippy," Prophet promised happily. "It's my God-given right as someone who's already lived through their teenage years."

Remy narrowed his eyes. "There's a tracker in the truck, isn't there?"

"That's a present from Uncle Crazy," Prophet said. Pointed up to the window where Mal was waving and signing. "He says you're welcome."

Remy smiled and waved, muttering, "I'm never going to be normal. Got no shot at it with you people."

"You're welcome," Prophet told him.

Tom added, "Be home by eight."

"Eight?" Remy asked.

"Right—that's late. Better make it seven," Prophet said seriously.

"Seven . . . like at night?"

"Yes," Tom said firmly. "Or I'll send these two to come get you."

"You're threatening me with Prophet and Mal?" Remy asked, looked between them, and said, "Fuck me, I see your point. Be home by seven."

"Don't say 'fuck,'" Prophet told him. They all stared at him. "What? I'm not going down to talk to those fucking teachers at his school every day when he gets in trouble for cursing. I've got shit to do."

"Like?" Remy prompted.

"I'll find shit to do," Prophet promised. "Like showing up at every party you get asked to."

"Fuck me," Remy muttered again. Prophet threw his hands up in the air and Tom? He just laughed.

While Remy and Prophet took a ride in what was now Remy's new truck, Tom was inside brooding, staring out the window, because he was definitely frustrated. Undersexed. Not that he and Prophet hadn't been having sex, protected at first when they'd both realized, after the initial shock, that John hadn't worn protection. Their tests had been clear—and they'd been really fucking grateful for that bit of luck—but the sex was all very ... calm.

It was mainly his fault—he knew that. He'd been treating Prophet like glass for weeks now, because both of them had still been healing. At least that's what he'd told himself. Also because Remy stuck to them like glue and they understood that and tried to be quiet. And understood when Remy insisted on sleeping on the floor next to their bed.

Mal was staying with them too, because he'd promised Remy he would come back and hang for a while, and, for the most part, he talked Remy back into his room, and he'd stay on the couch cuddling with his C-4.

Tom turned and Mal was there now, on the couch. With the C-4. "It's not even six—you're going to bed already?"

Mal shook his head. *No, but you should. With Prophet—as soon as he gets home.*

"Now you're managing my sex life?"

Someone has to because I've heard nothing.

Tom rolled his eyes. "Yeah, I'll fuck Prophet so you have a soundtrack."

Thanks. That'd be great. I'm not used to being a monk.

"Then why are you?"

For Remy. Same as you. Well, partially the same. You shouldn't let yourself get pushed away.

Tom nodded. Pushing away was Prophet's specialty, especially when he thought it was for said person's own good. "I was ... It was ... He was hurt."

He's still an asshole though.

"True, but ..."

Mal's hands interrupted him. *Prophet's default switch is asshole. Yours isn't, so you need to flip his switch. On a regular basis.*

Tom sighed.

Mal continued. *Tie him up and fuck him. I know it works. Firsthand experience.* His eyebrows rose suggestively.

In the past, Mal would get a rise out of him by saying *firsthand* ... and it still did, so Tom shot him the finger and Mal nodded approvingly. *My work here's almost done.*

"This isn't . . . goodbye, is it?" Tom asked.

Like you'll cry if I say yes?

"And then you have to go and ruin it," Tom muttered.

Yes. That's what I do. Mal looked exasperated. *I'm not leaving this second though, so hold back your tears. And Remy has my number too. Speaking of Remy, I'll take him to a movie while you fuck Prophet, so you don't scar the kid for life.*

"Asshole." But yeah, not a bad idea. Still, he frowned, because the same question had been bothering him since they'd left John's warehouse. "Hey, Mal? What happens when the war's over and you go home? Because I'm here . . . and I'm still not sure."

That's easy, Mal signed. *Because the war's never over. Not out there. Not in here, either.* Mal touched a finger to his head. *At least if you're lucky.*

"Lucky?"

It's what keeps you alive. Stop waging war? Men like us? They die, Tom.

And when Mal turned to go, Tom suddenly added, "You'll call though, right? When you leave, you'll call—especially if you get into trouble." Mal frowned, like he couldn't process that. "Just fucking keep in touch, you psychotic asshole."

Mal smiled widely. *Finally, you're talking my language. Maybe when I get back, we'll go get pierced together.*

He left the room on that note and Tom swore he heard the echo of Mal's laughter, Boston accent and all, inside his brain.

CHAPTER FORTY-ONE

M al and Remy left for the movies, and when Tom went to clean up the dinner plates, he found a note from Mal.

Left you a present. You can thank me later.

And the thing was, it could be anything, including a bomb. So he held the paper carefully, like it could explode on its own, and he went to find Prophet. The TV was on in the main room, loud as hell, and when he turned it down, he could hear Prophet cursing from the bedroom.

"Proph?" he called and went in to see what was wrong . . . and hoping it wasn't another nightmare.

It wasn't. It was Prophet, wrists tied to the bedposts, bare-chested and sweats hanging low on his hips. One of his ankles was tied as well, and Prophet's teeth were bared as his fingers attempted to reach the knots. In lieu of that happening, he was just shaking the headboard as hard as he could.

"I'm going to kill Mal," Prophet swore, before Tom could say a word.

"Mal did this," he said slowly, more to himself than to Prophet.

"Do you think I'd do this to myself?" Prophet demanded, then paused. "Well, I might've, to prove a point. But I didn't. So can you get me out of this shit so I don't have to break the bed?"

Tom shook his head and pulled his own shirt off. "As long as I have you here . . ."

Prophet's eyes narrowed. "You're in on this together. You fuckers!"

Part of Tom wanted to kill Mal for this, but hell, that was because tying Prophet up and fucking him was what he should've done a while ago.

He stripped his pants off and purposefully strode over to the side of the bed. "I think I need to keep your mouth busy for a while."

Prophet frowned for a second, until Tom climbed onto the bed and put a leg over Prophet's shoulders so he was straddling Prophet's face, his cock brushing Prophet's lips. Prophet swallowed him down, his eyes fucking Tom the entire time and dammit, he'd make Tom come too fast.

Then again, there were plenty of other things he could do while he recovered enough to fuck Prophet into the mattress.

So he pulled back and came, all over Prophet's chest and neck and shoulders, his body jerking as he watched his come covering his man. And then he rubbed his come into Prophet's skin, and Prophet's lazy drawl of "Marking me?" made them both smile.

"Always," Tom promised. He slid down and laid his full weight on Prophet. "Now I'm going to fuck all that worry out of you."

"I'm not worried. Not one fucking bit," Prophet insisted, but once Tom stroked down the length of Prophet's cock, ran a finger along the tip, swirling the drop of come, and made Prophet suck in a harsh breath through his teeth, he seemed willing to do anything.

"Tom— Fuck."

"We'll get there," Tom promised.

"I'm going to kill Mal. And then you."

"Don't be like that, babe."

"Still fucking . . . treating me . . . like . . . glass. Dammit," Prophet told him. "What the fuck are you waiting for?"

"That." Tom leaned in and kissed Prophet—hard. A punishing, promising kiss that hadn't happened since before John had come to tuck that damned envelope behind the dumpster. Prophet responded in kind, relief palpable. And they kissed like that for a long while, until Tom's dick hardened and Prophet was arching up against him, looking for friction.

Tom crawled down Prophet's body, stopped when he was at Prophet's cock. And then he smiled up at Prophet. "Ready for more?"

Prophet had been unconsciously tugging at the bonds, which made Tom glance up at him predatorily from his position between Prophet's legs to tell him firmly, "Don't struggle."

Prophet figured, yeah, why? Because there were different kinds of helpless and this kind? Definitely had its benefits.

Mal had tied him and then looped extra rope so he could easily be turned onto his stomach.

Bastard. And still, Prophet tucked the knowledge away for a later date. When he got free.

When he wasn't looking to come hard enough to see stars.

"C'mon, Proph—turn over. You know you want it," Tom urged.

Prophet shook his head. "I'm not making this easy on you."

Tom's smile was enigmatic. "Why would tonight be any different?" And then he leaned down, flipped Prophet onto his belly, and shoved Prophet's untied leg out of the way so he could bury his face in Prophet's ass.

Prophet arched, away from Tom's tongue, or tried to, anyway, but Tom held him fast, rimmed him until Prophet was goddamned blushing . . . partially at how exposed he felt and mainly because he couldn't stop a random string of sounds and groans from escaping. It was agonizing, the slow tongue-fucking that had his cock twitching with need.

And then Prophet stopped fighting, because his entire body was out of his control, especially when Tom smacked his ass hard, several times in a row, and then continued licking him. He repeated that pattern as Prophet buried his face in the pillow, ass in the air, fighting that pleasure-pain line that Tom loved riding along . . . and he was putting Prophet there purposely, forcing him to just stay and feel, the way he'd done countless times before. But this time? Prophet was learning his goddamned lesson, didn't have a choice, not with Tom centering him, making sure he—and nothing and no one else—stayed in his mind as Tom held him open, licking him, rimming him until he couldn't even recognize the long, low moaning ripping from his throat.

Tom's hand snaked under Prophet's body to tweak his nipple ring, twisting, pulling until Prophet cried out *Tom* and *fuck* and *more*.

"Might have to pierce this one," Tom murmured as he moved to roll the unpierced nipple between his thumb and forefinger, and fuck, Prophet hadn't remembered being that fucking sensitive. But his skin was hot, pricking, nerve-endings firing nonstop, and every place Tom touched tingled, left a burning sensation that was only going to be quenched with Tom's dick inside of him.

"Or maybe I need to pierce here." Tom's fingers played along Prophet's frenulum and an involuntary shudder raced through him. "Ah, you like the thought of that."

"I'm not playing that game," Prophet ground out. But fuck, he did, and his mind and body were on a runaway train, flooded with emotions. His reactions were giving him away, selling him out, and there was pre-come dripping from his cock and no real way to hide it from Tom.

But why would you want to hide anything from him?

He didn't. Not anymore. Tom knew everything.

Everything. And Tom? Was still here.

Tom bit his ass cheek to get him out of his head again, then speared his tongue into Prophet's ass, and he let the pleasure overwhelm him, paralyze him. And finally, Tom was lining his body up behind him, grabbing his shoulder for leverage as he pushed inside of Prophet, not worrying about resistance or the pinch of pain, and then he was settled, his balls against Prophet's ass as Prophet let out a plaintive cry of relief.

"So tight. So full. Fuck, you love that, right?" Tom leaned forward and bit his shoulder—hard. Prophet's face was hot—fuck, was he blushing? And Tom knew it. "Look how sweet and calm you can be when my cock's in you."

Prophet opened his mouth to make some kind of smart remark but all that came out was, "Fuck, Tommy . . ."

Tom pulled back and pushed in again, stretching him, taking him, gliding and grinding against his gland. Prophet was going to lose his mind, dammit, and his dick? Didn't give a shit as long as it got to come.

"Come on—don't stop. Please." Prophet was begging, which was against all his better judgment. Rocking, fucking himself with

Tommy's piercings, which added to the delicious friction and yeah, it was all good . . .

Until Tom held his hips still.

"Fucking not fair," Prophet growled, and enough of this shit. His wrists came out of the rope and he had Tom on his back in seconds.

"How the hell?"

"Still underestimating me? Guess we'll have to do something about that. Now, are you going to fuck me, or what?"

"Asshole switch definitely needs flipping."

Prophet's eyes narrowed suspiciously. "Is that what Mal told you? Because he's definitely the asshole."

"True, but I'm not interested in flipping his switch. So fucking ride me, asshole."

"Thought you'd never ask." Prophet raised his hips slightly, his hand circling Tom's cock, and then he eased himself down onto it and for a second, they both just stilled.

"Mine," Tom told him, in no uncertain terms.

"Yeah, Tom, yours. All yours. Was . . . from the beginning."

Tom got onto his elbows so he could get better leverage and he was fucking Prophet, his hips pumping up and down, and Prophet moved in time with him and finally, he was coming, spurting over Tom's chest and neck in white ropes, marking his man and rubbing it in even as his body shuddered from the aftershocks. When he finally lay down on top of Tom, he heard the frantic beating of Tom's heart against his cheek, matching his, and Tom told him, "Yes, all mine," against his ear.

"I'm sorry," Tom said, when they'd both recovered sufficiently enough to breathe.

"For fucking what? Tying me?"

He smirked. "Definitely not that."

"Yeah, me neither. So what, then?"

"I should've done it earlier."

"Yeah, well, I probably should've too, but it didn't seem to be in your comfort zone," Prophet admitted.

"My comfort zone?"

Prophet gave him a small smile. "I've said it before, T, and I'll keep saying it until you believe it. It's not about sex. It's about power . . . with Lansing, with John—they just used sex as their delivery method. We've both been fucked in other ways, by people looking for control."

Prophet was comforting him when Tom knew it should be the other way around. "But what they did—it's personal."

"Anytime someone tries to take something or someone away from you, it's personal. Anytime someone tries to break you, it's personal." Prophet rubbed Tom's cheek with his knuckles. "I'm all right, Tommy."

"You knew what he'd do."

"Yes."

"Did it help, knowing ahead of time?"

"Helped me to plan. It was a tactical move."

"One way to look at it."

"If you let him win, T—because he did it to hurt you. To break us. If you let him . . ."

"He didn't." Tom's words held a reassuring urgency.

"Then put it out of your mind. It was no different than any fight I've been in. Another form of torture." That wasn't exactly true, but Prophet wasn't going to let John get the final word.

Tom smiled. "Say goodbye to your ghosts."

"Say hello to a partner you can't kill."

"If I can't kill it," Tom started as he entered Prophet again—not too roughly, but not babying Prophet either.

"Marry it," Prophet finished with a gasp.

"Yes," Tom told him.

"Yes, Tommy. Yes."

CHAPTER FORTY-TWO

Mal had taken Remy to the movies three nights in a row after that, but last night, they'd all stayed home together and watched movies.

Now, feet propped on his desk at EE, Prophet rubbed his chest and felt the bandage in his way. He'd nearly forgotten about it.

Earlier that morning, before going into EE, Remy and Tom had approached him—accosted him, really—and told him he was getting another tattoo.

"What for?" Prophet had demanded. "I won't be able to see them."

"But I can," Tommy said softly, rubbed Prophet's shoulder.

"I'm supposed to go through pain so you have something pretty to look at?"

"I already have something pretty to look at," Tom pointed out. "But I want to mark you."

"You did that last night."

"TMI," Remy said loudly.

Tom ignored him. "Permanently."

Tom wasn't getting any more tattoos, because Prophet needed to picture him the way he remembered. Every night, he closed his eyes and mapped them out on Tom's body. It was his way of counting sheep, and usually, it led to neither of them sleeping, at least not right away, but neither one of them had any complaints.

"Go for it," he'd said to Remy, who tattooed Prophet a compass. Prophet could still see it, and hell, maybe he'd always be able to. Then again, maybe not, and he'd prepared for that.

The hardest part would be letting others do things for him. At times it would be vaguely frustrating, and others, terribly embarrassing. Soul-baring vulnerability, Dean called it, and Prophet hadn't understood the implications of it until right then.

When he'd told that to Tom, Tom had asked, "And you're okay with it now?"

"It's never going to be perfect," Prophet had explained. "It shouldn't be. It *can't* be. But you know what? It'll be okay."

"More than," Tom had murmured, his drawl heavy.

"Yeah, more than," Prophet had echoed.

Now, he smiled and continued trying to saw his cast off. With a letter opener. He hadn't moved into Phil's office yet, and neither had Tom. Instead, he was in his old office, with Tom's desk across from his, where it all began.

And that was very okay.

As Tom watched, Prophet tucked the phone between his shoulder and his ear. A tarp was half on *whateverthehell* he was building—the few times Tom had tried to investigate it, Prophet had sworn it was some kind of remote bomb-robot hybrid—and he was halfheartedly trying to saw his newest cast off. With a letter opener. Which only seemed to succeed in making the edges rougher.

Tom's back bore the scratches as evidence.

Prophet even had a pile of mail on his desk, like that would somehow fool anyone. But when he looked up, Tom just smiled. Checked his email to see Cillian's email—and a video attachment. "Does this mean he's okay?"

Prophet shrugged. "He better be or I'll kill him . . . unless Mal gets to him first. What's it say?"

"'Figured this would make up for the last one,'" Tom read out loud.

"Better not be the couch," Prophet said, rolling up next to him decisively.

He was still holding the letter opener and Tom tried to ease it away from him under the guise of holding hands. Until he saw the video playing.

It was more of a still taken from a video, a slideshow, with the first frame showing Prophet sitting at the kitchen table, leaning in toward Remy, and then one of Tom watching, smiling . . . and then Remy and Prophet hugging and finally, Prophet and Tom hugging and Remy, covering his eyes and laughing.

Tom bit his bottom lip. "It's definitely better than the first video he sent."

"Yeah, that's right," Prophet said softly. Tom slid his hand into Prophet's . . . along with the letter opener. "We're back where we started."

"After a million miles in between," Tom managed, although there was a hitch in his voice.

Prophet smiled, and then demanded, "Now stop being sappy and help me get the damned cast off. And hurry, before Doc comes back."

After a brief hesitation, Tom did exactly what Prophet asked. Because if he was going to be in trouble, doing so with Prophet was the most fun of all.

"He's still an asshole for spying," Prophet grumbled.

"Aren't you still spying on him?"

"Yeah, but that's different."

"How?"

"Because it's me doing it," Prophet said as if that completely justified it.

Somehow, it did.

EPILOGUE

One week later . . .

Cillian blinked and wondered if the drugs were that good . . . or if Mal was really standing there.

He reached out and winced. Mal's hand met him halfway.

"If I'm going to die, you'll be the one to kill me. That's what you came here to say, right?" Cillian managed, and Mal nodded solemnly. "Fuck, at least you're honest."

Not going to do it now. Too easy. Fish in a barrel, Mal signed.

Cillian laughed . . . even though it hurt.

Mal continued, *Guessing you didn't find Ahmet.*

Cillian shook his head. The failure of that, and of letting LT get the best of him? He took it as a personal affront. "You?"

Dead fucking end. Like he disappeared into thin air. I went to the facility Karen had been in and asked around with King and Ren. Opened up walls and shit. Traced the phones. Either she had a lot of help or she was really goddamned good. Mal's fingers paused. *There was one thing, though.*

"What's that?" God, Mal looked so good—the phrase *a sight for sore eyes* made so much more sense right now, and Cillian wanted him to stay. But then again, he'd never ask him to.

There was an alarm set up to go off at random intervals. It was weird. Like she was structuring her day in an already super structured environment. Like she was training for something.

"And she was successful. I'm sure Prophet's taking it hard."

Mal nodded. *He's running EE now, with Tom. We'll get her back, and Ahmet too.*

"I'll take that bet." Cillian paused, not sure he wanted to know the answer to the next question, but he asked anyway. "Who really sent you?"

You've got a lot of people looking for you. I came by myself.

"I heard SB-20's gotten in touch with you."

MI6 actually gives you intel?

Cillian smiled. "I'm not even sure they really want me alive. I got that intel from a source I've got in here."

Mal didn't even bother to ask why MI6 rescued him. Smart man. *SB-20 wants me to work with them—with you as my handler.*

"And you said yes?"

I didn't agree to anything yet. But I can't work for Prophet. Can't bring my family shit into Remy's life. It's not safe.

"What kind of deal did you make to get Ren out of trouble?"

I asked them to bury Ren's files. In return, I'm going to help them with my family.

"That's insane, Mal." He hadn't meant to give away what he knew about Mal's family, but Mal had to assume he'd dug . . . especially after everything that had happened in Amsterdam.

Mal simply shrugged. *You planning on hanging out here much longer? When are you being released?*

Cillian didn't push the family issue, instead just glanced at the glass partition. "I don't exactly know what MI6 means by 'being released.'"

And you're just going to lie here and wait to find out?

Cillian glanced up at him, then pulled the sheets back to show he was dressed in jeans and boots. "Shirt's by the window."

Mal frowned. *Give me a minute.* He came back and said, *Got your meds.* He was wearing a white coat, complete with a doctor's ID badge, and scrubs, pushing a wheelchair. This way, he could take his IVs with him and let them finish out. *We're going out the front door. Simple.*

Simple. Despite the fact that there was *nothing* simple between him and Mal, he couldn't deny that, sometimes, the simplest plans were actually the best.

Explore more of the *Hell or High Water* series:
riptidepublishing.com/collections/hell-or-high-water

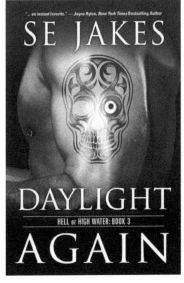

Dear Reader,

Thank you for reading SE Jakes's *If I Ever*!

We know your time is precious and you have many, many entertainment options, so it means a lot that you've chosen to spend your time reading. We really hope you enjoyed it.

We'd be honored if you'd consider posting a review—good or bad—on sites like **Amazon, Barnes & Noble, Kobo, Goodreads, Twitter, Facebook, Tumblr,** and your blog or website. We'd also be honored if you told your friends and family about this book. Word of mouth is a book's lifeblood!

For more information on upcoming releases, author interviews, blog tours, contests, giveaways, and more, please sign up for our weekly, spam-free newsletter and visit us around the web:

Newsletter: riptidepublishing.com/newsletter
Twitter: twitter.com/RiptideBooks
Facebook: facebook.com/RiptidePublishing
Goodreads: tinyurl.com/RiptideOnGoodreads
Tumblr: riptidepublishing.tumblr.com

Thank you so much for Reading the Rainbow!

RiptidePublishing.com

ACKNOWLEDGMENTS

As always, it takes a village, and mine includes Rachel Haimowitz, May Peterson, Alex Whitehall, L.C. Chase (another gorgeous cover!), and everyone else at Riptide who helps to ensure my releases go smoothly.

A special thanks to Madeline M. (aka Mad who owns Blue), who gave the perfect name to one of the CIA agents in this book, ensuring he'll show up in other, unexpected places in future books.

Also, to my readers who understood my (unplanned and unexpected) hiatus and hung in there, and to my family, who I couldn't do this without. More to come, and I hope you all love the final installment of Prophet and Tommy as much as I do!

ALSO BY SE JAKES

ABOUT THE AUTHOR

SE Jakes writes m/m romance. She believes in happy endings and fighting for what you want in both fiction and real life. She lives in New York with her family and most days, she can be found happily writing (in bed). No really . . .

SE Jakes is the pen name of *New York Times* best-selling author Stephanie Tyler (and half of Sydney Croft).

You can contact her the following ways:

Email: authorsejakes@gmail.com

Instagram: instagram.com/authorstephanietyler

Website: sejakes.com

Tumblr: sejakes.tumblr.com

Facebook: Facebook.com/SEJakes

Twitter: Twitter.com/authorsejakes

Goodreads Group: Ask SE Jakes

Truth be told, the best way to contact her is by email or in blog comments. She spends most of her time writing but she loves to hear from readers!

Enjoy more stories like
If I Ever
at RiptidePublishing.com!

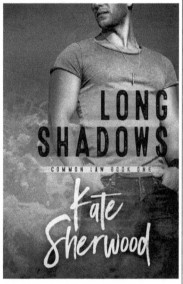

Risky Behavior

Long Shadows

When inexperience is paired with difficult, things start heating up.

Sometimes a bad decision is so much better than a good one.

ISBN: 978-1-62649-526-5

ISBN: 978-1-62649-565-4